L. MCSIMON

Ghosts in the Wires

Copyright © 2025 by L. McSimon

All rights reserved. No part of this publication may be reproduced, stored or transmitted in any form or by any means, electronic, mechanical, photocopying, recording, scanning, or otherwise without written permission from the publisher. It is illegal to copy this book, post it to a website, or distribute it by any other means without permission.

Ghosts in the Wires is a work of fiction. Names, characters, places, and incidents are either the product of the author's imagination or used fictitiously. Except in the case of historical fact, any resemblance to actual events, locales, or persons, living or dead, is entirely coincidental.

First edition

ISBN: 979-8-26-910069-2

This book was professionally typeset on Reedsy. Find out more at reedsy.com

To Fergal,
My brother and my hero.
Rest in peace, little brother.

Chapter 1

The sea was calm but restless, the steady rhythm of the waves broken only by the metallic creaks of *The West's Awake* fishing trawler as it swayed in the early morning darkness. Patrick Molloy, the eldest of the crew at 52, adjusted the throttle, his weathered hands steady despite an unusual unease tightening in his chest. Beside him, his younger brother, Liam, muttered something about the sonar glitching again, his voice a thread of concern barely audible over the drone of the engine.

Below deck, Patrick's son, Eoin, was hauling nets with his cousin Sean. They worked in practiced silence, the dull light catching the sweat on their brows. Outside, the cold Atlantic whispered against the hull, and a distant seabird's cry cut through the gloomy skies.

Then it happened. A groan—deep and guttural—rolled through the trawler like a death knell. The boat shuddered violently, knocking Sean off balance. Eoin grabbed the nearest handrail, heart pounding.

"Up top! Now!" Patrick's shout rang out.

Scrambling onto the deck, the younger men were met with chaos. The boat pitched wildly, as though caught in an unseen grip. Waves were no longer gentle; they churned with unnatural force.

"What's happening?" Sean yelled, panic lacing his voice.

Liam was at the helm, pale and rigid. "It's the engine—it's not responding!"

Patrick grabbed the radio, his voice measured but strained as he sent out an S.O.S. But there was no time to provide details, no chance to explain. Beneath their feet, the trawler heaved again, the stern sinking lower.

Eoin's breath caught as seawater spilled across the deck. "We're taking on water!"

Patrick's face hardened. "Get the life vests! Now!"

They moved as fast as their terror allowed, but the ocean was faster. A rogue wave slammed into the side of the trawler, nearly sweeping Sean overboard. He clung to a railing, gasping as icy spray drenched him.

The boat's bow lifted sharply, a futile struggle against the force dragging it down. Patrick locked eyes with Liam, a silent exchange between brothers, one born of decades at sea. There would be no escape.

Eoin's voice broke, raw with fear. "Dad—"

"Stay together!" Patrick roared, his command a final defiance against the inevitable.

The trawler groaned again, its hull twisting under immense pressure. Within seconds, *The West's Awake* plunged, swallowed whole by the churning Atlantic, the icy water closing over the fishermen, silencing their cries forever, all the while another ghostly vessel glided silently beneath the chaos on the surface—an enormous shadow in the depths, its form

CHAPTER 1

indistinct but undeniably there. For a fleeting moment, the fishermen's lifeless vessel seemed almost tethered to the dark shape below, drawn downward by an unseen force. Then, with a final, almost reverent pull, *The West's Awake* vanished completely into the abyss, leaving no trace of its passing but the ripples spreading across the surface, and the chilling question of what truly lay beneath the endless, unforgiving sea.

*****

It had been one of the most majestic, yet hidden vistas in County Mayo on the west coast of Ireland, known to few other than the locals. Halfway along the stretch of the Wild Atlantic Way that lay between the seaside town of Westport and the famed beauty spot of Achill Island, the shoreline at Mulranny village was easy to overlook, unremarkable along a coastline of spectacular scenery. It was a landscape both breathtaking and bleak, shaped by centuries of storms and solitude. And yet, that was precisely its allure for Robyn Mayhew, a journalist at *The Mayo Herald.* It was a place of silence, of space, where the Atlantic stretched endlessly to the horizon, where a person could stand alone on the strand and feel as if they had stepped beyond the earthly realm.

Driving out of Westport town one summer's evening after finishing work at the newspaper, she was in search of somewhere quiet to breathe in the sea air to ease a stress headache that had come on after a hectic day at the paper just before it went to press. Tall, with a narrow build and unusual colouring—pale skin with dark eyes, but grey not brown—Robyn carefully made her way across the shingle, pausing to look out over the Atlantic just as the sun began to dip below the horizon, casting a pink glow over Clew Bay and its myriad of tiny islands. As she drank in gulps of sea air, letting the vastness of the sea quiet her restless mind, she turned around to take in the wooded hillside above the roadway just behind her.

And that's when she saw it.

Half-lost in the trees on the hillside stood the ruins of the old Great Southern & Western Railway Hotel, its fairytale castellated roofline catching the last light of day. Time had not been kind to it. Its stone walls, once grand, were crumbling, encased in thick ivy, its windows frames dark and empty. And yet, even in decay, it was magnificent—an echo of an era long past, watching over the coastline, bearing silent witness. It was one of the most beautiful backdrops the county could boast of, even along a coastline of many, a hauntingly beautiful scene that was to draw Robyn Mayhew back time and time again, whenever she was desperate to escape life's pressures into the embrace of nature.

It had always been a place steeped in memory, but now its beauty carried a deeper sorrow. Standing on the same strand months later, freezing cold beneath a grey sky heavy with January rain, Robyn could almost feel the weight of the recent tragedy in the air. The loss of the local fishing trawler, *The West's Awake* had cast a heavy, mournful air over the village. Four men—two fathers, two sons—taken by the sea without warning, without explanation. No wreckage, no bodies. Only questions.

The Atlantic had always been a giver and a taker, but there was something different about this loss. It was not just an accident, not just another name added to the long ledger of

CHAPTER 1

those claimed by these waters. There was something deeper, something darker that Robyn could not shake.

As her gaze drifted back to the majestic ruins on the hill, she thought to herself, this place had seen no shortage of tragedy before. She had heard the stories in the pubs of Westport, told in reverent tones over pints of Guinness. The stories of the old Achill Prophecy.

It was a tale that stretched back as far as the 1600s, to a man named Brian Rua O'Cearbháin, gifted—or cursed—with the power of foresight by God after having shown great kindness to a widow and her children in their time of need. He had spoken of things impossible for his time, of "carriages on iron wheels with smoke and fire" long before the first railway was ever conceived. But it was not this vision that haunted the people of Achill. It was the warning that came with it.

"The first and last trains to Achill will carry home the dead."

For centuries, it was just a story, an old superstition passed down through generations. Until the day the prophecy came to pass in 1894, just as the new railway line came to completion. Thirty-two young people set out on a fully loaded boat from Achill Island, crossing Clew Bay to Westport, where they were to board a steamship bound for Scotland to work on the annual potato harvest. Tragedy struck when their boat capsized, and all thirty-two souls drowned. The very first train to travel the new railway line carried the bodies of those lost at sea home to Achill Island for burial, just as the prophecy had tragically foretold.

Decades later, as train travel declined, the line faced closure but not before the final, tragic chapter of Brian Rua's prophecy transpired. In 1937, a tragic fire in Kirkentilloch, Scotland, claimed the lives of ten more young potato harvesters from

Mayo. Once again, the remains were carried home to Achill, but this time on the railway's final trip before the line closed forever, bringing the ancient prophecy to its sorrowful conclusion.

But as Robyn stood in the damp, grey light of that January afternoon, she couldn't shake the feeling that the past was stirring once more. The sea had taken *The West's Awake* without a trace, and the village was haunted by a silence that felt almost foreboding, that worse was yet to come.

Robyn Mayhew had no idea how right she was. The spirit of *The West's Awake* was whispering to those willing to hear: to find the cause of its demise before the entire nation sank with it.

Was anybody listening?

But just as some warnings are never fully heard, some prophecies are never truly finished.

*****

On the afternoon of January 14th, Dublin city traffic was heavier than usual for that time of day. But it was of no consequence to the team of Garda motorcycle outriders, poised like coiled springs at the gates of Government Buildings on Merrion Square. A sleek black ministerial Mercedes idled behind them, its tinted windows concealing Taoiseach Liam Varley, the Irish Prime Minister, whose stony expression offered no clue to his destination as the cavalcade departed.

With their sirens screaming through the city centre, the Garda outriders quickly cut a path through the traffic, as vehicles pulled to the side where they could, in answer to the sirens. Pedestrians paused mid-step, heads turning to catch a glimpse of the commotion. Some, sharp-eyed and politically attuned, pieced together the puzzle in seconds. The direction of the convoy told them everything they needed to know.

A small number amongst the witnesses to the commotion were quick-witted enough to pop into a bookie's office to lay a bet on the outcome of that journey. They may even have chosen a betting office a few streets over, out of earshot of the sirens, so that their bet wouldn't be refused if the proprietor had the same suspicion themselves. The slightly more cautious amongst them, although gamblers were hardly synonymous with caution, would have waited inside a pub or coffee shop along the Quays somewhere for a speedy return journey by the Taoiseach's Merc in order to be certain of their bet. Because it was only a very short journey to his destination—Áras an Uachtaráin, the President's residence in the bucolic setting of the Phoenix Park in the west of the city. But it was a journey that was laid down in the Constitution of Ireland as one that must be made in the circumstances Taoiseach Liam Varley found himself in.

As he arrived at the presidential residence, President Martin T. Goggins stood waiting outside the front portico, his presence commanding respect and authority. At his side stood Síle, his wife and confidante, whose formidable political acumen had been instrumental in shaping her husband's career. It was the very same portico that was believed to have been the model for Irish architect James Hoban, who designed The White House years later in Washington, D.C.

After handshakes and pleasantries were exchanged, the President and Taoiseach made their way to the state drawing room, where they quickly got down to official business. The purpose of the Taoiseach's visit? To seek the dissolution of the 32nd Dáil, the principal chamber of the Irish parliament before calling a much-anticipated general election. Without hesitation, the president granted the dissolution as requested. In a matter of minutes, the wheels of democracy were in motion.

Then, with a sense of urgency, it was straight back to Government Buildings for the Taoiseach. On the dais in front of Leinster House, home to the Irish parliament, Varley made the official announcement to the assembled press who had been on election footing for weeks. A general election would be held three weeks hence on February 8th, 2020. Not that there was any surprise. A frisson of excitement had passed through the corridors of Leinster House when word quickly spread that the Taoiseach was making his way to the Phoenix Park. After the formal announcement, it was straight down to work for the Taoiseach, his aides and advisors. The gears of election machinery were now fully engaged. Across the city, a handful of punters gleefully returned to the bookies to collect on their bets, their quick observation handsomely rewarded.

But as the nation prepared for the campaign trail, no bookie or punter—not even the most seasoned political strategist—could have predicted the seismic shift that lay ahead, and how changed utterly the country would be before the ballots even began to be counted.

*****

A raucous cheer went up in the newsroom of *The Mayo Herald* in Westport, County Mayo as word came through that the election had finally been called. Speculation had been mounting for months that a general election was imminent

CHAPTER 1

and journalists the length and breadth of the country were worn out with the wait. General elections are usually looked forward to with much anticipation by political hacks, it was their battleground, their finest hour. But this one was proving to be even more riveting than usual. A sudden spike in the polls a number of weeks ago showed the once pariah, Irish Republican Party had undergone a sudden surge in popularity, which most commentators were attributing to a tipping point having been reached in the country's housing and healthcare crises. (The Irish Republican Party was now the main political front of the IRA or Irish Republic Army, having been formed from a breakaway Republican faction during the Northern Ireland Peace Process in the 1990s when the IRA agreed to a ceasefire bringing an end to their thirty-year campaign of bombing and murder against British rule in Northern Ireland. But it had never found much favour with the electorate in previous elections until now due to its candidates having been drawn from the ranks of its paramilitary "stars".) The backlog on public housing and hospital waiting lists had been at the forefront of the electorate's mind for years, but successive governments had failed to achieve any measure of success in solving the sectors' problems, despite pouring copious resources into each.

But *Mayo Herald* journalist, Robyn Mayhew wasn't so certain such a "tipping point" had been reached. As her first feature article of the general election cycle, she was planning a deep dive into the poll results across all parties in an attempt to figure out why the Irish Republican Party was the only opposition party "benefitting" from the dual crises in healthcare and housing. There was a lot more to this story, her intuition told her.

But her editor had other plans. Storming out of his office to quell the roaring, shouting and high-fiving, Jack Leahy barked at his journalists: "Knock it off and get the hell back to work. It's an election that's been called not a free round of drinks."

"Mayhew," he added, "Into my office. I've a job for you to do first."

Deflated, Robyn took a seat in front of his desk or what she approximated was the front of his desk. Such was the mountain of files, newspapers and books that abounded, one couldn't be quite sure.

"What's more urgent than getting down to the election coverage?" she asked him, out of genuine interest rather than the disrespect it at first seemed to engender.

"This trawler tragedy off the Mulranny coast," he replied.

Her jaw dropped. "You're telling me a three-week-old story that we've covered to death is more pressing than a general election? Have you lost your mind?"

"That's enough," he snapped. "If I tell you I want you to cover a story, then you cover the damn story. End of. Now get out to Mulranny and start knocking on doors. I can't for the life of me understand how nobody has a clue why that trawler sank. Someone somewhere must know something and if my reporters were anywhere near as good as they think they are themselves, they would have gotten to the bottom of this well by now. The only reason I'm sending you, by the way, is because you don't take no for an answer. So, get yourself out there today and use that special skill you have for being as annoying as hell."

"I get it. Jesus. If this is what general elections do for your mood, I hope I'm not around for the next one." She grabbed

CHAPTER 1

her bag from her desk and stormed off out of the newsroom. Usually, she loved any excuse to be out of the office but today was an exception. She felt like the only kid in school not invited to the party.

*****

Three weeks earlier, the small, seaside village of Mulranny was visited with a shocking tragedy. A local fishing trawler, *The West's Awake*, had put to sea from Cloghmore pier on the south end of Achill Island in weather that was unremarkable for the time of year. Manned by four Mulranny natives— two brothers and their sons—the boat sent out a brief SOS before capsizing 14 nautical miles off the west Mayo Coast. Experienced fishermen all, their bodies had tragically still not been recovered.

But it wasn't just the shocking loss of life that was haunting the villagers but the circumstances in which those lives were lost. The trawler had seemingly plunged into the depths of the ocean with alarming speed and without any apparent reason. Not a single rescue boat had a chance to be launched and the distress signal came as a fleeting, mysterious call for help, tragically devoid of any information or even the coordinates of the boat, such was the speed at which it sank.

The media had kept a respectful distance from the families, but neighbours and fellow fishermen had been canvassed for possible answers multiple times over. It was into this difficult situation that Robyn Mayhew found herself thrust that afternoon. She felt sick to the pit of her stomach at having to question the locals yet again. It was a fool's errand, knocking on doors, digging into a wound that hadn't even begun to heal. So she thought better of it. A walk along the beach in Mulranny would help her clear her head and figure out how to get around her editor's demands without harassing the traumatised villagers any further.

As she pulled in on the roadside just above the pier, the village had the air of a place holding its breath. The pier was empty, save for a few boats moored in silence, their hulls shifting uneasily against the tide. It was as if the place had not yet exhaled since the night *The West's Awake* vanished. Robyn picked her way across the shoreline, the stones shifting beneath her feet. The sea was calm, lapping at the sand with a deceptive gentleness, but she knew better than to trust its stillness.

A southwesterly wind had just started to blow in from the Atlantic and its refreshing breeze sparked an idea in Robyn's head. Instead of badgering the villagers for answers they didn't have, a stop-off at one of the local boozers in Newport, a picturesque small town along the road from Westport to Mulranny, would probably yield a decent round-up of the latest speculation, she figured. Stories had a way of surfacing with pints.

The Newport Arms was quiet for a late afternoon, the warmth of the peat fire battling against the damp that clung to the air. Behind the bar, the proprietor, Fergus O'Malley was pouring a pint for one of his customers, his sharp eyes turning towards her as she entered.

"Well, well, well, look who it is. We haven't seen you around in a while," Fergus smiled at his old friend. "What will it be? The usual—a pint of Bud?" he asked.

"No, it's more of a hot whiskey kind of day. I've just been for a walk on the beach at Mulranny so I need a bit of warming up."

"Well, that's the life!" he teased. "A leisurely walk along the beach in the middle of the afternoon followed by a nice quiet drink to round it off. Any more jobs going at *The Mayo Herald*?" he added jokingly.

At least it made her laugh. She knew Fergus through his girlfriend who was an old college friend of hers. He had grown up in the UK but moved to Ireland to follow his dream of opening a pub in his parents' birthplace where he had spent many summers as a child. He was a giant, hulking man in his early thirties but looked a lot older—weather-beaten from his enjoyment of outdoor pursuits. His love of the place had endeared him to the locals and his pub did a roaring trade at the weekends and even had a decent crowd mid-week. Normally Robyn loved to pull up a seat at the bar and chat to random punters, but today she just wanted a quiet word with Fergus. He got the hint when she took a seat on her own at the far end of the bar instead.

"What's up?" he asked. "I thought you'd be up to your eyes in election madness."

"I would be," Robyn replied, "if Leahy hadn't sent me chasing ghosts." She didn't have to explain further.

"I've heard he's a handful alright."

"He's under pressure to get the sales figures up so I guess that wouldn't do much for anyone's personality," she confided in him.

"Still, I don't know how he expects you to find out what happened when men with forty years' experience fishing those waters can't, for the life of them, figure out what went wrong that day and why those men were lost. It's shocking. No one can get over it. And it will be a long time before anyone does."

"Are there any theories even?" she asked.

"The only one I've heard fellas talking about is whether the line might have gotten caught in a sandbank."

"But surely the lads would have known where the sandbanks were?"

"Sandbanks can pop up anywhere. So, it's possible there was a newly formed one they didn't know about. The water's not that deep where they were. It's the only theory going around at the moment. And it will probably be weeks before the Marine Casualty Investigation Board gets divers out there to investigate. They use fellas from the Naval Service and they're undermanned at the moment. So, weeks could turn into months."

"That's so hard on the families," Robyn said.

"It's heartbreaking for them—not having a clue how they lost their sons and husbands and then not even having bodies to bury. All of this is 'off the record,' by the way."

"Of course, Fergus," she concurred, nodding to him. "Our usual terms and conditions. But if you hear anything further, can you give me a call? It would take Leahy off my case a bit."

"Of course I will, Robyn. Are you ready for another?"

"Better not. We're three weeks out from an election. I'll need to at least show my face back in the office, even if it's only to turn off my computer," she joked. "But thanks for the chat, Fergus. You're a star."

As she turned to leave, he said: "Hang on a minute. There is one guy you could talk to," leaning on the bar as he lowered his voice. "German Joe, they call him. He moved here from Germany in the '90s. Quiet fella, doesn't have a lot to say. He's in about his early eighties now. He lives in the cottage

CHAPTER 1

down by the viaduct, next door to Frankie O'Keefe. He's often out on The Point birdwatching with a telescope."

"Birdwatching?" she enquired, with a raised eyebrow.

"Well, that's what he says anyway. But it crossed my mind the other day whether he might have seen something. He probably would have said it to someone by now if he did but he's a quiet fella so it wouldn't hurt to call in on him to double-check."

"See, I knew you would come good, Fergus!" Robyn chimed. "You've never let me down yet!"

"All right. Get out of here and get some work done for Christ's sake. See ya, Rob."

Robyn took leave of The Newport Arms and headed down the town towards the old railway viaduct that once carried the steam trains of the Great Western Railway through Newport on the way to Achill Island. Spanning the famed salmon fishery of the Blackoak River, it was the focal point of the town and lent it a wonderfully idyllic setting, particularly as evening fell when floodlights beneath the arches illuminated the viaduct in a warm, white glow, casting an enchanting aura over the town that captivated all who saw it.

The cottage where German Joe lived was exactly what she pictured a foreign expat in Ireland would be drawn to—a thatched roof, whitewashed walls and very quaint. Robyn tried knocking on the solid wood door hoping to speak to him but there was no answer. Undeterred, she nipped around the back to see if there was another door she could try but there was no joy there either. She slipped a note under the door with her phone number asking the gentleman, German Joe to contact her at *The Mayo Herald*.

Chapter 2

By the time she got back to the office in Westport, the newsroom at *The Mayo Herald* was in full swing, the scent of stale coffee and newspaper ink thick in the air. Phones rang, keyboards clacked and half-shouted conversations overlapped as the team scrambled to put together the next edition.

Robyn shrugged off her coat, weaving her way through the maze of desks and towards her own workspace. She barely had time to open her laptop before the voice of Jack Leahy came slicing through the air.

"Where the hell have you been?"

Jack Leahy loomed over her, his face flushed with a mixture of exasperation and disbelief. His tie was already loosened, and his shirt sleeves shoved to his elbows, evidence of a long day that was far from over.

"I've been trying to reach you all afternoon, Mayhew! Ever heard of breaking news? It's the reason we *keep* our mobile phones *on*, for Christ's sake."

Jack was only five years older than Robyn's twenty-seven, but his relentless pursuit of news had aged him well beyond

CHAPTER 2

that. Tall and wiry, with a shock of brown hair that always looked like he'd just run a hand through it in frustration, he was a journalism wunderkind—poached from a rival paper and fast-tracked to *The Herald*'s news editor position before he'd even hit thirty. His problem? Robyn Mayhew didn't respond well to being managed. Her utter disregard for authority figures was like a match to Jack's short fuse, and their clashes were the stuff of office legend.

Before she could shoot back, Michael Davy—her colleague at the next desk—leaned in with an uncharacteristic seriousness.

"Marie Mulhall was caught with drugs in the Dáil."

"Drugs in the Dáil? The TD?" she exclaimed, laughing. But Davy wasn't laughing. "What are you talking about?" she asked. Marie Mulhall was a stalwart of Mayo politics, despite her relatively young age of thirty-eight years. A solicitor by profession, she was a diligent advocate on behalf of those in her constituency and was well regarded by all in the Fine Gael party.

"Seriously. Marie Mulhall bought Valium on the dark web and had it sent to her office in the Dáil," her colleague reiterated. At just 5'4" and with big brown eyes, Michael Davy had an impish charm that endeared him to everybody.

"You're joking me?" Robyn laughed. "Any clown could have sent that to the Dáil. Who put the story out?

"It was that blogger guy, Mike Mulcahy, who broke the news. You know, the guy from Meath that started that political blog, *Tales from the Dark Side*? He claims he got a tip from a hacker who hacked the site that sold her the drugs. He released details of any drug or gun purchases by prominent people to the media in their country of origin, apparently. It was the parliamentary address that tipped him off in this case. He even sent Mulcahy the Bitcoin receipt for the drugs purchase."

"Jesus, if this story checks out, it's some scoop," Robyn replied. "How do those guys on that blog get these great stories and why does no one ever send me a tip like this?"

"Jealous, Mayhew?"

"Damn right I am."

"Mayhew! In my office. Now," came the barked order from the editor's office again. This time she didn't hang about.

Leahy was planted behind his desk amid the stacks of files that littered it.

"I want you to get on the phone and figure out what the hell is going on. Drop that trawler story. I want to know by close of business this evening who's bloody high in Dáil Éireann and who's not, so drop the trawler piece."

"Got it," she replied. This time she didn't argue. She knew a huge story when she saw one, hoax or not. But still, that trawler sinking had been gnawing at her. A routine fishing trip shouldn't have ended with four dead men and a boat swallowed whole by the Atlantic. But this was a front-page scandal. The trawler story would have to wait.

"And why weren't you answering your phone for God's sake? I've been a full hour trying to reach you."

"My phone was on," she shot back. "There's no reason why you wouldn't have been able to reach me. There mustn't have been coverage out there."

"You mean you stopped in for a liquid lunch along the way and didn't want to answer the phone to your boss with pub noises in the background?"

"No, I'd have answered my boss if the phone rang in the pub because you already know that's where all my good stories come from."

"Well, for all your boozing you didn't get this story. So, I'd reconsider my methods if I were you. A two-bit blogger can out-scoop you these days."

She didn't bother arguing any further. But instead of heading back to her desk to start working the phones, she grabbed her car keys and stepped back out into the cold evening air. One of the lessons she'd learned from all the biographies of the newspaper greats she had read was that the best way to crack a story was to *follow the money*. That was where all great stories came from. So if there was a Bitcoin receipt for the alleged drug purchase, then that was the thread she needed to pull.

Problem was, her knowledge of cryptocurrencies was patchy at best. She understood the basics—decentralization, digital wallets, blockchain—but the finer details? That was another story. If she was going to chase this angle, she needed to swot up fast. Online research was always a last resort. Too many rabbit holes. Too much noise. Instead, she relied on the old-school approach—talking to experts or reading solid books on the subject. Just as well she was a speed reader.

As she turned the key in the ignition, she was already planning her next stop: the county library in Castlebar. If she was going to dig into this properly, she needed to start with the fundamentals.

The drive inland from the coastal town of Westport to the more subdued county town of Castlebar where she now lived was one Robyn had come to treasure. It offered the perfect window of solitude, a rare pause to let thoughts settle before arriving home recharged for the evening.

Castlebar hadn't been her first choice as a place to live

when she took the job. Her heart had been set on Westport—the postcard-perfect town with traditional shopfronts and window boxes spilling over with a blaze of summer flowers. But *The Herald*'s general manager had insisted she base herself in Castlebar to bolster readership in the county town. The trade-off was that she only had to come into the office in Westport on Mondays, the day before the paper went to press.

The library, situated a few streets over from the town centre, just off The Mall—a park that had once been a cricket ground for the notorious town landlord of yesteryear, Lord Lucan—was her first stop. But it wasn't like most libraries. Bright and open, with shelves no taller than four rows high, it was designed as a social space to encourage conversation between booklovers, rather than hush it.

So it wasn't a surprise to Robyn when a stranger approached her as she perused the "Biographies" section of the library that evening.

"I see you're a Russophile then," he said, nodding towards the Vladimir Putin biography she was leafing through.

"Well, I like the Russian people and learning about their country and its history. I'm just not so mad about their leader," she replied with a smile.

He was a man in his late seventies or thereabouts, she guessed, about average height and with a strong build, balding slightly.

"I see you were out at my place earlier today," he continued.

Startled, Robyn was taken aback. "Eh, are you German Joe then?"

"That's what they call me."

"Em, I wanted to talk to you about your hobby," she said with uncharacteristic awkwardness, after being caught unawares. "I heard you're a keen nature-lover and bird-watcher."

"I am," he confirmed, not giving much away.

"Eh, I had been looking into the trawler tragedy for *The Mayo Herald* and somebody mentioned to me that you spend a good bit of time out on The Point with your telescope," she continued. "I was wondering if you might have noticed anything that could possibly have led to the sinking of *The West's Awake* or if you had any theories even as to what might have happened?"

This was where the openness of the library worked against her. Their conversation attracted a few curious looks from nearby browsers. German Joe picked up on this too.

"Come across to Daly's," he said, referring to the historic Georgian hotel across The Mall.

Robyn didn't need telling twice. German Joe turned to leave and Robyn went straight to the desk to check out her books. He was a man with a plan for sure. Robyn had always admired decisiveness as a quality in people. And it boded well for the conversation that he may have had something interesting to share with her when he appeared to need privacy to talk.

When she stepped inside Daly's bar, her suspicions were confirmed. Instead of taking a stool at the counter, he was seated in one of the snugs at the back of the bar with a pint of Guinness in front of him. As she approached, he rose to get her a drink, but she waved him away.

"Not at all, Joe. I'm getting this. By the time I'll be back you'll be nearly ready for another one of those," she said, nodding at the pint of Guinness in front of him.

"No, I'm only staying for one," he said. "I've got to get back."

A bit deflated that this wasn't going to be the long chat she had hoped it would, she got a drink at the bar and joined him at his table.

"You haven't been long at *The Mayo Herald*," he said. "I haven't seen you around. You mustn't live in Westport," he added.

"You're spot on," she told him. "I live here in Castlebar and I'm pretty settled in at this stage so it would take a lot to get me to move elsewhere, if I'm being honest."

Since he had made it clear he was in a hurry, she decided to cut to the chase.

"I was talking to Fergus O'Malley earlier," she began, carefully choosing her words. "I asked if there were any theories floating around about what might have caused the trawler tragedy last month. He said it could take months before the Marine Casualty Investigation Board sends divers out there, and even then, there's no guarantee the families will get any real answers. But he mentioned that he saw you regularly out on The Point with your telescope and figured if anyone had noticed anything unusual, it would be you."

She let that hang in the air, watching his face for a reaction. She hoped her pitch to him, telling him where she had gotten his name and why it had come up, would build some trust and hopefully he would feel more comfortable opening up to her.

Joe exhaled slowly, leaning back in his seat. "I know it's a sensitive time for the families," he admitted, his voice quieter now. "That's why I haven't said this publicly. And to be honest, I don't want my name attached to it. People might think I'm a madman." He hesitated for a second, then met her gaze. "So as long as this is 'off the record,' and you give me your word on that, I'll tell you what I saw. Because someone needs to look into it."

Slightly stunned by the import of what he was saying, she muttered: "Of course. You have my word. No one will hear your name from me."

He studied her for a moment, then gave a slight nod.

"Alright. About four and a half weeks ago, I was out watching the Arctic terns coming in over The Point. It was about 10 a.m. when I saw what I first thought was a humpback whale breaching the surface." He paused. "I waited a few more minutes, and then I saw it again. But this time, I knew it wasn't the fin of a whale I was looking at."

Robyn leaned in slightly. "No?"

He shook his head. "It was the fin of a sub." He took a gulp of the pint of Guinness in front of him, before setting the glass back down gently.

She blinked. "The fin of a sub?" she asked, puzzled.

"The fin of a submarine," he confirmed.

"Eh... how would there be a submarine in the waters off County Mayo?" It almost sounded ridiculous when she said it out loud, and she felt an involuntary urge to laugh—but quickly smothered it.

"That's exactly what I thought," he said. "The Irish Navy barely has enough ships, never mind submarines. And as for the Brits—their subs are based at Faslane in Scotland. Sometimes, they pass by Northern Ireland along the Donegal coast before heading out into the Atlantic. But a submarine passing this close to the Mayo coast is...bizarre."

"OK, let's say it was a sub you saw surfacing..."

Cutting her off rather testily, he said firmly and clearly annoyed, "It was a sub. I know what they look like."

"Ok, fair enough," Robyn quickly conceded. "But that was

a few days before the trawler tragedy. So how are the two connected?"

His jaw tightened slightly. "The sub may have still been in the area on the day of the tragedy. Or maybe it left and came back. Either way, if it was in those waters when the trawler sank, there's a chance the boat's nets could have gotten caught in it. And if that happened, all it would take is for the sub to dive." He paused, letting the implication sink in. "It would drag the trawler down with it. Fast. There would be no chance to react, no time for a proper SOS."

Robyn exhaled. "Jesus."

A long silence settled between them.

"That's one hell of a theory," Robyn said finally.

Joe met her gaze.

"It's happened before, in the English Channel many years ago. There's actually a code of practice for submariners if they find themselves near a fishing vessel in distress—they're supposed to surface, stay on scene, and assist with the rescue. And there's supposed to be an investigation."

"You seem to know a lot about this," she replied. "Were you in the Navy?"

"No. I'm a fisherman." He said it simply, as though it should explain everything. "That's what I came to Ireland for, thirty years ago. The fishing."

"Deep sea fishing?" she asked.

"No, inland."

Something about that struck her as odd. An inland fisherman keeping such close tabs on submarine activity? But he didn't seem inclined to elaborate, and she decided not to push it.

"So then—whose sub do you think it was?"

CHAPTER 2

"I've no idea," he admitted. "But that's where you come in—to investigate that."

He stood abruptly, draining the last of his pint. "I have to head off. But remember our deal. And good luck. I'll follow the story in your paper with much interest."

Robyn stood up and shook his hand, but as soon as he left, she sank back into her chair, her mind racing. The conversation had ended so abruptly, leaving her stunned by what she'd just heard. This could potentially be a huge story, but for now, it was nothing more than a possible sighting and a theory—hardly enough to go on. There was no solid evidence, and to make matters worse, she had no contacts within the Defence Forces. That meant her first port of call would have to be the press officer at the Department of Defence. But experience had taught her that government press offices were typically only good for two things—issuing flat-out denials or trotting out the well-worn "no comment." Still, she would have to run it by them. Stepping outside, she made the call. It was just after 5 p.m., so she hoped to catch someone before they left for the day. But as the phone rang endlessly with no answer, her hopes dimmed. Now she'd have to resort to sending an email—a method that only made it easier still for them to brush her off with one of their two frustrating stock responses.

As Robyn ended the call, her gaze drifted to a weathered plaque mounted beside the hotel's entrance, its bronze surface catching the pale afternoon light. The inscription marked this very place as the birthplace of the Irish Land League—the movement that abolished the rule of landlords in Ireland and set the country on an irreversible path to independence. It was here, in 1879, that the first embers of revolution were kindled, and from those flames, the Irish Free State was born nearly half a century later.

Crossing The Mall towards her car outside the library, Robyn's thoughts swirled. There was something profound about standing on the very ground where history had been shaped—especially today, the day a general election was called, almost a century since the foundation of the state.

Without warning, a strange unease settled over her. Was it the weight of the revelation that a foreign country's submarine, an interloper in Irish territorial waters, may have caused the death of four Irish people? A revelation in the very spot where Irish history had been made?

An urge, quiet yet insistent, pulled at her, urging her to turn and look around.

Perhaps it was nothing. Or perhaps it was the ancient voices of those who had once gathered here, their struggles woven into the very fabric of this place. Michael Davitt, the Land League's great firebrand, had walked these same streets as he fought to free Ireland from foreign rule. She turned to look once more at the old hotel, its stone walls steeped in memory. Whatever lay ahead—truth, controversy, or something more dangerous—Robyn felt as though history itself was breathing against her ear, whispering for her to pay attention.

Chapter 3

The ghost of Michael Davitt, however, was nowhere to be found when Robyn emerged from her editor's office the next morning. Jack Leahy had just finished tearing her story to shreds, and the newsroom was still reverberating from the force of his fury.

"These are grieving families we're talking about—people devastated by the loss of their loved ones," he thundered. "And you think *The Mayo Herald* is going to add to their pain by publishing this harebrained theory? A submarine, a GODDAMN SUBMARINE," he bellowed, his voice bouncing off the walls, "sank that trawler? And without a shred of evidence? The Cold War has been over for thirty years, for Christ's sake. And Ireland's never even been a NATO-aligned country. This isn't *The National Inquirer* we're running here, Mayhew! Now get to work on the Marie Mulhall story and figure out if it's a hoax or not. I can't bloody believe you sometimes."

Robyn stormed out of his office, barely noticing the quiet hush that had fallen across the newsroom. She knew they'd all heard her getting chewed out—nothing new there. It wasn't even that he'd rubbished her story, it was that he genuinely thought she was so callous, so lacking in basic human decency, that she would run a wild conspiracy theory without considering the grief of the fishermen's families. That cut deeper than anything. Just the insinuation that she didn't care about the people involved? That stung.

The evening before, she had contacted the Department of Defence for comment on the reported submarine sighting off the west coast, well within Irish territorial waters. Predictably, they denied it outright. But she hadn't expected them to confirm anything. If a British or even a French sub had been patrolling those waters as part of a joint anti-drug operation, would they really admit it? The Irish Navy was severely undermanned, with only one of its three vessels at sea due to a staffing crisis. Pay and morale had been so poor for years that they were haemorrhaging personnel.

Admitting to the Irish public that the government had to rely on the British for patrolling Irish waters would be a bitter pill to swallow. But the French? They were fellow EU members—why the secrecy there? It wasn't as far-fetched as Leahy made it out to be. Still, she knew when to pick her battles, and today wasn't the day. The boss was in a foul mood, and the last thing she needed was to dig herself into a deeper hole. For now, she'd shelve the submarine story.

instead, she'd focus on the "Drugs in the Dáil" scandal and make herself useful. If she could find something big, maybe she could claw her way back into Leahy's good books.

She was still in the middle of her Bitcoin research and planned to finish the book that night, but before diving into that, she needed to do some digging into *Tales from the Dark Side*, the political blog that had broken the Marie Mulhall

CHAPTER 3

story.

The best person to consult on this? Charlie Lohan.

Charlie had been a senior reporter with *The Western People* in Ballina before retiring. Despite working for a rival paper, he had been a mentor to Robyn in her early years, taking her under his wing when she was still a cub reporter. A former president of the National Union of Journalists, he had spent years fighting for better pay and working conditions for journalists. To Robyn, he was nothing short of a saint—a legend in his own right, and always good craic on a night out. The man could do no wrong.

She picked up the phone.

"Hi Charlie, it's me" she said, her voice unusually subdued.

"Mayhem! How the hell are ya?" came the booming reply. His voice was as big as the man himself—tall, broad-shouldered, still sporting a full head of thick hair at seventy, and in better shape than men half his age with his favourite hobby hill-walking in Connemara when he wasn't holding court in a pub somewhere.

"I'm okay. I've been better. I'm in trouble with the boss—what else is new? Anyway, I wanted to pick your brain about something."

"Fire ahead. I'm just having a cup of tea and a look at the paper. So, what's up?"

"It's this Marie Mulhall story. What do you make of it?"

"Absolute nonsense. I know that girl likes a night out as much as the next person, but she's a rock of sense behind it. I'd bet the house that it's a load of rubbish. But I'm surprised those gurriers at that blog fell for it. They had solid evidence for the other two TDs they took down, but I'd say they've gotten cocky after their first big hits and standards have slipped."

He was referring to the two government TDs who had resigned after *Tales from the Dark Side* exposed planning irregularities. Those stories had catapulted the blog from obscurity into the national spotlight, earning it credibility and influence almost overnight.

Robyn frowned. "Why do you say 'gurriers,' Charlie?"

"Because that's what they are."

She laughed. You had to admire Charlie's straight-out-with-it manner of saying things.

"It's funny, isn't it? They expect politicians to declare all their business dealings, yet they don't declare theirs. We're supposed to believe a blog that came out of nowhere can afford to pay three full-time journalists from website subscriptions alone? Please. You and I both know how hard it is to get people to pay for news. Even legacy newspapers struggle with subscriptions. Someone is funding them—big money, big political money—and they're not being upfront about it."

Robyn's interest sharpened. "Good point. Investigative journalism like that is time-consuming and expensive. Maybe that's the angle I'll take. Thanks, Charlie. You're a star."

"You can get me a pint next time I see ya."

"Of course, Charlie. Catch you soon."

As soon as she hung up, she felt a renewed sense of purpose. But just as she was about to dig into the story further, a text pinged on her phone.

David O'Hara.

She had messaged him the night before to meet up—back when she still thought she'd be chasing the submarine story. It was coming up on lunchtime now, so she figured she might as well go meet him anyway.

CHAPTER 3

David was an old college friend and now a Garda with the Drugs Squad in Castlebar. Meeting Garda contacts was always tricky for journalists, so they had agreed to meet outside Westport at The Tavern in Murrisk. The village was nestled at the base of the famed pilgrimage site of Croagh Patrick mountain, which rose steeply above the surrounding landscape, its rugged slopes veiled in mist and legend, offering panoramic views of Clew Bay and drawing pilgrims and hikers alike to its revered summit all year round.

As she arrived into the pub, the aroma of seafood chowder made the instant decision for her as to what she'd be ordering. West of Ireland seafood was second to none, and a hot bowl of chowder with fresh brown bread was the region's equivalent of soul food.

David arrived just as the waitress left with Robyn's order. At 6'3", he had to duck slightly to avoid hitting the low-hanging timber beams that gave the place its rustic charm.

"How's life?" he asked, settling in.

"Oh, don't ask. Boss is on the warpath as usual. What about you? I haven't seen you down at the courts in a while."

"I've been working nights. Watching a few lads."

Robyn knew not to pry too much even though she'd kill to know who was under surveillance. But she had to keep a professional distance when he asked for it in his signature, understated way. Ever since their college days they had collaborated on info. They were both doing a post-graduate LLB law degree in the evenings at NUI Galway when David was moved from his Garda posting in Galway to Castlebar. His new job location meant he missed out on many evening lectures, and Robyn had always helped him out by sharing lecture notes even when other classmates were too competitive to do so. David never forgot this and now regularly returned the favour by helping her out with information whenever he could without breaching the Official Secrets Act.

"So what's this about? You said it was more off-the-wall than your usual requests. You have me intrigued," he said laughing.

Well, it's definitely one for the books. Have you ever heard of any submarines off the Mayo coast?"

"Submarines?" he spluttered, laughing. "Can't say I have."

"Yeah, it was a bit of a long shot, alright. The reason I ask is I was looking over that sunken story again. A fella told me he was out on The Point a few days before the boat went down and he saw what, he thought at first, was humpback whale. Only when he looked further—he had a telescope—he saw it was the fin of a submarine surfacing."

"You're joking me?"

"No, I'm not. And this guy seemed fairly solid. Not one of the usual attention-seeking, crackpot types who come into the office with their so-called 'tips.' He didn't come to the paper with it either. I happened across him. So, he had kept it to himself until I approached him."

"Unless the Irish Navy were running joint drug ops with the Brits, but I can't imagine they would be and the DS wouldn't know about it," he said, referring to the Drugs Squad. "The Navy do liaise with the EU's Maritime Surveillance Operation based in Portugal on ships with possible drugs cargo coming in from South America or West Africa. But by 'liaise' I mean the Navy would escort the ship to shore by boat. We don't even have subs."

"So there's no possibility of the French or anyone following a suspect vessel by submarine? Let's say a ship off-loaded

CHAPTER 3

drugs cargo onto a smaller vessel out at sea and then a French sub, for instance, tracked that vessel to the West coast?" she asked.

"I like how you're thinking," he said, "but if drugs were landed or there was even an attempted landing anywhere along the Mayo coastline, we'd definitely be in the picture. The only other scenario is—and it hasn't happened yet but, for argument's sake, I might run your possible reported sighting up the chain—but have you heard of narco subs?"

"Narco subs?" she looked at him blankly but interested.

"The cartels in South America have been building their own submarines to take shipments of cocaine up the coast to North America. Colombia's coastline has lots of inlets covered with thick jungle and so they use these hidden, coastal rivers as undercover shipyards to build the subs."

"Gosh, I had no idea drug running had gone so high tech."

"That's the thing. They're not high tech at all. They're just made out of fiberglass and intended for one shipment only. They can carry about ten tonnes of coke, so the building cost is minimal by comparison. And because they're made of fiberglass, they travel barely under the surface of the sea and are nearly impossible to detect by sonar or radar. They've even managed to evade infrared heat detection by piping their exhaust along the bottom of the hull to cool it before venting it. They can be spotted by air sometimes, but even this is tricky because the hulls are painted blue to camouflage them against the sea."

"So, it's only a matter of time before we'll see them crossing the Atlantic to Europe?" Robyn guessed.

"Spot on. Ireland has definitely been a target for the South American cartels for a while now. It's common knowledge that the Irish coast is pretty much unprotected. The Navy's down to one boat and we have no primary radar monitoring us from overhead. We just have what's called 'secondary radar' for the airports. So, we're reliant on tip-offs from allies about boats coming in with possible drug shipments. And maybe now subs, too. No, seriously. I doubt this sighting is real. If it was a sub, it wouldn't be coming this close to the coast. They'd be unloading the cargo to a fast boat much further out at sea. So I'd say it was a whale your buddy saw that day. But I appreciate the tip all the same. I'll let the higher-ups know, in any case."

"Well, thanks for your professional opinion anyway, David. So, I can cross submarine off the list of possible causes of the sinking."

His phone rang and he popped outside to answer. Robyn mulled over what he had told her. It turned out her editor was right to blast the story as nonsense, as much as she hated to admit it.

When he returned, she asked him if he had trouble with phone coverage out this side of Westport the past few days.

"No, I haven't, but I'm not surprised to hear you have," he said.

"Why?" she asked.

"We nabbed a guy the other day trying to sabotage one of the phone masts out near Newport," he revealed.

"Deliberately?" she asked.

"Yeah, he was a real clown. He was all decked out in camo and armed to the teeth like Rambo with a shotgun and knives."

"I don't believe you," she replied laughing.

"No, seriously. He was one of these nuts brainwashed on social media. When we brought him to the station, he was quoting all these conspiracy theories off the internet. That 'Q' said that 5G masts are giving us cancer, autism, Alzheimer's, freckles and everything under the sun. 'The only brain damage he had was from social media,' we told him. It wasn't even a 5G mast the clown was attacking—it was a 4G one." The 'Q' David was referring to was the American far-right internet conspiracist who came to fame with claims that a cabal of Satan-worshippers from the US Democratic party were behind 'Deep State' attempts to bring down Donald Trump.

"That's a great story, Dave. Can I publish it?"

"Yeah, off the record of course. Your readers will get a laugh out of it at least."

The chat with her old college buddy had done her the world of good. The two parted company and agreed to meet for a pint the following month. She needed to get the election out of the way, and he hoped his undercover op would be well wrapped up by then. Heading back to the office in Westport, Robyn felt relaxed and refreshed. She wrote up the mast sabotage story and sent it on to the boss who came out of the office happy for a change.

"Good story, Mayhew. A few more like these and I'll start to take you seriously again."

Five thirty p.m. rolled around fast and the staff all started to peel off, one by one, on the way home for the night. Robyn was the last to leave and, as she switched off the lights, she contemplated pulling an all-nighter in order to get the Bitcoin book finished, so that she could dive straight into the 'Drugs in the Dáil' story first thing in the morning.

The drive home to Castlebar went by in what seemed like seconds, her mind consumed with the stories she was chasing. But as she neared her home on Rathbawn Road, instead of turning right like she usually did, she made a sudden U-turn on the road. There was someone else she needed to see, someone who might hold the missing piece to what really happened out at sea the day *The West's Awake* was swallowed by the depths.

Chapter 4

The morning sunlight hung low over Westport, a pale gold misting the rooftops along The Fair Green. Robyn Mayhew stepped from her car with a weariness that clung to her like the morning mist. Four hours of sleep had done little to dull the fog behind her eyes, but she was grateful for even that.

As she walked the short distance to the office, she looked across at the picturesque Carrowbeg River as it calmly ebbed its way down through the town. When it came to workplace locations, Westport was jokingly known as "the death of ambition"—once you worked there, you lost all desire to move to Dublin or bigger cities, no matter how big the promotion you were offered.

The newsroom was just starting to get lively, with journalists and advertising staff already on phone calls, and production staff shouting across the floor, looking for copy and pictures they were urgently waiting on. It was chaos, but a chaos that she loved and even in the middle of it, she could think more clearly than in any silence.

"Jesus, Mayhew. What the hell happened to you?" her fellow reporter, Michael Davy, remarked on the bags under her red eyes. "A late night down 'the Planning Office,' was it?"

"The Planning Office" was the nickname given by journalists to The Irish House pub in Castlebar. On a slow news day, the actual planning office at Mayo County Council could be a good source of news if a new planning application had just come in for an interesting new development in the county. However, it wasn't always a guaranteed source of news, so a journalist could just as easily come up empty. And so it had become the legendary cover story for any hack who wished to disappear off for a sneaky pint or two in the afternoon. The Irish House in Castlebar was the porterhouse of choice, being a convenient spot for journalists from the three Mayo newspapers to convene.

The eye drops she had popped into her eyes before getting out of the car hadn't worked as well as Robyn had hoped, but she pointed to the book peeping out of her handbag as the excuse for her weary appearance.

"Up late reading about Bitcoin for this damned 'Drugs in the Dáil' story," she replied to Davy.

"I'm getting worried about you and this new level of commitment to the job you're showing, Robyn. It's not like you at all."

"Don't worry, it won't last," she assured him. "I'll be back to my usual laid-back self soon. Just dying to get this story out of the way so I can finally get down to the election coverage properly."

"But that is an election story," Davy said. "Marie Mulhall will lose her seat for Fine Gael for sure unless someone can

CHAPTER 4

prove that story is a hoax. I met her father at that filling station outside Ballina the other night, and he said she's devastated and completely panicked about how to prove the story wrong. She's seeing her GP for daily drug tests to prove to the electorate she's clean, but she doesn't know if that will be enough to prove herself to the voters. The damage might be already done."

"If it's a malicious hoax, it's a vicious thing to have happened," Robyn replied. "She's a super hard-working representative, and I'd hate to see that being done to somebody like her. I'm going to dig into the story today and see if I can turn anything up. But I'm not optimistic, to be honest."

"All you can do is your best, Robyn. I'm off to Claremorris to cover the court today, so I'm no help to you. But give me a buzz in the afternoon if I'm not back, if there's anything you want me to help with."

Turning on her computer, the best place to start, Robyn figured, was with LinkedIn. The platform had been a gift to the journalism profession since it was established. Prior to that, chasing down contacts and spokespeople had been an eternal nightmare for journalists, whereas now the profession had a veritable database of open-source contacts for every news story under the sun.

There were three guys behind the *Tales from the Dark Side* blog, and two of them, rather helpfully, had posted full CVs on LinkedIn. It never ceased to amuse Robyn how people thought nothing of posting every single detail of their personal life on the internet. Having a sceptical view of Big Tech, it wasn't something she did, only having social media accounts under pseudonyms for research purposes. But she wasn't naive enough to think there weren't private details about her being collected by every website she visited on the net, no matter how many times she clicked "no" to cookies on the sites she visited. But that was a story to dig into for another day.

Two of the bloggers, Vincent Peters and Dermot Mullane, had studied law at a private college but never progressed past the title of paralegal. Not surprising, Robyn mused—the entrance exams for the solicitors' and barristers' professions were tough. She had taken and passed hers after university but had never used them. Journalism had called louder.

The editor of the blog, Mike Mulcahy was a journalism graduate but had a much sparser résumé than his colleagues. He listed work experience with two of the national papers in Dublin, followed by various "research" gigs, freelancing, and traveling for the five years since. For guys who had uncovered three substantial political scandals over the past year or so, you certainly wouldn't have guessed it from their CVs.

When she was done being surprised, Robyn picked up the phone to Caroline Feeney on the news desk at *The Irish Observer*, where Mulcahy had interned a number of years ago. Caroline was the editor she dealt with when she syndicated her work to the national title. They had become good friends over the past two years and met regularly whenever Robyn was in the capital. Caroline always had the lowdown—and a memory that never failed her.

"Mike Mulcahy?" Caroline laughed when she picked up. "That fella? I couldn't forget him if I tried."

"Why was that?" Robyn laughed.

"Strictly off the record—the guy was a bloody nightmare. He had an ego the size of the EU. Everything you asked him to do, he had an attitude about. I thought it was because he was one of these assholes who didn't want to work for a female boss, but when I passed him off to some of the other editors, the lads had the same problem with him. He thought he should be writing the editorials and everyone else should move aside for him. I know there are a lot of big egos in this business, but Jesus Christ, this guy took the biscuit. I'm not one bit surprised he started his own blog because he wouldn't work for anyone other than himself."

"But he has gotten some serious stories over the past year. Did you see any of that promise in him at the time?"

"Not a sign of it. When I did try to give him some more substantial assignments to see if he would live up to his ego, he didn't rise to it. He had no news instinct or insight to talk of. We practically had to shove him out the door."

"You didn't hear of him turning up anywhere else after that? His CV on LinkedIn is pretty vague," Robyn asked.

"He was heading off to Eastern Europe, traveling for a while. We never felt so sorry for Eastern Europe. We were going to ring around the embassies and warn them."

"So you would never have expected him to be breaking stories of this calibre?"

"He'd have been the last person on earth I'd have expected it from. The only way he can be getting stories like those is if he's well in with the Opposition. The Republican Party must be getting those stories from insiders in the local councils in question. But where they got this drugs story on Marie Mulhall, I've no idea. It's allegedly from a hacker that reached out to them. It sounds a bit too much of a journalistic fairytale to me. Even if the Irish Republicans leaked him the planning stories, it's funny that they would give it to a friendly blogger rather than one of their TDs just stating it outright in the Dáil."

"What about money? Any indications he came from a wealthy background and would have been able to self-fund a blog with a full-time staff of three?" Robyn pressed her.

"Not that I could see. But I wouldn't have known him that well to even know one way or the other. Look, I've got to run, Robyn, but I'll ask around here and see if anyone has any theories and if they do, I'll come back to you."

Robyn thanked her and hung up, her mind racing. She called the other paper where Mulcahy had interned. The same reaction—arrogant, underwhelming, and then vanished.

If she couldn't crack Mulcahy, then perhaps his co-bloggers Peters or Mullane might yield answers. She sent messages to old classmates from law school and looped in her sister's legal contacts too. Dublin's legal scene was tight-knit, someone would know something.

For now, though, she had to get on the road. A special awards ceremony was being held in Belmullet, North Mayo, to belatedly recognise the efforts of a 98-year-old heroine of World War II. Her story was an amazing one, and Robyn was looking forward to meeting her. The journey from Westport to Belmullet took just over an hour and traversed some of the most rugged and scenic views of the West of Ireland. At the northwest tip of the country, the town of Belmullet always seemed to Robyn as if it was perched on the edge of the world. If you looked out over the vast expanse of the Atlantic Ocean from the beach in Belmullet, there was nothing but open ocean stretching endlessly before you to an unseen shore.

A strange sense of timelessness often came over her on the journey to the peninsula, luring her into a deep trance that regularly produced some of her best stories and ideas. As she set out on her journey, she thought more about what

CHAPTER 4

Caroline Feeney had suggested about the *Tales from the Dark Side* blog possibly having Irish Republican Party connections. Like all journalists, they probably didn't declare their party affiliations or take up party membership, but it didn't mean they weren't political. Aside from being the source of their insider leaks, could the Republican Party also be the source of their funding?

After all, the party was awash with cash. For years, money had poured in from the US from the Irish emigrant community over there, where the party had milked the Troubles for all it was worth, romanticising the fight for a united Ireland—safe in the knowledge that the Yanks were at a distance from all the murders, disappearances, kneecappings, and bombings.

For decades, it had been common practice for a bucket or a hat to be passed around the Irish pubs of New York, Boston, and Chicago for the "widows and orphans" of IRA men "fighting the good fight." Anyone who failed to contribute was considered a marked man or woman, even though it was well known that the money for the "widows and orphans" was actually money for guns and bombs.

On top of that slush fund, there was also the money from the Northern Bank robbery—over £26 million sterling. At the time, it was the largest bank robbery in the history of the UK. And it was such a huge haul that the PSNI (Police Service of Northern Ireland) in the North believed the IRA, in the end, didn't even know what to do with it. They had systems long in place for laundering money from the proceeds of crime, but this mountain of cash overwhelmed even those systems. Most of it was sent down south and just buried in the ground for years to come.

But it created a huge political storm. Politicians in Dublin and London were of the belief that senior figures in the Irish Republicans, who had been party to the Northern Ireland peace process, had advance knowledge of the heist and even sanctioned it. But a few months later, the IRA announced an end to its armed campaign and then completed the decommissioning of its weaponry. Those moves were welcomed on all sides, but the suspicion remained that the IRA had cynically raided the Northern Bank to secure a pension plan for its members after the armed struggle ended.

It wasn't a stretch to consider that some of these IRA/Republican Party funds were used in the years to come to establish and fund a political website with the aim of taking down the government in the South so they could take over.

As she arrived in North Mayo, Robyn was met with a warm welcome. The rugged, remote setting along the wild and windswept Atlantic Way seemed to shape the character of the Erris Peninsula's people, who embraced visitors with an uncommon warmth and genuine hospitality whenever they made the journey to their remote town.

The reception for the lady of the hour, Eileen Heaney, was in no way marred by its setting—a local nursing home. Now with silver-blue hair and a frail build, Mrs. Heaney's family and the people of Belmullet were bursting at the seams with pride for the historic role she had played in World War II. At just twenty-one years of age, when she had secured Belmullet's place in the history books for centuries to come with her game-changing weather forecasting for the D-Day landings. Now, decades later, her contribution was finally recognised. Letters and medals were bestowed, but it was her smile, wry and knowing, that Robyn would remember.

As Robyn drove back to Castlebar afterwards, she decided to

CHAPTER 4

dictate the story to her phone as she drove. She couldn't afford two hours of dead time for the full round trip to Belmullet when work was piling up back at the office.

"In a quiet, windswept corner of County Mayo, a 98-year-old Belmullet woman was bestowed with a rare honour by the US House of Representatives," Robyn wrote. "Her name was Eileen Heaney, a daughter of Co. Kerry, whose legacy was now woven into the tapestry of world history through her humble yet momentous contributions to weather forecasting.

"In the shadow of World War II, the remote Blacksod Lighthouse and Coastguard Station stood sentinel, its beacon not only guiding ships but also illuminating the path of destiny. Among those stationed there were Ted and Eileen Heaney, diligently recording the shifting winds and gathering clouds that would unknowingly alter the course of World War II.

"It was June 3, 1944, when Eileen, at just 21 years old, detected the approach of an Atlantic storm—a foreboding harbinger that would delay the Allied invasion plans by two critical days. From the quaint confines of the Blacksod post office, her weather reports were dispatched, their significance unbeknownst to the local populace amidst the chaos of distant battles.

"D-Day, the pivotal juncture in the war's theatre, was thus postponed, granting General Eisenhower the wisdom to wait for fairer skies. In the annals of history, Eileen's inadvertent contribution granted Eisenhower the confidence needed to embark upon the greatest amphibious assault in history.

"Decades passed before the true gravity of Eileen's actions became known to her and her family. It was a revelation that sparked both pride and laughter as Eileen recounted with amusement the frustration of the generals who, despite meticulously planning every aspect of the invasion, found themselves, in the end, completely at the mercy of nature's whim.

"In a poignant ceremony at Star of the Sea nursing home, Eileen received a letter of commendation from the World War II Museum in New Orleans, alongside a personal note from Congressman Jack Bergman. A medal, symbolising her "Laudable Actions," was placed upon her lapel—a tangible token of gratitude from a nation across the Atlantic.

"And amidst the strains of music and verse, Mayo's D-Day heroine sat, her weathered hands clasping memories that spanned continents and decades, a testament to the indelible mark one woman could leave upon the canvas of history."

As she finished up dictating the story, Castlebar's lights appeared on the horizon and her thoughts returned to Caroline Feeney's theory on Mike Mulcahy. Could the *Tales from the Dark Side* blog be a Trojan horse, funded by Irish Republican Party money? She thought of the American donations, the whispers of the Northern Bank heist, the slush funds buried beneath peace and rhetoric. It was plausible—but how could she prove it?

Pulling into Castlebar, Robyn pulled her scarf closer to her, still cold from the coastal chill that had seeped into her bones. She thought about what Eileen had said when she asked her views on climate change: "For all the talk of the climate getting wetter, warmer, and stormier, there's no mention of the east winds that are on the increase. When I was a girl growing up, it was a rare day you would feel an east wind," she recalled. "Maybe it's because I'm older now that I'm feeling the cold more. I haven't measured it scientifically, but the old

CHAPTER 4

weather forecaster in me definitely thinks those cold winds from the east are on the rise."

Robyn didn't doubt it.

The woman had once changed history with her eyes on the sky.

And she was watching it still.

Chapter 5

The morning crept in, grey and sullen, over Castlebar. By 9:00 a.m., Robyn was already at work on her laptop, coffee in hand, concentrating intensely. Monday's deadline loomed and she welcomed the solitude of working from home before then, in the calm before the inevitable storm.

She was deep into her research into the ownership of the *Tales from the Dark Side* blog. An online search of the Company Registration Office records showed the blog to be owned by a company incorporated by the three founders, Mike Mulcahy, Vincent Peters and Dermot Mullane, plus another company called interestingly, Darker Limited. The name alone bristled with bravado, almost like a taunt, daring anyone to come looking for the real owner behind it.

The company wasn't registered in Ireland so a phone call to her cousin, who worked in one of the Big Five accountancy practices in Dublin, might help get to the bottom of who owned it, Robyn thought to herself.

"Morning, Cuz. I need a quick favour. Could you run a company search through Lexis for me?" Lexis Nexis was a

CHAPTER 5

huge database of corporate resources. Most national media organisations had subscriptions, but smaller newspapers like *The Mayo Herald* were shoestring operations which unfortunately didn't boast access to such resources.

Robyn wasn't exactly a morning person herself, but her cousin was even less so. "Rob, you know I'll always help if I can, but I'm drowning at the moment. I can't do it right away, but I'll get back to you later on it. Who or what is it?"

"A company called Darker Limited. I owe you one."

"You owe me millions of ones at this stage. I'll ring you later."

Now that the company search was underway, Robyn turned her attention again to the journalists at *Tales from the Dark Side*. She had a response on WhatsApp from one of her former college classmates who knew of blogger, Vincent Peters. Adam was practicing at the bar now and the Law Library was always a hive of gossip, so she gave him a ring to see what the story was.

"Hi Adam. Robyn here. Can you talk for a quick minute?"

"Sure can, stranger. I haven't heard from you in a while."

They exchanged small talk, the kind rooted in years and distance, before Robyn cut to the chase.

"This guy, Vincent Peters, that I was messaging the group about yesterday. He's one of the founders of the political blog, *Tales from the Dark Side* that's broken a few big stories recently about politicians up to no good. I'm doing a story on the four founders of the blog. So, you've come across him then. What do you know about him?"

"Yeah, I knew him when he worked with Lancaster O'Keefe Solicitors on the Quays. He was a paralegal with them for a good few years. He did law at Griffith College but never managed to pass the Law Society entrance exams. It was always constitutional law he got stuck on. I think he sat it four times and failed it four times before he gave up. But maybe the law's loss is journalism's gain."

"You don't know if he had any particular political leanings, Adam?"

"Not that I know of."

"Or did he come from a well-to-do family background? I'm trying to find the source of the funds used to set up and run the blog."

"If he did come from money, he didn't show it. He always seemed to be a fairly down-to-earth fella."

Great, so no story there with Vincent Peters, Robyn thought to herself. Other than it being ironic that he was making a career out of launching judicial review proceedings against any government body that refused him access to information sought by his blog. Judicial review was one of the main subject areas in constitutional law, so it was kind of funny that it was this exam he repeatedly failed.

The other law grad member of staff at the blog was Dermot Mullane, and he was coming up empty as well. Two of her former classmates knew him but he didn't seem to be wealthy or political either. So, she'd have to wait on her cousin to see if she turned up anything with the company search for Darker Limited.

It was time for another caffeine hit to jolt her out of her morning brain fog, but she was interrupted by the phone ringing. On the other end was an out of breath Fergus O'Malley, owner of *The Newport Arms*.

"Hi Fergus," she answered, half laughing. "I'm not used to hearing from you this time of the day."

CHAPTER 5

"Robyn, I was out for a quick walk along the beach and," he said, pausing to catch his breath, "it's a shocking sight."

"What is?" Robyn replied, clearly concerned now.

"There are loads of them. I can't get over it."

"Loads of what, Fergus?" she said, trying to make sense of what he was telling her.

"Dolphins. Dead dolphins. Washed up on the beach here in Mulranny. It's shocking. The beach is covered in them. It's like an apocalypse."

"Dead dolphins. What the hell, Fergus. What happened?"

"I've no idea. But there must be forty or fifty of them at least lying dead all over the beach."

"Jesus."

A silence stretched between them, heavy and stunned.

"Is the coastguard there? Or the Department of the Marine?" Robyn then asked.

"Yeah, they're here. There's a good crowd gathered. I thought I'd give you a ring to come down to see yourself and if you want to bring a photographer."

"I'll be there in twenty minutes, Fergus. And thanks so much for the call. I appreciate it."

Robyn was still in the t-shirt and yoga pants she slept in, but a quick change of clothes and she was out the door. Her morning shower would just have to wait until later.

When she got to Mulranny village, the usual peacefulness and solitude of the beach had been shattered by the morning's grim discovery. Thirty-eight lifeless dolphins lay scattered along the shore in a nightmarish scene from nature. A large crowd of local people had gathered in shock and disbelief, murmuring amongst themselves as to possible causes. Officials from the Department of the Marine had already arrived, donned in hazmat suits as they began their examination of the animals and the surrounding scene. Seagulls circled overhead, their calls adding to the eeriness of the unnatural scene below.

Robyn pulled one of the officials overseeing the investigation aside and identified herself with her press card. But predictably, there was nothing of use he could tell her at this early stage. She tried to press him on a possible cause—was it pollution or disease—but he wouldn't be drawn further.

She walked the length of the beach, each lifeless form a stark reminder of the fragility beneath the waves. No oil, no visible toxins, no signs of a fish kill of any other species either—just death without explanation—once again on this stretch of the Mulranny coastline.

She left her photographer at the scene to record the event and drove back to Castlebar, still disturbed by the sight she had seen—thirty-eight dead dolphins that lay witness to the fragile balance between humanity and the natural world.

As much as she could have done with a caffeine fix, Robyn had to head straight to the courthouse when she arrived in Castlebar. A long day of boring district court reporting lay ahead. But maybe the act of concentrating on something else would help take her mind off the scene she had witnessed earlier.

She usually hated the tedium of court reporting—the same old tedious public order offences and the same old offenders, or in this case, young offenders—over and over again. But council and court reporting was the "bread and butter" of provincial newspapers. Council reporting certainly turned up interesting stories on local government, but the courts rarely did, apart from the odd big criminal case, at circuit court level. But the district court was the dustbin of court reporting.

CHAPTER 5

Despite her many requests to be reassigned to other tasks, Robyn's frequent protests fell on deaf ears.

Court went on without a break for lunch from 10.30 in the morning right through until mid-afternoon—five hours of continuous note taking, her hand cramped from shorthand, her mind only half-present. As with council meetings, no recording equipment of any kind was allowed so notes had to be taken by hand and then typed up all over again later—a double waste of time.

After court finally adjourned, Robyn slipped into The Welcome Inn. Soup and a toasted sandwich in the familiar warmth of the pub offered a brief respite. The hotel was one of the town's most distinctive buildings. Its mock-Tudor exterior with half-timbered black beams and a steep, gabled roof imbued it with a wonderfully old-world charm. The front bar at the hotel was the unofficial headquarters of the Fianna Fáil party in the town, with the other main political party, Fine Gael, taking up residence at Coady's Bar around the corner. The Republican Party hadn't yet established a semi-official presence in any of the pubs on the town, but it would only be a matter of time.

Rain ticked softly against the windowpanes as she stared out and her thoughts drifted to the earlier distressing scene on Mulranny beach, a wave of melancholy washing over her. Robyn knew all too well that when she let herself sink into serious contemplation, it often led her to darker places than she cared to explore. Today was no exception. Caught off guard, she found herself descending into a mood that was heavier than she'd anticipated.

With the bar empty after the lunchtime rush, Pat O'Mahony the barman, who was also a local town councillor, wandered over to her table for a chat. At first glance, his stocky build and receding hair made him look middle-aged, but he was still only in his thirties, not long married and with two little kids.

Sensing her quieter than usual mood, he ventured: "Man trouble?"

Surprised, Robyn turned to him. "I guess. But not that kind of man trouble. No, it's my brother I'm thinking about." She cast her eyes down. "We lost him twelve years ago."

"My condolences, Robyn. I didn't know you had a brother that passed away."

"No, he didn't die, Pat. He disappeared."

"Disappeared?" he replied, clearly taken aback. "That must have been tough."

"It was unbelievably hard," Robyn acknowledged, quietly.

"It's probably hardest on the ones left behind," he commiserated.

"No, it was definitely hardest for him. That's what's breaking my heart."

"Will you have another cuppa, Robyn, or something stronger? On me this time."

"Thanks, Pat. I appreciate it. But I have to get back to work for a while."

As she rose to leave both the premises and her dark mood behind, her phone began to ring. It was Jenny, one of her closest friends since her early school days. She was the first person she called that morning when the dolphins washed ashore. She had been working in the Coastal Erosion Section at the Department of the Marine for a number of years since she finished her engineering degree. Robyn hoped she might be able to give her the insider track on what the thinking was

CHAPTER 5

inside the Department on the dolphin kill.

"Hi Jenny. Thanks for calling me back. You probably know what I'm ringing you about."

"Yeah, I've a fair idea."

"Can you talk there at the moment?"

"Yeah, I've gone outside. There's no one within earshot," her friend replied.

"You must have something interesting to tell me so. What's the verdict there on the cause?"

"Look, Robyn. I'm deadly serious here. But there can be absolutely no way that what I'm about to tell you will ever be traced back to me or my job is gone. OK? Not to your editor—nobody. OK?

"Of course, J. And no one there in the Department knows you have a friend working in the media, right?

"No."

"And always keep it that way, Jenny. Otherwise, you'll get blamed for every single news leak even if it never had anything to do with you. I tell that to everybody I know. Never tell anybody that you know a journalist. All it will do is cause trouble for you."

"Right, I better make it quick," Jenny almost whispered. "But there's major shock in the Department over the dolphin kill off the west coast. The toxicology tests aren't due back until tomorrow, but the Department's vets are already pretty sure from their examination of the animals as to the cause of death. The dolphins had bleeding from their eyes and ears and this is consistent with only one thing," she paused. "Injury from intense deployment of sonar."

"Sonar?" Robyn replied, slightly confused. "Like what they have on ships? How would that have caused a mass dolphin kill?"

"Dolphins and whales are very sensitive to sonar and it's known to cause internal haemorrhaging at intense levels."

"At the risk of sounding incredibly stupid, Jenny, but there are ships at sea all the time. Why, all of a sudden, would they cause dolphins to die?"

"Merchant ships and fishing vessels use what's called an echo sounder. Most people think that is sonar but it's not. True sonar is used by military ships, but the Irish Navy hasn't been down the west coast in the past few days. And no other Navy would be in those waters. This is going to sound crazy, Rob but the only other type of vessel that deploys sonar would be, em," she faltered, "a submarine."

Chapter 6

For one stunned heartbeat, Robyn's mind froze as the weight of Jenny's words slammed into her. It was several seconds before her thoughts staggered back into motion.

"A submarine?" she finally managed, her voice low and disbelieving.

"Exactly," Jenny said, her voice sharp with the same stunned urgency. "The government's in a total spin over it. You can tell—none of the Secretary Generals are answering their phones. The departments are jammed up with high-level crisis calls."

"Would they have sanctioned the Brits or the French to do a run down the West Coast as part of a drug smuggling surveillance op? Is the government genuinely clueless about it or are they just claiming to be?" Robyn questioned her friend.

"Well, the Department of the Marine is certainly clueless about it. Unless Defence sanctioned a joint op with the British and are keeping it quiet. I've no idea."

"I'm in shock to be honest, Jenny because there's another

part of this story that I need to tell you about. But I need you to keep it on the down low for now."

"Another part? Like what?" she asked, surprised.

"A couple of weeks back—you probably heard about it on the news— a trawler sank off the Mayo coast in unexplained circumstances and four fishermen lost their lives, two brothers and their two sons. The weather was what you'd expect for the time of year, and they were experienced fishermen all. The boat went down suddenly with barely three seconds of an SOS. They didn't even have a chance to radio coordinates to launch a rescue boat. People were at a loss for an explanation as to what happened, and the bodies haven't been recovered. Anyway, last week, about a month after the tragedy, my editor asked me to do another trawl for information to see if anything had come to light. One particular guy, a keen birdwatcher who's out on the coast with a telescope a lot, told me that a few days before the sinking, he saw what he thought was the fin of a humpback whale appearing out on the water— only to realise it wasn't the fin of a whale, but the fin of a submarine. He was pretty shocked about it and hadn't told anyone because he thought he'd be dismissed as a lunatic. But now, after what you've told me about sonar being the likely cause of the dolphin kill and there being no military ships in the area, it's all pointing to that guy being correct in what he saw."

"That's shocking, Rob. When did you find that out?"

"Just a week ago."

"I can't believe you didn't tell me last weekend!"

"In this job, Jenny, you actually end up keeping more secrets than spilling secrets, believe me."

Jenny was silent for a moment. "How are you going to find

out what's going on?

"I've absolutely no idea. I'll have to have a think about it and see."

"Well, I'll leave it with you for now, Robyn. I better get back to work. But if you need anything give me a ring and I'll give you a quick text back. And keep me posted on anything you find out."

"Will do, J. And thanks for taking a risk on me. I'll make sure nothing ever gets back to the Department from me."

Robyn took a deep breath as she hung up the call, her mind still reeling from what she had just learned. She needed to talk to her editor and share her discovery, but first, she had to carefully plan how she would pitch it to him. He would inevitably demand to know her source, but she was determined to protect her friend, no matter how much of a tantrum he threw. Convincing him to run the story would be a tough sell, especially since he had fiercely rejected it just last week. His ego would now be an obstacle, preventing him from admitting he was wrong.

She went back inside the bar and settled up the bill. At least the drive from Castlebar to the office in Westport would give her some time to steel herself for the showdown with her boss.

But as she drove, Pat's words about the loss of her brother echoed in her mind: "It's the ones who are left behind."

The families of the missing fishermen were the ones left to suffer after the trawler's sinking in this case, possibly dragged down by a submarine that wasn't even supposed to be in Irish waters. Robyn felt a sense of duty to those family members to put up the best fight she could to get the story published, so that pressure would be on the government to investigate the matter fully. She silently vowed to keep asking questions for their sons and brothers—because she hadn't and she lost her brother because of it.

But as she drove into Westport, instead of turning left onto Distillery Road for the newspaper office, she kept driving through the town and took a right onto the Newport Road. She decided she was going to approach this head on. Rather than pleading with her editor to take a chance on the story, she was going to go directly to the people it mattered to most: those who were left behind after the trawler tragedy.

But first, she needed to get one other person on board.

German Joe answered his door almost immediately, peering at her with the wary suspicion of a man used to keeping to himself.

When she explained why she'd come, he hesitated only a moment before nodding gravely. "Aye. They deserve to know."

Robyn exhaled in relief. As they climbed into the car, she quickly dialed Caroline Molloy's number, her hands slightly trembling.

"Mrs. Molloy?" she asked gently when the call connected.

"Yes?" she answered softly.

"Hi, I'm Robyn Mayhew from *The Mayo Herald*. My apologies for interrupting you this afternoon. And my condolences on the recent loss of your husband, son and extended family."

"Thank you," she replied, her voice tinged with the weight of her grief.

"I've been looking into the circumstances surrounding the trawler's sinking and I've come across some information that I'd like to share with you and your sister-in-law, Geraldine. I have someone with me, a neighbour from just outside the town, German Joe—who made one of the discoveries. Would

CHAPTER 6

it be ok if we called by to talk to you and Geraldine about this? Or if it doesn't suit, maybe another time?

"What kind of information did you find?" she said, her voice filled with a desperate hope for any new details about the loss of her loved ones.

"It would be better if we could explain in person, Mrs. Molloy, if we could."

"Ok. That's fine. I'm at home at the moment. I'll ring Geraldine to call over as well. Do you know where we live?"

"I do. I'm just on the Castlebar Road, so I'll be there in five minutes or so."

"That's fine. I'll see you then."

Caroline Molloy sounded anxious on the phone so Robyn appreciated that she would have to tread very gently in this situation. The family were obviously traumatised by their loss, their nerves on a knife's edge while they waited for their loved ones' remains to be recovered. Sadly, those remains would probably be washed ashore somewhere along the coast in the coming weeks, unlikely to even be intact after being in the water for weeks. It was a harrowing situation for any family to endure.

Conveying this to German Joe, she said: "Joe, we're going to have to tread very delicately here. If you let me take the lead at first and then you can describe what you saw yourself. But I've also uncovered some additional information since that will be of interest to you as well. But I'll share it with everyone together."

"You've found out more? About the submarine?"

"Possibly."

German Joe inhaled deeply, concerned about what he might be about to hear.

As they pulled into the Molloys' driveway, Geraldine Molloy arrived too, her small frame rigid with anxiety.

The house, a modest, neat fisherman's cottage painted white with blue window frames, radiated an aching kind of resilience. Robyn noticed a small boat on a trailer parked beside the house and nets awaiting repair in the yard, sorrowful reminders of maritime lives frozen mid-breath by tragedy.

Inside, the Molloy home was warm and clean, the kind of ordered place that said the family was doing their best to hold on. A fresh pot of tea, neatly arranged cups, and a plate of biscuits sat on the table—a kindly effort by a woman in the grip of cold, hard grief. They settled into the living room, sunlight streaming in through windows framed by early-blooming snowdrops, giving hope at a time of such loss.

Robyn decided to get straight down to business: "I won't keep you in suspense any longer. My editor asked me earlier this week to revisit the circumstances surrounding the trawler tragedy and see if I could uncover anything new. On foot of my enquiries, I was directed to German Joe who, as you know, is a keen birdwatcher and spends a lot of time out on The Point. What he told me left me floored, to be quite honest. Joe, I'll let you explain from here."

Joe took a deep breath, clearly uneasy about what he was about to say. "A few days before the trawler went down, I was out on The Point, scanning the horizon. At first, I thought I saw the fin of a humpback whale emerging from the water in the distance. But when I adjusted my scope and looked again, I was shocked by what I saw. And I realise this might sound crazy, which is why I didn't come forward sooner—I just didn't think anyone would believe me."

CHAPTER 6

"What did you see?" Geraldine asked, leaning forward anxiously.

"It wasn't the fin of a whale I was looking at," he paused, shifting uncomfortably in his seat. "It was the fin of a submarine."

"A submarine?" both women echoed in disbelief.

Joe nodded. "Yes. I know the Irish Navy doesn't operate submarines, and there shouldn't be any foreign subs in the waters off the west coast of Ireland. UK submarines usually pass along Northern Ireland on their way out to the Atlantic from their base in Scotland, but there's no reason a sub should have been where I saw it that day."

"Are you saying that a submarine could have collided with the trawler, Joe?" Caroline asked, her face suddenly pale.

"Not exactly. Submarines are equipped with advanced systems to avoid such collisions. But there's a more plausible, though still unconfirmed, scenario. It has happened in European waters before—a submarine could have unknowingly become entangled in the trawler's nets. If the sub then dived to deeper depths, it could have dragged the trawler down with it. That would explain why the crew only had seconds to send out an SOS before they were pulled under."

Caroline gasped audibly, clearly shocked. Geraldine reached out and grasped her hand, her own expression mirroring her sister-in-law's shock.

Robyn took a moment before speaking again. "I brought this story to my editor last week, but he refused to publish it because it was based on a single, uncorroborated sighting. He was concerned that it might be more traumatising for your families if the story turned out to be unfounded. But something happened yesterday that might change his mind."

She continued, "You both heard about the beached dolphins on the strand in Mulranny?"

Everyone nodded, but half in fear of what was to come next.

"I was following up on this story for the paper and I contacted a source I have within the Department of the Marine. And they told me that the Department's vets examined the animals and found that they were bleeding from their eyes, ears and noses. There could be only one cause of this—not pollution, not disease—but sonar, like that used by military ships, none of which were on the West coast in recent days. The only other type of vessel that would deploy sonar is a submarine."

Joe's eyes widened as the realisation hit him. "Damn it," he muttered, his voice filled with regret. "That's what took them down. I should have spoken up sooner."

Caroline and Geraldine were now quietly crying, the weight of the revelation settling in. Robyn apologised for upsetting them, but Caroline shook her head.

"No, we needed to hear this. It's shocking, yes, but we've been waiting for weeks for answers, and all we've gotten is silence."

"Well, I'm afraid that's all I'm getting from official channels too," Robyn said. "I've reached out to both the Department of the Marine and the Department of Defence for a statement, and all they've done is deny everything. It's clear the government is covering up the presence of a submarine off the West Coast. I don't know why—maybe they've asked the UK for help patrolling the coast for drug smugglers, given that our Navy is down to just one ship operational at the moment. And perhaps they want to keep it quiet for PR reasons. Even though it's been public knowledge since after the September

11th attacks that we have a military arrangement with the UK for the Royal Air Force to protect our airspace in the event of a threat from the skies. So I just don't know what's going on, to be honest."

Robyn paused before continuing. "Publishing this story in the press might put pressure on the government to come clean, but I don't want to give you false hope. They could just as easily ignore our call for answers or say they will investigate and publish a report in due course. When a government wants to bury an issue in red tape, they can and will."

"And there's one other thing," she added. "My editor. He rejected Joe's story last week because it was only one person's account. He thought it was too risky to publish something so sensitive without corroboration. But now that I've spoken to you, I'm hoping he'll reconsider and publish the full story this week."

"That would be a great help, Robyn," Caroline said, her voice thick with emotion. "Any pressure that could be applied in order to get answers would be welcomed by our family."

"And thank you, Joe, for coming forward with what you saw," Geraldine added. "I know it wasn't easy."

"I just wish now I had come forward sooner," he said, downcast.

"I get it, Joe. It wasn't an easy decision," Geraldine reassured him.

As they got up to leave, Robyn promised to keep in touch with any updates from official sources.

Robyn dropped German Joe home and she thanked him personally for bringing the story to her. "If it wasn't for you, those families would still be aching for answers. But at least they have something to hold on to. I hope we're able to get further with it, but I'll let you know Joe over the next while if I find out more. And thanks again for trusting me with this."

"No problem, Robyn. I'll be back on coast watch tomorrow and if I see anything, you'll be the first to know."

Robyn waved him goodbye, feeling a mix of determination and unease about what lay ahead. Now came part two of her challenge: convincing Leahy to publish the story. With the families backing her, he had little reason to refuse, except perhaps out of anger that she had gone behind his back, defying his authority. This could be explosive, but she had no choice—she had to steel herself and face the music.

"Jesus Christ, Mayhew. Last week, you came to me with some crackpot submarine story from some nutcase you met in the library. Now you're back with another nameless source claiming a submarine killed forty fucking dolphins. What is it with you and fucking submarines?"

Editor Jack Leahy was in one of the worst moods she'd ever seen him. What a day to have brought this story to him. If she'd known he was in such a stinking mood, she'd have held off pitching the story until over the weekend.

"You've pulled a fast one by going to those families first with this story, giving me no choice but to publish. But if you pull that one again, you can pack up your desk and leave. I'm not having any reporter in this office undermining my editorial decision-making. We're three weeks out from an election and this is all you have for doing? You're skating on thin ice, Mayhew. Get a damn election story for me and have it on my desk before Monday's County Council meeting."

As Robyn walked out of his office and onto the newsroom floor, she had never been so relieved that it was Friday evening at last and the weekend was here. What a bloody week it had

CHAPTER 6

been.

Chapter 7

Monday morning broke grey and hostile over the West of Ireland. Robyn stumbled through it, raw and hungover after a weekend she barely remembered and already regretted. She'd planned to write up the week's court cases on Sunday evening, but the task had loomed too large, and she had kicked the can down the road until morning. Now, weighed down by fatigue and regret, she was about to pay the price.

The newsroom pulsed with the usual Monday madness, but this morning it felt even crueler. The guys in production shouted for her reports before she even dropped her bag, some of them grinning as they did it, knowing how it irritated her. It was half-past midday before she banged out the last line of her court write-ups, her head pounding, her nerves frayed. She wasn't ready to start on her election story, not yet. She needed to breathe.

She took her laptop and slinked off next door to Tony's, the

CHAPTER 7

pub that she thought of as her living room in Westport. It had seen better days, but then again, so had she.

Chris was behind the bar polishing the well-worn countertop. His floppy fringe hung low over his eyes. He clocked her mood as soon as she walked in.

"A coffee, Robyn?" he asked, instinctively knowing it wouldn't be a beer when she had her laptop bag with her. As much as she could have done with a "hair of the dog" pint, it just wasn't a good look for a journalist to be spotted in a pub writing up the news reports whilst sipping on a cold pint. It was acceptable to meet a contact in a pub and have a drink, but typing up news stories under the influence was a definite no-no.

"I'll have it down the back, Chris."

"One of those days?" he enquired.

"Sure is," she said, exhaling deeply.

The laptop stayed closed for now. As she waited for her coffee to cool down a little, she stared into the worn timber and low-beamed ceiling of Tony's, grateful for the way the outside world dulled here. She needed a plan, but her mind spun in circles.

It was time to get stuck into that election story she had been trying to get to for the past week. But where to even begin? The country's electorate seemed to be giving the Irish Republican

Party a pass on the dark, murderous past of its military wing—the IRA—and the decades it had spent maiming, bombing, kneecapping and murdering in the name of a united Ireland. The Commissioner of An Garda Síochána had only recently reiterated his view that the party in the Republic was still subject to the orders of the IRA Army Council. Yet, somehow, the party's violent history was slipping quietly into the mist of forgetfulness.

The support from younger voters in particular—many of whom were born in the '90s and after and had no direct memory of IRA atrocities—was a significant factor, but it didn't fully explain the party's sudden, spectacular rise to the top of the opinion polls in the past few weeks.

Just five months ago, the party had been decimated in local elections, securing only 9% of the vote. Now, they had skyrocketed to 25%, leading the polls. The media at large were quick to attribute this rise to a tipping point having been reached in public frustration over the country's ongoing housing and health crises. Yet these crises had remained stagnant since the summer, and none of the other left-wing parties had seen a similar surge in support. The argument lacked sufficient analysis, and the media seemed unusually willing to accept the poll results without probing deeper into the reasons behind this extraordinary shift, too distracted by the pressures of "churnalism" and the 24-hour news cycle.

But Robyn was convinced there was a bigger story at play here. The Cambridge Analytica scandal in the UK two years ago had exposed how the Leave campaign in the Brexit referendum had exploited psychological profiles of voters, harvested from their Facebook accounts, to manipulate them into voting Leave. Ever since then, every despot in the world was alerted to the potential of data harvesting as a means to sway elections. The Cambridge Analytica firm closed their doors in the wake of the scandal but no doubt, many more opened theirs. The lure of using of data harvesting from the internet was just too tantalising for many political figures and campaigns to resist. Could the Irish Republican Party, the wealthiest political party in Ireland by a mile, with unlimited funds from the Northern Bank robbery and North American fundraising, have enlisted such specialists to tip the scales in their favour? And more specifically, if they had, how could she prove it?

Frustrated, Robyn sipped on her coffee. It was at times like these that she questioned the wisdom of her decision to work in the provincial press down West. She hadn't pursued the possibility of moving on to a national paper in Dublin because she was just so comfortable where she was. But it had its downside in terms of occasionally feeling sidelined from all the action in the capital. Especially when it came to access to the people who mattered. But being based in the West never stopped her before, so she wasn't going to let it now.

The only way she could investigate this hypothesis was by getting inside the Republican Party. Robyn had never cultivated contacts within the party, having always felt reviled by the IRA's violent history. But it was easy to ignore them when they were political pariahs. Now that they were considered rockstar politicians by the younger generation, she knew she would have to get her hands dirty and infiltrate their ranks.

Using a virtual proxy server to access the party's website, Robyn signed up as a volunteer under her fake identity, Lia Hyland. She had created the alias years ago as a journalism student, backstopped with fake social media profiles and a LinkedIn account.

For added security, she had even acquired a pretty convincing counterfeit driver's license through some shady connections of college friends. When the showboating sports editor of *The Mayo Herald* had begun a campaign to feature journalists' photos alongside their bylines, Robyn had steadfastly refused. She was determined to maintain her privacy, knowing that once it was lost, it could never be regained. Now, as she prepared to delve into an undercover political investigation, she was grateful she had stood her ground.

Once she had signed up to volunteer, all she had to do was wait for them to get back to her. In the meantime, she would write up the bones of her story on the Republican Party's meteoric rise in the opinion polls, questioning how it surged so dramatically in the space of just five short months. She would get quotes from local politicians on all sides of the political divide at the county council meeting she was covering later that evening. With those in hand, she intended to have the finished piece on Leahy's desk by tonight.

Then she'd follow up her hunch on her own time and out of Leahy's hair. She couldn't stand having an editor breathing down her neck. This was probably why she hadn't made the

CHAPTER 7

move to a daily paper and stayed down the country instead. She didn't have to account for every second of her day like her colleagues in the capital, even at the expense of sometimes feeling like she was missing all the action.

Now that she had gotten her bearings, it was time to go back to the office to show her face there for a while before she had to leave again for the County Council meeting.

She thanked Chris on the way out the door, adding: "I've sent you on a story you'll be interested in," she said, referring to the story about submarine sonar being the likely cause of the trawler sinking and the dolphin kill. "It's the unedited version. The boss might chop half of it before it goes to print, but that's the uncut edition for you, Chris." It was the one advantage of working in a bar next door to a newspaper office—you often got a heads up on breaking news stories.

Chris smiled. "Cheers, Robyn, I'll have a look at that. That was a great one last week about Rambo versus the phone mast, the plonker."

She laughed properly for the first time that day. It was always nice to get positive feedback from readers, especially since feedback usually only came in the form of complaints from district court offenders who weren't thrilled to see their names and misdeeds published in the local paper and blamed the journalist for printing it. It always lifted her spirits knowing that she had at least one appreciative reader out there, even if it was only Chris next-door.

She was barely back at her desk when her phone rang. It was her cousin, Emma, calling with an update on her investigation into the ownership of the *Tales from the Dark Side* blog.

"Hi Ems, how are you getting on?"

"I'm ok. Can we talk or do you have an audience there?"

"Just hang on and I'll go outside," Robyn told her.

"Jesus, those bloggers weren't joking when they called that holding company Darker Limited," Emma quipped. "I had to assign three trainees to it for the past few days to try to unravel the ownership. There was shell company after shell company after shell company."

Robyn winced. "I'm sorry, Ems. I didn't know it'd be that bad."

"Don't worry," Emma said dryly. "I had some credit built up from my Caymans days."

"From your Caymans' days?" Robyn sounded alarmed. Emma's two years working in the tax haven had given her a Rolodex of contacts who could unpick even the most tangled of shell companies. But those bloggers had a serious backer if he was hiding his shareholding behind layers of shell companies in the secretive Caribbean tax haven, she thought to herself.

"Are you sitting down for this?" she warned her cousin.

CHAPTER 7

"Standing outside in the rain," Robyn told her. "Fire ahead."

"It's Jimmy Costello, the hedge fund owner."

"Jimmy Costello? The guy threw a big hissy fit at his friend the Taoiseach when he didn't grant him the custom tax breaks he demanded for having established his hedge fund in Dublin—that Jimmy Costello?"

"Yep, the very one," Emma confirmed. "*Tales from the Dark Side* is a Jimmy Costello production."

A cold knot tightened in Robyn's gut. Jimmy Costello was a ruthless operator.

"Sneaky bastard," she breathed.

"This is serious, Rob," Emma warned. "He's not a guy you want to go up against unless you have your i's dotted and your t's crossed."

But Robyn knew that herself. She thanked Emma for the breakthrough and ended the call, staring into the leaden sky, the rain dripping from her hairline down her face.

Gosh, what a news week it had been for Robyn—two major news stories—a foreign submarine as the cause of the trawler sinking and now, the uncovering of the financier behind the blog taking down government TDs. Both were serious scoops that she would be able to syndicate to the national papers. But she wasn't patting herself on the back just yet. The "Drugs in the Dáil" story was far from over, and time was bleeding away fast. If she didn't clear Marie Mulhall's name before election day, the political machine would crush her like roadkill.

Still, the Costello revelation gnawed at her. She hadn't expected him to be behind the blog. Yes, he was a sworn enemy of the Taoiseach, but she had been almost certain that it was going to be a Republican Party supporter who was the moneybags behind it. Costello was bitter, but he definitely wasn't Republican. That would conflict with his capitalist mores. So, while it was a big story in its own right, it had unfortunately disproven Robyn's theory that it was someone on behalf of the Republican Party who had set up TD Marie Mulhall with "drugs in the Dáil" so she would lose her seat in the forthcoming election to the benefit of their candidate. She'd have to change tack now and examine the story from a different angle. And fast.

No time to wallow. It was almost four, and County Hall beckoned. And given that it was the last county council meeting before the general election, there were bound to be fireworks with politician after politician grandstanding and fighting it out for votes on behalf of their parties. It was the type of political scrum that Robyn really looked forward to. This day was turning out to be way better than it had started out.

It was two minutes to four when Robyn pulled her car into the car park adjacent to County Hall in Castlebar and ran up the steps to make the meeting on time. It was a cold, frosty evening with not much sign of spring in the air—a terrible

CHAPTER 7

time of year for an election, not just for the politicians and canvassers out on the stump, but also for election day itself and the detrimental effect the cold and the rain could have on potential turnout.

Robyn nipped inside just on time to take her seat on the press bench where all her colleagues were already situated and looking forward to the evening's theatrics. Though they were technically competitors, there was such a great camaraderie amongst the journalists in Mayo that Robyn regarded them all as friends. But that didn't stop plenty of good-natured ribbing about each other's stories, nonetheless.

Robyn was still buzzing from the scoop she'd landed that afternoon and she itched to share it with her fellow reporters. But there would be no time for celebratory pints after the meeting. The clock was ticking, and everyone was under pressure to pull together a lead story from the evening's proceedings before the papers went to print. In the journalism world, it wasn't common practice for journalists to share scoops before they hit the newspaper stands, but there was a certain old-school courtesy among her more seasoned colleagues that she deeply respected. Their word was their bond, and they upheld an unspoken code of integrity that she admired. She still missed Charlie Lohan, who had retired a year back. Charlie had been a mentor to her, guiding her in the right direction on more than one occasion. It was his advice that had set her on the right path in tackling the "Drugs in the Dáil" scandal by steering her to investigate the financial backers behind the *Tales from the Dark Side* blog. She would definitely be getting him a bottle of his favourite whiskey as a gesture of thanks for his generous encouragement and guidance.

Proceedings got underway and there was nothing remarkable to report for the first hour of the meeting. But when they hit the motion tabled by Cllr. Richard Duffy, the sole Republican Party councillor—to launch compulsory purchase orders against derelict properties in the county—she sat up straighter, pen poised.

Duffy. Now there was a man who could turn hypocrisy into an art form.

For years he had fought tooth and nail against housing developments in his electoral area, accusing anyone in favour of being "in the pockets of developers" when it curried favour with the public to do so after the property crash of 2008. His sharp U-turn in the opposite direction once the housing crisis became a burning issue with the public, was nothing short of sensational. Once the champion of "Not In My Backyard" or NIMBYs as they were known, he had suddenly positioned himself as a crusader for housing as if he hadn't spent years stalling the very solutions he now claimed to support. His reversal was as stunning as it was unchallenged, much like the Republican Party's stratospheric rise in the polls—a phenomenon equally shrouded in silence and a lack of scrutiny. The irony, however, was impossible to ignore. Duffy, who had once been a key obstacle to much-needed development during a time when the construction industry was already on its knees, was now pointing fingers at the government for their alleged short-sightedness. Yet, his own shortsightedness was evident in his years of opposition and so he was a clear contributor to the current housing crisis.

But this wasn't just a local issue—it was a national trend. The Republican Party had adopted this populist stance in councils across the country, seizing on public discontent wherever they could, and Duffy was merely one player in a much larger, more cynical game.

Predictably, one of the independent councillors seconded his motion and so, it was deemed passed, but not before Fianna Fáil and Fine Gael councillors added to the debate with their handwringing over the crisis too. She jotted down quotes from both sides of the debate, but she still wanted to pursue it further with Cllr. Duffy. She would try to nab him on the way out of the meeting later.

By the time "Any Other Business" rolled around, the councillors were shifting restlessly in their seats, but Robyn's attention sharpened again. The Chief Executive raised a fresh concern—an unexplained power outage across North Mayo. Unscheduled, widespread and alarming.

"Industry in Ballina is concerned the effect such outages could have on production," he told the meeting. "And while most plants, hospitals and critical facilities had backup generators, there were hundreds of smaller businesses who didn't, never mind the inconvenience to the general public."

A representative from ESB Networks was introduced, and Robyn was pleasantly surprised to see that it was none other than Donnacha O'Brien, an old friend from when they were kids. They had lost touch when Donnacha's family moved to Sligo in their teens. But seeing him now, she was struck by how little he had changed since they were fifteen, still with a lanky build and spiky dark hair. With a warm sense of nostalgia, Robyn made a mental note to catch up with him too after the meeting.

Donnacha revealed to those assembled that a fire at the Moy substation in Ballina had been the cause of the outage. They were still investigating the cause of the fire as it wasn't immediately clear what had happened, but they had engaged outside experts to assist with the forensics. A further report would be provided to the council at the next month's meeting.

Robyn's curiosity was piqued. ESB Networks had a reputation as a solid public company, offering excellent pay and working conditions, largely due to strong union representation. It was the kind of place where employees settled in for life, accumulating decades of experience in their respective fields. This was precisely why she found it odd that the company had felt the need to bring in outside consultants to investigate the fire. There was more to this fire than met the eye and that the company weren't letting on publicly.

As the meeting drew to a close and attendees began gathering their belongings, Robyn noticed Donnacha making his way toward the press gallery. His usually easygoing demeanor was replaced with a more serious expression.

"I can't talk here, but give me a ring when you can," he said,

CHAPTER 7

winking and discreetly passing his business card to her before taking off.

That was strange, Robyn thought to herself, making a mental note to follow up with him when she got a chance.

She milled around near the exit to see if she could grab Cllr. Duffy for a word, but he seemed to be deep in conversation with two of his fellow councillors. Although she had been covering these council meetings for a while now, she'd never actually spoken to him directly. He didn't come across as the friendliest but then, it was probably a pretty lonely position to be in—the sole member of your party on the entire council and a party with murky past, at that. She resolved that she would treat him fairly, but firmly. The questions she planned to put to him would probably ruffle his feathers, but it was her job to ask tough questions. Most politicians, even those under scrutiny, understood this and could still maintain a respectful, if not cordial, working relationship with the journalists who covered their activities. She hoped Cllr. Duffy would be the same, but she was prepared for the possibility that he might not be.

She tapped him on the shoulder and he indicated that he'd be another minute or two and he'd meet her outside in the corridor. With a receding salt-and-pepper hairline and a rounded middle, he looked a lot older than his 40-something years. And his perpetually furrowed brow didn't help either. Robyn paced up and down the corridor for at least half an hour before he finally emerged.

"Cllr. Duffy, Robyn Mayhew from *The Mayo Herald*," she introduced herself. Do you have time for a few quick questions?"

"Fire ahead," came the brusque reply.

"You spoke about the housing crisis this evening and the effect it's having on your constituents. Do your regret the part you played in allowing the housing shortage to build to its current level?"

Cllr. Duffy looked at her stunned.

"The part I played?" he replied, laughing at the idea of it.

"Yes, Councillor, the part you played. I have checked the planning records since 2008. You objected to every single housing estate and apartment development in your electoral area since the property crash in 2008."

The mask cracked. For a flash, he looked genuinely rattled.

Then, it was Robyn's turn to be shocked.

"That's not true," he snapped.

"But I've checked the records in the planning office, Councillor. I know what your record on housing development is. Now you're going to blatantly lie about it?"

His face tightened, the lines around his mouth turning harsh.

CHAPTER 7

"You'd want to be very careful, Miss... What did you say your name was?"

"It's Mayhew and it's Ms.," she replied, tersely.

"You'd want to be very careful, Ms. Mayhew. If any of these unfounded allegations of yours are printed about me in your paper, then I will be instructing my solicitor to immediately sue for defamation. Do you hear me, Ms.?"

"Do you hear me, Councillor? The objections you've lodged against every single housing development in your area since 2008 are a matter of public record. Each one, signed by you, is there in black and white. So, no matter how hard you might try to spin it, this isn't a situation where you can pull a Donald Trump and deny the facts. The reality is staring you in the face, and it's not going anywhere. And I don't take well to your threats of a lawsuit either. That will also be in the paper. And it's not just you—your entire Party has contributed to this housing crisis. They objected to the 'Help to Buy Scheme' that so many young people desperately need to buy a first home. And in the North, your party wouldn't support rent controls to give young people a chance to try to save for a deposit to buy a home. You supported rampant capitalism at their expense instead. The Republican Party might be used to the rest of the media falling under their spell, but I haven't. I'm very up to date on your party's history on both sides of the border and I won't be giving you the 'kid gloves' treatment that other journalists have. So, I've one more question for you: have the Republican Party deliberately tried to maintain the housing shortage in order to gain from it politically?"

"That's preposterous," he guffawed. "Now, I've had enough of your abuse. So, I'd advise you to think carefully about your words. Because once spoken, they can't be taken back."

"And once written, Councillor, they most definitely can't be taken back either. Like in the planning files of all those developments you objected to," Robyn retorted, walking away from him.

She got into her car, shaken by the exchange. Of the thirty councillors on the council, she had never encountered such hostility before. Every single one of the other councillors had always been courteous to a fault, no matter how hard the questions were. Her line of questioning had been tough, but this guy was blatantly lying in the face of written records, clearly denying reality and threatening a journalist. This guy had just torn up the rulebook.

As she started the engine to move off, she looked into her rearview mirror to reverse, then suddenly froze. There he was—standing right behind her car—taking a photograph of her licence plate.

She just hoped he hadn't gotten a picture of her as well. It would put paid to her plans to infiltrate the party under a false identity.

And while there was no recording equipment allowed within the council chamber, both Cllr. Duffy and herself were outside by the time Robyn surreptitiously put her mobile phone to use as well—switching it on in time to record Duffy's menacing

Chapter 7

threats.

Chapter 8

The passenger's journey began under the cover of nightfall, when the shadows conspired with secrecy. As she stepped out into the cold night air, she paused, before turning around. The silhouette of the house was visible against the moonlight, with darkened windows like hollow eyes that watched her leave. The stillness of the hour seemed to hold its breath along with her. It was 2:00 a.m. and the world was asleep.

Her blonde hair was barely visible beneath her hood and would soon be disguised with a dark wig waiting for her in the van that had arrived for her. The vehicle was crammed full of old furniture. The plan was to conceal herself amongst the furniture, lying on the floor between two towering bookshelves that pressed against her sides like a straitjacket. It was far from a comfortable hiding spot, but comfort was a luxury she could not afford on this mission.

The van's driver, a heavy-set man with a grizzled beard, had given strict orders for her to stay still and silent. If the van was stopped at a border checkpoint, the guards might not bother to look too closely, assuming the cargo was nothing more than a mundane delivery. But the passenger knew that a single suspicion from a diligent border guard could spell disaster.

The journey was arduous, a test of nerves as much as endurance. The van rattled along the rough country roads, avoiding main roads as much as possible. Every two hours, the driver would pull off down one of the narrow, twisting laneways that wound through the dense forests in this part of the world. Here, in the depths of the countryside, the passenger could take a few precious moments to stretch her stiffened limbs, her breaths coming in deep, grateful gulps of cold night air.

Despite the relative quiet of the main road, they knew better than to trust it. The driver was relentless in his caution, eyes darting to the rearview mirror at every turn, as though expecting pursuit at any moment. Their mission was too important to be jeopardised by complacency.

Days later, after a harrowing journey that seemed endless, the passenger found herself standing at the edge of a rugged coast, the salty tang of the sea in the air. A fishing trawler, its hull weathered and worn by years of battling the elements, waited to carry her onwards to her next destination. The sea was choppy and the small vessel tossed about like a cork in a storm. But she held firm, her gaze fixed on the horizon, where her destination and her mission awaited. After hours of battling the relentless waves, they finally docked in the early morning light in the quiet port of Piraeus, Greece. The scent of fresh fish mingled with the briny sea air as the fishermen unloaded their catch, oblivious to the secret passenger who had slipped ashore to the EU.

*****

The day the paper hit the newsstands was usually a slow one at *The Mayo Herald.* It was an unofficial day off for the sports team who, more often than not, spent their weekends on the sidelines of pitches around the county covering matches. But the "sports team" actually included the entire news team, bar her. When she took the job with *The Herald* the boss had warned her not to express any interest in covering sports to the Sports Editor or he would have her reporting on camogie matches in every corner of Mayo for the rest of eternity. But it wasn't difficult for Robyn to keep her mouth shut about sport. She knew next to nothing about it anyway, except for basketball. The editor had been clear: the paper already had a robust sports section, which was, in fact, the main reason most people bought *The Herald.* However, this strength came at the expense of the news section, which had been struggling to keep up. Hiring an extra news journalist was a deliberate move to bolster the news coverage and to bring balance back to the paper.

"We'll give you six months," the managing editor had told her, "And then we'll know by the circulation if you're paying your way."

It was her first job in journalism, and she felt the pressure. But the six-month deadline came and went and nobody even noticed. No appraisal, no new contract, nothing. Things were very "ad-hoc" at *The Herald.*

Today she had to make an appearance at the office in Westport because she was pencilled in to interview a local dignitary. Joe Heskin was the owner of a diverse portfolio of businesses in Westport and, as befitting his status as a big employer in the town, the editor thought he should be afforded a full-page interview in the newspaper. Not that anyone in the town would be the slightest bit interested in reading it. The man was born and bred there, and everyone knew him on first name terms. There was nothing new under the sun to say about Joe Heskin. But somehow Leahy thought Robyn might squeeze some interesting details out of him, like juicing a lemon. But he made it clear it was to be a friendly interview, not some "exposé" of the kind to which she was accustomed. Luckily for Robyn, she could squeeze news out of stone. But she hated writing fluff features. It bored her to tears.

"Jesus Christ Mayhew, we didn't expect to see you in here with your kneecaps intact," Pat Flynn, the advertising manager exclaimed when she walked in. "I thought it was the IRA that carried out execution jobs, not journalists," he added, laughing.

Pat's desk was the very first one inside the newsroom entrance. As soon as anybody entered, regardless of who they were, they were always greeted with mirth and banter at the doorway from Pat. He always kept the mood light in the office, even if his jokes veered towards being off-colour, on occasion. Not everyone could get away with it, but Pat Flynn usually did.

Robyn's first election story of the campaign had hit the printing presses last night and was now out there to be read—and attacked—by the Republican Party's newly energised fan base. The sheer volume of backlash she received online was a testament to how unquestioned the party's meteoric rise in the polls had been until now. Her story, which peeled back the layers of the party's past and present, seemed to jolt its supporters out of their complacent reverie. Suddenly, basic truths—like the fact that the Irish Republican Party was the only political party in Europe with a paramilitary wing—felt almost taboo to mention.

The reaction was as if she had broken some unspoken rule, like pointing out the drunken antics of an alcoholic uncle at a family wedding, something everyone noticed but nobody acknowledged out of politeness. How had the country arrived at such a bizarre state of affairs in just a few short months? The question hung in the air, unsettling and unresolved, as Robyn braced herself for, what was sure to be, an intense few days ahead.

"Did you check under the car with a mirror for a car bomb this morning?" Pat's colleague in advertising at the next desk, chuckled. He spent his life trying to imitate Pat's natural wit but never hit the mark.

She gave him a withering look. Muppet, she thought to herself.

"You're a brave woman to be taking on those fellas," he persisted.

"Not as brave as fools like you are to be voting for them," Robyn hit back, hoping to nip any more smart-assed comments in the bud.

Suddenly, Leahy rounded the corner out of his office. "A word please, Robyn," he said, with way more reserve than she was used to. She couldn't be in trouble already at this stage in the day, she thought. It was as if someone had died, his demeanour seemed so serious. She followed him into his office, not sure what tragedy she was about to hear.

"Take a seat there for a minute, Robyn," he said.

Robyn was shocked. Was Leahy actually being nice to her? And why was he calling her "Robyn" instead of his usual,

CHAPTER 8

angry "Mayhew"? Now he had her really worried.

"Look, this Republican Party piece you did for this week's paper has gone down more of a bomb, excuse the pun, than I thought."

"What?" Robyn asked, both puzzled and relieved no one had died.

"It's serious, Robyn," he said, in the quietest tone he had ever spoken to her. "Have you been on Twitter yet this morning? There have been threats against you, Robyn, on *The Herald's* Twitter account. Threats against your life."

"Threats against my life?" she exclaimed, laughing. "Gosh, that's when you know you're doing something right!"

"I'm serious, Robyn."

"Will you stop with the 'Robyn' stuff. It's creeping me out."

"I've been over to the Garda Station this morning. I've reported the threats directly to the Superintendent. We can't overlook this. It's my job as editor to take it seriously."

"Jesus, Leahy. I thought you'd be offering to help them take me out."

"Robyn, I'm not joking. There have been rape threats against you as well. Really savage, vile stuff." At this, she fell silent. "Kill" was a word that got thrown about in everyday language. "Rape" wasn't.

"The Super said he'll tell the boys in Castlebar to keep an eye on the house at night. They'll drive by a few times to make their presence felt until the election is well out of the way. I gave them your address."

"Eh, thanks boss," she muttered, still taken aback.

"Are you ok?"

"Of course I'm ok. There are always nuts on the internet threatening people every day of the week."

"These aren't just any old nuts. These guys have the IRA behind them. So this is serious, Robyn."

"Ok, I get it, Boss. Thanks for being concerned and looking out for me. I do appreciate it. But I won't be backing down either."

"I wouldn't expect anything else but just keep an extra eye out for your safety and if anything seems out of sorts or you're in any way worried about anything, ring 999 straight away. They're on alert to the situation."

"Gosh, I'm not wrong in what I'm saying about this party if we're actually having this conversation."

"Exactly, Robyn. I had the same thought myself this morning."

"Ok, well I'm going to step out for an early coffee break just to get a break from these jackasses out there," she said, nodding towards the newsroom.

"Ok. But don't forget about the Heskin interview later," he reminded her.

"No problem, boss."

"Hang on a second—I nearly forgot with all this IRA crap—the radio shows have been on to me to get you on-air about the submarine story. Who'd have thought that a bleedin' election story would overshadow a submarine story? Never saw that one coming. And the Jimmy Costello story too and his funding of *Tales from the Dark Side*. They want to interview you about that one as well."

"Boss, you know my feelings on doing radio. I've had a tough morning. Can we drop the radio interviews for today without our usual row about it?"

Leahy couldn't argue with a journalist who had just received a death threat. For someone who rarely stopped talking,

CHAPTER 8

she always put up a hell of a fight over having to do a radio interview on one of her stories. Her argument was that she took a job as a newspaper journalist, not a radio journalist. It just wasn't her medium. She preferred to hide behind the pen. Blah, blah, blah. He'd heard it all before. The paper could do with the extra publicity when one of their stories hit the national headlines, but he'd drop it for today and just do the radio interviews himself on her behalf.

As Robyn walked back out to the newsroom, another 'RA fan accosted her over by the printer.

"Are you our "Anti-Republican Party" correspondent now?" Jerry O'Hara, one of the production guys asked her, smirking. Trendy and in his twenties, he fancied himself as the hip and happening guy of the production team and normally Robyn enjoyed the banter with him, but today wasn't the day.

"I don't know, Jerry. Are you going to be our head-wrecking pro-IRA colleague today? Do I stand around bugging you about what bloody fonts and colours you'll be using doing your job?"

"Jesus, alright," he said, taken aback.

"No, it's not alright," she countered. "If the polls are to be believed, we're sleepwalking towards a Republican party government in this country in two weeks' time. So they should be getting tonnes of extra scrutiny from the press, so people know who they're voting into government. Jesus Christ, we'll be handing over the Gardai and Army to the murderers and bombers. How can we expect them to respect democracy if they haven't done so in the past? They bombed their way into getting their political goals met. Wake up, people or we'll have terrorists in government in two weeks' time," Robyn all but shouted to her colleagues around the office. Heads were raised from their keyboards, but no one could argue with her logic.

It wasn't just the grief she was getting from all her colleagues about her election story that was bugging Robyn, as she stormed out of the office. It was a dry, bright morning so she left the car where it was and took a walk in the fresh air to clear her head. It was too early for Tony's bar next door so she'd get a coffee down the town instead. She was so annoyed that there was a story about a submarine off the Mayo coast on the front page of the paper, but all anyone had to talk about was one of six election stories buried inside the paper. What planet was she living on? She had told the families of the missing fishermen that media scrutiny would put pressure on the government to come up with answers, but now she felt she had let them down by publishing what seemed to be a more explosive story alongside it. Even the story about Jimmy Costello being behind the blog that took down Marie Mulhall had disappeared in the explosion of indignation for the Republican Party. She had been between two minds whether to hold back that story from the boss for another week to cover her tracks in case she had to spend a day or two in Dublin "volunteering" undercover with the Republican party, without him knowing. But since Emma had a team of four researching the shell companies, she thought it would be too much of a risk in case the story got out in the meantime. Two great scoops, but such wasted effort.

As she walked along The Mall—the two streets bordering the Carrowbeg River—she drew in long, deep breaths. The crisp morning air, tinged with distant sea salt, filled her lungs, soothing her frazzled nerves. Each exhale felt like a small release of the tension and, with every step she took, she allowed the peacefulness of her surroundings to seep into her.

Westport was one of the few planned towns in Ireland, its Georgian design and elegant symmetry setting it apart. The tree-lined streets lent it a graceful air and the Carrowbeg River, gliding gently through the town under a series of stone humpback bridges, made the setting fairytale-like. Rising in the background was the majestic Croagh Patrick mountain, a famed pilgrimage site where St. Patrick himself was said to have spent forty days fasting on its summit. It was almost as if "the Reek", as it was known to the locals, watched over Westport, its natural splendour casting an otherworldly beauty over the town.

Stepping out of her reverie for a moment, Robyn remembered she needed to send flowers to Emma to thank her for all the great help she gave her with the *Tales from the Dark Side* story. Even though Emma wouldn't have much interest in flowers, she thought. Pity you can't get booze sent to people as gifts. But come to think of it, you could probably get a Tesco delivery to her office. Great, she'd send over a bottle of vodka to Emma and a slab of beer to the staff. She hoped Emma's boss wouldn't be annoyed. She knew Emma wouldn't be.

Where would she be without friends and family in this job? When she was younger, she couldn't bear formal education, either school or college. She was an avid reader all her life but just wasn't a fan of formal education with a teacher or lecturer standing at the head of the class and students learning by listening, an education system that hadn't changed in centuries. Come to think of it, she still wasn't a fan of lectures. Or listening. But at least her education had left her with a big, fat contacts book of old school friends and college friends in a whole host of jobs, that she could call on for stories. But she believed in showing her appreciation to those people and not just taking people for granted. All her cousins as well were always so helpful.

As she strolled down the town of Westport to go get her morning coffee, she thought to herself—family and friends—that's what it was all about. But even in the brightness of the morning sunshine, an invisible shadow lingered, casting a pall over her as her thoughts automatically went to her missing little brother, as it always did and forever would. The thought of him was an unshakeable ache, a void that followed her everywhere, whether under a bright sky or beneath distant stars. It was a sorrow she carried with her always, and no matter where she was in the world, she knew it would always be there—an emptiness that no amount of sunshine could ever fully dispel.

Chapter 9

Robyn was just in the door on time to get a prime window seat at The Coffee Bean Café, just as another patron stood to leave. Greeted by the comforting aroma of freshly brewed coffee, Robyn settled in with a warm, frothy latte and a berry muffin, taking a few moments to herself to relax and switch off, letting the cadence of café life lull her into a gentle detachment.

Ten minutes slipped by unnoticed before she cracked open her laptop, dragging herself from comfort into the grind. Her story list blinked back at her from the screen, the week ahead mapped out in bullet points. Yet a stubborn, insistent whisper crept in—Twitter. The comments. She shouldn't. She'd long promised herself never to look at abusive content online. But she was weak.

She clicked. Slowly. Reluctantly.

And there it was—over six thousand comments.

Her eyes narrowed. Six thousand? That was unprecedented for *The Mayo Herald*. Even if every resident of Westport logged in to hurl abuse, they'd barely scrape that number. This was something else. Something national. Maybe international.

Robyn braced herself and scrolled through a few of the comments. The notorious "RaBots"—as the Republican Party's online army of "activists" were known—an aggressive swarm trained to descend on anyone who dared publish anything remotely negative about their party with a barrage of vitriol had swung into action as soon as the paper was published online last night. But if they left it at "vitriol", she could take that. But some of the comments on there were pure filth. Social media, once the tool of the curious and connected, had become a complete cesspit, amplifying and rewarding the worst voices in society, like rats scurrying around in a sewer.

She lasted all of thirty seconds before snapping the laptop shut. Her heart pounded a little faster. Her jaw set a little tighter.

She looked up from her laptop and exhaled deeply. She needed to call her old friend, Donnacha, who had given her his card at the County Council meeting. Now would be as good a time as any, she thought. After the darkness she had just glimpsed online, talking to a decent human being would be the antidote she needed to bring her back from the abyss she had just stared into.

She dialled.

"Hi Donnacha, it's your old buddy, Robyn."

"Well, well, well. I couldn't believe it was you when I spotted you at the council meeting the other evening. You haven't changed a bit," he said, laughing.

"God, that's depressing," she joked. "And I can't believe how tall you've gotten. I was towering over you last time I saw you. I don't know how I feel about you being bigger than me now. You must have shot up after we turned fifteen."

"Yeah, I kept growing until I was 21, so I'm 6'2" now."

CHAPTER 9

"Yeah, that's kind of what I thought. So, how've you been? Is your Mum still as wired as ever? I always remember what good fun she was when we were kids."

"Yeah, she's great. Still daft as a brush. What about your Mum?"

"She's still daft as ever too. She was talking about Elaine at Christmas and meeting up again, so I'll let her know I've bumped into you and I'm sure the two of them will arrange something."

"Well, I'm glad to hear she's doing ok. She hadn't been herself for a long time after you guys lost little Alex. It was heartbreaking what you went through, and the little guy as well."

"She still has days where she is so haunted by what happened. But like all mothers, she's doing her best for the sake of the rest of her family. But I'll let her know you were asking for her, Donnacha."

She paused for a moment.

"So anyway, you're an engineer with the ESB now?"

"Yeah, I've been with them since college," her friend replied. "It's a handy enough gig. Glad to see you went into journalism. I remember you talking about it since you were a kid."

"Yeah, it's going well so far. I didn't think I'd be in Mayo, but I'm so settled here now it would take a lot to get me to move away from here. But what I'm ringing you about is this fire. Can you let me in on anything further? It sounds a bit strange that you're getting outside experts in. I'd have thought the ESB would have all the expertise in this area in-house themselves."

"You could always smell a rat from a mile off," he said,

laughing. "No wonder you're in the job you're in."

"So, am I right? Is there more to this than meets the eye?"

"Look, don't quote me on this, whatever you do. It won't go down well if I've briefed a journalist before the council. That's why I just slipped you my card quickly in the meeting the other day and took off. I didn't want to be spotted talking to the press. But yeah, it's looking like this fire was a bit out of the ordinary."

"How do you mean? And of course I won't mention your name. You have my word on that."

"Just as long as you don't confirm to anyone that I gave you the inside track, that will do. But yeah, that outage was a funny one. We had calls coming in from the public across all of North Mayo that day saying their power was gone. But when our engineers went out on site to the substation, everything was in order. So they left and went back to the office. Then, bizarrely it was *afterwards* that we got the alert on our system that there was a fire at the substation. The engineers went back out and extinguished the fire. But they couldn't understand it. They had been there minutes before and couldn't find a reason for the reported outages, which baffled them. Then minutes later, just after they'd left, a fire broke out. None of it made sense."

"Yeah, you're right. I'm lost completely."

"The only possibility we can see is, and what we have the security experts looking into is..."

Robyn cut him off: "Security experts? I thought it would have been forensic fire investigators that were looking into it? she asked, puzzled.

"No, it's cyber guys we're talking to. I'll explain. Looking at the series of calls we got, a few came in at first, saying their power was out. But there was nothing amiss at the substation.

CHAPTER 9

Then an alert came in saying a fire had broken out. Then a massive number of calls came in saying they were without power. The sequence was out of place completely. How could we have gotten calls before there was actually a problem? So, the only way this could have happened is if the problem started at the other end. For instance, if a decent number of smart meters were all switched off simultaneously, and there was significantly reduced uptake of electricity as a result, that could theoretically cause the supply network to overheat and a fire to break out. The only organised way in which a few hundred smart meters could be turned off all at once is if they were hacked—an AI-powered hack. People don't realise it, but all their smart appliances at home have very little built-in security. There needs to be much more awareness about it."

"That's crazy. So you think this is a prank by some hackers? Some kids messing around?"

"Well, that's the working theory. But the investigation isn't completed yet. I'll be presenting the final report to the council in a few weeks so couch your article in language that it is a working theory only at this stage. It's not the final word."

"Thanks so much, Donnacha. I really appreciate you giving me the heads-up on this one."

"No problem, Rob. I'll keep in touch and if I hear anything further, I'll give you a ring."

There was a pause.

"Hello. Are you still there Robyn?"

"Hi Donnacha, no I am. I just got distracted there for a minute. Sorry. No. I'd love to hear from you Donnacha if anything comes up and if not, I'll see you at the next council meeting. But of course, I don't know you. Never saw you. Never spoke to you. Nothing," she joked.

"Bye, Rob, ya nutter."

Something had caught Robyn's eye as she was finishing up her call with Donnacha. A guy sitting across from her in the coffee shop had left his laptop open as he got up to order another coffee. It was the meme on his screen that caught her eye. *"Don't Vote. It Just Encourages The Bastards!"* Was this a one-off or was there more of this kind of stuff floating around on social media?

She opened RevEye, her favourite reverse image tool, and traced the meme's reach. Thousands of shares. Across accounts. Across platforms.

It could be just a dumb joke going around online—it was taken from the title of book by American political satirist, P.J. O'Rourke. But organised campaigns of voter suppression had been a big problem in elections in the US. Had it spread to this country? And if so, who was behind it?

The clue to this was usually provided by asking the question: who would benefit from it? Younger people were more likely to see this online. Who would benefit from discouraging young voters? They were more likely to vote for the Republican Party or left-wing parties. Could the government parties be engaging in voter suppression to counter the Republican Party's chances of political success? As much as Robyn personally despised the idea of the country being governed by the Republican Party, she couldn't ignore this potential election interference story. Interference in democracy, no matter by whom, would have to be called out.

It reminded her of something else she had almost forgotten about too. Yesterday, she was talking to the *The Mayo Herald* receptionist, Mary and it came up in conversation that she was voting for Republican Party this time round, which shocked

CHAPTER 9

Robyn. A flame-haired, single lady in her late sixties with usually conservative leanings, she told Robyn she had seen something on social media that asked: "What have Fine Gael ever done for you?" which stopped her in her tracks and made her really think. She was now considering voting for the Irish Republicans instead.

She couldn't come up with specifics on the spot, but she told Mary what the government party, Fine Gael, *hadn't* done for her. They hadn't maimed, killed, murdered, knee-capped and bombed their way into politics. That made Mary pause and think. But it still preyed on Robyn's mind that people were being influenced by such shady tactics.

She decided to do a quick hashtag search of *#WhatHaveFine GaelEverDoneForYou?* And predictably, thousands of accounts had been sharing memes like this as well. This type of negative campaigning by political parties was rife in the US too, but Irish parties had historically avoided negative campaigns by mutual agreement. But once something happens Stateside, it's only a matter of time before it crosses the Atlantic.

She decided to download the list of all the accounts sharing these memes, as she had done with the *"Don't Vote, It Just Encourages The Bastards"* meme. That phrase had drilled into her thoughts, and now it became a data point—one of many. TweetDeck made the gathering easier, a quiet companion in her search for patterns in the chaos. But this was only the beginning.

She had a plan—methodical and precise. Next, she would pull the latest press releases from each political party, compile them, and map the accounts that had amplified them. With enough overlap, she might uncover a coordinated pattern. Find the accounts pushing both official messaging and the darker, more subversive content. If the lines intersected, she'd have a thread worth tugging. The working title already rang in her head: "Dirty Tricks: Election 2020." It had weight.

Feeling a bit braver then, she decided to take a look at Twitter again. With a steadying breath, she opened TweetDeck. It was time to face the swarm again—death threats, slurs, the full spectrum of online hate. She harvested tweets, retweets, metadata—everything. Lunatics or not, their words might one day be evidence.

Apart from her own analysis, she wondered if an industry insider might be able to shed more light on these election practices. An ex-employee of a social media company might be the best person to talk to, she figured. LinkedIn as always was a great source of information. But its search capability didn't extend to a search as specific as she required. She emailed a developer that she worked with from time to time that she had found via a freelancing website. She asked if he had a tool, or could create one pretty quickly, to search LinkedIn for a recent ex-employee of a named social media company. Always on the ball, Deepak in India was straight back to her, despite the time difference. He worked principally for UK clients, so he tended to work during the night instead of daytime hours, in order to accommodate his UK clients. He would have the tool ready for her within two hours, he promised.

While she was logged into her email account, a message came through from Sam Donlon at the National Union of Journalists: "Dear Journalists, protect yourself, your information and sources in the run-up to Election 2020 by downloading this program to give yourself an extra layer of protection."

Robyn stalled, just a millisecond away from clicking the

CHAPTER 9

link.

Sam Donlon always began his emails with the salutation "Dear Members", not "Dear Journalists."

She sent a quick message to her colleagues to warn them not to click on it and forwarded the suspect email to the *The Mayo Herald's* IT guy. Then, she sent it to Sam Donlon as well in case he was, in fact, the author and had just happened to change the usual salutation in his email.

"Hey Rob, how's the going?" a voice interrupted.

She looked up from her laptop. It was Dara Wall.

He was one of her very first friends in Castlebar when she moved there. Coincidentally, the night before she packed up her stuff to move, she was on a night out with friends in Galway and Dara was in their company—a friend of one of her friends. They got to talking and he mentioned he was from Castlebar. Robyn laughed and told him she was moving there the following day, so they agreed to meet for drinks the following evening. And so, they had been meeting for drinks ever since.

Dara was an engineer by profession but his real passion in life was boating. His slight build belied the strength he had acquired from his hobby, his wiry frame hiding a surprising reservoir of power. Brown hair, tousled and unassuming, framed his face, while his deep brown eyes held a quiet intensity that hinted at the discipline and determination honed through years of dedication to the sport.

Robyn smiled. "Dara! What are you doing on dry land?"

"Just grabbing a quick cuppa and heading out to the pier. I'm going on a hunt for this submarine of yours," he joked.

"Alright, smart-ass. Knock it off. There's more to that story than you think."

"I'll take your word for it."

"But it's good to hear someone is reading something other than my damn election story. Jesus, the grief I'm getting over it."

"Really?"

"Yeah, bloody death threats and rape threats."

"You're joking me."

"No, I'm deadly serious. The boss had to report it to the Superintendent this morning."

"Talk about lunatics out there. Are you okay though, Robyn?"

"Of course, I am. It will take a bit more than that to intimidate me."

"Good on you, Rob. But, on the subject of lunatics, I met two yesterday."

"Yeah? What particular flavour of lunatic are you talking about?"

"These two Swedish fellas who chartered the boat from me to take them out to dive a shipwreck. Except they couldn't tell me the name of the wreck and, I know for a fact there isn't one in the spot they dived. Talk about two loopers. But they were two funny sorts all the same."

"Maybe they were looking for drugs thrown overboard if they had to ditch a run into the bay previously?" Robyn ventured.

"I doubt it because then they'd have a witness then to the drug bales being brought on board. Plus, those fellas usually have beacons on the bales, so they'd have their own equipment to locate the drugs. Still, it taught me a lesson not to be picking up strangers on the pier. Anyway, I have to run. I'll be back in Castlebar this evening though, if you're worried about anything. Or there's any creeper about, just give me a shout and I'll be round to you in minutes."

"Aw, thanks Dara. That's kind of you."

"But, come to think of it, what house would I go to?" he said laughing.

"How do you mean?"

"Word is your car is now parked outside a rented house further down Rathbawn Road these evenings. Must be a new fella on the scene," he said, enjoying making her squirm.

"Jesus Christ. Tell Don Murphy not to be snooping on his neighbours so much." Don was a mutual friend of theirs, who ran one of the pubs they frequented in Castlebar and was an old school friend of Dara's."

"Well, is there?"

"No, it's just a friend from Galway staying there."

"Is he a good-looking friend?" Dara teased.

"Get lost. It's a girlfriend."

"Ooh, kinky."

"I mean it. Get lost, Dara."

"Ok, I'm outta here. I'll keep an eye out for that sub for you."

"Please do, Dara. I'd be delighted for you to find it."

It wasn't easy to get work done around Westport, either in the office or out of it.

Dara disappeared into the blur of morning foot traffic, and Robyn turned back to her laptop. The IT guy's email had landed. As she feared—it was a spear-phishing attempt. The NUJ hadn't sent that link. She'd been right to trust her gut. Now, she had to report it to the Union itself to warn others. God knows how many had already clicked it.

She rubbed her temples. It was getting harder to stay ahead

of it all.

*****

As Robyn Mayhew got back to work in The Coffee Bean Cafe in Westport, elsewhere in Dublin businessman Tom Doherty was grappling with an increasingly unmanageable workload. A highly skilled statistician, Tom had left Opinion Sphere Research, the nation's top polling company, a year earlier to establish his own outfit. The venture had taken off swiftly, attracting a wave of new clients, particularly from the multinational sector. Success seemed assured until autumn, when everything began to unravel.

Tom had been conducting political polling for several U.S. companies interested in the political forecast for Ireland. But to his dismay, his data was consistently at odds with the results published by the larger polling firms. The discrepancy was glaring—his polls showed the Republican Party at only 10% of the vote, while the big players reported figures as high as 25%.

Despite the mounting pressure, Tom was confident in his work. He had meticulously reviewed every aspect of his process, from the data collection to the final calculations, staying late into the night in his Merrion Square office. Yet, each meeting with his clients grew more and more tense, with them smacking his reports onto the table in front of him with frustration, questioning his credibility. The temptation to tweak the results, to align them more closely with the industry giants plagued him, but he resisted. His clients were on the verge of walking away, and he could feel his grip on his fledgling business slipping.

CHAPTER 9

But Tom stood firm. He knew his data was flawless, even if he couldn't yet explain why it diverged so sharply from the others. Desperation haunted him as he searched for answers, determined to uncover the truth before everything he had built came crashing down.

Chapter 10

The *Mayo Herald* office was a whirlwind of activity on Wednesday. The full news team had been drafted in for a critical assignment—interviewing every candidate vying for a seat in the Mayo constituency in the general election. The energy was electric, the atmosphere charged with the weight of the day's responsibilities. The rhythmic clatter of keyboards commingled with the murmur of urgent conversations. Journalists were hunched over desks cluttered with notepads, coffee cups, and stacks of papers. Graphic designers beavered away at their workstations which, in contrast to their colleagues', were completely free of paper and clutter.

When Robyn arrived at her desk that morning an email was waiting for her in her inbox, the subject line sparking immediate curiosity. She had tracked down an ex-employee of one of the big social media companies via LinkedIn, with the help of a custom search tool created by a resourceful developer she had enlisted for the job. She messaged him via Proton Mail, an encrypted messaging platform trusted by journalists for its security. He had responded quickly, suggesting he was

CHAPTER 10

eager to share his experiences at the social media company, possibly even revealing something significant.

Wasting no time, Robyn shot back a reply, and they quickly arranged to meet the following afternoon in Dublin city centre at Frank Ryan's Pub—her old watering hole from when she used to live in Smithfield in Dublin city centre. The prospect of a story with real impact hung in the air, adding an extra layer of intensity to an already demanding day.

And there was another email waiting for her in her "Lia Hyland" inbox—an invitation to an orientation meeting for new Republican Party volunteers. Handily enough, that was also scheduled for tomorrow evening at Party HQ in O'Connell Street. So she could kill two birds with the one stone in the one trip to Dublin. She didn't have to be there until 6.30pm but at least it gave her plenty of time to meet and chat with her ex-social media company contact. It was shaping up to be a productive day, with the opportunity to gather crucial information from both encounters.

Her day was off to a perfect start and Robyn Mayhew was in superb form. She asked around the office if anyone had come across IRA memes in the run-up to the election. Her colleagues didn't disappoint, offering up a disturbing selection of the most "popular" ones —grotesque tributes to the IRA's violent history. Just as she had done yesterday, she saved the data from all the accounts sharing and commenting on the memes for cross-analysis later, against the voter suppression and negative campaigning memes that she had been investigating also. This would be a job to finish at the weekend with a good friend of hers who was staying in Castlebar for a while. She was an IT expert who could conduct an analysis of the data in minutes for her. It would just take up too much time to try and muddle through it herself at work. And Leahy would be breathing down her neck the whole time wanting to know what she was doing and bashing it before she even got a chance to investigate it properly. The less he knew, the better.

"Mayhew, which of the candidates are you interviewing today?" came his voice from behind her.

Jolted out of her deep thought, she responded: "I thought you were in hospital today for an operation?"

"It got bloody cancelled. All elective surgery is off for today, so I have to wait until I hear back from them when it's rescheduled. So annoying. They didn't even give a reason why. Normally they say if it's due to A&E overcrowding or whatever."

"Sorry to hear that, boss. I hope you get a date for it again soon. And it's Declan Ryan I'm meeting at 3.00pm."

"Good. But don't go easy on him. I know you like the Green Party but I'm trusting you to give him a good grilling."

"Leahy, do you not think I'm capable of putting my political beliefs aside when I'm doing my job?"

"Ok, well you better. I'm keeping an eye on you."

Great. Now Leahy wouldn't be at home tomorrow recuperating from his operation after all. Since she was going off reservation for this story—"Dirty Tricks Election 2020" as she was calling it—she'd have to ring in sick in the morning because there's no way Leahy would sanction her heading off on a jolly to Dublin for the afternoon.

In the meantime, Robyn needed to knuckle down and dig up some stories for next week's paper. One story in particular kept nagging at her—something about what Dara had mentioned the other day. He'd told her about two

CHAPTER 10

Swedish guys who had chartered his boat out at the pier, and something about the whole situation just didn't sit right with her. Determined to get to the bottom of it, she called the Clew Bay Historical Society to see if there had been any recent shipwrecks discovered in the Bay. The answer was no, but they did point her toward the Wreck Inventory of Ireland database, which held details on over 18,000 wrecks scattered around the Irish coast. It sounded like a treasure trove of fascinating history—stories of pirate ships, Spanish Armada vessels, and shipwrecks laden with Caribbean rum meant for Scottish estates, blown off course to the wild western shore of Ireland.

As much as she wanted to dive into those rich tales of the past, she simply didn't have the time right now. She knew that Dara, with his deep knowledge of the bay, would know for sure if there was a known wreck where the Swedes had been diving. But the mystery still bugged her. What were those two up to? They certainly weren't out there recovering bales of drugs tossed overboard for later retrieval—Dara would have spotted something like that a mile away. Robyn let her mind wander for a while to try and figure out another reason, unable to shake the feeling that there was more to this story than met the eye.

Then she thought of it. Eileen Heaney, the lady weather forecaster she met last week at a special ceremony honouring her contribution to the Allied victory in World War II, had spoken to her about the lighthouses of Erris. There were four around the peninsula. Despite Ireland's official neutrality, one of them had actually been attacked by a German bomber during WWII with the glass panes of the lantern having been shot out completely.

"But," she said to Robyn, "it's not the lights in the lighthouses we need to worry about if war was ever to break out in Europe again." Eileen broke into a cough and it took her a few moments to get her bearings again.

"What would be need to be worried about, Eileen?" Robyn pressed her, eager to hear this wise lady's advice.

"It's all the lights beneath the sea," she told her.

Robyn was puzzled. "What do you mean 'the lights beneath the sea?'" Robyn asked her.

"The lights flashing through the fibre optic cables under the sea, all the way across the Atlantic. Like the cables coming ashore in Killala and Clew Bay."

Of course—the transatlantic cables. Yep, that lady was sharp as a tack and didn't miss a beat, Robyn smiled to herself as she thought back to their conversation.

She picked up the phone and dialed Dara's office. But she got a surprise when a lady's voice answered.

"Hi Teresa, I didn't expect you to answer today," Robyn said cheerfully. Teresa was Dara's mother who worked part-time with him in his office on her days off from her other job as a part-time theater nurse at Mayo General Hospital in Castlebar. Dara and his mother were carbon copies of each other—the same small, wiry build, the same shock of tousled brown hair, tanned skin and bags of energy. It was almost comical when you saw them side by side, they were so alike. "I thought you'd be called into work today. I hear its bedlam in the hospital at the moment," Robyn said.

"Well, em," Teresa murmured.

"The boss was supposed to be having a routine operation done today but all elective surgery was cancelled," Robyn added.

CHAPTER 10

"Look, you didn't hear it from me Robyn but there was some cock-up on the admin side. The surgeons and theater nurses were all in work, gowned up ready to go but the theaters were empty. There were no patients. A text went out in error last night notifying all the patients that elective surgery was cancelled and so nobody showed up today."

"You're joking me," Robyn said, flummoxed.

"I know. Such an absolute waste of resources. And all the desperate people on the waiting lists for operations."

"That's shocking. How the hell could a message like that go out in error?"

"I've no idea. But it's amazing the things management can find to 'eff up', things that were previously thought 'un-eff-up-able.'" Robyn laughed.

"Anyway, I presume it's Dara you're looking for, not myself, so I'll get him for you."

"Thanks, Teresa."

Dara came on the line. "Hey Rob, what's up?"

"Hi sunshine, quick question for you. Remember those guys you picked up out at the pier the other day?"

"Well, I don't like how you phrased that question. I didn't 'pick up' any guys out at the pier, Robyn."

Robyn laughed. "Ok, my apologies, sir. The guys that picked you up out at the pier."

"Now, if you're going to be a smart-arse, Mayhew," he warned, jokingly. "Yeah, what about them?"

"Any chance you'd still have a record of the coordinates of their dive spot?"

"Yeah, I would. Why?"

"I'm wondering could they have been diving some point along the fibre optic cable that comes ashore here in Westport?"

"I doubt it. The companies that own those cables would have their own boats and crew doing any maintenance or checks. Those two didn't even ask for a receipt. No, they were up to no good all right. Just not sure what that 'no good' was."

"Could you humour me and just check the coordinates, and I can cross-check it against a map I have of the cable route here online," she asked.

"God, the things I do for you, Mayhew. I won't be out on the boat until this evening but I'll let you know."

"Good stuff, Wall. Add that to my tab of pints that I owe you."

"We're running at two thousand and..."

"Get lost. Ok see ya, D.

"Bye, Rob."

Leahy popped up behind her again. "Mayhew, this water notice has come in from the County Council. It not the usual "boil water" notice when there's an *E.Coli* outbreak or something like that. This one is to do with high mineral levels in the water—a naturally occurring mineral called manganese. At certain levels it causes damage to the nervous system. And boiling the water won't fix the problem. The county council will be sending water tankers out around the county and people will have to collect their water. It will be a massive problem for people and businesses," he said, shaking his head. "But it seems to cover an awfully big area, Robyn. Will you double check with the County Council if that's right and when they expect the problem to be rectified?"

"Yep, will do," Robyn replied.

"Yeah, and what was that I heard you talking to someone

about shipwrecks? Was there a new wreck found?" Leahy was a big history buff so he couldn't help himself. Robyn almost felt bad to have to disappoint him.

"Eh, I was just checking with the Historical Society if there were any wrecks around the area where the trawler went down last month. Em, in case its nets could have gotten caught in a wreck on the sea floor...." she trailed off, knowing she was reaching. She couldn't tell him about the two guys her buddy met on the pier. He'd have written her off completely.

Leahy rolled his eyes. "God, I'll be expecting a UFO story from you one of these days, Mayhew."

Chapter 11

Morning broke over Castlebar the following day with a pale wash of light, the town still rubbing sleep from its eyes as Robyn reversed out her driveway and drove through the town. Her mind was already racing ahead—to Dublin city centre, anticipating the conversations ahead, the gentle probing of a whistleblower, and the deception she would have to wear like armour before walking into the Irish Republican Party headquarters. She barely noticed the bleary morning haze lifting off Lough Conn as the sun rose behind her.

Nor did she notice the car following in her wake.

It was the kind of vehicle no one remembered—unremarkable, forgettable, designed to vanish into the ordinary. When Robyn's jeep turned onto the open road towards Dublin, the vehicle behind her peeled off at the roundabout, the driver pausing just long enough to watch her go. Then, without hesitation, it slipped away toward the grey sprawl of the Moneen Industrial Estate, swallowed by warehouses and anonymity.

The buildings there were blocky, grey, and utilitarian—

CHAPTER 11

warehouses with dust-coated windows and rust-stained signs. The driver's destination lay at the far end of what seemed to be a dead-end, deep within the industrial estate. But this cul-de-sac was deceptive. At its very end, there was a hidden turn left, leading to a secluded premises that faced on to a desolate stretch of waste ground. The area was utterly isolated, and crucially, remained hidden from any prying eyes.

The industrial unit the car parked in front of was unremarkable from the outside, blending seamlessly with the surrounding buildings. But it had a distinct advantage in that it was perched above a quiet, rarely visited warehouse. No one had any reason to turn that final corner of the cul-de-sac, unless they were specifically headed for the warehouse below. This meant that anyone lingering outside, or any unexpected visitor would be easily noticed from overhead.

A metal staircase clung to the side of the building, leading up to the windowless unit at the top. Inside, the atmosphere was stark and sterile. The walls were painted a dull gray, and the only light came from a series of fluorescent fixtures overhead, casting a cold, harsh glow on the room's contents. A single workstation, where three computer monitors flickered with streams of data, lay just inside the doorway. One of the screens displayed a live feed from the surveillance camera mounted on the building outside. The camera's lens captured the entrance to the cul-de-sac, ensuring that anyone approaching would be seen long before they reached the top of the stairs.

A glass partition divided the space in half, and behind that lay rows and rows of computer servers on tall metal racks, their blinking lights and humming fans creating a rhythmic pulse in the high-tech labyrinth. The server room had its own advanced air-conditioning system to prevent the servers from overheating and components from wearing out. The unit was also wired with a high-voltage power supply to handle the massive electricity load required to feed the computer stack and its tireless data processing.

Security was tight. The door to the server room was secured with a cyber lock that required both a physical key and an encrypted code to open. But that wasn't the only measure in place. A security team of two, their expressions grim and alert, stood guard inside the unit. They were professionals trained to be vigilant, knowing theirs was the first line of defence against anyone who might stumble upon the operation. Occasionally, one of them would step outside to take a drive around the industrial estate, circling the area to watch for other watchers. For now, there were none. This remote unit, hidden in the industrial shadows of Castlebar, was a fortress, designed for secrecy and security.

And it was here, the blonde-haired lady who got out of the parked car and who had traveled so far across many countries, carried out her mission, day after day until the operation was up and running, only requiring the occasional adjustment and security check from her. For the rest of the time, the unit lay empty as the hum of the servers continued, the only sound in this warehouse in the West of Ireland, designed to keep its secrets so well-guarded.

*****

It felt like an omen.

Traffic on the M50, the ring road motorway around Dublin City Centre, was mercifully light, and Robyn made swift progress through the city's arterial roads. Heuston Station

CHAPTER 11

passed by on her left in a blur of sandstone and classical grandeur, its Renaissance-style façade catching the late morning sun. Even the usually murky River Liffey almost shimmered for a moment too. She followed its course along the Quays, gliding through a city that, just for once, wasn't fighting her every inch of the way. By the time she reached Smithfield Plaza—her old neighbourhood just off the Quays—a parking space just steps from the back entrance of Frank Ryan's pub, opened up as if it had been waiting just for her. The day was off to a pretty great start so far.

As she got out of the car and stretched, the expanse of Smithfield Plaza opened before her—still cobbled, still proudly rough-edged in places, despite the glass-fronted apartments and hotels that had crept in over the past decade.

A strange memory surfaced, one that had lodged itself firmly in her mind from years before. She remembered the old pub owner telling her, pint in hand, about the time *The Spy Who Came in from the Cold* had been filmed there, the adaptation of the great John le Carré novel. Smithfield Plaza, in its stark stony expanse, had stood in for Checkpoint Charlie, the infamous crossing point between East and West Berlin where Russia had faced off against the West during the Cold War. Robyn had walked these streets every day back then, fascinated by the fact that she was living in the echo of Cold War drama.

Now, years later, she wondered if spy games in Dublin was still just the preserve of movies whether they had quietly bled into real life—camouflaged by algorithms, carried out behind screens, and waged not with guns, but with data.

As she stepped through the back door of Frank Ryan's—still a traditional Dublin pub, where many in the city had been replaced by trendy hotspots—another wave of nostalgia washed over her, pulling her back to the many carefree student nights she had spent here. Laughter, music, and the easy camaraderie of those days seemed to echo in the dimly lit corners of the pub.

She approached the bar. "Is Paul around?" she asked.

The new bartender, barely out of his twenties, shook his head. "Paul's gone back to Meath. Family stuff, I think. I don't have a number for him, sorry."

She nodded, disappointed but not surprised. Life moved on. Still, she made a note to try and track him down. Paul had been a good laugh, and more than once, a sounding board during tough times.

For now though, she resigned herself to the present. She ordered a cold pint of beer and carried it to one of the small round tables just inside the front door. She sipped her drink with memories swirling in her mind while she waited for her contact to arrive.

She thought back to how much the city had changed since when she was a kid in the '90s, when it would have been murder coming through Dublin traffic on the Quays, the air thick with diesel fumes and tension. Poverty and deprivation would have been rife in the inner city and still was, in some pockets. Many areas, like the one she was in now, would have been considered no-go areas due to the heroin epidemic in the '80s that had carved scars into entire communities. Smithfield, back then, was a place you passed through quickly—if you passed through at all.

But urban renewal, and the tax breaks that went with it, had swept through the inner city with glass and chrome and changed the old neighbourhoods completely. There were still plenty of people living there from the old days for whom not much had changed but, for the most part, all the apartments along the Quays were populated with young twenty and thirty-somethings living their best lives.

She took a slow sip of her pint and thought of Galway.

Her hometown remained the black hole of Irish traffic. Even now, it was being reported as one of the worst cities in Europe for congestion. A place where four hours a day vanished into commuting purgatory, robbing parents of their evenings, children of their time, and lives of their rhythm.

Only that morning, before Robyn set off for Dublin, her mum had been on the phone telling her of the chaos that had hit Galway City that morning as she tried to make her way to work. The usually crazy traffic of morning rush hour had morphed into apocalyptic traffic when all the traffic lights in the city simultaneously malfunctioned overnight. But a news report on Galway Bay FM revealed the bizarre cause of the problem: traffic lights in the city had been turned off at 3am to allow giant-sized wind turbines on huge transports to pass safely through the city and on to Cloosh Valley in the west of the county where the vast, new Galway Wind Park was in development. But when city engineers tried to restore the lights afterwards, the system wouldn't reboot. The city choked for hours. As of midday, they were still scrambling to find the cause of the problem. It didn't bode well for the government parties in next week's election, Robyn thought to herself. Chaos to that extent, burned into the public's collective memory, had a way of resurfacing at the ballot box.

The pub door creaked open, pulling her attention back to the present.

A young man stepped inside—late twenties, pale olive skin,

dark eyes and dark-rimmed glasses. His movements were hesitant, searching. Robyn recognised the uncertainty. It had to be him.

"Matteo?" she called.

He turned, surprised. "Yes?"

She stood. "Hi, I'm Robyn. Thanks for coming."

"Nice to meet you," he said, eyes flicking briefly up before returning to the floor.

The poor guy must have felt either very intimidated or very conflicted meeting a journalist to talk about his former employer. He might have been questioning whether he could even trust her, and scared that he could be signing a death warrant for his own career. Robyn would have to put him at ease pretty quickly or this interview wouldn't go far.

From Italy originally, he was just one of the thousands of bright young things from around the world that had flocked to Dublin's "Silicon Docks," as it was known, to work in one of the several major tech giants that had their EMEA (Europe, Middle East & Africa) Headquarters in Dublin.

"What can I get you, Matteo?" she asked, nodding towards the bar.

"Just a coffee, please. Milk and no sugar."

"Sure. Would you like anything with that? Any snacks?" she asked.

He shook his head. "Just the coffee. Thanks."

"You can take a seat here, Matteo. And thanks again for agreeing to meet with me. Just to reassure you, this conversation is completely off the record. I'll never use your name—not even with my editor. I won't reference your job title, or the fact you recently left, in my story. Nothing traceable."

Matteo gave a faint nod. "I appreciate that. But honestly, it's a churn machine in there. Contractors come and go all the time. Nobody notices."

He was referring to his role—one of thousands who filtered trauma and hate every day as outsourced content moderators for a social media giant.

"And I understand if you're feeling overwhelmed, Matteo, so take your time."

"Ok, thank you," he said softly.

There was nothing for it but to dive right in and get it over with as quickly as possible. The coffees arrived and they got started.

"So, I told you in my email that I came across some political memes, IRA glorifications, that were troubling. They are concerning in any context but especially in the context of the upcoming election where politically inexperienced young people might be swayed to vote Republican out of bravado.

"I'm sure you are familiar with the whistleblower revelations from the US regarding voter suppression, negative campaigning and election interference in their elections over there," she continued. "There is evidence from the UK and the Continent that these practices have now spread to this side of the Atlantic also, for example, in the Brexit campaign in the UK. I fear they are now being used in this country and the general public just aren't aware of these practices and how they are used to manipulated voters into voting for someone they wouldn't ordinarily do so."

Matteo spoke in a low voice. "Yes, I agree. People are happy to blindly use social media without considering what the social media companies are getting out of them. The message I'd like to get out there is how easily they can be manipulated and how 'dark posts' in particular prey on them on social media platforms."

Robyn tilted her head: "Dark posts?" she said. "Are they a subliminal message of some sort?"

"No, they are a kind of secret post that is there for some people to see, but not others. Only a very small number of people can see them—those who have been targeted because of their particular vulnerability to its message."

Robyn looked at him quizzically.

"They were originally developed by the social media company for legitimate business reasons," he said. "For example, if companies wanted to test different versions of an advertising campaign to see which version performed better. These so-called 'dark posts' allowed them to do this without lots of different versions of an ad appearing on somebody's page making the company look ridiculous. They could target one campaign at, let's say, the first 1,000 users and another campaign at the next 1,000 users. Each group would only see their ad and not the other group's ad. So, when the social media company developed dark posts, it was purely for commercial reasons. They never foresaw that they would be used for political propaganda campaigns as happened in the US with the Trump campaign."

"Clever," Robyn commented. "But creepy."

Matteo nodded. "And now they are weapons. Especially when combined with micro-targeting. You can micro-tailor political messages for maximum effect on just the right kind of person—the angry, the disillusioned, the suggestible."

Robyn felt a chill settle in. "So you mean... different people can be shown completely different realities?"

He nodded. "Exactly. Two friends sitting side by side, on

the same app, scrolling through what looks like the same timeline—but one sees a campaign about immigration reform, and the other sees a meme linking immigrants to crime. One sees voter registration drives. The other sees posts implying the vote is rigged and not to bother voting."

"Jesus," she whispered.

"That's the thing, everyone suffers from this same mass delusion on social media. They believe scrolling through the news on social media is the same as reading a newspaper online or any other website—where everyone sees the same thing. But on social media you don't. You see what the social media platform, and those who pay them, want you to see. Whether it's to convince you to buy a particular pair of trainers or buy into anti-immigrant/Far Right beliefs. People all think they are seeing the same thing on social media but, like I said, it's a mass delusion. Even two best friends sitting side by side or two family members will have completely different feeds, but they think they are just at different stages of scrolling. And that illusion that everyone is seeing the same thing makes manipulation effortless.

"And this is what is causing such polarisation in society as well," he explained, "because we think the 'other side' is seeing the same information as us and are just coming to a different conclusion, but they're seeing different messages in their feeds completely. They're only seeing the information that's being fed to them by whomever is paying the platform to manipulate them."

"Jesus," Robyn replied. "I knew social media was dragging people down rabbit holes of extreme beliefs, but I never realised how strong the forces were that were dragging them there. I thought we all had some degree of agency or control over our social media consumption, but now it looks like we're being controlled like puppets on a string."

"That's exactly it," Matteo replied. "And once you start viewing content of a specific nature you get fed more and more extreme content on that topic. For instance, if you start to search for pages or videos on vegetarianism, after a while you'll start to see pages on veganism appearing in your feed. Or if a young man starts commenting or engaging with anti-immigration content, then after a while he'll start seeing content from the Far Right, then from neo-Nazis. It's destroying society."

Robyn shook her head: "No wonder the Far Right are gaining a hold in Irish society. It's down to the social media companies pushing this content."

"That's the other danger of social media that people don't realise," he warned, "the endless scrolling function on social media pages. It lulls people into a hypnotic state and they're even more prone to easy manipulation when in this state of mind."

Robyn exhaled deeply, clearly stunned by all she'd learned.

She looked up at Matteo. "So as a journalist, what kind of content do you think I would be vulnerable to?" she asked, half scared by what the answer could be.

"You could be targeted by a political party with one of these 'dark posts.' It could be promoting, for instance, a voter registration, civic engagement or a 'Get Out The Vote' campaign. And naturally, you think this post is being shown widely on social media.

But it isn't.

It's a 'dark post' just for the media's benefit, but the electorate might be seeing something completely different.

CHAPTER 11

"And the reality?" Robyn asked.

"The reality might be voter suppression. Or targeted disinformation aimed at people least likely to vote for their campaign, those who vote for their opponents. In the U.S., Trump's campaign specifically targeted African Americans, young women, and liberal whites. To discourage them from voting at all. Because they were more likely to be Hillary Clinton voters."

"When you talk about 'voter suppression' posts,'" she asked, her voice steady though her stomach had tightened, "what kind of content would this be exactly?"

Matteo's tone didn't waver. "Smears, falsehoods. Take Hillary Clinton, for instance—her 2016 campaign was bombarded with targeted lies. Not just to make people hate her, but to make her own supporters feel demoralised. Defeated. Like their vote wouldn't matter."

"It's as easy as that?" she asked, incredulous.

"Yes. It's as easy as that. People have no idea the control social media has over their thought processes. It's like you said: we're puppets on a string. We just can't see the strings that are pulling us."

Robyn leaned back in her chair, rattled. Not surprised, exactly. But unsettled by how much of what she'd suspected was now confirmed.

"So just hypothetically," she began, speaking slowly, carefully, "if the Irish Republican Party—who are polling strongest right now—wanted to kill the vote for their main rivals, they could run a series of 'what have they ever done for you?' campaigns. Aimed at different demographics. Undermine the loyalty of Fine Gael, Fianna Fáil, Labour, Greens—each in their own way. Urban middle-class voters who lean Fine Gael. Farmers loyal to them for decades. Older voters still clinging to Fianna Fáil. Working-class Labour supporters. Drain the faith from all of them. Turn their voters passive. And win."

Matteo didn't hesitate. "That's exactly the strategy. Trump didn't just win because his base showed up. He won because Clinton's didn't. The key wasn't rallying supporters—it was suppressing everyone else."

Robyn felt a sick twist in her gut.

"And if it's happening in the US and the UK," she said quietly, "it's already here."

"I'd be stunned if it wasn't," Matteo said, without blinking.

"How would I find out for sure?" she asked.

He gave a small, apologetic shrug. "That's the thing. You won't—unless people in those demographics show you their feeds. Unless they physically let you look over their shoulder. Otherwise, these dark posts are invisible. They vanish into the ether. No trace. No public archive. That's what makes them so effective. So dangerous."

Robyn nodded slowly, processing the full implications.

"I know you left the company before the campaign season properly began," she said, "but did you see anything that pointed in this direction?"

"No," he admitted. "It was too early. These campaigns only go live when they'll leave a fresh imprint close to election day. Any earlier, and the effect wears off."

She sighed, "Well, I've learned a hell of a lot here today, Matteo. More than I expected. And honestly, it's terrifying. These dark posts are being used to set different sections of society against each other. It's like a scalpel being used as a sledgehammer. It's tearing society apart."

CHAPTER 11

"I know," Matteo said. "That's why I came. Even if I can't prove anything about what's happening here in Ireland yet, I wanted people to understand the method. Once you understand the tool, you start to see how it's being wielded against you."

"And I give you my word," Robyn said, meeting his eyes. "None of this goes on the record. No names. No identifiers. Not even with my editor."

"Thank you, Robyn. I will keep an eye out for your article online and I hope it alerts people to what's happening in their social media feeds and how they're being taken advantage of."

"I'll say goodbye for now Matteo, and we'll keep in touch."

They stepped outside together. The winter light was thin, the sun already lowering behind the brick rooftops. They parted quietly, no handshake, no lingering glance. Just a quiet understanding between two people who had briefly shared the weight of something much larger than themselves.

With that, Robyn slipped into the crowd and made for the Luas tram stop at Smithfield.

She'd have preferred to walk—she needed the air, needed to steady herself—but it would have been cutting it too fine for her meeting at the Irish Republican Party HQ. The last thing she wanted was to arrive late and attract any unnecessary attention. The tram journey to Abbey Street was short, just a few stops, and from there, it was only a brisk walk around the corner to O'Connell Street.

The party's building was inconspicuous, but its front door stood out—painted green in a nod to the party's nationalism. Not the cheerful Kelly green of parades and flags, but a darker, more solemn shade. Military green. The kind worn to memorials of IRA members by their masked paramilitaries, standing at the gravesides of those who died with guns or bombs in their hands.

Or maybe the colour of the doorway was a coded threat to those that didn't belong there—a threat dressed as nostalgia?

She paused, took a deep breath, and then stepped inside.

Chapter 12

The bell was answered quickly, and with her nerves masked by a confident tone of voice, Robyn gave the name she had rehearsed a dozen times: "Lia Hyland." A brief pause followed, before the door buzzed, signalling her entry. She pushed it open and walked into the dimly lit hallway, her pulse quickening.

The meeting was already underway in the first room just beyond the entrance. As she slipped inside, her eyes quickly scanned the room, taking in the crowd. There were about seventy people packed closely together, an eclectic mix of faces, most of them young, likely in their twenties or thirties. A couple of older individuals, perhaps in their early forties, stood out like anchors of experience in the sea of youthful enthusiasm. Groups of young women chatted amongst themselves, while the men appeared more solemn, as if weighed down by the gravity of the cause that had brought them all together.

At the front of the room, a poised young woman stepped forward, commanding attention with the quiet authority of someone accustomed to leadership. A tall, thin brunette, she introduced herself as a senior executive officer of the Party, her voice steady and clear. She began by expressing her gratitude, thanking everyone for their willingness to volunteer, for dedicating their time and effort to what she described as the essential work of transforming the country.

She spoke first about housing, laying out the bleak realities without embellishment—rising costs, entire communities priced out of their own neighbourhoods and the dire lack of supply. Then she moved to healthcare, outlining a system in need of root and branch reform: people waiting months for basic care, staff stretched thin, and the difficulties in even recruiting staff in this country.

But it was her third point that made Robyn straighten in her seat, her heartbeat quickening as she leaned in to listen more closely.

"As soon as the Republican Party takes the reins of government, our top priority—aside from addressing the critical issues of health and housing—will be to hold a border poll aimed at achieving a united Ireland. There has never been a stronger momentum for this historic change. The time is now: a vote for the Irish Republican Party is a vote for a united Ireland."

The room erupted in applause and cheers, the energy palpable as the speaker's words resonated through the crowd. Robyn joined in, clapping and smiling as if she shared in their excitement, but inside, she was reeling. The sheer boldness of the announcement left her stunned. Nowhere in the media had there been any hint that a border poll was on the immediate agenda. Yet here it was, unveiled by sleight of hand as a top priority that could suddenly shift the entire political landscape in Northern Ireland if the Party won the

CHAPTER 12

election down south in the Republic.

She knew, of course, that a future border poll was provided for in the 1998 Good Friday Agreement, the result of the Northern Ireland Peace Process. The conditions would arise for such a referendum if the Northern Secretary (the Secretary of State in the UK government with overall responsibility for Northern Ireland) believed that a majority in the North no longer wished to remain part of the United Kingdom. And with the growing Catholic population, that day would likely come eventually.

But it wasn't here yet. And so any attempt by an Irish Republican Party government to force the hand of the Northern Secretary and push for a border poll now could dangerously escalate tensions among Unionists, whose patience was already being sorely tested by Brexit, and the precarious position in which it left Northern Ireland within the United Kingdom. It could even risk dragging Northern Ireland back into the dark days of violence.

As Robyn sat there, absorbing the gravity of what she had just heard, she realised the significance of being present at this meeting. Even if she learned nothing else tonight, hearing the Party's covert prioritisation of a border poll was invaluable. This would be news to virtually the entire electorate, she thought to herself, her mind racing with the implications.

At the sound of the applause, a man in his forties stepped into the room from a side entrance, immediately drawing attention. Fit-looking and of medium height, he had dark eyes, but they weren't brown. Instead, they were a dark piercing grey, an eye colour that is even rarer than green eyes anywhere in the world. The lady at the front introduced him as Goran, the Party's social media manager. Surprisingly for a party so rooted in Irish history and the Irish language, Goran spoke in an Eastern European accent.

After his introduction, he began to explain that the volunteers would be focusing their efforts on social media to support the campaign in these last critical days leading up to the election. He emphasized the urgency of gathering more data for the Party's canvassers. With only a week and a half remaining, he said, it was crucial to target the "undecideds"—those who might still be swayed to vote Republican if nudged in the right direction—rather than wasting time on voters already aligned with other parties.

"This," he said, "is where we win or lose."

The volunteers, Robyn included, leaned in.

His tone was brisk, unapologetic. They were to dive into Facebook. Engage. Interact. Extract.

"Find out who they're voting for," Goran said. "If they sound like they're leaning Republican, that's your green light."

What followed sent a quiet alarm through Robyn's mind.

Once a likely Republican voter was identified, volunteers were instructed to get their general location—through comments, messages, whatever worked. Then, by cross-referencing the name and general location with the Party's own database, they could pinpoint the person's exact address.

The ease of how the Republican Party could find out where someone lived was deeply unsettling, Robyn thought to herself.

Goran didn't hide his satisfaction as he explained it all. The Party's database, he said, held the full electoral register—but more than that, it included extra layers of data the Party had "acquired" on each voter. What kind of data, he didn't say.

CHAPTER 12

How it had been collected, he didn't say. But the implication was loud enough to be heard through the things he left unsaid.

Robyn caught herself glancing around. No one else seemed to flinch.

Goran's voice grew more animated as he described the process—how simple, how effective. His confidence flirted with something darker, almost gleeful in its disregard for ethical and likely legal boundaries.

At the end of the meeting, he promised, all the volunteers would be given access to the system. They'd receive credentials, walk-throughs. Everything they needed.

Once you had a name and an address, he said, you sent it to a dedicated email. After that, the Party's canvassers would take over.

Robyn kept her expression neutral, but the whole process left her cold as ice.

So this was how it worked, she thought. No regard for privacy laws. No accountability. Just data, tactics, and a willingness to cross the line if it helped nudge the numbers in the right direction.

Data privacy and data protection seemed to most people to be a completely abstract issue, but its roots were far from abstract and were based some of the darkest chapters in European history. In the 1930s, the Nazis pioneered the automated mass processing of population data using early IBM technology. By registering people according to ethnicity and other criteria, they created the means by which they could later sort the *Untermensch* or "inferior people", from the rest of the population, ultimately facilitating the Holocaust.

After the war, the Stasi secret police in East Germany built vast and meticulous archives on its citizens which became tools of surveillance and subjugation, enforcing conformity through fear. Information, once again, was power—and punishment.

It was no accident then that modern data protection laws first took shape in Germany during the 1960s and '70s. Those closest to the abuses of unchecked data had learned the hardest how dangerous data could be.

And now, as the Republican Party edged further into power—where mainstream politics began to blur with paramilitary ambition—data protection was never more vital.

"And," Goran added, "make sure you encourage all young people you come across, those in the 18-35 age bracket, to take the '*FindMyTribe.ie*' political quiz. It will help them decide who to vote for."

"Will that be the Irish Republican Party?" Robyn shouted up jokingly, to laughter from the room.

"No, it's not run by us," the social media manager said, rather sourly. "But we do have access to the information from the quiz."

"How do you have access if it's not a Republican Party quiz?" she asked, instantly regretting it in case it raised suspicion.

"We buy the data from the owners of the app," he replied, thankfully not having taken any notice of her question, but immediately wondering if those who took the quiz were even informed that data on their political beliefs was being sold on to those who sought to influence their vote.

But feeling emboldened now, Robyn decided to throw another one at him.

"Just one last question," she said. "This Pat Quirke story. I see it's all over the mainstream news, but it hasn't hit social media so far. How do we make sure we keep it off social since this is where most young people and Republican voters get their news?"

Goran seemed pleased she asked and impressed with her loyalty to the Party. Pat Quirke was 20-year-old man who had died a brutal death in 2007, widely acknowledged to be at the hands of the IRA. He had been beaten with iron bars and nail-studded wooden bats for over half an hour. Every bone in his body was broken and he died two hours later. No one was ever convicted of his death and by 2020 his family had been campaigning for justice for thirteen years. Questions over the murder were raised again by the media in the run-up to the election. Specifically, they related to recent disrespectful comments made by a senior Republican Party politician who insinuated that the young man was involved in illegal diesel smuggling and had tried to move in on someone else's patch — the IRA being the main player in the business in the North. Despite the furore in "the mainstream media" about the killing leading up the election, social media lay completely silent on the matter.

"We have a way of taking care of this on social media, don't worry. But if you do see it popping up anywhere, make sure you downvote it if you can so it doesn't gain any traction. We can control social media to a certain extent, but there's nothing we can do unfortunately about the bastards in the mainstream media."

The crowd sniggered approvingly of his term for the press. It took every ounce of self-control Robyn had not to ask what 'their way of taking care of it on social media' was. She'd have to try and find out what this meant from somebody else with expertise in the area. She'd definitely blow her cover and expose herself as a "mainstream media bastard" if she tried asking Goran there and then.

The meeting only lasted half an hour. Time was clearly of the essence when the Party was on election footing. The crowd were invigorated and ready to swing into action on behalf of the Party by the time it was over. They eagerly stood in line to add their email addresses to the list for database access and Robyn found herself standing next to the lady who had introduced the meeting, making small talk.

She remarked that Goran was very on top of things and that his strategy would make a big difference in laser-focusing the Party's efforts the last week of the election campaign.

"Oh, yeah," she agreed. "We were very lucky to get him. He's made an enormous difference."

"Is he one of the new Irish?" Robyn asked. "One of the wave of Polish people who came here in the Celtic Tiger years? His English is excellent."

"Oh no. Goran is only here since the autumn. And he's not Polish, even though everyone thinks he is," she said laughing. "He's Serbian."

Robyn shot her a look. "Serbian?" she stumbled but recovered fast. "Em, I've never met a Serbian person before."

"Well, there you go. There's a first time for everything."

Chapter 13

Westward toward Castlebar, the road lay still and solemn, a dark vein pulsing through the heart of the country's sleeping landscape. Robyn got home at midnight, the journey from the East Coast had taken two and a half hours—longer, perhaps, in weight than in time. There was little traffic, no need for stops, yet the stillness of the landscape had not stilled her thoughts.

Sleep did not come easy that night. She slid between the sheets hoping for the comfort of rest but found only the echoing weight of everything left unresolved. Her body lay motionless, but her mind was a tempest, thoughts spinning too fast to grasp, too many to count. The unsettling events of the day cast a dark shadow over her consciousness: the sinister 'dark' social media posts that marked her and many others as targets, watched, vulnerable. The way the Republican Party baited unsuspecting users through social media, only to appear at their doorsteps like ghosts materializing from the screen. They knew where you lived. They knew what you thought. And all of it unfolding beneath the surface of ordinary life, invisible yet insidious.

What kind of world were we living in? she asked herself that night. A surveillance state, where privacy was an illusion, and unseen forces pulled the strings? The night continued as it began, as Robyn restlessly tossed and turned, unable to shake the unease that had taken root deep within her.

By morning, the sky hung low, swollen with unfallen rain, the light a dull, aching grey. Robyn dressed without thought and left Castlebar behind, driving toward Westport—not to the familiar chatter and noise of *The Mayo Herald*, but somewhere stranger, quieter. Old Head Beach awaited, though it was winter, and the beach was no place for leisure now.

Normally, she would have chosen Mulranny—secluded, windswept, a place where the roar of the Atlantic could drown out even the noisiest parts of her mind. But not today. Today, something else called her. Old Head was a summer beach, a place of laughter and barefoot evenings. But now it felt different. The shoreline was deserted, the tide out, the horizon blurred beneath a slow-moving front of rain.

But as soon as she stepped out of her jeep, the salty sea air filled her lungs and immediately took effect, giving her the sense of calm she always craved. She stood still for a few moments and just inhaled deeply to soak in the healing effect of the ocean. There was a biting cold breeze, a reminder that winter still had its grip on the land. The rain was holding off for now, but not far away, lurking just over the horizon.

Robyn took in the rugged beauty of the beach for a few moments, her eyes tracing the line where the waves met the shore. Then she turned around and set about the task to hand. She took out her mobile phone and pulled up a map on screen.

Then she set off down the beach holding the phone in front of her until she reached her destination—a weathered manhole, nestled in the grass above the beach, roughly three-metres-by-three in dimension.

Suddenly, the phone rang and interrupted her thoughts. She answered quickly, shielding the phone from the wind.

"Hi Dara, I was just thinking about you," Robyn shouted into the phone, raising her voice to compete with the fierce wind that whipped in from the sea.

"Same here, Rob. I just got hold of the coordinates you asked me for the other day—for the spot where those two guys dived."

"Thanks Dara. I appreciate you checking for me. I have my notes up on screen here on the phone and the map I was talking about. What were the coordinates you have?

"Well, I have that same map you were talking about open as well. And, as usual, Mayhew you were spot on. Those guys were diving right over the cables."

"You're joking me, Dara?" she shouted into the phone. "Are you serious?"

"Yeah, I'm afraid I am."

"What the hell business had two Swedes doing diving that cable?"

"It a strange question alright, Robyn. I'm baffled. I've no idea. I don't think they were trying to tap the cable. Everything is encrypted these days so it would be pointless."

"Or could it be a rival cable company? Who owns these cables? Wasn't it a Google/Facebook consortium that laid the cable?"

"Yeah. But who would be their rival? The Swedes are industry leaders in mobile phone tech but I don't know much about the cable laying business. So there could be a major Swedish company in the business for all I know, or not. I'm afraid I'm no help there."

"I'll look in it to it, Dara. Would you mind if I share this information? Or if I have to use your name in connection with it?"

"No. Fire ahead. I think it's definitely something that needs to be reported either to the company that owns the cable or maybe even the Gardaí, if needs be. I'm fine with making a statement either way, Robyn."

"Ok, thanks Dara. That makes things a lot easier for me."

"No problem. Look, if you find out anything, let me know and if you need to know anything else, just give me a shout."

"Will do, Dara. And thanks again for the info. You're a star."

The rain had begun its slow advance from the sea, a fine mist at first, gradually growing heavier. Robyn felt the first few droplets and quickened her pace. Not wanting to get drenched, she broke into a jog, her shoes sinking into the wet sand with each step. By the time she reached her Jeep, the downpour was just behind her, sweeping across the beach in sheets.

She sat inside for a few minutes while she looked up more information on the cable that was the source of all the drama: the AEC-2, short for America-Europe Connect 2. A single cable, stretching beneath the Atlantic, from New Jersey and Long Island to the shores of Ireland. From there, it coursed onward through the seabed to Denmark—Blaabjerg, its final European port. The cable was a digital artery, carrying data from tech giants' servers across the ocean floor, feeding the pulse of the world's communication. AEC-2 served as a critical link between the large-scale data centers on the US East Coast and those in Ireland and Scandinavia, where the cool climates were particularly favorable for such infrastructure. The cable was owned by Aqua Comms, a consortium that included tech giants like Google and Facebook. Aqua Comms also owned two other cables under the Irish Sea, connecting Dublin to the UK, and another major cable that linked Europe, the Middle East, and India. AEC-1, the other transatlantic cable connecting New York to Killala in North Mayo had been operational since 2016. Other transatlantic cables, owned by different operators, also connected the US, Ireland, and Europe, making landfall in Cork and Kerry. Ireland's shallow continental shelf made it uniquely well-suited for landing undersea cables and had transformed the country into a key global hub in telecommunications, linking continents and facilitating the vast flow of digital data across the Atlantic and beyond.

If AEC-2, the cable the divers were interested in, made landfall in Denmark which was a Scandinavian country, maybe the two Swedes had some legitimate interest in the cable, Robyn thought quietly to herself.

If the cable ended in Denmark, Robyn thought, maybe the Swedes had a reason to be interested. But why here? But then, why all the "cloak and dagger" behaviour? Something about it just wasn't sitting right with Robyn. She stared at the rain streaming down the windshield, mind whirring. Eileen Heaney's words floated back: "the lights beneath the sea." That same woman had helped save D-Day. Her instincts had been right then. Robyn felt, with growing certainty, they still were.

There was someone else Robyn had to meet that morning. She rang him to see if he could meet her for coffee in Newport and he was already in town doing some errands. It wouldn't take long but she needed to talk to him about her discoveries the previous day.

When she pushed open the door of *The Newport Arms*, the aroma of breakfast and coffee greeted her. The windows fogged slightly from the warmth within, and in his usual seat by the window sat German Joe—stoic, familiar, waiting. Two mugs of coffee parked were parked in front of him, and he offered her a small nod of welcome.

The pub was hushed. The fire had not been lit. Fergus O'Malley, the proprietor was conspicuous in his absence, replaced by a younger barman who moved with the slow ease of a quiet shift. Beyond the glass, the sea broke softly against the quay wall breaking the silence within.

With a nod of acknowledgment, Robyn slid into the worn leather seat next to German Joe. He passed one of the mugs of coffee over to her and she was glad of it, savoring the heat as seeped into her chilled body. She glanced around the room once more, to make sure nobody was within earshot before she broached the topic she had come to discuss with him.

"Well," he said. "What can I do for you, Robyn?"

"There are so many things going through my mind at the moment, Joe, that I just can't reconcile."

"Yeah? Like what?" he asked.

"Do you remember," Robyn began, her voice low, steady, "that day you told me about the sub you saw out at sea?"

German Joe didn't answer immediately. His gaze drifted out the window, past the fogged glass and into the grey beyond. Then he turned back to her, brow creased slightly. "Yeah. Of course I do. Why?"

"Did you tell me everything that day?" she asked, the words hanging between them like mist.

He tilted his head, caught off guard. "What are you getting at?"

"I mean," she said, leaning forward slightly, "was there anything you left out?"

A pause. The faint clatter of a glass behind the bar. Then, "Left out like what?"

"The full extent of your suspicions," she said quietly. Her eyes searched his face. "Whatever it was you were afraid to say."

"Robyn," he said, straightening, "I honestly don't know what you're talking about. You'll have to stop talking in riddles.

"Fair enough," she replied, exhaling slowly. "I'll spell it out."

He waited.

"This election," she began, voice now just above a whisper, "something's not right. I've had doubts about how the Republican Party surged so fast in the polls over the past few weeks. So I did something, probably reckless. I created a false identity, signed up as a volunteer, and attended one of their training sessions yesterday. At headquarters. In Dublin."

German Joe's lips twitched into the faintest hint of a smile. "Go on."

"That's confidential, by the way," she added, her tone sharp.

He nodded once. Understood.

"What I found out is that they have some pretty suspect ways of electioneering. They're not just running ads. They're hunting. They comb through social media looking for swing voters—people unsure, frustrated, or just quiet. Then they cross-reference everything they find out about them online with the electoral register and unspecified "additional data" they hold on people. Names. Addresses. Profiles. And then they go to them. In person. Stand on their doorsteps. Apply pressure."

She paused. "But there's more."

Joe raised an eyebrow, waiting.

"Their social media manager had an accent. So I asked someone where he was from."

"Yeah? Nothing wrong with that—have an accent myself," German Joe commented, half-laughing.

"Turns out he's Serbian."

Silence fell across the table like a dropped curtain. German Joe didn't flinch. He didn't blink. But something behind his eyes shifted—something instinctual. Robyn watched him closely.

"You ever meet any Serbs in this country?" she asked.

He shook his head. "Not one."

"Neither have I."

Another long silence.

"I never told you about my brother, did I?" she asked him.

"No. What about your brother?"

"This is going to be a long story. I'll get another coffee," she said and went to the bar to order two more.

Chapter 14

Halfway down the hushed length of The Newport Arms, across scuffed floorboards and age-stained tabletops, a man sat alone. A half-empty mug of coffee cooled in front of him, untouched for some time now. His thumb moved slowly over the face of his phone, scrolling without urgency, eyes locked on the screen with a vacant intensity. He had occupied the same seat for over an hour, unmoving, his presence fading into the quiet pulse of the room like a ghost that no one had noticed entering.

After some time, he rose and walked towards the bar, his footsteps quiet on the worn floorboards. The young barman, polishing glasses with mechanical patience, glanced up and offered a remark meant to pass for friendliness. But the man's reply was curt and uninterested. The bartender, getting the message, nodded once and said no more.

Without waiting for his refill, he returned to his seat. The barman brought the coffee to his table a few minutes later and simply said "enjoy". He understood the look—the inward stare, the closed door of a man who had no interest in conversation. No further pleasantries were offered, none expected.

Around him, the few other patrons carried on in their own small orbits—two tradesmen in workwear talking in low tones, an elderly woman reading a newspaper. None gave him more than a passing glance. That was the kind of man he was. Of medium build, with dark brown hair already retreating above the temples, his features bore the anonymous quality of someone easily overlooked, just another presence in a quiet corner of the pub.

Robyn finally stood up to leave, shaking hands with German Joe and heading for the door. Preoccupied with all the thoughts swirling in her head, she didn't notice the quiet figure at the far table also standing up at the same moment.

As she pushed open the thick, oak door of The Newport Arms and stepped outside, the gentleman slipped out behind her, almost unnoticed, as if he were simply a shadow following in her wake.

*****

It was just after lunchtime the next day in Don Murphy's Bar in Castlebar. Robyn was sat at the bar in front of a pint of Budweiser. Her notebook and pen also lay on the counter unused. She sipped on her drink, lost in the churn of her own thoughts. Outside, Castlebar carried on its usual weekly rhythm, but inside the bar felt like a welcome pause between breaths.

All this time she was spending in pubs, Robyn thought to herself, couldn't be good for a girl. But she had all these shady characters to meet and pubs were neutral ground, public yet private. These were the places people relaxed and talked,

CHAPTER 14

and if you were a journalist who knew how to listen, the pub was still the best newsroom in the world. So, decision made. Hanging out on bar stools and at back tables in pubs was just a job hazard that came with the territory. So no cutting down on pub-time for now, she smiled faintly to herself, just as pleased with her decision.

Robyn Mayhew was, in many ways, one of the last of a dying breed—a young journalist drawn to the legend of the olde Fleet Street journalism, what was considered the profession's golden age when newspapers still mattered and the men and women who wrote them did too. Fleet Street was more than just a location where all the newspapers and press agencies had their offices, it was a street that ran through the heart of London like a main artery, once thick with the lifeblood and ink of the British press. But that was before a new generation of ruthless cost-cutting newspaper barons banished the papers to industrial estates outside the city.

But to belong to the world of Fleet Street journalism was to live your life in dim, windowless rooms, lungs filled with cigarette smoke and coffee fumes, your fingers black with ink and your nerves frayed by the relentless tick of the deadline. It was a hard life, unforgiving, but one that burned bright with purpose.

And the pubs—those were their sanctuaries. Just around the corner or down the alleyway, where a journalist could slouch at the bar beside a rival, pass notes over pints, trade stories for scoops and where friendships were built on the rough-edged trust that only shared exhaustion could breed.

That time had faded now. The presses had been hauled out in the '90s and the offices shuttered. Fleet Street's heart still beat, but faintly—its arteries diverted to industrial parks and glass towers far from the ink and history. Still, its spirit lingered in the hearts and minds of generations of young journalists since. And for journalists like Robyn, it wasn't just nostalgia, it was her job and she loved it. The pursuit. The pulse of something hidden, just waiting to be uncovered.

Don Murphy, barman, proprietor, and one of Robyn's oldest friends in Castlebar, was craning his neck to see out the window, trying to get a look at something further down the street. From behind the bar, his height gave him the advantage—six-foot-two, lean with short, dark hair and a face that wore charm like a second skin. People liked talking to Don. Most came into the bar just for the chat.

"Do ya hear that?" he asked, still looking out the window.

Robyn glanced up from her notebook. "Hear what?"

He tilted his head, listening again. "Some kind of banging."

Just then, the door creaked open and a punter with an un-lit rollie tucked behind his ear stepped back into the bar.

"Looks like a protest coming up the street," he said, his voice carrying more curiosity than concern.

Robyn immediately brightened. "A protest?" she snapped her notebook shut. "I'd better have a look," she said, hopping off her bar stool enthusiastically.

They all followed. Don grabbed his jacket from behind the bar, the smoker held the door, and two others from the snug drifted out behind them, half-drawn by the noise, half by the break in routine. Outside, the air was heavy with distant rain and a chilly breeze. Robyn squinted up the street. The sound was louder now—drums, chanting, all folding together into a single advancing pulse.

"Well," she said, shading her eyes with one hand. "That's a nice bit of excitement for Castlebar. First protest I've stumbled on since I got here."

"They're rare enough," Don agreed. "Wonder what they're shouting about?" The crowd was still too far to make out properly, their chant came in waves.

"'No direct... what?'" Don repeated, brow furrowed.

Then it came—loud, raw, unfiltered.

"What do we want?"

"No 'Direct Provision!'"

"When do we want it?"

"Now!"

The group at the pub's entrance fell silent for a moment, taking it in—the rhythm of voices, the thump of bongo drums, the defiance in every shout.

"Jesus, these boyos are a lively lot," one of the other customers remarked at the roar of the protestors.

"They've fight in them too. I wouldn't want to meet any of them down a dark alley at night," Robyn shouted to their huddled group.

"Yeah, they're definitely not the usual protest crowd you see at environmental protests and the like. These fells look like they want a war," Don acknowledged above the roaring, shouting and pounding of bongo drums.

The crowd was closer now, the chants louder. Robyn pulled her phone from her coat pocket and switched to video, already framing the shot.

In recent years, a quiet but charged resistance had begun to take root across the Irish countryside, coalescing around the establishment of "Direct Provision" centres in rural towns—usually in shuttered hotels or long-vacant properties that bore the weight of economic decline. On the surface, the protests appeared grounded in local concern. But beneath that

uneasy surface, something darker stirred. The Far Right—
still embryonic in Ireland but growing bolder—had found
its foothold in the shadows of these grievances. Wolves
in sheep's clothing, they cloaked their xenophobia in the
rhetoric of human rights, parroting the Left's long-standing
criticisms of "Direct Provision".

It was, after all, an undeniably broken system—one that
warehoused asylum seekers for years in poor conditions,
forbidding them from working, robbing them of agency. But
the Far Right had no interest in fixing the system. Their aim
was exclusion, not reform. And so, with a disturbingly deft
sleight of hand, they reframed their intolerance as empathy,
their hostility as humanitarianism. The message was simple,
if deeply cynical: We're not against the people—we're against
the system. But in small towns like Castlebar, where questions
outpaced answers and fear found easy purchase, that lie was
already beginning to take hold.

The scene of the most recent protests had been in Achill,
County Mayo along the rural west Mayo coastline. Scare-
mongering Far Right agitators descended on the community
spreading fear that their local services—schools, doctors,
post office, shops, housing—would be overrun by foreigners
who would take over their community.

While the system was flawed and needed to be overhauled
urgently, having a "Direct Provision" centre locally, on the
contrary, benefited a rural community. Payment for asylum
seekers' accommodation and the provision of food services
brought money and jobs into a rural area, especially in a
place like Achill where hardly a soul visited during the winter
months. Asylum seekers themselves often contributed to
the local economy by shopping at local businesses, and they

enriched the community culturally by introducing diverse perspectives and traditions. Moreover, their presence could foster a greater sense of solidarity and humanitarianism, challenging prejudices and promoting inclusivity. But this barely received a mention in any media coverage of the xenophobic protests. Fear, often founded in ignorance, could just as easily be countered by education about the benefits of immigration which would go a long way towards quelling the social tensions being deliberately stoked by the Far Right. But this rarely happened.

But such perspectives rarely made it into the headlines. The media often failed to investigate the instigators, reporting happenings instead of examining roots. Fear, born of distance and disinformation, spread faster than truth. And yet, there was a way forward—education, conversation, clarity. These things, slow as they might be, could pierce the fog of suspicion. In the face of manufactured outrage, the facts still mattered. And so did compassion.

Robyn decided to nip inside and gather up her belongings. She was going to follow the protest along the footpath to find out more. Before she left the relative quietness of the pub, she put in a call to one of the paper's press photographers in town to see if he was available to take pictures.

"Beat you to it, Mayhem," Michael McInerney said as he answered the phone. "I'm already out in front of the protest snapping away." McInerney was a towering 6'4" man, lean to the bone and always wore a suit with an open-neck shirt on any of his press photography jobs. He had worked in Dublin for years and so was well practiced with media scrums, still enjoying the buzz from the job, although nearing retirement age soon.

"Wow, you're on the ball, Michael. I'll leave you to it. I'll be following along on the footpath and I'll catch up with you wherever they end up."

Robyn said her goodbyes with a few quick nods, then peeled away from the huddled group outside Don Murphy's. She kept to the footpath, walking parallel to the march, careful not to become part of it but close enough to feel the heat of its momentum. Within minutes, the quiet streets of Castlebar were transformed—swallowed by a pulsing mass of movement. Hand-painted banners rose and fell like sails in a stiff wind, their slogans stark against the grey sky. The screech of a loudhailer pierced the air, followed by the relentless rhythm of bongo drums and the guttural chants of protestors, each beat and bellow amplifying the anger in the air.

It was one of the loudest, most visceral demonstrations Robyn had ever witnessed, louder even than those she'd covered as a student chasing stories through the city streets of Dublin. But this was something else. Castlebar was not a place accustomed to spectacle, much less confrontation. And now, the protest surged like a wave through its centre, jarring the daily rhythm. Elderly shoppers sheltered in doorways, clutching bags, their eyes wide with unease. A few stepped back inside the nearest shopfronts, startled not by the cause perhaps, but by the fury in the air—the sheer volume of it, unfamiliar and raw.

The marchers had already covered much of their route by the time they reached Robyn and her friends at the pub. As they reached the top of Main Street, the crowd turned onto Market Square where the leader of the march mounted the steps of the civic space and, his voice rising above the din,

CHAPTER 14

delivered a final tirade to the gathered crowd. At about forty years of age, with a receding hairline of brown hair and of medium height and build, he could have been Joe Anyone, a man you'd pass on the street without looking twice. He could have been a neighbour, a schoolteacher, someone you might chat to in the queue at the post office. Not the kind of man you'd expect to be standing where he was, lending voice to the language of division. There were no tattoos, no skinned head, no visible threat. And that, Robyn thought, was part of what made him dangerous. He didn't fit the picture most people had in their heads. He slipped beneath their radar—until it was too late.

His words were laced with the coded language of obvious "dog whistles"—phrases that are designed to sound innocuous or even reasonable to the general public but carrying a more sinister appeal to those "in the know." But the message was unmistakable. In thinly veiled rhetoric, he expertly exploited fears about "the dilution of our Irish heritage" and the need "to defend our way of life", spreading misinformation and xenophobia to inflame the protestors. But it was a clear rallying cry against foreigners, designed to harden hearts and close minds. The crowd, packed tightly in the square, cheered on in agreement—their faces a mix of anger and determination—a reflection of how potent and dangerous this anti-immigrant rhetoric had become.

Robyn stood at the edge, clearly taken aback as she realised the hold the Far Right had taken in Irish society, if it had already permeated all the way down to a small town in the West of Ireland like Castlebar. How had a country who had, as recently as 2017, elected the first Irish government leader from an ethnic minority group, come to this? Former

Taoiseach Leo Varadkar was born in Ireland to an Indian father and an Irish mother. He was also Ireland's first gay Taoiseach which was also a cause for much celebration in Ireland at the time.

But as Robyn watched the protest end, the acrid atmosphere lingered, heavy and charged with the unsettling echoes of what had just been said. Though she had no intention of giving the Far Right a platform in *The Mayo Herald*, Robyn knew better than to let the moment pass without trying to find out who the speaker was and where he was from. She moved quickly through the dispersing crowd, eyes fixed on the man who had stirred it into motion. But true to form, he was slippery, one of the new breed of agitators who understood all too well the value of anonymity. They knew how to thread the line between visibility and deniability, always careful not to out themselves to press or police.

Robyn introduced herself briskly, holding out her press card. "Robyn Mayhew. *Mayo Herald*."

His eyes flicked to the card, then back to the crowd. "The people have spoken," he said, gesturing with a sweep of his hand as though a hundred protestors on a sleepy Friday afternoon represented the voice of a nation.

Robyn didn't flinch. "One hundred people on Main Street isn't exactly 'the people,'" she replied, her tone dry, deliberately needling. She hoped to provoke him into saying more than he meant, but he didn't take the bait.

He scoffed—quickly, disdainfully, as if he knew better—and then he was gone, melting back into the crowd. Robyn watched him disappear between the shoulders of the last stragglers, then made a mental note. She knew someone who could help.

CHAPTER 14

Organisers of marches through towns or cities had to notify Gardai in advance so they could put a traffic plan in place, so her Garda friend, Dave could probably get this guy's name and address for her.

But Robyn watched as he slipped off, blending into the crown. Then, she set off after him at a measured distance. Something in her gut stirred—a mix of instinct and curiosity, sharpened by years of chasing stories that didn't want to be caught.

As he walked alongside a group of the marchers making their way, it seemed, towards the church car park on Chapel Street, Robyn followed in their wake, careful to stay on the opposite side of the street, her gaze down, her steps slow. When she reached the entrance to the car park, she hesitated, choosing not to venture inside. Instead, she opted for a more strategic approach—perching on the low stone wall outside.

Shivering in the cold with her breath forming small clouds in the frigid air, she took the maniacal decision to remove the jade fleece she'd worn all morning, a beacon of colour in the otherwise grey day. Wearing a black top underneath and with a black baseball hat he had found at the bottom of her rucksack tugged low over her brow, it was all she could muster by way of a disguise to lessen the chance of the march leader spotting it was her.

One by one, the cars began to file out. She waited for the right moment, just as each driver paused at the junction, eyes darting left and right for traffic—and then, click. A discreet snap of the registration plate. Another. And another. It was a small step, but it might offer some insight into the origins of the crowd. Dave had mentioned before that a core group of far-right supporters traveled around the country to attend these protests, masquerading as locals. She suspected this might be the case today. And whilst registration plates from outside County Mayo didn't exactly offer proof that the car owner was from outside the county, it would be a strange Mayo march that didn't include any Mayo plates.

She worked quickly, hands stiff with cold, camera steady. Thirty-two cars in all passed, with plates from Dublin, Meath, Galway, Cork. A smattering from the Midlands. But only four out of thirty-two bore the tell-tale "MO" of a Mayo plate. Hardly an outpouring of local fury, she thought grimly. Just a carefully staged spectacle, orchestrated by outsiders. A travelling circus of hate. She hugged herself against the cold, teeth beginning to chatter. If she caught the flu over this, so be it. The story would be worth it.

But chilled to the bone by now, Robyn resolved to head home, where she could finish the day's work at her kitchen table without distractions. Once at home, she immediately cranked the central heating, eager to banish the lingering cold. She filled a hot water bottle, nestling it in her lap, hoping its warmth would chase away the icy grip that had seeped into her bones.

At the kitchen table, she flipped open her laptop and typed a brief email to Michael McInerney, just a quick thank you for his swift follow-up on the protest and a note that she'd pop into the office later in the week to go through the photos. She hit send. Then, just as she leaned back, her eyes caught the familiar flicker of a notification in the corner of her screen.

A new message had landed in her Gmail: "We've detected suspicious activity on your account. Your Gmail was accessed from Dublin yesterday. Was this you?"

Robyn frowned. "Lordy, is there anything Google doesn't

know about me?" she muttered under her breath, more amused than alarmed.

Her cursor scrolled over to the blue hyperlinked text that simply said "Yes "and she clicked, confirming it was indeed, just herself.

The message vanished, and she closed the tab. She reached for her hot mug of coffee, oblivious to the shadow she had just let in.

Because Google never asks you to click on a link that says "Yes"—they ask you to type it.

*****

It had been only yesterday that Robyn passed through Dublin, unaware that by the following evening, another traveller would be retracing her steps—though for very different reasons. He came from Mayo too, but where her curiosity had been open and urgent, his was silent, deliberate. A man of few words and many secrets, he boarded the afternoon train with little ceremony and fewer plans, save for the one that had brought him here.

By the time he stepped onto the platform at Connolly Station, dusk had begun its quiet descent over the capital. The walk to where he was going was not that far and although he was a man in his early seventies walking through the inner city at night, he was not a man easily unnerved. Too many years in darker places had dulled the edge of fear.

The city was alive with the pulse of a Friday evening. Shop shutters clattered closed and office workers made for the bars embracing the weekend revelry. The pubs spilled over with laughter and clinking glasses, the air heavy with the scent of cigarettes and the hum of conversation.

He blended into the crowd until he reached O'Connell Street, broad and defiant, the capital's spine. It was here, more than a hundred years ago, that the first blows of Irish independence had been struck, the ghosts of the 1916 Rising still clinging to the façades, if one knew where to look.

His journey concluded at a dark green door, an elegant example of Georgian architecture in a classic shade of heritage green. Without hesitation, he pressed the intercom. A moment later, the door clicked open and he stepped inside.

The Republican Party Headquarters. A place where whispers lingered and secrets thrived—on the very street where Irish independence was born.

Chapter 15

Saturday dawned but not with the usual stillness that came with a Saturday morning, only the hush that comes before something big happens. Robyn sensed it even before she heard the phone ring, a weight in the air, the unmistakable feeling of unrest rising again.

This time it was Michael McInerney himself, the seasoned press photographer, who was calling to alert Robyn, his voice clipped with urgency. He'd caught the morning traffic update on Midwest Radio: another protest was assembling, this one set for noon. Not a sequel to yesterday's Far Right march, but a rebuttal. A rally against racism. A gathering of people determined not to let hate march unchallenged.

Robyn didn't hesitate. Though her weekend had already been surrendered to the chaos of election week with stories half-written and facts still to be confirmed, this assignment was one she greeted with relief, a chance to quiet the unsettled feeling that had taken up residence in her mind since yesterday. The nastiness and viciousness of the Far Right march had sickened her heart and the old quote kept rattling around in her head all night that "the only thing necessary for the triumph of evil is for good people to do nothing." Now she had her chance.

With time already in short supply, Robyn decided to catch the march at the top of Main Street instead of following it all the way through the town. Then she'd take in any speeches or address to the crowd at Market Square. She'd grab a few quick words with the organisers and file a story more deserving of front-page space than yesterday's angry rabble, who'd refused even to speak with the press.

They came just after eleven. A stream of voices and feet, emerging from Linenhall Street like a tide of colour and conviction. There was no menace in this crowd, no hostility. The mood was earnest, almost hopeful. Families stood shoulder to shoulder with students and retirees. Children perched on shoulders. One loudspeaker. Fewer drums. But a spirit as fierce as what Robyn had seen yesterday.

A rough count placed them at around one hundred and thirty strong. A solid number, considering the late notice. But even in that moment of collective resolve, Robyn felt it, the ache of symmetry. The Far Right, too, had drawn similar numbers. That thought chilled her more than she cared to admit.

The marchers had just passed the halfway mark up the street when Robyn noticed small groups of young men, mostly in their late teens to early thirties, loitering on either side of the footpaths. They began shouting at the protesters as they passed. Robyn couldn't make out their words, but the reaction from the marchers was unmistakable—the expressions on their faces changed sharply, as if being taunted. Alarmed, Robyn hurried down the street towards them get a closer look.

That's when she heard it. A sharp whistle cut through

the air above her, a firework hurtling straight toward the crowd. It exploded right at the front of the march with one young lady grabbing her face and shrieking in pain, clearly injured severely by the blast. Chaos erupted as glass bottles were suddenly hurled toward the marchers. Robyn ducked instinctively, taking cover in a doorway. With her hands trembling, she pulled out her phone and dialed 999, urgently requesting an ambulance and the Gardaí.

Minutes seemed like hours as she waited for their dispatch, from just literally around the corner where both the ambulance base and Garda Station were located, just off The Mall.

"Where the hell are they?" she muttered in frustration, before quickly calling her Garda friend directly on his mobile, desperation clearly evident in her voice.

"We're here," he answered. And hung up immediately due to the unfolding circumstances.

Robyn turned to look up the street and squad cars had arrived. The Gardaí got out with batons already drawn. Whilst most of the protesters had fled in the opposite direction as soon as the firework was thrown, pockets of chaos erupted with scuffles breaking out between some of the male protesters and the those who had turned up to fight and chant Far Right slogans from the footpath: "Ireland for the Irish", "Ireland's Full", "Foreigners Out", "F**k the Foreigners." The Gardaí rushed to break up the brawls and tackle the violence, but the streets of Castlebar descended into scenes of shocking violence that afternoon.

Robyn's blood ran cold. This was no spontaneous outburst. This had been planned.

Shaken to the core, Robyn ran the short distance, less than fifty feet, to take shelter at her friend, Don Murphy's bar.

She ducked inside just in time as Don quickly locked the door behind her. Inside, the patrons sat in shock and kept away from the windows, but Robyn couldn't resist the reporter's urge to look.

She asked Don if there was any way to get access to the roof above for a better view, but his lease was only for the ground floor premises. So unless she could shimmy up a drainpipe, he told her, there was no access onto the roof.

Robyn's thoughts then turned to Michael McInerney, hoping that if he had managed to capture some of the chaos on camera, he did so without getting hurt. She tried calling him, but his phone went unanswered, each second of silence heightening her anxiety.

The situation had done a complete one-eighty from the previous day, when they had all spoken of how rare it was to even have a protest in Castlebar at all. Now, Garda cars and ambulances were stationed in the middle of Main Street, with blood spilled on the street and shattered glass strewn everywhere. It was almost as if the town itself was wounded. How had things descended into such violence and so quickly?

But Robyn knew the answer, as shocked as she was by it. There were sinister forces now at work in Irish society, determined to dismantle the country's humanitarian policies towards those fleeing war, drought, famine and torture in their home countries. The violence had been planned in advance by those who turned up to intimidate those marching in support of immigrants.

Ireland, with its own horrific history of famine and oppression, had lost millions to emigration and as a result, and naturally become a supporter of humanitarian policies for those fleeing unimaginable horrors in their homeland.

CHAPTER 15

That empathy was now under siege. Sinister currents were moving beneath the surface of Irish society, whispering lies, cultivating fear, and feeding it to those gullible enough to believe it.

But the question gnawing at Robyn was: who were the architects of this hatred? Who was pulling the strings from the shadows, stoking the flames of division and bigotry?

Answers, if there were to be any, might come at that evening's late night special sitting of the District Court, hurriedly convened by the Courts Service at the Gardaí's request, to deal with the large number of offenders arrested following the breakout of violence. The Courts Service notified the editors of the three newspapers and two radio stations in the county. Jack Leahy, Robyn's editor had put through a call to her, asking her to be at the court sitting that night at 9pm to get the full story. Although, she was now doubly behind with her work, there was simply no getting around the matter.

The cold east wind from yesterday was still rumbling down Chapel Street when she arrived at the District Court that evening. The rest of her colleagues who covered the courts had already assembled and were not happy about having their Saturday night being disrupted over the thuggery from earlier that day. Robyn relayed her eyewitness account of the violence and, despite their protestations at their weekend being disrupted, they understood the gravity of the situation. The town's solicitors had all turned out as well and looked less than thrilled to be there also. Judge Cynthia Healy was a no-nonsense judge but was known to enjoy a good night out, so she wouldn't have been best pleased by the turn of events either.

Name after name echoed through the courtroom as the

court clerk called each case. Solicitors rose in turn, most offering guilty pleas on behalf of their clients. In mitigation, again most claimed their client had never been in trouble with the law before, save for the occasional defendant with a prior public order or traffic offence. The majority of the cases called involved the minor offenses from that chaotic day, a bit of pushing and shoving, nothing more. Where the charges weren't contested, very little additional detail was provided beyond the defendants' names and addresses and a brief description of the offence by the Garda Superintendent who represented the prosecution, leaving much unsaid.

But the case Robyn was most eager to hear, disappointingly, didn't get a mention at all at the evening's court sitting. She was desperate to find out the identity of the culprit behind the horrendous firework incident. But as name after name was called, no one was charged with the firework attack. The Gardaí were likely still in the investigation phase for the more serious offences, gathering evidence, taking statements, and conducting forensic tests. Justice for the poor victim of the shocking firework attack would just have to wait a while longer.

One case did catch Robyn's interest though. Here the defendant was a twenty-year-old UCD history student who had been down home in Mayo for the weekend. He pleaded guilty to the public order charge against him, but his solicitor went into a bit more detail in his plea of mitigation to the Judge before sentencing.

"Judge, my client has never been before the courts before or come to Garda attention in any way. He is a studious young man who plays Gaelic games for his local club and also at college level. He is also an accomplished fiddle player

CHAPTER 15

and a member of Ceol Eireann, the traditional Irish music association. Today's events were extremely out of character for him," his solicitor informed the court.

The Judge looked down from the bench at the defendant, who had wisely dressed in a suit and tie in a show respect for the court. His anxious looking parents sat either side of him and, a young girl in her late teens or early twenties sat with them, possibly a girlfriend or sister.

"In fact, Judge, before today my client had never been to a protest of any nature for any cause," his solicitor elaborated. "When I asked him how he came to be at the scene today he told me that he had been seeing posts on social media about how Irish music, GAA and Irish culture in general would become diluted and eventually wiped out by foreigners coming to this country and, I quote, 'taking over the country'. The posts made spurious claims that this had already happened in other countries. My client said he felt deeply saddened and angered that this could potentially happen here according to the posts he was reading."

He paused, choosing his words with care.

"It would appear, Judge, that my client, possibly due to his age and his stated interest in Irish music and culture, was more vulnerable to such outlandish claims and maybe even targeted for these reasons. We all hear in the media these days about social media algorithms pushing polarising content in order to get reactions from people to boost so-called 'engagement,' and therefore bring in more advertising revenue for the social media companies. The algorithms tailor outrage, push polarising content, and feed users what keeps them engaged—not what's true. He is not the only one. These platforms, knowingly or not, are creating echo chambers where disinformation flourishes and young minds are primed for radicalisation."

He continued earnestly.

"I do not excuse today's events, nor do I downplay the violence. But I ask the Court to consider the context. My client was drawn into something far larger than he understood, by actors with agendas far darker than he realised. And if we're to prevent days like this from happening again, we need to begin by acknowledging that manipulation and by holding those responsible to account."

"I believe my client, and possibly even more of the young men here today, were preyed upon by the social media companies, in cahoots with those wishing to spread xenophobia, and fell victim to false narratives online. While I'm not in any way, shape or form, condoning the violence in Castlebar today, I believe that there was pressure deliberately placed on my client and others online, to engage in certain behaviour offline, and society needs to acknowledge that this real and this is happening in our society. I would respectfully ask you, Judge, to give consideration to this in sentencing my client today."

It was a hell of a mitigation from his solicitor, Robyn thought.

Judge Healy's expression was unreadable.

"Today's events were of the utmost seriousness," she said. "And while I acknowledge the effect social media is having on society today, including what is akin to radicalising people of different political persuasions, your client still exerted his free will in choosing to engage in disorder on the streets of Castlebar. Given that he has no previous convictions however, I am prepared to give him the benefit of the Probation Act on this occasion, but I do not wish to see him before my court again. I will not be so lenient on the next occasion."

A look of relief washed over the defendant's face, followed by hugs from his family. They got up to leave as the court clerk called the next case. Robyn decided to follow them out even though she'd miss the next case as a result. Her colleagues glanced at her assuming she was just taking a toilet break. But Robyn had other ideas.

"Excuse me—sorry—could I just have a quick word?" she called after them, weaving past members of the public gathered in the foyer. The young man turned, his jaw tightening when he saw the press badge. They kept walking.

"Sorry, if I could just have a quick word?" she continued. "It will be off the record?" she called after them. As always, the magic word worked.

"Look, I've nothing to say to you," he said, turning around.

"I get that," Robyn said gently. "I'm not looking for a quote. My report on your case will be just the basics, I won't be adding anything to it. But I'm doing a separate piece on the kinds of social media accounts fueling this sort of thing. You won't be named in it. I just want to understand where it's coming from. If people are being whipped up into doing things that are totally out of character, someone needs to look at that."

The young man glanced at his father, who gave a reluctant nod.

"'Ireland for Ourselves,'" he muttered.

"That's the page you saw it on?"

"Yeah. They said the 'woke crowd' was letting the country be taken over by foreigners."

"Did they specifically ask people to turn up in Castlebar today?"

"Yeah, they even said 'there will be fireworks' but I didn't expect someone to throw an actual firework into the crowd and injure somebody."

"Did you tell this to the Gardaí this?" she pressed

"No. I was just so in shock over being arrested," he said, looking at the ground.

"It's not my place," she said as gently as she could, "but I bet it would mean the world to that poor girl who was injured if, whoever was behind that page, got justice."

"I'm not saying anything to the Gardaí. Then they'll be after me."

His father interjected angrily. "You said you won't link his name to any of this."

"And I won't. I give you my word on that. I appreciate you talking to me and I'll give you my card in case you want to talk further."

"I won't," he said curtly, before grudgingly taking it, as his father started to move off ahead of him, clearly saddened that his son had been brought before the court that day.

*****

As the young man and his family turned the corner onto Chapel Street, a dark SUV eased past them, silent, deliberate, unnoticed. Its engine barely murmured. The windows were tinted deep, rendering the occupants no more than shadows.

Two men sat in the front. Broad-shouldered and in their early forties, their eyes, glacial and alert, scanned the street with clinical precision—ahead, to the sides, behind, always watching. There was nothing casual in their manner. These were not ordinary men, but elite operatives, part of a covert

CHAPTER 15

security detail forged in the quiet corridors of Europe's most secretive agency, the External Action Service. It was the EU's answer to shadow wars, its reach likened to the CIA's Ground Branch. These men were now embedded within An Garda Síochána's Special Detective Unit, their assignment hidden beneath layers of deniability.

Their mission: the protection of a single passenger.

The External Action Service had orchestrated a covert and perilous escape for their passenger and protectee from Minsk, the capital of Belarus. Disguised and hidden amidst junk furniture in the back of a battered van, she endured a tense, claustrophobic 16-hour journey overland, traversing desolate backroads to avoid detection. Their destination was the port city of Odessa in Ukraine. Under the cover of night, she was smuggled aboard a small fishing boat and for seven long, grueling days, she remained concealed in the boat's cramped, dim quarters, the air heavy with the smell of the fish cargo. As they made the slow and cautious journey along the Black Sea, they skirted along the coasts to avoid navy patrols. Eventually, they reached the small fishing port of Piraeus in Greece and crucially, the safety of the EU. From there, the Service whisked her away to a secluded airfield in the Greek countryside, where one of their Gulfstream jets awaited, bringing her swiftly to Ireland, landing in the middle of the night at Ireland West Airport in County Mayo.

But who was this woman, forced to flee Belarus under such desperate circumstances and smuggled into the EU under the cover of darkness? Svetlana Volkov, or Lana as she was known to her friends, was no ordinary citizen. A brilliant network engineer by profession, she had become entangled in the complex and dangerous world of Belarusian politics due to her husband, Vasily Volkov, the leader of the only opposition party that existed in Belarus.

Bordering the European Union and lying just east of Poland, Belarus had long been under the iron grip of Europe's most enduring autocrat, Dimitri Lukopetrov. Since 1994, he had maintained an unyielding hold on power through elections, widely condemned by the international community, as neither free nor fair. His latest "victory" in the January 2020 presidential election, in which he claimed to have won an implausible 90% of the vote, sparked a wave of mass protests across Belarus. The streets filled with demonstrators calling for change, but the regime responded with its usual, brutal force. The European Union and the United Kingdom refused to recognise the election results and swiftly imposed sanctions in a show of condemnation. The leader of the opposition, Lana's husband, facing imminent death was forced to flee into exile in neighboring Lithuania.

Being his wife, Lana was also urged to flee but for her, however, this exile came with an additional mission. During the post-election chaos, the website of Belarus's largest independent newspaper, the only lifeline of information during the protests, was crippled by a cyberattack, widely suspected to have been orchestrated by Lukopetrov's regime. To prevent future digital blackouts, the paper's publisher decided to establish backup servers in a European country, ensuring the continuity of the press should another attack strike. Lana, a highly skilled network engineer, was entrusted with this critical task.

When asked which European country she would choose within which to take refuge and set up the servers, there was no question for Lana which country it would be: her childhood

CHAPTER 15

safe haven, Ireland. In 1986, when the Chernobyl nuclear disaster in neighbouring Ukraine spread radioactive dust clouds all over southern Belarus, thousands of children suffered from health issues for generations as a result. An Irish charity, committed to aiding the victims of this catastrophe, had flown many of these children to Ireland for respite, offering them clean air and a summer holiday. Lana Volkov was one of those children.

When it came to choosing a town in which to go into hiding and carry out her mission to set up the vital servers, she chose the town in which her dearest childhood friend was living. The town was Castlebar, and her best friend of all those years, was Robyn Mayhew.

Chapter 16

That kid wasn't wrong. Robyn could see how impressionable young men and women—young men in particular spoiling for a fight—could get roped into violence by the social media pages of the so-called "Ireland for Ourselves" organisation. And typically for such hate spewing accounts, there was no information on who the organisers were hiding behind it.

The level malice and vitriol now directed at foreigners coming to Ireland was sickening. It struck Robyn deeply, especially considering Ireland's own painful history of emigration. Millions of Irish people had been forced to flee their homeland to escape the Great Famine in the 1850s, and for over a century and a half since, poverty had driven waves of Irish emigrants abroad.

Even today, many still chose to emigrate simply for better job prospects, a more appealing lifestyle, or simply for a better climate. Over 70 million people in the United States alone claimed Irish ancestry, not to mention the vast numbers of Irish descendants in the UK and Australia.

CHAPTER 16

And after the 2009 recession, another wave of young Irish emigrants left to find work elsewhere. Yet, here at home, so many Irish people now lacked the compassion and heart to welcome those who arrived on our shores, fleeing from situations far more desperate.

These new arrivals weren't simply seeking a better life — they were escaping the ravages of war, drought, and famine — disasters exacerbated by climate change. The painful irony was that climate change had largely been fueled by the industrialised economies of the developed world, but it was Africa and Asia that was paying the highest price.

Images of desperate African migrants packed onto inflatable boats, dangling over the edge, haunted the nightly news. These people risked everything to cross the Mediterranean, driven by sheer desperation to escape unbearable circumstances. Week after week, stories surfaced of boat loads of immigrants who had drowned, turning the Mediterranean into Africa's largest unmarked grave.

But it wasn't only Africans that were fleeing desperation. Robyn couldn't shake the haunting images of Afghans clinging to the wheels of US military aircraft, desperate to escape as the Taliban reclaimed power in their country. The scenes left an indelible mark on her mind forever, people so terrified of their future under the Taliban that they risked their lives in this horrific manner in a frantic bid to leave.

The growing number of people joining in on the hate was maddening, especially when one considered Ireland's urgent labour shortages. Professions like construction, medicine, nursing, private home care and nursing home care, dentistry, teaching, cheffing, hairdressing and mechanics profession and all trades were crying out for workers. It was baffling that so many couldn't see the irony: the very people being scapegoated for society's ills were the ones most needed to keep it running. Perhaps it would take something as personal as not being able to get their cars fixed, their hair cut, houses built or arrange creche care for their children or nursing home care for elderly parents to make people realise how manipulated they were by the Far Right's toxic, Nazi rhetoric.

The pension crisis was another looming catastrophe. With Ireland's rapidly aging population, there was no hope of sustaining the country's pension reserves without a fresh influx of young, taxpaying workers. Foreigners coming to Ireland were not a burden—they were a lifeline, essential to filling the gap left by an aging society. Yet, despite this obvious truth, so many were blinded by prejudice, caught up in a cycle of fear and hatred.

Seeing how susceptible Irish society had now become to racist ideologies, it brought her back to documentaries she had seen on the rise of the Nazi party in Germany. She now understood how easily Hitler's anti-Semitic bile had gained traction, leading to World War II. As a child, Robyn had always been horrified that such widespread hatred could have festered and exploded into global conflict, especially so soon after the devastation of World War I. It seemed impossible to her that people could allow themselves to be swept up in such blind hatred. But now, witnessing the rise of racism in her own country, she realised how quickly people abandoned their better natures, using hate as an outlet for their own frustrations with life.

While the courts had intervened this weekend, holding a small group of young men and some in their forties accountable for their actions, Robyn knew this was only a

Chapter 16

temporary solution. The real danger lay with the thousands of others, quietly 'liking' and following hateful pages online, remaining unchallenged and uneducated about the racism they were fueling. These people would continue to spread division, unchecked by any legal consequences, reinforcing a dangerous undercurrent that was seeping into everyday life. It was a chilling reminder of how easily societies could unravel if left unchecked.

It was Sunday morning, and Robyn found herself in a bleak mood, weighed down by thoughts about the troubling direction the country was heading in. But she couldn't afford to let it consume her. The election was less than a week away, and after a whirlwind week of news, her work was far from done. She'd have to push through the weekend to make sure everything was written up in time.

She already had five stories finished from earlier in the week. First, there was the story of the death threats that had poured in after she published the story on the Republican Party's meteoric rise in the polls with no apparent reason for their sudden popularity. Second, there was the unnerving spear-phishing attacks on journalists around the country under the guise of protecting themselves from, ironically, just such attacks. It was strange and disconcerting to be featured in these two news stories herself. She was supposed to write the news, not be the news. But she couldn't dwell on it. These were stories that needed to be told, and she had to push forward.

Her feature interview with a local businessman was also completed, though she had hoped to polish it a bit more. Sadly, with time running out, any chance of rewriting it was off the table. At least her profiles of the election candidates turned out well with probing questions that led to candid, sometimes fiery, responses that made for an engaging read.

Then there was the "manganese in the water" story which was relevant to everybody and was causing havoc in the town. It covered the largest geographic area ever of such a water alert for the county and there was still no update on when it would be lifted.

Then she had three more pretty sensational stories yet to write up: the hacking of electricity smart meters across the north of the county as the likely cause of the substation fire that led to recent massive power outage; the unexplained cancellation by text of elective surgeries at the hospital despite doctors, nurses and theatres all being available on the day; and the Far Right's arrival in county Mayo and their violent attack on a counter-protest yesterday.

On top of that she had the election feature she was calling "Dirty Tricks Election 2020" to write up as well yet. This was the story on the Republican Party tactics she had uncovered at the training seminar for volunteers: the Republican Party baiting undecided voters on social media to elicit their name and home address, which when combined with information on the electoral register, enabled Republican supporters to turn up on their doorstep to make sure they voted Republican; the use of 'dark posts' to mislead the media into believing they were encouraging all sections of society to get out the vote; the use of micro-targeting to spread IRA memes amongst young people vulnerable to Republican radicalisation; micro-targeting to spread disaffection with other parties amongst their supporters; the purchase of data on people's private voting intentions, that she had since discovered was being sold illegally without their consent, by the owners of the

CHAPTER 16

supposedly 'impartial' FindMyTribe app; the establishment of a fake polling company by the Republican party to conduct "impartial" polling on people's voting intentions without revealing that they, the Republican Party, were behind it; the media management of the Pat Quirke murder story and how the Republican Party were keeping it off social media and away from their young voters' eyes.

It was explosive stuff, and Robyn knew that when the paper hit the stands on Tuesday, the national media would have a field day. The coverage would be relentless, and the stories would dominate headlines for days. She had covered plenty of high-profile criminal cases throughout her career, and never once had she worried about her personal safety. But last week's paper had sparked a vicious backlash—death threats, rape threats —all for questioning the sensational and suspicious rise of the Republican Party in Ireland. Now, as she prepared to release much more damning revelations, she couldn't help but wonder what she'd be facing this time. She shivered to just think about it. What if this week's stories provoked an even more dangerous response? What if the threats turned into something real? The fear gnawed at her nerves, but there was no going back now.

She couldn't un-know what she now knew. The Republican Party wasn't just rising in popularity by chance. They were conning the Irish public, manipulating the very fabric of democracy. Robyn knew that stepping back or turning a blind eye, would be a betrayal of everything she stood for as a journalist. For a brief moment, she entertained the thought of walking away, but it was only a split second of doubt. She exhaled deeply then turned back to her laptop. She had a job to do, and no amount of fear was going to stop her from doing it.

She had three other stories that had to be followed up on further before they would be ready to be written up. The first one, the Marie Mulhall "Drugs in the Dáil" story, was at a dead end for now but she would follow up on this as soon as she could get a break from writing because it had an urgency about it with the election only a few days away.

The second story involved the two strange guys out at Rosmoney Pier the other day. It didn't seem like much at the moment, but her instincts told her to keep digging. However, it was low on her list of priorities for the moment, so she would circle back round to it next week, after the election, and investigate it further.

But the third story had consumed most of her energy this week. She'd been working on it well into the early hours of each morning this week. It was a story that grew out of the vicious rape threats and death threats she had received via the newspaper's Twitter account the previous week. Against her better judgment, she had sneaked a look at some of the abusive comments directed at her, as well as the accounts they came from. But, in truth, she hadn't just peeked. She actually ended up doing a deep dive into these accounts, pits of horror though they were.

She downloaded the full list of accounts posting abuse directed at both her and the paper. There were even threats to burn the newspaper building down. The accounts seemed to be run by some of the vilest creatures on earth, but also the most political creatures on earth, spewing hatred toward every major Irish political party, except for the Republican Party, which they seemed to fervently support whilst trolling every other political party and jumping on anybody who dared

CHAPTER 16

support them. It was if the IRA's fearsome reputation on the ground had transposed itself to their online army and people were just as afraid of them there.

The deeper she dug, the stranger it got. Part of her was intrigued whether these accounts may have had official sanction from the party or even be run by the party. She copied headlines from the Republican Party's press releases and cross-checked them with the profiles posting abuse. Sure enough, the same accounts were sharing official party material. That couldn't just be a coincidence. Her gut told her these profiles were more than just supporters—they were connected to something bigger.

Driven by that hunch, she continued to dig further. She ran a search for the accounts sharing the "What Has Fianna Fáil Ever Done For You" meme and hashtag, and then searched by replacing Fianna Fáil with each of the other political parties, as well. And there they were again. Each time, the same profiles appeared. Something wasn't right.

A closer analysis confirmed her suspicions: these accounts were bots. They posted over fifty times a day and, like clockwork, each account posted at the exact same times for that account, each day in a clear pattern. And, each of the suspected bot accounts seemed to have Twitter handles or usernames that followed a set formula: six digits followed by a first name.

And the profile pictures? Reverse image searches revealed they were either stock images or stolen from real social media accounts. Even more incredibly, each of the twelve accounts had the exact same number of likes, tweets and retweets. It was clear evidence of not just automated activity, but concerted automated activity. It wasn't just twelve bot accounts she had found, but a network or "botnet" of twelve accounts, working in concert with each other to amplify and spread disinformation.

One of the accounts had an associated YouTube channel with millions of views which mostly came from clips of 90's TV sitcoms uploaded in 2017 but which was now strangely posting industrial quantities of Irish Republican Party content. It was a sneaky way to gain access to people's YouTube feeds — lure them with funny sitcom clips then once a regular viewer, start sneaking in political messaging. But it was a method that clearly worked.

Another one of the Twitter accounts linked itself to the so-called "Men's Rights" movement, pushing the narrative that men should be dominant over women, women should be submissive to men, men deserved greater pay for the same work and an elevated position in society. It posted free invites to a porn site interspersed with political propaganda for the Republicans. Another siren call to young men.

But the upshot was that this concerted botnet of twelve Republican Party-supporting pages, bouncing all the same memes and stories between them, had artificially boosted the newsworthiness of their posts, getting more likes and shares than established media by far. Just twelve accounts operating in this manner managed to generate an astronomical 27 million views between them, far in excess of the number of views for paid political ads by all of the political parties in Ireland. It was a stunning level of influence for whomever was behind the operation.

Robyn's instincts led her to believe that the Republican Party's social media manager, who had boasted of having methods to "take care of" the Pat Quirke murder story on social media, which Robyn suspected at the time meant using a bots, could possibly be behind this botnet as well. It was definitely within his wheelhouse, given all the other dirty tricks he was engaged in.

But proving it was a different matter. She needed evidence, something concrete, ideally a digital forensics expert to confirm the botnet's origins. But time was short, and money even shorter, to hire someone to look into her hunch for her.

Determined to do the work herself, Robyn dived even deeper into the accounts' histories, going back as far as 2018. But what she found didn't just blow her theory out of the water—it completely baffled her. These accounts, which had been so fiercely pro-Irish Republican, had also been tweeting in favor of the UK government's pro-Brexit policies. How could that possibly align with the Republican Party's anti-Brexit stance?

She was gutted that her hunch was blown. It's not like she was stuck for something to write this week, but she had put so much work into analysing the accounts. All that work, all of that missed sleep, felt wasted.

Then things took an even weirder twist.

Not content to stop at 2018, she decided to look into the very first tweets published by each account. Three of them had, bizarrely, published content relating to Ukraine, a country in Eastern Europe and a place few Irish people would have even been able to point out on a map. The county had zero relevance to Irish politics at that point in 2020.

The other nine accounts had strangely deleted their entire first year of tweets. Again, without any apparent reason. Robyn also spotted that all twelve of the accounts were created within the same week in January 2017, in more evidence that it was a concerted botnet.

But not a solely Irish Republican concerted botnet, unfortunately. Frustrated and exhausted, Robyn knew she had to let this one go. The botnet's origins would remain a mystery for now.

As her stomach began to rumble, softly at first, it was a subtle reminder of her growing hunger. She tried to ignore it, focusing on the task at hand, but the rumble soon escalated to a grumble, impossible to overlook. Robyn sighed, realising she hadn't yet had time to grocery shop that weekend, leaving her with no choice but to step out for a quick takeaway brekkie, despite how super pressed for time she was.

She craved her go-to comfort foods—a thick, berry smoothie bursting with tart-sweetness and a warm, blueberry muffin—always optimistically hoping the healthiness of the first would balance out the unhealthiness of the second. Normally, weekends were for tea—her preferred way to unwind—but this weekend, a latte with a double shot of espresso was essential to keep her mind sharp. And as much as she longed for a peaceful walk down the town to clear her head, the ticking clock urged her otherwise. With a reluctant glance down the tree-lined street, she grabbed her keys instead and jumped into her jeep, given the weekend it was.

A short while later, Robyn found herself standing at the counter of the nearby filling station. While paying for her breakfast, she spotted the sandwich rolls on display and added one to her order for lunch as well to carry her over until dinner. The young cashier's friendly energy broke through Robyn's haze of hurried thoughts, pulling her into the present.

"Is that everything?" she asked, a slight young kid, brunette and about college age.

"Yeah. Just those three, please," Robyn replied, pulling her

CHAPTER 16

card from her jeans pocket.

"You wouldn't by any chance have cash on you?" the shop assistant asked hopefully before explaining: "It's just our machine is on the blink this morning and we have to enter the long numbers manually to put through transactions."

"Oh no. Shoot. I don't have anything else, I'm afraid," Robyn offered.

"Don't worry. I can put still put it through if you don't mind hanging on a second."

Robyn shot an apologetic glance at the two customers behind her, but they seemed to be in an obliging mood and didn't give her any annoyed looks in response.

"Enjoy your brekkie," the shop assistant said to her handing back her card. "And have a good day!".

"You too," Robyn smiled. "Take care."

Then just as she was putting her key in the ignition of her jeep, it came to her.

The sudden realisation that the long string of numbers from her debit card that the shop assistant had entered into the machine, resembled something she had been staring at for over a week now.

The bitcoin transaction number from the "Drugs in the Dáil" scandal.

The words of advice of Charlie Lohan, her old friend and mentor, echoed loudly in her mind: "always follow the money". For days, she had been feeling as though she was hitting dead end after dead end. But now she finally had a breakthrough. This could be the thread that tied everything together. Her pulse quickened, not from caffeine or hunger, but from the adrenaline of discovery. Finally, she had direction and a new hunch to follow.

Chapter 17

"Robyn, are you at home?"

It was Michael McInerney, the Castlebar-based press photographer whom the paper worked with on stories in the county town.

"Sure, Michael. Have you got something for me?" Robyn answered, thinking it strange that he called her by her first name, instead of the usual bellowing of "Mayhew" down the phone line, instead of "hello".

"Just something I want to run by you, if you don't mind me calling round to the house."

"Of course not, Michael. I'll have the kettle on."

Robyn was intrigued but the fifteen minutes that it took him to get there flew by with all the work she had to do on her laptop. "Well, Man of Mystery, what have you got for me?" Robyn grinned happily, as she answered the door.

"It's a bit a funny one."

"You know I'm a sucker for a funny one."

"Well, this is one of the funniest ones I've seen in a long time." He produced two photo prints from an A4 envelope. That in itself was unusual. Thumbprint photos on screen were his usual stock in trade.

"Must be a special occasion!" Robyn joked.

"See if you can spot anything unusual in these two images," he challenged her.

"Oh, they're the pics of the protests. Are they Friday's or Saturday's protest?" she asked

"This one is Friday's: the anti-immigration march. And this one is Saturday's: the march in support of migrants."

"Mmmm," said Robyn as she studied first one image, then another, then back again. "Mmmmm." This went on for about twenty seconds.

"Jesus, Mayhem. I thought you'd be better than this."

"Michael, you're going to have to give me some sort of clue."

"Ok, look. See these two guys here?" he said, pointing to two guys in about their early thirties at anti-immigration/Far Right march.

"Yeah?" she said, not knowing where he was going with it.

Pointing to the second picture of the march in support of migrants, he said: "And here they are again."

He gave it a second to sink in.

"What are two Far Right protestors against migrants doing at a march in support of migrants the following day? And I mean *in* the march. They weren't on the sidelines throwing insults or bottles."

Robyn glanced down at the two pictures again. "Jeez, you're right Michael. Same two guys. And yeah, different days on the time stamps." She looked again at the images. "Unless they're undercover cops, maybe," Robyn ventured.

"Well, the cops I was talking to on traffic duty after the first march on Friday—the Far Right march—told me the station wasn't notified of the protest. And organisers of protests almost always notify the cops in advance so the they can put a traffic plan in place," McInerney filled her in.

"Unless they were undercover cops from Dublin and they didn't want to blow their cover by letting the local station know they were in town. I have a good contact that I can run it by. Would you mind if I held on to these to show them to him?"

"Be my guest. The whole thing just looks fishy to me," McInerney added, as stood up to leave.

"Hey, are you not staying for a cuppa?"

"No, I've got to run. I have a match to get to that your sports editor wants shots of. Another time."

"Ok. I'll let you know if I find out anything, Michael. And thanks for bringing it to me. I always appreciate your observations. You're always on the ball."

"No problem, Mayhew. I'll talk to you soon."

She always enjoyed Michael McInerney's company. His main business was sports photography, but he had a keen eye and ear for news journalism too, so their chats were always interesting. But today was different. Robyn had a bee in her bonnet to pull up the files on her laptop for the "Drugs in the Dáil" story. Her investigation had been stalled all week and it was tormenting her that she hadn't gotten any leads and was close to admitting defeat on this one.

But she had one last line of enquiry that she hadn't thought of previously. At the petrol station paying for her breakfast, the shop assistant had to key in the long number from her debit card. The long sequence of numbers set off a train of thought in her brain that led to one of those rare light bulb moments that she absolutely lived for.

Robyn opened the JPEG file containing the bitcoin receipt that Marie Mulhall had allegedly received for her dark net drug deal. Her eyes immediately zeroed in on the long sequence of numbers at the top—the bitcoin transaction number. This was the key.

Next, she downloaded a bitcoin "explorer" to search the blockchain for the specific information she was looking for. The blockchain was the public ledger that stored the history of every bitcoin transaction ever made. It was accessible to anyone, a transparent system meant to ensure traceability. It was an intricate system, but one that offered undeniable proof of a transaction. Hopefully the bitcoin explorer app would pull up the results she needed. Otherwise, she'd have to download the entire blockchain which would take hours on end, possibly even run into days.

She entered the details of the Marie Mulhall drugs transaction number. Then a tense few moments passed as Robyn scanned the ledger. And there it was, or more correctly, there it wasn't—there was no such transaction number at all. Someone had created a fake transaction number and "receipt" to frame Marie Mulhall, fabricating the entire "Drugs in the Dáil" scandal in a calculated effort to destroy her, just before the election.

Robyn sat back in her chair, stunned. This wasn't just a mistake or a misunderstanding—it was a deliberate smear campaign, a setup designed to destroy a top-performing politician's reputation. The implications were enormous.

Editor Jack Leahy was ecstatic when she rang him. Although it was a Sunday, he always went into the office at the weekend to write his editorial for the next edition of the paper, while he had some peace and quiet.

"This is top class, Mayhew!" he exclaimed, when she recounted her morning's findings. "But how are we going to prove the Republicans are behind it?"

"I don't know if I will be able to, but they're the ones that stand to benefit if Marie Mulhall loses her seat. Their candidate, Rita Collins was polling just behind her and would take the seat if Mulhall doesn't recover from this scandal."

"Well, hopefully giving her a front-page splash on this will help make up for the lost ground and she'll benefit from a bounce, when people sympathise with what was done to her. But there will always be the few begrudgers who'll still slate her for it, but hopefully what you've uncovered, is enough to win back her seat for her."

"Can I ask you a favour, boss?"

"Can you ring her to give her the good news because I'm so up to my eyes trying to get this week's stories written up. I've a few more on the boil at the moment and I literally don't have a second to even to pee this weekend."

"Mayhew, you're some tulip for always ducking out of the spotlight, but I'll do it if you want me too. But I'm sure she'll still want to have a word with you to thank you in person."

"Yeah, that's fine. I'll take her call Tuesday once the paper's put to bed. But if you just fill her in on the all the details and give her an explanation on how the blockchain works it will save me a ton of time."

"Will do, Robyn. Keep up the good work, and who knows— we might just let you stick around a bit longer," he quipped, his voice dripping with his trademark sarcasm.

"Ok, cheers boss. That's good to know. Appreciate it," she replied, every bit as sarcastically, right back at him.

CHAPTER 17

The rest of Sunday went by in a blur for Robyn as she scrambled to write up all she had uncovered that week. Having detailed notes on a story always helped the writing up process, but sometimes, an overwhelming amount of detail made it harder to formulate an approach to a story that was readable and interesting for the public. As the evening wore on her brain was getting more and more sluggish, but she did get a really heartfelt phone call from Marie Mulhall which really lifted her spirits. It was midnight before Robyn turned off her laptop that night, having to be up for 7am and ready for an early start again the next day.

Monday went by at its usual frenetic pace. It was the day before the paper went to press and journalists, the advertising team and production staff were always in a mad dash to fill the pages of the paper. Robyn was making good headway with her week's news stories, but her one frustration was that she couldn't get hold of her Garda friend, Dave. She desperately wanted to run the two protest pictures by him to see if he could shed any light on who the two guys were who turned up to both marches. He must have been on a surveillance op. His phone was off all day and evening. Even when he had time off, he was usually always reachable, so it was probably for operational reasons that he wasn't that day.

It was 10.30pm and Robyn was about to call it a night at the office when Paddy Dunbar, the production manager walked all the way over to her desk from the far side of the newsroom, instead of shouting over like what he usually did.

"Have you done any work at all this week, Mayhew?" he enquired, tongue-in-cheek. "Only messing, Robyn. You didn't upload any of your stuff to your pre-press folder."

"No, I did, Paddy. It's all there," she replied, clicking the folder open on her laptop. "What the fu...?" she said, clearly irritated. "I've been uploading stuff all day. The last one just fifteen minutes ago. I saw the 'upload complete' message and on all the other stories in the folder too. Hey, is someone taking the mick?" she shouted around the office to the few sports staff and one of the production team that still remained.

But all she got were blank expressions, convincingly blank ones too. And Monday night had never been prime prank time in the office before. Everybody was usually well beat at that stage of the night.

"Jesus, where's Leahy?" she said clearly exhausted and in no mood for disappearing news stories during the week of an election. She stomped off into his office but when she told him, she got the same blank expression back that she received from the rest of the lads. He came out onto the floor with her and over to Paddy Dunbar's desk to see what was going on.

"How the hell could her whole folder of stories have disappeared?" he asked. "I thought those upload folders could never be deleted accidentally."

"They can't," Paddy replied, clearly confounded. "The folder's still there. There's just nothing in it."

"Look, we have to get to the bottom of it," came Leahy's pronouncement on the matter. "That copy has to be found or we have no paper tomorrow. I'll ring Seamus Mullaney to come back in and find it on the system, wherever it's gone. You go home guys, but Paddy, I'll need you in at 6.00am to have the pages ready on time to go to print. Robyn, you keep your phone on in case we need to ring you later."

Seamus Mullaney was the paper's IT guy. Bald, middle-aged and looking it, he was always moody around the office and no one ever approached him with an IT issue unless it was

CHAPTER 17

life or death, which was probably his actual intention.

"Alright, thanks Jack," Robyn replied. "But if you find all the stories, can you send me a quick text, because I don't know if I'll even be able to sleep tonight unless they're found."

"Will do. Now off you go while you can."

Jesus, what a nightmare way to end the best week of her career, Robyn thought to herself as she walked dejectedly out the door, dumbstruck by what had just happened. But the night was only just getting started for Robyn Mayhew. It was a phone call at 1.30am that broke the bad news to her.

"Robyn, I'm sorry for waking you." It was her editor, Jack Leahy, again. "But it's bad news. The deleted files are nowhere to be found on the system. And Seamus has gone through your desktop and laptop and they're wiped from that as well."

"You have to be joking me, Jack? Please tell me this is just a really, really bad joke?"

"I'm afraid not. Look it breaks my heart Robyn to tell you this but if you can re-write the Marie Mullhall story from memory for the front page. Then the rest of the election stories, if you're able to re-write from memory, you can give to the daily papers this week instead. They're of too much public importance to hold off on until after the election is over for our next edition in a week's time. It kills me to do that but we have no choice."

"How the hell could all of this weekend's writing just disappear in a puff of smoke?" Robyn asked, heartbroken.

"Seamus couldn't find any trail of evidence tonight but we'll have to get computer forensics specialists in to see what happened. It's just crazy. It's the best week of your career Robyn and it's just been wiped out," he commiserated.

"I'm gutted, Jack. I just don't know what to say. I'm going to come over to the office because I won't be able to sleep now anyway. Do you have a spare laptop I can work off or can Seamus lend me one?"

"Yeah, he will have one for you. Take your time coming over, Robyn. There's only so much we can do at this stage now anyway."

"Okay, I'll be there in forty minutes or so."

Robyn wracked her brain on the drive to Westport, desperately trying to figure out how things had gone so catastrophically wrong. Could she have accidentally downloaded a virus? It seemed impossible. She had been so vigilant, especially with the surge of spyware attacks targeting journalists in the lead-up to the election. She couldn't think of a single suspicious email or file, other than the hoax NUJ email, which she spotted instantly.

She had no way of knowing but the Google security alert email she received a few days ago, asking if she had accessed her device from Dublin, wasn't from Google. Google always asked you to type your answer, not click on a link saying "yes" or "no." That one slip, that single click, and she had walked straight into a trap. Now everything was unraveling before her eyes and she had no idea why.

Chapter 18

Robyn could barely summon the strength to drag herself to the elegant Knockranny Park Hotel, a stately establishment gracefully perched on a hilltop just outside the town of Westport. Earlier that morning, her close friend, Garda Dave O'Hara, had seen a series of missed calls from her on his phone. He rang her immediately to see if there was any emergency. He was relieved to hear her anxiousness to get hold of him was only for a story about the Castlebar protests. He had missed her deadline unfortunately, but they agreed to meet at the hotel bar outside town, as per their usual preference for meeting in quiet spots, away from prying eyes.

Inside, the lobby of the hotel exuded elegance and warmth, with plush seating arranged around a grand fireplace. Soft lighting, rich wood accents, and tasteful décor added sophistication, while large windows bathed the area in natural light, offering glimpses of the beautiful surroundings outside. The bar, cozy yet refined, featured dark wood paneling and leather armchairs. Its intimate atmosphere made it the perfect spot for a quiet drink.

Robyn recounted the night's events and it was obvious from Dave's facial expression that he was worried.

"Robyn, it's definitely not a coincidence that your stories were wiped off the server just a few days before the election. They're political stories with big implications for the Republican Party. This means you're on their radar, just on the basis of the polling story from that last week, and you were deliberately targeted. I'm pretty sure the IT forensics specialists will find malware implanted in the paper's systems. What scares me for you is that your stories this week are much more explosive and to be honest, I'm worried for your safety."

"I'm fine, Dave. You don't need to be worrying," Robyn quietly reassured him.

"Don't look now, but there's a guy at the table over in the corner that came in after you. Maybe take a walk out to the ladies and say hello as you're passing and see if you've seen him anywhere before."

Robyn was surprised Dave was so immediately concerned, but she turned to reach into her handbag hanging from the back of her chair as an excuse to take a furtive look: "I got a glance at him there. No, I haven't seen him before. Why? Do you think he's following me or something?" Robyn asked. He was the only other customer in the bar.

"I don't know. It's strange for someone to come all the way out of town and go into a hotel bar at 11.30am for a coffee. He's not a resident, because I saw him come through the front lobby."

Dave wasn't wrong. And Robyn clearly didn't recognise him as one of the patrons in *The Newport Arms* when she met German Joe last week, but then, few would.

"I'll keep an eye out, Dave," Robyn, in her blissful ignorance, assured her friend. "But to be honest, I'm only a minnow in the journalism world. I'd find it hard to believe I'd be on the Party's radar, never mind that they'd have the IRA surveilling me. But come to think of it, did I tell you what happened after the County Council meeting the other night?"

"No. What happened?"

"I had a run-in with the Republican councillor, Richard Duffy."

"What sort of run-in?"

"I approached him after the meeting to ask him a few questions about the party's housing policy. He left me waiting for nearly three quarters of an hour and the place was cleared out by the time he came to me. I had some tough questions for him and he wasn't taking it. Threatened me with a lawsuit and everything if I even printed the questions I had asked him. Basically, he had objected to every house and apartment development in his electoral area since the recession up until recently. So I asked him if his party had been deliberately objecting to developments for years in order to create a housing crisis and use it to get elected. He flat out lied and denied he had objected to all these developments even though I told him I had seen every single one of his objections in writing at the planning office. Anyway, as I was reversing out of the car park, I looked in my rear-view mirror and got the fright of my life – there he was standing right behind my car videoing my registration plate, the freak."

"You're joking me," Dave replied, clearly stunned by the councillor's actions. "That's typical IRA intimidation tactics – the asshole. Good job you told me that. When the election's out of the way Robyn, I might get you down to the station to make a statement. That needs to be on record."

"Oh, it's on record alright. You know we can't use recording equipment inside the council chamber. But something told me to have my phone at the ready when he came out to talk to me and I had just switched it on. So I have it all recorded."

"Good. Keep a few copies of it in a few different places. I know he made a big show of recording your reg plate, but at the same time, we can't just assume it was for intimidation purposes only. He may well pass on your plate to the boys themselves," Dave told her, referring to the IRA.

"Ok. I'll keep a good eye out on who's behind me on the road."

"But getting back to last night, what happened at the paper was definitely no coincidence, believe me. I think you and Leahy need to have a sit down with the Superintendent today to keep him in the loop. Don't wait for the results of the forensics to come back. For Christ's sake, you were even getting death threats and rape threats just last week with a much tamer story."

"That's social media, Dave. They're all nuts on there."

"Yeah, and those nuts are taking their causes onto the streets and into real life. Politicians are being targeted on the ground now as well. The Gardai have had to give security briefings to the politicians in the Dáil and Seanad only recently."

"Ok, well I'll take it on board, Dave and keep a look out for people or cars that might be tailing me. But getting back to what I was calling you about…" Robyn said to him as she reached into her bag to pull out an envelope. She took out two photos and laid them on the table before him.

"This is a photo of the anti-Direct Provision/Far Right protest on Friday. And this is a photo for the counter-protest

CHAPTER 18

the following day in support of immigrants in Ireland. See these two guys here?" she said pointing to the first protest. "They're here again at the protest the next day as well. Which is extremely strange. Why would someone be Far Right one day, and in support of immigrants 24hours later? It's bananas. So I'm wondering if they're undercover cops? I know you probably can't confirm if they are for operational security reasons but can you confirm at least if they're not?" Robyn asked.

"No, they're definitely not our guys. No one had any idea this march was taking place in Castlebar on Friday. We were notified about the second one on Saturday, but the Far Right march wasn't even on our radar. But you're right. Why the hell would Far Right protestors be supporting migrants at march the following day. It doesn't make sense. Can I take a photo of those pictures?"

"Yeah, sure. They're from Michael McInerney but I've already cleared it with him. It was he who spotted those two fellas."

"Well spotted, too. I just can't figure out what's behind it."

"Neither can I. But I think I'm going to keep an eye out on the Far Right social media, as sickening as it will be, to see if they have any other protests or actions planned for Mayo. I was genuinely shocked that march even took place on Friday and then even more shocked how they attacked the counter-protest the following day."

"As sickening at the Far Right is in itself, there's another even more sickening angle to it," Dave hinted.

"Another angle?" Robyn quizzed him.

"Yeah. A link up between the Far Right and the IRA."

"You're joking me?" Robyn spluttered on her coffee. "I

thought the Republicans were supposed to be on the left of politics?"

"'Supposed to be' being the operative words. They've needed to be on the Left to get the vote of ordinary people so far, but now that they've built up a following, they'll start turning to the right. They have a military wing after all, so being on the right of politics would be more their natural inclination. Anyway, out the country people here are more suspicious and less welcoming of foreigners than in the cities, where people tend to be more open-minded. And IRA fellas are jumping on the anti-immigrant bandwagon. Anywhere there's a fight, they want to be involved. The higher ups in the party are officially in support of migrants because they want their vote when they become citizens. But they seem to be turning a blind eye to their supporters on the ground fighting for the Far Right. The so-called Far Right fellas are really the IRA—we know this because they've the same tactics as the IRA. They ring in false crime reports to draw the Gardai away from the scenes of their protests or violence. That's why there was delay in the Guards turning up at the protest in Castlebar last week. So basically, the IRA and Far Right are one and the same these days. Total hypocrites, the lot of them."

"Jesus, I'm shocked Dave. I didn't see that coming. But it's happened before if you look back in history."

"When?"

"The Nazi party in Germany," she replied. "Nazi was short for National Socialist Party. Like you said about the Republicans, they're on the left when they're trying to get the vote of the ordinary person, but once elected, they could turn sharply to the right. On the continent when that happened, we ended up with Nazi Germany and the Holocaust against the Jews and foreigners."

"That's the worry about the Republicans entering government," Dave continued. "They can't be trusted. The IRA fellas on the ground aren't going to stay in the shadows, are they? They're going to want a piece of the action, a piece of the prize. But we don't know what form that will take yet. The Garda Commissioner himself has said that the party in the Republic operates under the direction of the IRA Army Council. So you can take it from that that if the Republican party is elected, the country will be governed by the IRA. Scary prospect."

"People don't even seem to realise that," Robyn stressed.

"The younger generation don't seem to have a clue. They're just in love with the idea of being radical," Dave agreed.

"You can see the party's authoritarian streak already in the way they control their members' social media. And they have legal proceedings underway against four journalists for articles they claim defamed their politicians. They're using the law as a means to control the media and scare them away from even writing about the party. Publishers and newspapers won't have the funds to defend a defamation action or sustain months of legal representation in the Four Courts for trial, so they'll just shy away from writing about the Party. So, like you said, they're already turning to the right of the political spectrum. There are scary days ahead for this country. But I'm not going to back down on reporting it. I will cover it every step of the way. Yes, I'll keep a better eye on my own personal security, Dave. But I'm not going to respond to their intimidation of journalists either."

"Look, just be careful, Robyn."

"I will, Dave. And thanks for always looking out for me. And for the chat. Don't forget our few pints after the election," she said, as they got up to walk out.

"No, I'm holding you to that. We'll probably be drowning our sorrows, though."

"I haven't given up yet, Dave, that the country will see sense."

"Hope you're right, Rob. I'll see ya."

"Bye Dave. Take care."

Robyn sat in her jeep outside the Knockranny Park Hotel, lingering in the stillness for a few moments. She gazed out over the sprawling countryside of West Mayo, bathed in the pale, wintry light of midday. The rugged landscape stretched toward Clew Bay, where scattered islands dotted the shimmering blue-gray water. The majestic pyramid-shaped peak of Croagh Patrick mountain rose steeply above the surrounding landscape, its peak shrouded in mist that day. Bare trees swayed gently in the cold breeze, their branches stark against the soft, silvery sky, with the town of Westport cradled by the unique beauty of the West of Ireland countryside.

As alluring as the landscape before her was, it failed to lull her into a state of relaxation and quieten the worries in her head as she had hoped. She was unable to shake the unease that had taken hold inside her since the violence of the weekend, an unease that only deepened with last night's cyberattack on the paper. With a sigh, she started the ignition and pulled onto the road towards Castlebar, hoping a shot of an energy drink she bought earlier would jolt her awake, enough to keep her alert for the drive home.

Her thoughts, however, kept circling back to the two men she'd seen on the pier in Rosmoney. At the time, her concerns had seemed trivial, almost laughable—the pair seemed like

CHAPTER 18

characters straight out of the old sitcom, *Only Fools and Horses*. But Robyn's instincts kept telling her that Dara's encounter with them was odd, extremely odd. And it was highly unlikely such an inept pair were from the cable company or their competitors. She regretted not mentioning it to Dave, thinking his insight could have shed some light on it. But with the election looming and his investigation consuming all his time, it would have to wait until next week.

Despite everything weighing on her mind, Robyn slept deeply that afternoon, her body finally succumbing to the exhaustion of being awake for thirty-six hours straight. She woke at 7pm, disorientated with the evening light shining through her bedroom curtains. It took her a few minutes to find her bearings, but once everything came into focus, she exhaled and yawned deeply, grateful for the few hours rest. True to form, she decided to get up rather than try to force more sleep. It was just how she was - once she woke she could never just roll over and go back to sleep, even on mornings where she might be hungover. She was just highly strung that way. She hadn't been able to have a lie in at weekends or on holidays ever since she was about ten years of age.

Stretching her arms, she thought of her friend, Lana, and decided to drop by to update her on everything. Just like Dave, Lana was someone she trusted completely. As she made her way down Rathbawn Road, where Lana lived just a short distance from her own home, she thought back to how long they had been friends, taking comfort in their history together. Knocking on the backdoor of Lana's house, she wasn't surprised when it was Mike, one of the two close protection officers assigned to Lana, who greeted her. His presence was a constant reminder of the heightened security surrounding Lana's stay in Ireland.

"It's yourself," Mike said, as he opened the door, taking in a wide sweep of the surroundings outside. "No one with you?" he said, half in jest and half not.

"No, just me as usual, Mike."

"Lana's down the kitchen."

"Great. Will you and Ger have a cuppa?" she asked

"Yeah, if you're putting on the kettle, I will. Ger's on the night watch tonight so he's not up yet."

"That was me last night, Mike, so I'm not long up myself," Robyn told him. "We'd some sort of virus or something at work so all my stories for the week got wiped off the system and I had to start re-writing them during the night."

"Bloody hell."

"Yeah, nightmare," Robyn added.

"What's that about a nightmare?" a voice asked, appearing from the kitchen. It was Lana, already in jammies, as was her way, her tousled, blonde shoulder length framing her pale face. Unlike Robyn, Lana definitely wasn't a night owl and liked to be in bed early and up early. Robyn filled her in on what had happened at the paper as the two of them sat down at the kitchen table.

"Robyn, the timing of that incident pretty much confirms it was a malicious virus. Just the night before going to print? That was no accident. The paper was definitely targeted. Some of the sports writers' work being wiped was just to cover their tracks, but it was your work they wanted to disappear. Were you able to re-write the 'Drugs in the Dail' story without notes?"

"Most of it, but I had to ring Marie Mulhall herself to get the bitcoin transaction number off the fake receipt. I don't think

CHAPTER 18

she minded too much being woken at dawn, considering we had proved she was victim of a hoax. Even though she must be exhausted from canvassing herself, she was very gracious about it."

"Yeah, I remember our own election campaign a few weeks ago and how exhausted Vasily and I were. People have no idea how hard politicians work."

"Yeah, and they take their democracy for granted until it's stolen from them," Robyn added.

"You're in a gloomy mood today. It must be after the night you've had and I don't blame you," Lana said.

"No, I'm normally in good form after having a chat with Dave, but things are getting heavy. I'm feeling the pressure of this election and I'm not even a politician. I've no idea what you and Vasily must be going through with all that's happening in Belarus."

"It's heart-breaking and I can't stop worrying about him. But I have to try and distract myself if I'm to survive this."

"It's the only way, Lana. You have to keep strong for him, but at the same time, I know how hard it is for you to fight the worry every single day."

"So, how was your friend Dave besides?" Lana enquired.

"He's tired. He's working long hours at the moment but he's hoping things will settle down with him next week too. We all can't wait until next week!" Robyn laughed. "I was to mention something to him, but I didn't because it felt a bit silly, but I regret now not asking him about it."

"What was it you were to ask him?"

"Did I tell you about the two guys Dara met on the pier at Rosmoney last week?"

"No, I don't remember you saying anything," Lana said,

trying to recollect.

"Two divers that hired him to take them out to a shipwreck that didn't exist?" Robyn added.

"A shipwreck that didn't exist?" Lana asked, laughing.

"I was sure I'd said it to you. My head is in such a spin these days I must have forgotten," Robyn explained. She recounted the full story at the kitchen table over hot mugs of tea and the marshmallow biscuits which had been their favourite since they were kids. Robyn explained why Dara and her and ruled out drugs thrown overboard as the motive for the guys' dive at that particular spot: they would have had a beacon on the drugs bale and their own equipment to locate it. Plus, they wouldn't have wanted a witness seeing them hauling a drugs bale on board the boat.

"Then we discovered that the spot they dived was just over the fibre optic cable running into the bay," Robyn explained. "But why would they want to dive to see the cable? To tap the data passing through it? But everything is encrypted these days so what would be the point of that?

"Well, not everything is encrypted," Lana added, "but usually anything of value would be. Definitely state emails would be or corporate secrets that could be the target of industrial research. Valuable academic discoveries would be too."

"Well, that rules out putting a tap on the cable as a reason," Robyn stated, deflated.

"Not entirely," Lana suggested. "It could be the metadata they're interested in."

"What's metadata?" Robyn asked, with renewed enthusiasm.

"It's data that describes other data," Lana replied. Robyn

looked at her lost.

"Metadata summarizes basic information about data. For example, let's say, the author of the data, the date it was created, when the data was last modified and the file size are examples of a document file's metadata."

"Why would that data be of any use to anybody?" Robyn quizzed.

"Remember, the Snowden revelations in 2013?

"Yeah, of course."

"Well, one the US government programs Snowden revealed was the Prism program."

"Yeah, I remember," Robyn replied, intrigued.

"It involved the NSA - the US government's cyber spying agency - collecting metadata from all the main internet companies like Google, Microsoft, Facebook, Apple, Skype, YouTube and more. And while the companies didn't divulge the content of emails or phone calls or other messages, they did reveal metadata which covered information such as who was messaging or calling who, when, for how long and how often. The government's justification for the collection of this data was the US Patriot Act which allowed government spying for the purposes of combating terrorism. You can see how this information could be useful to a terrorism investigation. For instance, if a suspected terrorist start calling another suspected terrorist more frequently and for longer, it could indicate that they were planning a terrorist action."

"I remember reading about it at the time of the revelations," Robyn commented, but still a bit bewildered as to how it related to the two Swedes on the pier that day.

"The terrorist threat seems to be in abeyance at the moment since Islamic State have been largely wiped out in Syria and

Iraq. Even though there are still some pockets of resistance there and some IS cells in other parts of the world - in Khorasan in Afghanistan/Pakistan and in part of North Africa and the Sahel."

"So why would two Swedes be interested in the metadata from an Irish undersea cable?" Robyn pressed her friend.

"Were they definitely Swedes?" Lana asked.

Well, that's what they said they were," Robyn replied, getting more and more baffled by Lana's line of thought.

"Would Dara know a Swedish accent if he heard one?"

"I doubt it," Robyn said, half-laughing. "Why?"

"Well, they could be from anywhere really. We don't really know."

"Why do you say that?"

"Because if the Americans already have access to metadata, who else would that information be useful to?" Lana asked rhetorically. "Instead of the metadata flowing into the United States, think of the data flows the other direction and who is would be of use to. For instance, if there was an increase in the number and duration of calls and emails between the US and its allies in the UK and Europe indicating the increasing likelihood of an imminent military action, to whom would this information be useful? China with it threat against Taiwan, Russia in its frozen war against the Donetsk and Luhansk provinces in Eastern Ukraine, Iran in its threat against Israel or North Korea in its threat to South Korea, could be any of our suspects."

"You really think those two Swedes were operatives from one of those countries?" Robyn asked incredulously.

"I've no idea, but it's not outside the bounds of possibility. Ireland is the fibre optic bridge for super-fast internet cables

CHAPTER 18

between North America and Europe. So it's uniquely placed for espionage opportunities, not like the cables making landfall in the UK or France where MI5 in the UK or the DGSI, Directorate General for Internal Security in France, would pounce immediately. Ireland has a much smaller counterintelligence complement by comparison meaning it would be a preferable location for this type of espionage."

"Wow, I had never even considered Ireland being a target for this kind of cloak and dagger stuff. I guess I better get onto the cable company pronto to report this. And I'm sure they'll want Dara to make a statement to the Gardai as well. Just as well we can have this conversation, Lana. You have so much more experience of this kind of thing being from Belarus and dealing with Russian interference in your political system. I was putting this cable story on the long finger until next week."

"Now that we're talking about this, it has given me another idea," Lana thought aloud.

"What?" Robyn enquired.

"Did you think about checking the metadata on the JPEG file of that fake bitcoin receipt?"

"I didn't even know what metadata was until ten seconds ago," Robyn quipped.

"When you go home, just right click on the file. Scroll down the menu to where it says 'Properties', then click on that and see if it reveals anything interesting."

"Like what? Robyn asked, unsure of what it was she was supposed to be looking for.

"You'll know if you see something."

Robyn didn't quite have the confidence in herself that Lana had in her. But it was getting late. She had to get the remaining deleted stories on the election re-written tonight and sent to the daily papers for the morning editions. Unfortunately, she would be pulling another all-nighter again. But she was grateful for the few hours' sleep she got that afternoon. It would tie her over until the morning. She decided to head over to the office in Westport instead of working from home that night. There was too much of a risk that she'd fall asleep on the couch at home. The office would be a safer bet. The artificial fluorescent lighting there would help keep her awake too, while she tried to re-constitute those stories that she had lost. It always did the job in keeping her awake on Monday nights when she couldn't nod off after a twelve-hour work day when the paper went to press. So hopefully it would do the trick this time for her, Robyn thought to herself.

The office was predictably empty when she turned up at just after 8.30pm on a Tuesday night. At almost twelve hours after the paper was put to bed, the office had likely never seen such a late visitor on a Tuesday night before. But these were troubled times. The office had never seen a journalist's entire week's work wiped from the system in the week of an election. She started to scribble a few bullet points from the Republican party training seminar story that was vital to get published before the election. But she was struggling to concentrate at this hour of the evening. Whilst she would never have described herself as a morning person, Robyn always believed in tackling difficult jobs or anything that required deep concentration, first thing in the morning before the best of her brain energy got used up on anything else. Today was in reverse but she didn't have the luxury of waiting until the morning. The electorate and the rest of the media would need the few precious days that remained

CHAPTER 18

before the election to digest what Robyn had to reveal about the Republican Party's dirty tricks.

But Lana's suggestion that she carry out one more check on the "Drugs in the Dáil" story kept circling around in her mind, refusing to be ignored despite her attempts to focus elsewhere. Eager for a distraction when concentration wasn't coming easily to her, she decided to take Lana up on her suggestion that she check the metadata in the fake bitcoin receipt. With a sigh, she went through the steps to open the metadata, sipping a comforting mug of warm coffee as she did so. It would probably be the usual strings of code and numbers that made no sense to Robyn – technical stuff, dull and unremarkable.

But her blood ran cold when she saw the screen in front of her. The document's hidden metadata wasn't written in English. It was written in Cyrillic.

Chapter 19

Robyn's heart pounded in her chest as she desperately tried to make sense of the incomprehensible string of characters she was seeing on the computer screen before her.

But she couldn't just assume the worst. She'd have to double-check. Other languages like those of Central Asian countries—Kazakhstan, Kyrgyzstan and others—used the Cyrillic alphabet. Bulgaria did too as far as she knew.

Then in her dazed state, she elbowed and knocked over her coffee mug, sending a cascade of hot liquid spilling across her desk. The dark brown tide quickly soaked into her papers and began creeping toward the keyboard.

"Damn it!" she swore under her breath, snapping back to reality. In a frantic rush, she darted to the staff canteen, yanking a handful of paper towels from the dispenser with trembling hands. Back at her desk, she frantically blotted the spreading mess, her hands shaky with urgency.

After she managed to contain the worst of the spill, she scrambled to open Google Translate, her fingers stumbling

CHAPTER 19

over the keys. She copied and pasted some of the text from the metadata into the translation app. Then she hit the "translate" button and closed her eyes. She was almost afraid to open them.

But her suspicions were on the money.

Google Translate confirmed she was looking at Russian text.

She tried to think of any possible reason why a document, which was written in English and issued by an English language website, would have metadata in Russian attached to it? Her brain, a worn-out mess by now, came up empty. The only reason would be if the document was created on a computer system operating in the Russian language.

How had the *Tales from the Dark Side* blog, based in County Meath and run by two Irish law graduates and a journalism graduate, financed by an Irish businessman with a grudge against the government, gotten caught up in publishing false allegations against an Irish politician that originated with a forged Russian document? They claimed the story came from a hacker who had hacked the dark web marketplace which had purportedly sold the drugs to Marie Mulhall. The story was that when the hacker noticed the parliamentary address on the receipt, he decided to spill the beans on what the elected representative was up to, in the interests of the Irish people.

But it looked like now that *Tales from the Dark Side* were sloppy in their due diligence, at the very least. What checks had they even made on who this hacker was and where he was from? They were the questions Robyn would be putting to their editor this week.

Or were they willing victims of the hoax for the headlines it would win, regardless of whether it destroyed a political representative's career and reputation?

Still, it seemed like a stupid move, a gamble like that could now wipe out their blog and their own professional reputations. Robyn was pretty sure Marie Mulhall would be instructing lawyers to launch legal proceedings against them, if she hadn't already done so. But their multi-millionaire backer had deep pockets to defend such an action, even if it was practically indefensible.

The clock had crept into the early hours of the morning, the quiet hum of the office settling into a kind of stillness that only the dead of night could bring. Robyn's entire body ached with exhaustion. She rubbed her tired eyes and groaned, knowing that if she was going to make any sense of this mess, she'd need more caffeine. With a sigh, she pushed away from her desk and made her way back to the staff canteen for yet another cup of coffee.

But it did little to sharpen her mind. Instead of clearing the fog, it only seemed to thicken it. But then, amid the clutter of half-formed ideas, one thought pushed its way to the front of her consciousness: hadn't one of those bloggers spent some time in Eastern Europe? She racked her tired brain, sifting through the fog for details. She went back to her desk and pulled up her notes, her eyes skimming over the pages until yes, there it was—Mike Mulchay, the editor of the blog, had spent a few years in Eastern Europe.

But there was just something about the Russian language having turned up in the metadata of a fake Bitcoin receipt, and his having spent time in Eastern Europe, that wouldn't leave her thoughts. Maybe it was just a coincidence, Robyn thought to herself. But her instincts were telling her otherwise, and in this line of work, instincts had a way of leading to answers— whether she liked those answers or not.

CHAPTER 19

But she just couldn't let it lie. When all else failed, a good old Google search was sometimes all you could do to see if it threw up any ideas. She entered Mike Mulcahy's name in inverted commas into the Google search box. Predictably all that came up were newspaper stories about him as editor of *Tales from the Dark Side,* his LinkedIn profile and his own bylined stories from the blog.

But a journalist whose work Robyn followed with great interest at *The New York Times,* had once given a simple but effective piece of advice to young journalism students: never underestimate the power of page 10 of Google Search results. Most people scroll down to the bottom of the first page of search results, but it's often those that keep scrolling through tens of pages of results who turn up the pot of gold at the end of the Google rainbow.

And today was that day for Robyn Mayhew.

There he was, Mike Mulcahy, editor of *Tales from the Dark Side*, appearing in a YouTube clip from *Russia Today*, or *RT* as it was known, the Russian state-controlled television station. Guess where he had gotten a job as a "researcher" during those "in-between years" after college and before starting the blog? He had conveniently omitted having worked for *RT* from his LinkedIn CV. But it was harder to scrub details from Google.

Robyn sat back on her chair for a few moments to think, stunned at her discovery and its implications. Everyone had thought that financier, Jimmy Costello, was the one pushing the agenda at *Tales from the Dark Side.* But now it looked like a case of the tail wagging the dog, with the Putin-sympathising editor as the tail, and Costello as the dog. Mulcahy had used his multi-millionaire boss and his grudge against the

Taoiseach and made a Russian stooge out of him.

But why would Mulcahy turn on his own country? Was he really that easily manipulated by the Russian government propaganda he was listening to in his job at *RT*? Weren't journalism students trained to be sceptical? Why would he even have taken a job with an organ of Russian state propaganda in the first place? Robyn thought back to what her friend, Caroline Feeney in *The Irish Observer*, had told her about him when he had worked under her at the paper. "He had an ego the size of the EU," she remembered. And she could understand completely how he chose to work for himself rather than an employer, even if it was just at his own blog.

Robyn remembered reading somewhere a few years ago how ego, and the feeling of being underappreciated by their own country or employer, was a common motive for state or industrial espionage. Maybe that was the case with Mulcahy, she thought to herself, musing at how egotistical it was for a young man only in his early twenties to feel underappreciated when he had barely started out in life. Maybe his nose was out of joint when his talents weren't immediately recognised and he wasn't able to secure paid employment in journalism in this country, she thought to herself, despite journalism being one of the toughest professions to break into.

Robyn glanced at her watch. It was 3.00am and she hadn't even started to re-write her lost work from last week. Her brain had turned to mush now and she couldn't focus on anything other than the fake Russian bitcoin receipt and the discovery that political writer, Mike Mulcahy, had worked for Russia Today.

With a deep sigh, she buried her head in her hands. She could feel the burning sensation in her eyes from tiredness turn to tears, slowly rolling down her face. It wasn't just the pressure of the last two weeks weighing on her, it was the exhaustion, as well. She would have to send an email to Leahy for him to read in the morning, detailing her discoveries and explaining why she didn't have the election 'dirty tricks' story ready to send to the daily papers. Would he understand? She prayed he would, given the gravity of her findings. But the election story was vital, a matter of national importance, and her failure to get it written for the morning sat heavily on her conscience. As she switched off her computer, resigned to the twenty-minute drive home to Castlebar ahead of her, the weight of unfinished work and missed deadlines followed her like a shadow, wrapping around her as tightly as her exhaustion.

The road was empty and the night eerie as she left Westport. She drove through the darkness, her mind artificially on alert by the shock of her discoveries that night. Why was Eastern Europe cropping up in her life so much in the past week? She had wanted to visit that part of the continent since she was in primary school and had learned about the fall of communism and the Berlin Wall in the 90s, but she had yet to get round to it.

Her mind thought back to internal Republican Party training seminar she had infiltrated last week when she learned that the party's social media manager was Serbian. It had set off alarm bells straight away in her brain. Serbia and Russia had been political and military allies for centuries.

Tonight's revelations were confirming her worst fears. A Serbian in a senior political position in Ireland, whilst unusual, wouldn't have been a shock prior to 2016 and the US presidential election, when Russian political interference in elections in the US, UK and Europe came to light. Could the Republican Party's Serbian social media manager have any connection with former *RT* journalist, Mike Mulcahy, now editor of the *Tales from the Dark Side* blog? Or was it just a coincidence that his work uncovering political scandals—some real, the latest a hoax—played into the Republican Party's hand?

All these disjointed thoughts churned restlessly in her mind, like puzzle pieces she just couldn't quite fit together. She found it hard to resist the urge to bring everything to a neat conclusion. But maybe there was no connection at all.

It's just that Ireland was an extremely small country, she continued to argue in her mind, and events like these were unlikely to be just coincidental. She thought back to something a retired detective had told her during an interview a few months ago: "The first rule of investigating is: there's no such thing as a coincidence. You just haven't found the connection yet."

Those words echoed in her ears as she recalled her weekend deep dive into the tangled web of posts from the botnet working to influence the Irish election. She had trawled through the early posts of some of the suspect accounts, and uncovered posts on topics as diverse as Ukraine, the UK and Russia. But the more she tried to piece it all together, the more any connection eluded her. She just couldn't figure out why an anti-Irish government botnet would be pro-Brexit and the UK government position, and then also push anti-Ukraine and pro-Russian narratives. The contradictions just ate away at her all weekend and drove her to the edge of madness.

Then suddenly, it hit her square between the eyes.

How had she not seen it before?

CHAPTER 19

The political positions weren't mutually exclusive, as she had first assumed. The point wasn't that you had to be anti-UK and anti-Ireland at the same time to be swayed by these posts. It was the source of the posts—the originator—who was both anti-UK and anti-Ireland. Who else fit that description and was also so vehemently anti-Ukraine? Only Russia.

The pieces began to fall into place. Ever since the UK had refused to extradite Russian dissidents in the early 2000s—culminating in the poisonings of Alexander Litvinenko, and later Sergei Skripal and his daughter, with radioactive agents on UK soil—the UK had been firmly in the sights of Vladimir Putin. The UK imposed retaliatory sanctions on Russia and Vladimir Putin's animosity towards the UK only grew. The Russian dictator was engaged in hybrid warfare against Ukraine in a frozen conflict since 2014. And he was the same Russian dictator who engaged in political interference in the UK Brexit referendum, backing the Leave campaign to destabilise Europe.

As for his interest in bringing down the Irish government? It mirrored his goals in France and Germany: to weaken the European Union, his most formidable adversary. For Putin, sowing civil disruption and upending the democracies of the EU wasn't just about breaking up the EU. It was also about proving to his own electorate that Europe was no utopia, which in turn reinforced his own grip on power in Russia. He had already interfered in the 2016 U.S. presidential election, and it was only a matter of time before he applied those tactics across the Atlantic. That day had now come for Ireland.

Robyn could feel panic rising in her chest as she turned the corner for home on the Rathbawn Road. She had no idea how she was going to get some sleep. Adrenaline was coursing through her veins and sleep was a dim prospect.

As she opened the front door when she got home, she dropped her laptop bag inside the living room door and threw herself on the couch. But something wasn't right. There was unusual stillness, as if the place seemed to be holding its breath. A haunting feeling crept over her that somebody had been in her house while she was out. She told herself it was just paranoia—too much coffee, too little sleep—and her exhausted mind playing tricks on her. But no matter how hard she tried, she couldn't shake the eerie sensation that somebody had been there whilst she was away.

She tried to push the thoughts out her mind, already spinning from the weight of the night's deeply unsettling revelations: Mike Mulcahy's work for Russian state-sponsored TV; a Serbian social media manager—hailing from Russia's staunchest ally—working for the Republican Party in Ireland; and a concerted botnet working to influence the Irish election, having previously posted content in support of Russian political positions. Yet, as tantalizing as these revelations were, Robyn thought, they remained disconnected. She needed more than just her gut instincts to prove a connection. She needed solid, undeniable proof.

But the longer she sat in the haze of exhaustion and disbelief, the more convinced she became that the Serbian social media manager was no ordinary political operative. She was almost certain the Republican Party had a Russian agent working for them. They were probably unwitting stooges for the Russians, but she couldn't rule out the possibility of collusion either. She had no clear evidence of it so far.

It wasn't surprising that Robyn Mayhew was the journalist

CHAPTER 19

to uncover Russia's "active measures" in Ireland. She and her family knew well the long arm of Russia and its leader, ex-KGB man, Vladimir Putin. It was Russia after all, via their close ally Belarus, who had disappeared her younger brother all those years ago.

Chapter 20

Alexei came to them as a four-year-old little boy in late 2014.

The Chernobyl disaster in Ukraine in 1986 had blown a radioactive cloud over neighbouring Belarus, leaving generations of babies born afterwards with severe health complications. There were many cases where the parents just couldn't cope with the severity of the child's health condition and tragically, these children ended up in state care. But in Belarus, even state care was a bleak prospect.

Despite being four years of age, Alexei's development level, cognitive and motor skills were that of a two-year-old. The Mayhew family quickly set about seeking a diagnosis for him, almost certain the little boy was suffering from autism, so that he could get the help he needed, as soon as possible.

However, what unfolded in the weeks that followed was both heart-warming and heart-wrenching. As Alexei grew more comfortable in his new home, the little boy who had previously barely interacted with the world around him, now began to blossom. He responded to hugs, showed affection, and his cognitive and motor skills flourished. After just two months, he stunned the family by uttering his first word—"Mama"—to Robyn's mother. The Mayhews were overjoyed, but it broke their hearts to realise that his delays hadn't stemmed from autism, but shockingly, from sheer neglect in state care. And to think that there could be thousands more children like him in Belarus was torture.

For a year and a half, Alexei was a cherished part of the Mayhew family. Then one day, out of the blue, they received a letter from the authorities in Belarus requesting that they attend with Alexei at his former orphanage to finalise the documentation for his adoption.

During this visit, Alexei was taken to another room for a "medical exam," despite their protests that as a minor, he should have one of his parents with him. But Alexei never returned from that medical exam. Instead, he was disappeared back into the state care system. The trip had been a cruel deception.

The geopolitical ripples from Russia's invasion of Crimea in 2014 had led to sanctions being imposed in response by the US and the EU. In retribution, the Russian leader, Vladimir Putin, convinced his ally, Belarus to halt international adoptions of children that were already in progress. And so, Alexei became a pawn in a political game and the Mayhews were powerless to stop it. They hired lawyers and investigators, anything to bring him back. But the Belarusian government blocked them at every turn. In the end, even their own lawyer had been an informant for the state. The family were broken by the loss of the beloved little Alexei—his adorable little face, blonde hair, sallow skin and bright blue eyes never to be seen by them again.

So Robyn Mayhew was in better position than most to understand the long arm of the Russian government. For many years she had read about the ruthless power plays orchestrated by Vladimir Putin. But this wasn't just a distant political narrative for Robyn—it had become painfully personal. The reverberations of those manipulative schemes had stretched across continents, their chilling impact felt by her own family as far away as the West of Ireland. Since then, the Russian leader had been uncovered as the political puppet master behind election interference operations in the US and throughout the EU. So Robyn was pretty sure whose hand was at play in the sudden change of fortunes of the Republican Party in Ireland.

The election of a party with a paramilitary wing to government would wreak economic havoc on Ireland, which was heavily dependent on multinational companies to provide employment. It's one thing international companies were wary of and that was political instability of any kind in the countries in which they operated. But the younger generations who had fallen for the lure of the Republican party's propaganda couldn't see that it was their own livelihoods that would be at stake if the Republicans came to power, jeopardised by the very political instability that Russia was working so hard to create.

Robyn dragged herself from the couch and wandered into the kitchen. Her hands shook as she poured a double shot of Jack Daniels, hoping the whiskey would dull her nerves and help her to sleep. The liquid burned down her throat, offering a momentary warmth, but her unease persisted. Suddenly, she thought she heard something in the hallway.

She checked, but it was nothing—just her frayed nerves

CHAPTER 20

on edge after losing her work and now fearing for her safety in a way she never had before, not even during some of the high-profile criminal trials she'd covered in the past.

She hadn't a single drop of energy left to give so bed was the only option at this stage. As the effect of the whiskey washed over her, sleep soon would as well. But it was a restless sleep, not the restorative kind, that renews your energy for another day. There was so much tumbling through her mind.

She woke half-dreaming about the weekend's protests, Dara and the divers. She checked the time on her phone and was disappointed to see she'd only had three hours sleep, but still, half-glad not to have lost too much of the day. Coffee and adrenaline would have to act as replacements for real energy for just one more day. A speedy shower would hopefully wash the cobwebs of sleep from her mind.

But as the water ran down her face, the divers that Dara had met on Rosmoney pier last week, just wouldn't vacate her mind. Then, as she was shampooing her hair—it came to her. She rang Dara as soon as she stepped out of the shower and dried herself off.

"Hi Dara, are you in Castlebar this morning?"

"Do I not even get a 'good morning' today?" he joked.

"I'm sorry, Dara. I haven't had much sleep."

He knew by the semi-depressed tone of her voice, that she was on the "struggle bus" today, and not from a hangover. "I get it," he said, understandingly. "Do you want me to come over?"

"If you can, that would be great."

"Have the kettle on so."

It was just coming up to eleven o'clock tea-break, so Dara was round in a flash. Robyn pulled out the two pictures of the protests from last weekend for him to see.

"Oh, that's them again," he said in a surprised tone, staring closer at the pictures.

"That's who, Dara?" she quizzed.

"That's the two divers I met out on the pier that I was telling you about. Where'd you get this picture of them?"

"Jesus Christ," Robyn said, putting her face in her hands, shocked by her friend's confirmation of her shower hypothesis.

"What?" Dara asked worried. "What is it, Rob?"

"This picture of them is at the Far-Right protest on Friday. Then they turned up again on Saturday, this time protesting *in support* of immigrants."

"I don't get it," Dara stated, looking quizzically at the pictures again.

"These two guys were out diving, right over one of our main fibre optic cables from the States, last week. What were they doing? Tapping it? Mining it? I don't know."

Dara looked at her alarmed.

"Then they show up leading a Far-Right protest in Castlebar, when there's never been a Far-Right protest in this county ever before. Then the following day, they join the counter-protesters where violence breaks out."

"That makes no sense," he responded.

"I'm afraid it does," Robyn replied. "I don't think they're Swedes at all, Dara. I think they're Russians. And they're in this country to carry out destabilisation ops before the election to ensure the Government gets kicked out and replaced with the Republicans."

Dara spat out his coffee, half-laughing, half in shock. "Robyn, now you've definitely lost me. In fact, I think you've

CHAPTER 20

lost *it*."

It took half an hour to go over all the details she'd uncovered in the past week, but by the time Dara left, he was pretty shaken. He suggested she come stay at his house until it blew over. Robyn thanked him for the offer but told him she was finding it hard enough to sleep at her own place, never mind at someone else's house. But if she felt spooked enough, she might take him up on the offer.

"And there's always the boat too," he added, "it can sleep four people." Robyn had half-forgotten how handy it was to have a yacht master as a friend, in case life ever required a speedy getaway.

After she waved him off, she retrieved her laptop from inside the living room door. Powering it up, she decided to go back into her bookmarks folder where she had saved a few pages from the Republican Party's website. A week ago, after the training seminar, she had decided to have a look through the party's archive of press releases. The Republicans, being a supposedly left-wing party, had long found common ground with Russia in international affairs, even refusing to condemn the Russian leader after the annexation of Crimea and the invasion of Eastern Ukraine in 2014. In her search, Robyn found a multitude of press releases from the past two decades stating political positions in support of Russia. She wanted to re-read them again in light of her findings that night.

But something was wrong. Each bookmark she clicked returned the same message: "The page you are looking for no longer exists."

She went through the party's website manually to try to find them again. She scrolled and scrolled for over an hour. Every single one of them had disappeared. Now she didn't even have proof that they'd ever been there in the first place, other than a bunch of empty bookmarked pages, which didn't prove anything.

But maybe it did. It proved that pages had been removed. But what had motivated the party to delete these statements and why now? Did something spook them? Or was it in case they were subject to more scrutiny if the party got elected this weekend?

What Robyn couldn't have known was that it was her own searches that had spooked the party.

Social media manager, Goran Vladic was doing a routine check of the party's Google Analytics account. This often showed up interesting information, for instance, which search terms visitors to the site were inputting into the search box. It was a reliable way to gauge the electorate's concerns — a snapshot of the issues gaining traction with the public. But the real treasure trove was the press releases page. The search terms on that page provided a valuable early warning system for the kind of media questions that were likely to surface in the coming days.

But one particular search term made Goran Vladic sit bolt upright: there appeared to be a number of searches for the word "Russia" on the website. Whilst Robyn had taken the precaution of searching the website using an "incognito" window on her browser to mask her IP address, she had still unwittingly given the social media manager a heads up that somebody somewhere had their suspicions.

Knowing it was likely a journalist if they were searching the press releases page, Goran Vladic sensed trouble. He made it his immediate priority to find whichever journalist it was. He might deploy the trick he had used earlier in the week on a nasty provincial journalist in County Mayo, spouting vitriol about the party. It was a good old-fashioned spear-phishing trick. He sent her a spoofed-version of the typical "Google has noticed your device was used in x location. Was this you?" Both the "yes" and "no" links, when clicked, deployed malware to their device. Then he was able to have a good old snoop around her computer and what she was working on, plus he got into her newspaper's system and deleted all her vicious articles so they wouldn't be printed. It was a great trick to have in his back pocket for journalists who made a nuisance of themselves.

But this time, when he set out to find the journalist who had been searching "Russia" on the party's website, he would find a lot more than he bargained for. His efforts on behalf of the party would be richly rewarded. It turned out that the journalist searching "Russia" on the party's website was, first of all, the same provincial journalist still making a nuisance of herself. But the real prize was the person in whose company she was spending much of her time.

No one would ever have guessed it, but right by her side was a high-value Belarusian dissident who, for weeks, had evaded a relentless global manhunt, outwitting the best of his country's foreign intelligence agents. Against all odds, she had been hiding in the remote corner of County Mayo on Ireland's West Coast, where no one would ever have thought to have looked, had her nosy journalist friend not led them straight to her.

Chapter 21

As she jumped into her jeep and headed further down the winding Rathbawn Road, Robyn hoped Lana would be awake when she got there. She also had been battling insomnia for the past few weeks, not just from being out of sorts from being on the run, but because every day brought worse and worse news from her home country. The police and army were clamping down harder and harder on the pro-democracy protests and thousands were languishing in prison awaiting sham trials. Every passing hour weighed heavier on her as Lana feared for her husband, and their family and friends' safety constantly, her helplessness gnawing at nerves more and more each day.

As Robyn pulled round to the back of the house, the sight of Lana's bedroom window with its curtains drawn open, filled her with relief. She had hit a dead end trying to untangle the layers of intrigue that surrounded the Republican Party's sudden surge in popularity. Something darker was at play and she was convinced Russia had a hand in it. But proving that connection seemed insurmountable.

Lana, however, was uniquely qualified to help. With her

CHAPTER 21

deep political acumen and years of experience grappling with Russian influence in her own country, Lana might be able to bring a fresh perspective to the problem. And, coming from a tech background meant she would have a different set of problem-solving skills to Robyn, seeing possible solutions where Robyn wouldn't. Together, they might just find the key to unlocking the truth. "Two heads are always better than one," Robyn's grandfather used to say, "even if they're only heads of cabbage." She smiled briefly as she thought of him and what he would make of the quandary his granddaughter found herself in.

One of Lana's security detail, Ger, was quick to answer her knock at the back door. He greeted her with a curt nod, gesturing for her to come inside before casting his practiced, sweeping gaze across the back yard. Robyn had grown used to this routine—the two Garda close protection officers always on edge and ever-watchful. Their presence, while comforting, was a constant reminder of the danger Lana was still in.

"Thank God you're up, Lana," Robyn said, greeting her friend with a hug in the kitchen.

"Not that long," her friend laughed. "I haven't even hit the shower yet."

"Before you do, can I run some stuff by you?"

"Sure, you must be in a rush?" she asked, growing a little concerned.

"Yeah, it's to do with this election in a few days and I'm running out of both time and ideas. I was hoping you might crack the problem for me."

"I can barely crack an egg these days, I'm such a basket case, but run it by me and I'll see if I've any ideas for you."

With two frothy lattes in front of them, the girls once again sat at the round oak kitchen table and Robyn poured out her heart to her friend. But Lana's reaction to Robyn's tale of probable Russian interference in the upcoming Irish election got a reaction—the polar opposite of Dara's—to the same story earlier that morning.

"There was never a question of 'if' there would be Russian interference in an Irish election, only 'when' it would happen," Lana's response was. "It has happened all over Europe already and, with Ireland in such a key position to affect British politics after Brexit, I should have been keeping a better eye out for the country."

"You don't know how much of a relief to me it is to hear that you get it, Lana. I've been beside myself with worry about how to get someone to listen. But how will I get the authorities to listen? I'm sure they're of the same mindset that Dara was this morning. This will sound like the stuff out of Cold War novels to the Irish government."

"We're going to have to provide solid proof. And I'll be able to recover the old pro-Russia statements from the Republican Party's website for a start. I know it doesn't prove anything, but it's at the very least suspicious, so it will be a help."

"How will you recover the statements if you don't have access to the back end of their website?" Robyn queried her.

"I won't have to for that part. There's an online tool called 'The Way Back Machine' that I can use to recover them. It's an archive of all web pages that have existed on the internet. I know, cool, isn't it?" Lana said excitedly at the prospect of putting it to use against the enemies of the state.

"Ok, that would be awesome," Robyn agreed, happy to see her friend's excitement, and more importantly, to see her distracted from her own worries. "But what do you mean 'for that part?'" Robyn quizzed her.

"Well, I am going to need access to their systems for the next part," she added, her initial excitement switching to seriousness. "We're going to have to find evidence of election interference on their own servers."

Robyn's own depression over events swiftly returned. That prospect was a complete no-go.

"Lana, I can't go back into their HQ pretending to be somebody else after I've already been there posing as a volunteer and talking to their social media manager. I'm done for if I try that."

"You won't have to go back into their HQ. You just need to go somewhere nearby."

Robyn looked at her, dumb-founded and depressed. She'd no idea what her friend was talking about and she wasn't in the form for riddles either. But within thirty minutes, that had all changed.

That was the length of time it took Lana to build out the gadget they needed. Then a further two and a half hours for Robyn to drive to Dublin and fifteen minutes to get parked up in the Arnotts multi-storey car park. Just ten minutes more and Robyn was seated with a latte and a laptop in front of her at the coffee shop right next door to the Republican Party Headquarters. With Lana's home-made gadget sitting in a large tote bag, deliberately left open on the seat beside her, Robyn had the bag's handle held firmly on her wrist, just in case an opportunistic pickpocket decided to exercise their skills. Robyn was still in disbelief over the scheme Lana had concocted and convinced her to participate in, both at the audacity and sheer genius of it, and potentially at her own stupidity, as well. It was highly illegal should she get caught, but she was hopeful a court would grant her leniency due to the civic minded motive behind her nonetheless, illegal act.

Robyn had watched spell-bound as Lana crafted what she called an "IMSI-catcher" from basic materials she found lying around in the garage of the house, as well as a couple of specialist items from her own tech kit. It would essentially work as a miniature, fake mobile phone mast to intercept mobile phone traffic from phones in the immediate vicinity. The gadget Lana had "MacGyvered" together was connected to a laptop in front of Robyn. The plan was that hopefully a staff member from the Party HQ next door would pop in for coffee at some stage, scroll through their phone whilst waiting in the queue, connect to their work VPN and the IMSI-catcher would hoover up their login credentials. Well, there was one more condition: that the staff member in question hadn't the most recent security patch for the VPN updated. That was three conditions in total—a Republican party employee turning up, there being a queue for coffee that would give them time to start scrolling on their phone, and that they hadn't the latest VPN update. It felt like a massive ask.

Row after row of data kept streaming down the screen in front of her, her eyes glued to the screen for any clue that one of the unsuspecting caffeine addicts in front of her could be Republican Party. Eventually eye strain got the better of her and she looked up from the laptop at the patrons around the coffee shop. Almost all of them were busy worker bees popping in for a late afternoon coffee to power them through into the evening, probably in order to stay working late. There was the odd retiree stretched out with a proper old-school newspaper, a reading habit Robyn herself found hard to let go of. She had been raised in a newspaper-reading family and

CHAPTER 21

it always reminded her of leisurely times at home with her parents. Then there was a smattering of city centre students availing of the cozy café atmosphere to study. A good mixed bag of the denizens of city centre Dublin, but none Robyn could identify as a Republican Party politico, just by looking at them. Bar one patron wearing Harry Potter-style spectacles with a preppy scarf and tweed jacket—a look that some of the Party's more upper-class "Gaelgóirs" or Irish speakers were going in for these days.

Robyn looked around to see if there were any newspapers left lying around the coffee shop to read. She spotted one about five or six tables away, but it was too much of a risk to get up from her mobile spy station to run over and nab one, so she sensibly chose to stay put instead. She pulled up the day's news on the RTE website, the national broadcaster. She caught one of the news bulletins in the car on the way to Dublin earlier, but she usually preferred music to talk radio when she was driving, so she only got the bare bones of the day's news.

It turned out, from what she was seeing on the RTE home screen, that the after-effects of Brexit were taking the biggest toll on Northern Ireland. While many people in the South had little to no interest in news from North of the border—even many of those who claimed they fervently wished for a united Ireland—some of the best books Robyn had read on journalism in this country were written by reporters who had cut their teeth on "The Troubles" in the North. So she had a more in-depth knowledge, and a continued interest in, Northern Irish affairs than was usual for those living in the Republic, south of the border.

So the Northern Ireland Brexit story was the first one she

dived into. Violent demonstrations were breaking out night after night in Belfast, protesting the post-Brexit customs arrangements at the five commercial ports in the North: Belfast, Larne, Derry, Coleraine and Warrenpoint. The main sticking block in the Brexit negotiations between the UK and Europe had been the unforeseen consequences it would have for Northern Ireland. Although it was more correct to describe the consequences as "unconsidered". The consequences could have been foreseen, if only the politicians in the UK had considered them.

In the context of the negotiations, Northern Ireland occupied a unique position. It was politically part of the UK, but geographically part of the island of Ireland. It therefore had the UK's only land border with the EU, along the Irish border between the North and the Republic in the South. This had to be protected from a customs point of view, otherwise the European market via the Republic, would be flooded with cut-price and inferior products, not manufactured to European standards. But politically, there could not be a return to a physical or "hard" border, with customs inspections posts re-instated between North and South, symbols of the bad old days of "the Troubles."

The only alternative was to move the inspection posts to the ports. This meant that, for all intents and purposes, Northern Ireland operated as if within the EU, but with an invisible border down the Irish Sea with the UK. But this was anathema to the Unionists. They perceived it as Northern Ireland operating as a second-class province of the UK—no longer fully within the United Kingdom. It was for this reason that, night after night, Protestant loyalists were raging against the new arrangements, with custom posts at the ports

CHAPTER 21

targeted with petrol bombs and arson attacks.

Suddenly, a notification on her phone alerted Robyn that Lana, via her connected device in Castlebar, had nabbed a set of credentials that worked to get her into the backend of the Republican Party's server. Robyn was elated. She resisted the urge to phone her for operational security reasons. In case they were prosecuted for their actions in the future, they needed to leave as few clues as possible behind, so they settled on the pass phrase "just having a cuppa with some coconut cream biscuits" as their mission accomplished signal.

Robyn was now free to pack up and leave and she couldn't wait. It had only been forty-five minutes of waiting, but it felt like hours when she knew she was engaged in a such an illegal activity. She almost jumped every time a middle-aged male walked through the door, scared they were an undercover cop heading to her table to arrest her. Once they continued walking past her table, she then switched to wondering if they were possibly the Party employee who would give up their login credentials. It was forty-five minutes of to-ing and fro-ing between those two psychological extremes. As she gathered up her top-secret spying handbag, she could have almost laughed at the craziness of it, were it not so serious. As she walked out the door of the coffee shop, she looked at each of the seated customers and wondered which one of them could, unknowingly, have been the conduit to potentially proving an election interference operation by the Russians in Ireland. They may be sitting there, sipping on a coffee, taking their place in history—a greater patriot than they could ever realised.

As Robyn walked back to the car-park, she carried out the age-old check for a tail that she had seen in so many movies—

but in disbelief, all the same, that she actually found herself in such a situation. She pulled up suddenly at a shop and stood in the doorway pretending to look at her phone occasionally, but really just checking to see who had been behind her, memorising their faces. Then she carried on again, keeping an eye out to see if any of the pedestrians who had gone on ahead, pulled the same trick as well—a definite sign of a tail. How had her life got to this point? she wondered. Her legs felt strangely light, despite her exhaustion. No doubt it was the adrenaline surging through her body from the high-risk mission she had just carried out. As she got into her jeep and pulled out of the multi-storey car-park, she chugged the bottle of Lucozade she had bought earlier. Powered by glucose and adrenaline, she set off on her journey west, first across the River Liffey, then across the country.

She thought of the trouble that had broken out in the North again. She checked the time and hoped she would make it home on time for the nine o'clock news. She had read about last night's protests in the paper but sometimes, for scenes like that, you actually needed to see footage to feel the full impact. There was something bugging her all evening about the intensity of the protests and the timing of their escalation, just in the past month. The Brexit customs arrangements for the ports had been in place for several months, so why were such violent demonstrations breaking out now? She had read through a few stories from *The Belfast Telegraph* as well while waiting in the coffee shop and there didn't seem to have been any changes to the customs inspections in the past month to precipitate such violence. It seemed to descend without warning. There was something niggling at her brain that she needed to check, but it would have to wait until she got home. She loved the freedom that came with being able to drive directly into the city centre when she travelled to Dublin, but she didn't love the dead time driving created. Travelling by train, you could work away on your laptop for a few hours. But by car, she was limited to dictating notes or stories on her phone using a speech-to-text app.

As she drove through the Midlands, crossing the mighty River Shannon at Athlone and into the West, her mind also drifted back west and to events there during the last few weeks. She thought back to the disaster on Monday night when her week's work got wiped off the newspaper's servers including the two biggest stories—the fake "Drugs in the Dáil" smear campaign against Marie Mulhall and the Republican Party's dirty tricks against the electorate. She still hadn't heard any update from her editor on any progress being made by the investigators. What if it was an inside job? How did she know who she could trust now at work?

Then there was another thought that she couldn't quell in her mind: how did she know if she could trust German Joe? It had never sat well with her the circumstances of their first meeting that day in the library in Castlebar. She had visited his house earlier that day in Newport and, when he wasn't there, left a note for him under his back door. But later that afternoon, he suddenly popped up on her while she was looking through books in the library. How had he known she was there? She checked with the receptionist at the paper: he hadn't phoned or called into the office looking for her. So nobody from work told him that he could find her at the County Library. The only logical conclusion was that he had seen her out at his house and followed her. It was a creepy conclusion to reach but she put it down to the suspiciousness of an elderly man, which seemed in keeping with his character overall. Despite many long conversations the two of them had over the submarine sighting and dolphin kill, he never volunteered any personal information about himself, even when Robyn opened up to him about what happened to her little brother, Alexei.

Now she regretted having told him she infiltrated the Republican Party and what she had found out about their underhanded electoral tactics. After he entrusted her with the submarine sighting story, she had thought she could trust him too in return. But maybe it was just a ruse to bait her—maybe he was a Republican party operative who wanted to get a journalist on-side in the run-up to the general election. But then he didn't try to spin her any political stories. The only thing he had ever said to her about politics was: "watch this election," which puzzled her. As a journalist of course she would be watching the election, so why did he feel the need to say that specifically? She remembered looking at him to see if he was joking, but he appeared deadly serious. She dismissed it as an oddity at the time and didn't think too much further about it. But now it was puzzling her again.

As her journey west brought her closer to the wild Atlantic west coast, Robyn Mayhew was not to know that she was indeed right: there was a lot more to German Joe than met the eye. He was a man who spoke very little yet carried the weight of many unspoken stories. German Joe wasn't even "German" Joe, after all. He was, in fact, Russian Joe.

Chapter 22

German Joe only acquired his "German" status when he arrived in Newport, County Mayo. When asked by the locals where he was from, he would volunteer a very literal response—stating the last place he had lived as where he came from, rather than his birthplace. Few in Newport would have recognised the ever so slight "Russki" intonations of his original Russian accent which still lingered, despite years of speaking German. The traces were so slight they could only be detected by another native Russian speaker. And so, the moniker "German Joe" stuck.

For Josef Vulkov or German Joe as he was now known, concealing his personal details came by force of habit—a survival skill honed from years of dangerous work. In his former profession, the slightest slip could have led to horrific consequences: torture at least, and death at best. Espionage was a career one never truly left behind. No matter where you fled, its shadow followed.

The fall of the Berlin Wall in 1990 brought a rare chance

for Josef Vulkov to escape his life as an undercover Russian agent embedded in East Germany's notorious secret service, the Stasi. Amid the chaos of reunification, many spies from across the crumbling communist bloc seized the moment to flee westward. Some sought to leave behind the grim life of espionage, while others ran from the fear of prosecution for the crimes they had committed in the line of duty. Once an honorable profession under the old regime, espionage now carried the risk of public opprobrium and revenge as the tides turned.

But while the future held uncertainty for many ex-spies, it also offered unforeseen opportunities for some. At his former posting in Dresden, one of German Joe's former colleagues had exhibited an even more ruthless streak than most, in a profession which prized ruthlessness. It was a characteristic that eventually propelled him to the pinnacle of global power, leading the world's second-largest nuclear nation. That, combined with his cold precision and calculating mind, had paved his way to success. But his colleague never forgot the lesson of his time in Dresden—how fast everything could fall apart. It was a lesson Vladimir Vladimirovich Putin held onto as he continually tightened his grip on power in Russia. And it was a lesson, his former colleague German Joe, never forgot either.

*****

Svetlana couldn't shake the unease— engaging in illegal activities felt like a betrayal of the hospitality and safety her host country had afforded her. Even though her ultimate goal was to safeguard the integrity of their electoral system, the plan required this illegal hack to gather the proof she needed. Without it, there was no way to expose the imminent threat to the election. The optics were terrible, but she hoped her kindly hosts would understand her position, especially given the time crunch she found herself in.

Suddenly lights lit up the back patio outside her kitchen window. Startled, she instinctively shut down her laptop. Ger, her security detail on duty that night, moved swiftly into the kitchen, positioning himself perpendicular to the back door, carefully out of sight from the car pulling up outside. Then suddenly, Svetlana's tension eased as she remembered it was just Robyn returning from Dublin, calling in to check on her friend's progress.

Ger stayed in his "on guard" position as Robyn knocked on the door and called out "it's me, Robyn." He swung open the door, letting her in, before taking his customary wide sweeping look outside.

The girls had agreed that they'd continue their work from Lana's kitchen. Moving to Robyn's would cause too much disruption to her security detail and raise unwanted suspicions from them also. Officially, Svetlana's role as a network engineer involved setting up servers in Ireland for her country's national newspapers, so discussing technical matters wouldn't attract much attention. But they'd still have to be careful and use codewords they had agreed in advance when discussing anything election related. The election was deemed to be "the debate" and the electorate, "the audience." Russia was "the producer" and Serbia, "the researcher." With a clear system in place, they could speak freely, without raising alarm—at least, for now.

"How was the journey, Robyn?" Lana asked her friend as

she came in from the cold.

"Long. Thought I'd never get here. How's work going for you this evening?"

"I got in," she said to Lana, with a knowing look. "The files are with the 'researcher.' The servers are with her."

Robyn looked startled. "The researcher" was their code for Serbia. Her friend was telling her then that the Irish electorate's personal information was being stored on servers in Serbia.

"So if the 'researcher' has the files, so has the 'producer,'" Lana continued.

Was Lana really telling her that Russia also had access to the Irish people's data via Serbia? Robyn asked herself in disbelief.

As if reading her mind, Lana said to her: "The staff of 'the producer's' office would have access to the files of the 'researcher' also. There is an excellent working relationship between both offices. But 'the researcher's' office wouldn't necessarily have access to 'the producer's' files."

Robyn's brain was scrambled after little to no sleep all week. She looked at her friend: "I got this new make-up at a pharmacy in Dublin earlier. Do you want to give it a try and see what it looks like on you?"

Lana knew instinctively that it was just a "let's go somewhere private" line from her friend, as absurd as it was given that they both had completely different skin tones and would be wearing make-up shades a world apart. But the security guys would be none the wiser. Robyn followed her into her bedroom and Lana turned on the TV so their whispers wouldn't be audible to security.

"The Republicans' servers are based in Serbia," Lana confirmed to an incredulous Robyn. "It's not illegal, but highly suspicious. But in saying that, they could explain it away as something their Serbian social media manager organised."

"How could you possibly explain away something like that?" Robyn asked.

"Maybe he got a good deal on hosting costs from a buddy or some excuse like that. I don't know. But we need more evidence if we're to have any credibility," Lana elaborated. "But going back to what I was saying earlier about 'the producer' having access to 'the researcher's files' and not necessarily the other way around, what I meant was that the Serbs could grant their ally—Russia—access to the data without raising suspicions here. Because the servers are abroad, the Republican Party would be none the wiser as to who was accessing their servers. So there's no evidence that the Party is colluding with the Russians to win the election. But equally, they could wilfully be turning a blind eye to the possibility that the Russians could be interjecting themselves into this election to boost the Republican Party's electoral prospects."

"I get you," her friend conceded, but clearly shaken at the idea the Irish electorate could be in the hands of Vladimir Putin. It was something she had been having severe anxiety about all week but had managed to convince herself it was just paranoia in the extreme. Finding out there could be something to her hunch after all left her heartbroken for her country.

"Hey, can you turn that up a bit?" Robyn interrupted her friend. Something had caught Robyn's attention, out of the corner of her eye, on the TV screen. The nine o'clock news was on and it was showing images of police in riot gear and petrol bombs being thrown. The news presenter was describing the breakout of violence for yet another night in a row at Belfast port. Tensions were high in the loyalist Protestant community over the Brexit customs arrangements which, they argued, treated Northern Ireland as separate from the rest of the United Kingdom. Politicians were working around the clock to defuse the tensions but with little success. The violence appeared to be getting worse night by night. But it reminded Robyn of something she had thought of earlier in the day, which she needed to look into.

"Lana, there's something bothering me about those riots that I want to examine further. Can you give me half an hour or so to get this off my chest and then we'll get back to deciding on how to proceed next with this whole election mess?"

"Sure. I'm hungry anyway. I think I'll make some dinner. Will you have some too?"

"I'm not that hungry to be honest, even though I haven't eaten," Robyn told her. "But maybe my appetite will return if get the aroma of food cooking. What were you thinking of?"

"Something quick, like pasta carbonara? I've had a craving for smoky bacon since I had a full Irish down the town the other morning with the guys."

"You got me there. I can never say no to carbonara!" replied her cheered-up friend.

Robyn hung back in Lana's room so she could concentrate on the task at hand, while Lana headed to the kitchen to begin rustling up her favourite pasta dish. Powering up her laptop, Robyn opened up one of the jewels of her journalistic toolkit— PimEyes—an invaluable app for reverse searching images across the internet and crucially, social media also, pictures from which didn't usually appear in Google image searches. Once signed in, she uploaded the images of the two guys who

CHAPTER 22

turned up at the protests in Castlebar at the weekend—the same two guys Dara had identified as the divers who had dived right over the fibre optic cables in Clew Bay. The few moments she had to wait for the search results felt like an eternity.

And bingo. There they were again.

Under normal circumstances, Robyn loved when a hunch of hers turned out to be on the money. But these weren't normal circumstances, and her hunches proving correct was in fact, proving more and more depressing and enormously stressful, these days.

But as strong as her hunch had been, she still couldn't believe what she was seeing on the split screen in front of her. Both guys had turned up in social media posts on the fringes of the riots in Belfast. She trawled and trawled through the search results and couldn't find any images of them engaged in actual violence, but their presence in Belfast at the disturbances was evidence enough of ill-intent, when combined with their presence at protests in the Republic as well. An *agent provocateur* was the name given to such actors in the field of espionage tasked with stirring up civil unrest in a target country to bring about regime change or the installation of a friendly government.

Robyn's stomach churned from the shock of seeing the evidence in front of her of her worst fears some true. Suddenly the prospect of pasta carbonara seemed like stomach torture. She called her friend from the kitchen.

"Lana, I'm not joking. Remember the news item I turned up the volume to hear? About the Brexit protests in the North? I had a hunch that I thought was off the wall, but it wouldn't stop niggling at me. I reverse image searched those two guys from the protests here in town and guess what? I found images of them at the protests in Belfast as well. I think we have found two *agents provocateurs* in the country. And my guess is they're not Swedish, but Russian. What Irish person would be able to tell the difference in the accent? We call everyone from the continent Polish."

"Are you serious?" Lana asked her, suddenly looking pale. The thought of her own country's enemy, also being active in Ireland, shook her to the core. She thought Ireland was so far away from Russia that she would never be found here. Now she wasn't so sure.

"I'm afraid I am serious, Lana. And I'm worried for you now."

"I think I'm going to be sick," her friend replied, as she rushed into the ensuite bathroom and heaved into the toilet bowl. Robyn came in after her to hold back her friend's hair as she continued to vomit from the shock.

"Lana, it's ok. We're just going to have to be extra careful," she reassured her friend, helping her back into the bedroom to lie down. "But we have to tell the guys. It's too much of a risk at this stage for us to be investigating this on our own. I know we don't have solid evidence that they're Russian, but if there's even the prospect of Russian agents in Castlebar stirring up civil unrest, that's way too close for comfort. If you happened to be out on the street that day, they could have grabbed you and disappeared you. I know you have security, but we need to put them in the picture."

"Robyn, this is Ireland. Russia isn't even on Irish people's radar. The authorities will just think it's paranoia because of what my country is going through with Russia. No one's going to take us seriously."

"Look at all the evidence we have so far—the Republican's

sudden rise to the top of the polls only a few weeks before an election; a concerted botnet at work on Irish social media posting pro-Republican and anti-government content, the same account having been based on anti-Ukraine, anti-EU, pro-Brexit content up until a few months ago; the Republican Party's election campaigning dirty tricks on the Irish electorate under the direction of a Serbian social media manager; all the Party's data on the Irish electorate held on servers located in Serbia, a close ally of Russia; then the two guys at pro and anti-immigration protests; the same two guys again turning up at Brexit protests in the North and discovered diving key fibre optic cables off the Irish coast. Just the evidence we have on those two guys alone is enough to go to the authorities with. We have solid evidence on them. We're not crazy," Robyn argued.

"Yeah, we have plenty of evidence that they're up to no good. But we have nothing yet to tie them to Russia," Lana countered. "Same with the Serbian guy. It's just suspicious, but we've no evidence of a link to Russia."

"But based on Russia's interference in the American presidential election, the UK's Brexit referendum and elections on the continent, common sense would tell you it's Russia's hand at play here as well," Robyn persisted.

"Yeah, if it was just some random Irish citizen reporting it. But when it's a Belorussian dissident and her best friend reporting it, it just looks like paranoia on our part. Look, we've engaged in criminal hacking of the Republican Party's systems, so we have to have solid evidence behind us if we're to avoid jail time over that. Just give me one more day to search for a link via their systems and then I'll go with you to the authorities anyway, even if I can't find anything," Lana pleaded with her friend.

"We can't afford to leave it another day, Lana. It's way too risky for you."

"Just one more night then. And by the morning we can go to the authorities," Lana argued.

"You can't stay up all night, Lana. You've just been sick. You need a night's rest."

"I'm not going to sleep knowing what I now know. So I might as well do something useful. I promise, if by midday tomorrow I haven't found anything, I'll give up."

"I'm not happy about this, Lana, but I'll wait until the morning then. But I'm not leaving it until midday. That's almost lunchtime. I'll give it until 9.00am but then I'm done."

"Ok, agreed. I don't feel like that pasta I just cooked if you want to finish it off."

"Yeah. I don't feel like food now either. But I need some sleep. I just can't cope anymore with all that's going on."

"You go to bed, Robyn and try not to worry until the morning. We'll hand it over to the cops or the government or whomever by then. Then it's up to them what they do with it."

"Ok, but can I ask you one favour?"

"Yeah, sure."

"Can I stay here for tonight?" Robyn asked. "I know I wouldn't be much use against an intruder if we had one, but I'll feel better just by being here."

"Of course, you can stay. The bedroom at the end of the hall is free and the bed is made up."

Robyn turned in for the night, leaving her friend to make one last desperate search for evidence of Russia's interference in Ireland's 2020 general election. It was a mammoth task

CHAPTER 22

but, as someone who had suffered directly at the hands of the Russian government, she couldn't leave her beloved adoptive country to fall prey to Vladimir Putin's ruthless manipulations, letting the Irish people become mere pawns in his twisted games of geopolitical chess, just puppets on a string pulled this way and that, against their very own interests.

Just as Robyn was turning out the light at Lana's house, elsewhere a flashlight was flickering to life.

It was at the back door of Robyn's house, just further along the Rathbawn Road. The beam was steady, focused on the keyhole of the back door as expert lock picking tools were inserted quietly. Robyn slept fitfully at her friend's house completely unaware that tonight, she was the target, and not her friend.

Chapter 23

The night was dense with silence, broken only by the soft tick of a radiator cooling in the corner and urgent tapping on a keyboard. The blue light of the screen before her cast Lana's pale face in an ethereal glow, with shadows carving deep hollows beneath her eyes giving her the appearance of woman both haunted and hunted.

Outside, the town slept fitfully beneath a low, wet sky whilst inside, Lana, hunched and rigid, fought the heavy weight of exhaustion dragging at her eyelids. But while her body longed for rest, her mind surged forward with determined focus, having just gained access to the Republican Party's servers in Serbia, thanks to the login details Robyn had surreptitiously obtained in O'Connell Street earlier that day. Lana's fingers trembled over the keys, but her nerves buzzed with the uneasy thrill of trespassing.

Now, inside the digital catacombs of the party's servers, Lana trawled through endless layers of folders, file upon file, rabbit hole after rabbit hole, each branching into darker warrens still. She didn't know exactly what she was searching for but prayed that her instincts would inform her of anything suspicious or that warranted further investigation if she came across it. Somewhere in all of this, she was certain, the truth was hiding.

Four hours passed in her search for paydirt before it finally surfaced. It was a folder with an innocuous name to most.

"Segmentation."

But given Lana's quest that night and her previous experience, it fog-horned menace to her.

And, just as she suspected, within that folder were two further folders, labelled "Persuadables" and "Non-Persuadables". Lana's pulse quickened as she clicked on each to reveal its contents. She instantly realised she had seen this structure before.

It was the exact replica of the notorious Cambridge Analytica method of election manipulation—the use of an individual's online data to tailor messages to them based on their personal vulnerabilities.

Lana knew this method, knew it far too well.

Cambridge Analytica was established in 2013 as the Western arm of parent company, SCL which for decades had moved unseen through fragile democracies in Africa and Asia, sowing unrest and influence for those who could pay: corporations, governments and billionaires with private stakes in the will of nations. Lana remembered being so shocked by the scale and audacity of the company when its operations were revealed. SCL had even claimed they could foment coups on behalf of their clients. Their fingerprints were global: Italy, Latvia, Ukraine, Albania, Romania, South Africa, Nigeria, Kenya, Mauritius, India, Indonesia, the Philippines, Thailand, Taiwan, Colombia. The list stretched across continents like a slow-spreading stain.

And at the centre of it all—data. Private, personal and plundered. Lana stared at the screen, trying to steady her breathing.

In 2018, the façade cracked when the *New York Times* and the British *Observer* exposed the rot. Millions of Facebook users' data had been siphoned off under the cover of an academic study by a researcher named Aleksandr Kogan who offered Facebook users a personality quiz called "This is Your Digital Life".

But hidden in the fine print, permissions bled outwards.

And so a few hundred thousand quiz takers unknowingly gave away access to all their friends' data too. That detail had always haunted Lana. And now more than ever, given that she was on the run from a repressive regime. It was never just the person who clicked. Everyone around them was caught in the net too, friends, family, anyone they'd connected with.

Eighty-seven million profiles were sucked into the scheme that way giving the app creator every single morsel of information about them. Five thousand data points per person. The ability to see not only who people were, but what they feared, what they doubted, what they wanted and what could break them. It was like being X-rayed through the soul.

Lana clicked deeper into the files. The entire Irish electoral register was right there on the Serbian server. Hundreds of thousands of entries. Names, addresses. And now, linked to all those names and addresses, deeply personal psychological analysis of every single person. Personality types. Traits. Psychological triggers. Segmented, categorised, stripped bare. Lana stared at the data, her breath shallow. It was like reading strangers' minds—and it felt shameful and voyeuristic.

Robyn had told her about a quiz, "Find My Tribe," that the

CHAPTER 23

Republican Party was promoting. Masquerading as a helpful guide as to which political party and candidate you should give your vote, it was little more than a trapdoor into voters' psyches. Personality-based questions disguised as politics. Friendly, harmless and effective. It was all coming together now.

But what about those who hadn't taken the quiz? How was their data obtained? Lana wondered.

Her mind raced back to the online developer boards she frequented where recent hacks of social media platforms had been discussed. Millions of social media accounts had been compromised, and the data was apparently available for purchase on the dark web.

And then there were the legal data brokers, hoarding and selling behavioural data on all of us to anyone with the cash. Making a living off our habits, moods and anxieties. All neatly packaged and monetised.

Combine the two sources, and the result was chilling: a complete psychological map of a population. A nation stripped of its inner lives and sold to the highest bidder. Lana's hands hovered over the keyboard. Her stomach turned.

But there was a deeper horror.

Modern data science, supercharged by AI, had even become clairvoyant. Studies showed it could deduce a person's sexuality, intelligence, even mental health—just from online activity. People lived unknowing, unaware of the manner and extent to which their private selves were being harvested and analysed by unseen hands, then sold onto the highest bid with ill-intent or otherwise.

Lana shivered. Even the machines could read people now, better than they read themselves.

She dragged her focus back to the screen.

The "Non-Persuadables" folder revealed its contents, bleeding its secrets as sub-folders named "Committed Government Supporters," "Over-Forties," "Rural," "Professional" and "Earners Over €70k."

Each was a weaponised list and accompanying strategy. It turned out the Republican Party didn't just ignore those unlikely to convert to its cause and vote for others—it actively sought to silence them. The strategy files revealed social media campaigns tailored to disillusionment, directed at voters for other parties. Subtle nudges, veiled doubt. "What did Fine Gael ever do for you?" Her friend, Robyn had spotted it weeks earlier, in viral social media posts that had spread like a mold on society. Lana remembered seeing them too. She'd scrolled right past—never realising their purpose.

Lana opened the next folder: "Persuadables." And here the darkness truly bloomed.

This wasn't merely data. It was diagnosis.

Each entry catalogued with cold precision: users flagged for "Neuroticism," "Closed-Mindedness," "Disagreeableness." They were the vulnerable ones, marked not by ideology, but by emotional architecture. These were the people whose fears, flaws and pain points could be molded like wet clay.

They were subdivided further: "Conspiracy Theorists," "Government Hostiles," "The Dis-Engaged Middle," "Heart vs Head Believers." Labels turned into levers. Traits turned into targets. The manipulation was surgical in its precision.

With that depth of insight into people's thought processes, Lana shuddered, the Republican Party doesn't just know who you are, they know how to turn you into the person they want you to be. Now that they were all neatly segmented

CHAPTER 23

as the Serbian files revealed, the Irish electorate were being manipulated like puppets on a string, but with well-placed whispers in a feed pulling the strings.

Lana's throat was dry. The implications came crashing down on her.

It was all there: how to break a democracy with nothing but data and algorithms. A system designed to reach past opinion, past ideology, past even thought—straight to the raw, vulnerable pulse of personality.

It was game over for the Irish election.

Not because the votes had been counted, but because the battlefield had already shifted. The campaign wasn't in the streets, or in televised debates. It was in memes and whispers woven into timelines, fear disguised as fact, comfort sold as truth. It was psychological warfare—personal, invisible, and devastatingly effective. Lana had read the playbook and now she was watching it unfold in real time.

And then that was where the Russian operatives would take over. Lana remembered the investigations that followed the 2016 US presidential election—how they revealed the murky world of Russia's self-described "Internet Research Agency," based in St. Petersburg, the Russian leader's home town.

The building it occupied at 55 Savushkina Street looked harmless from the outside, a grey office block surrounded by post-Soviet flats and newer office complexes. But Lana knew it was far from harmless. Inside, it was a factory. A factory of lies. A state-run "troll farm" that was said to have industrialised the art of trolling.

Back in 2016, it was staffed by 250 or so party workers who were mostly made up of "failed journalists and English language students." The staff worked long hours maintaining a multitude of sock puppet accounts each—fake social media profiles with manufactured lives— using these accounts to hijack reality and spread Russian propaganda wherever required around the world. Working in concert, they were able to create the illusion of a massive army of supporters for whatever viewpoint or propaganda they were pushing.

Lana remembered reading how they operated in teams, where one sock puppet account was nominated as "the villain" stirring controversy or planting the seed of a disinformation campaign. Then other members of the team would back up the original poster or ask questions pretending to be sceptical, only to "come round" to their way of thinking in the end. The story could then be picked up by state-sponsored media such as RT (Russia Today) or amplified further by the Russian news agency, Sputnik. But what looked like spontaneous public sentiment was, in fact, carefully plotted fiction. Workers there were required to work twelve-hour shifts and post 135 comments per day, feeding chaos into the bloodstream of democracy.

One of the Russian trolls who worked there spoke to the media and what she had to say stood out in Lana's mind because so many young people, in recent years, had fallen under the spell of psychics and other con artists online. One of her alter egos at the troll factory was a fortuneteller named "Cantadora" who issued daily affirmations and astrological predictions. Through the spirit world, Cantadora claimed to gain insights on topics like relationships, weight loss, feng shui, and weirdly, even international politics. But the "energies" she sensed on the latter would always predict failure for Western politicians such as Barack Obama and his allies in Europe and the UK. It was propaganda disguised as whimsical spiritual advice. And the goal was clear—to subtly embed propaganda into what seemed like the casual, nonpolitical thoughts of an ordinary person.

But all that was back in 2016, Lana thought, and with advances in artificial intelligence since then, much of the "trolling" and spreading of disinformation was now done by AI-powered armies of bots, instead of armies of people. Bots didn't have to sleep, they learned faster, scaled wider and worst of all, they adapted. And so, the extent of the disinformation crisis has exploded exponentially.

She remembered hearing from those who grew up in the 1970's and 80's about the fears back then about children watching too much television. That too many hours in a daze before a television screen could affect their brain development. The same fears were even raised about radio, and its hypnotic hum, a few decades earlier. But now, Lana realised, the threat was far more disturbing. The processing power of today's computers had gone up by a trillion times, whereas our brains hadn't evolved at all, and we were no match for the computing power of social media.

This processing power, coupled with the almost total control our phones had over our lives, was a vista from hell, she thought to herself. The level of detail that social media companies and internet giants had on us was nothing short of frightening. She remembered reading in white papers and developer forums about the kind of "engagement metrics" that social media companies captured on us including what photos you stop to look at, how long you look at each picture, if you're depressed, if you're lonely, if you're looking at pictures of your ex-partner, what you're doing late at night. And all of that, Lana knew, was linked to your name and address. Social media companies know more about you than you know about yourself.

Those same companies then used that data to predict behaviour— what triggered someone emotionally, what site they'd visit next, what they'd do even when they logged off. With our location data tracked also, phones had essentially become our ankle monitors, Lana thought to herself angrily. They kept us under constant surveillance, all for the benefit of platforms and advertisers fighting for our attention.

She had long resented the level of control the social media companies had over people. If you were on, what they knew was your break at work, and you weren't on the network, they would nudge you with a notification such as "your friend Tom just tagged you in a photo" to get your attention and get you to comment. And so you were sucked in again. Once your scrolling speed slowed, they predicted your session was coming to an end and they would pull back up friends' and family's posts in your feed to keep you interested or a post by someone you had a crush on, and once you were engaged again, they'd show you an ad.

It was a carefully engineered spell, one that Lana had seen cast hundreds of times.

How many times do you see two people having a conversation with each other and as soon as one of their phone's beeps, they do as commanded and go check it, regardless of whether they were in the middle of a conversation with somebody, and regardless of how rude it was. We constantly do our phones bidding as commanded by these companies and those who pay them to control our attention, she despaired.

Like the man who orchestrated Russia's troll empire.

He had a name that was as darkly ironic as the enterprise

itself. "The Chef," they called him. Yevgeny Prigozhin. To outsiders, the moniker came from his catering company, the one that supplied meals to the Kremlin. But those in the inner circles of Moscow power knew the real truth: Prigozhin wasn't called the Chef because he fed people with food, it was because he fed them information. Carefully plated lies, spiced with paranoia, served en masse to Russia's enemies through their own digital feeds.

Later, the world would know him for his role as head of Wagner, the brutal mercenary outfit responsible for atrocities in Syria, Ukraine and Africa. But before the guns, there were memes. Before the bloodshed, there were bots. When he died in a fiery plane crash following his failed coup against Putin, no one in Moscow was surprised. The Chef had served one too many poisoned dishes.

His propaganda campaigns usually all began in the shadows, Lana recalled reading, in online spaces that were anonymous and allowed people to post without discourse. Like 4Chan, an online message board populated by mostly by teenagers, young men and gamers, posting content that was considered by most to be distasteful, but even anti-social and shocking at times. Discord, the app used by gamers to communicate, was also used to seed disinformation campaigns.

Lana had mapped out before how these Russian campaigns unfolded in her country and in Eastern Europe in the past. Platforms like 4chan, 8chan and Discord would be used to share specific details about coordination of online campaigns, such as "we're going to try to get this particular hashtag to trend," or "use this meme to respond to today's events on social." The coordination often then moved into large Twitter DM groups or WhatsApp groups, where nodes within a network spread content to a wider group of people. It might then move into communities on sites like Gab, Reddit or YouTube. From there, the content would be shared into more mainstream sites like Instagram, Facebook or Twitter at large as it spread outward like spores in the wind.

And then came the fatal amplification—when journalists, sometimes unwittingly, picked up the poisoned thread because they didn't realise the provenance of the content and decided to use it in their reporting without sufficient checks. Even when they tried to debunk it, the headline still echoed the lie. It still lived and still multiplied.

Lana had traced the patterns many times. She knew the language, the pacing, the cadence of online manipulation. It moved like weather. It could start on the fringes in places like Gab or Reddit, sweeping through YouTube rabbit holes, and finally pouring down on the mainstream: Instagram, Facebook, Twitter. A storm dressed as conversation.

One tactic had stood out to her in the Belarusian election that was particularly duplicitous: warping the results of post debate polls. People could be startlingly simple in the run-up to elections, many just wanted to be on the winning side. If a poll told them who was "winning," they would lean towards that, rather than voting on the basis of their own values and beliefs. Such voters were easy prey and the most vulnerable to manipulation. So the troll factories stacked the comments, inflated the likes, manipulated the reactions. They forged a tide, and the tide carried people with it.

Political manipulation had long gone beyond leaflets, speeches, or TV ads, Lana sighed. Now it was a game of data, algorithms, and psychological profiling, played in secret, far from public scrutiny.

CHAPTER 23

Cambridge Analytica had shown just how easy it was to manipulate opinion using Facebook's "audience like this" feature on the advertising platform. For instance, a political party could go into a conspiracy theory group on Facebook, then buy ads featuring, for instance, disinformation they wanted to spread about the government. Then, they select the "audience like this" option to target these conspiracy theorists, before hitting them with more conspiracy theories and watching their disinformation campaign spread like wildfire.

Those wildfires burned out of control in the 2016 US presidential election and again in 2020, in Brexit and in countless other elections around the world. Lana had watched as it eroded trust in institutions, sowed doubt in science, painted journalists as propagandists and teachers as ideologues. It polarised families and communities until it seemed there was no such thing as shared truth anymore

Lana stared blankly at her screen, her mind reeling.

She could see it all now. The genius of it wasn't in the technology—it was in the manipulation. You didn't need to stuff ballot boxes or hijack voting machines to rig an election. You didn't even need to change the vote. All you had to do, Lana realised with despair, was change the voter. And with the right data, the right algorithm, and the right nudge at just the right moment, you could do exactly that.

And the worst part? People never knew when they were under attack. Because the messages didn't come from official campaign pages or politicians themselves. It came from "concerned citizens" or from community pages, from anonymous posts that looked like they came from a neighbour or a parent or a colleague. Because once the algorithm knew you—your politics, your insecurities, your weaknesses—it knew exactly what kind of messenger you'd trust.

This was how democracy died, not in a blaze of violence, but in a flood of content. You wouldn't hear the end of the republic coming, Lana thought to herself. You'd scroll right past it.

That was the dark brilliance of it. Disinformation didn't look like propaganda anymore. It looked like someone's stories, a viral tweet, a community post from a page you didn't even remember liking. Propaganda shouted, but this whispered.

And it worked. It worked because people weren't being confronted. They were being comforted. The stories that appeared in their feeds didn't challenge them, they confirmed them. They made them feel right, righteous, empowered. And, perhaps most importantly, not alone.

That was the secret of virality in the modern age, Lana thought to herself, it wasn't about truth, it was about belonging. You didn't share an article because it was accurate. You shared it because it reflected who you were or wanted to be

And it wasn't just fringe actors weaponising this. It was built into the platforms themselves. Instagram, Tik Tok, YouTube, Twitter, Facebook, Twitter—these weren't passive mirrors of society. They were amplifiers, accelerants. They didn't show you the world. They showed you your world. A curated, manipulated version of reality designed to keep you angry, engaged, and clicking.

Because outrage, as it turned out, was good for business.

Lies spread six times faster than facts, Lana remembered reading. Not because people were stupid, but because the truth is often dull, complicated, or inconvenient. A simple, emotionally charged lie was easier to digest and far more fun to share.

The result? A world where vaccines were doubted, elections were discredited, and scientific consensus was just another "opinion." A world where facts were up for debate, and every piece of evidence could be dismissed as "fake news" if it didn't fit the narrative, you'd already been fed.

Lana thought back to the MMR scare in the 2000s and the lies about vaccines causing autism. The panic it caused. How parents were terrified into inaction. Even after scientific study after study debunked the claim, the fear lingered. Because the lie had emotion, the truth had footnotes. And in a battle between those two, the lie usually won. That was why it was so dangerous. Because people didn't just believe lies anymore, they defended them. They built their identities around them. And once your identity is wrapped around an idea, no amount of evidence can pull it loose.

And if a lie is repeated often enough, people begin to believe there's truth in it after all, no matter how outlandish it may first seem.

Lana had seen and heard it firsthand: parents continuing to put their children's health at risk by refusing to vaccinate them and protect them from deadly diseases like measles, mumps and rubella because they believe the fake news instead of the truth. The conspiracy theorists had more influence over them than actual doctors and scientists. And the fake MMR vaccine/autism conspiracy was a particular favourite of Russia's trolls in St. Petersburg. It continued to cause a fall-off in vaccination uptake in the West putting their populations at risk whereas, in Russia, vaccine uptake was much higher where society hasn't been targeted by this false conspiracy and their children were better protected as a result.

What chilled Lana most wasn't just the existence of these tactics, it was how normal they had become and that it was now global. From Brexit to Trump, from Ireland to India, from conspiracy groups to political parties, disinformation wasn't just something that happened. It was designed, strategised, tested, measured, and optimised like any other product.

The campaigns didn't even have to be rooted in reality. One that stood out in her mind in particular was a campaign Cambridge Analytica devised when working on the Leave side during the UK's Brexit referendum. It started with a fake news story posted on social media about a poultry factory on the Northern Ireland border in which, it was claimed, the Irish workforce was allegedly replaced by two hundred foreign workers. It was supposedly an example of immigration directly affecting low-skilled jobs. Eastern European workers had undercut existing terms and conditions, it was claimed, and so no Irish people were working there anymore.

But when a journalist went to visit the factory to follow up on the story, it turned out that there was no such factory. It just didn't exist. However, due to the pressures of "churnalism" where the online environment had created a never-ending 24-hour news cycle, journalists simply don't have time to check out the veracity of stories on the ground. And with the loss of local newspapers due, in turn, to the loss of ad revenue to online behemoths like Google, Meta, Twitter/X and the like, there were fewer and fewer local journalists on the ground to investigate news stories locally.

What mattered, Lana realised, was that the story felt true to the people it was meant to reach. It played on their fears, their grievances, their sense of being left behind. That emotional payload was what made it spread.

CHAPTER 23

This fake news story was an example of what those working on the Leave campaign for Cambridge Analytica called "shitposting", where they would completely fabricate "news" stories and post them online, knowing the likelihood of them ever being fact-checked was slim. She still couldn't believe it, but this was the disturbing new reality of the "news" we were consuming on social media. Local newsrooms had been hollowed out by Big Tech siphoning off ad revenue. Churnalism was the new norm—articles aggregated, click-baited, and pushed online without verification. By the time anyone bothered to check the facts, the fake story had already gone viral.

That's what the disinformation architects counted on. Throw enough garbage into the stream and eventually it contaminates the water supply.

And yet, Lana thought, most people still thought they were in control of what they consumed. That illusion of agency was perhaps the greatest trick of all. People believed they were freely navigating information, when in reality they were being guided, nudged, programmed.

Lana had read about how YouTube could even radicalise someone without them realising it. You start with a basic video—a political commentary, a news clip, a debate. Then the algorithm nudges you forward with more videos lined up to watch. One click leads to another, each one a little more extreme. Before you know it, you're down a rabbit hole of xenophobia and hate, then conspiracy and onto neo-Nazism and Holocaust denial. And you think you got there on your own. But it was a path you were lead down.

That was the real brilliance of it and what made it so dangerous, she thought. Because if you don't know you're being manipulated, you don't resist. You believe it was your idea. That you figured it out. That you're too smart to be duped. But the truth was, the smarter you thought you were, the more vulnerable you probably were.

But it wasn't just about extremism. Even innocuous interests could be manipulated. Watch enough vegetarian cooking videos, and you'd be funneled toward veganism, then animal rights activism, then disturbing footage of slaughterhouses. The algorithm didn't care what path you were on, it only cared about keeping you on it. And that meant pushing you further. Harder. Deeper. Whatever you watch, it's not hardcore enough for YouTube. It remains as one of the most radicalising platforms of the 21st century.

And it's not just YouTube and the social media companies which are heavily influencing us. She knew, from the ads she saw online, the deep surveillance she was under by Google and other search engines. As soon as you would visit an online store and look at a product you may be thinking of buying, Google would chase you around the internet for weeks, shoving ads for that product in your face until you relented and bought it.

But it wasn't just its pervasive surveillance that was creepy. What most people didn't realise, Lana remembered, was how we were influenced by Google when performing just a simple Google search, something you would think is completely within our own agency and control. Most people didn't know that Google showed you results based on where you're from. This was logical if you were looking for local services like shops and restaurants, but Google bases our search results on our location for general search terms too. For instance, a study in the US showed that when people from the East or

West coasts typed the term "climate change" into the Google search box, Google auto-filled the search to read "climate change a threat to humanity." The auto-filled search term is just a suggestion but is still very influential. However, when Americans from the South searched "climate change", Google auto-filled the search to "climate change is a hoax." Because most people on the East and West coast accepted climate change as a threat to humanity, this was the suggestion they were shown when searching. And because the opposite was the case in the South, people there had "climate change is a hoax" suggested as search term when Googling the topic. And we wonder why our society is so polarised and at war with one another? Lana sighed. Social media companies were without doubt to blame, but Google wasn't innocent either.

Even the smallest groups could be reached and manipulated now. Lana had read how Meta's micro-targeting tools allowed political campaigns to whisper directly into the ears of groups as small as just fifteen people in a town if they wanted to. Tell each one what they wanted to hear. Promise each one something different. Nobody would ever know, except the algorithm.

And that, Lana thought, was the ultimate perversion of democracy. Not just that people could be lied to—but that they could be lied to individually. That every voter could be told a different version of reality, tailored precisely to their psychology, all under the guise of "engagement."

So imagine the power this gives a political party in a constituency or electoral area where the gap between two candidates is so small it could go either way. This level of micro-targeting gives political parties huge scope to bring in every single voter by just telling them what they want to hear, with the vast amount of data they have access to on them.

But this had always been the business model of social media. They offer a free service to help you stay in touch with friends. In exchange, they get total, 24/7 surveillance of your mind. Your thoughts. Your emotions. Your habits. Your fears. Your dreams. All of it for sale to anyone who wishes to manipulate you.

After all, the saying was, she remembered: "if you're not paying for the product, then you *are* the product."

She sat still. The screen glowed. A chill settled over her as she considered the night's revelations.

And then she thought of the man who had started it all—the founder of Facebook. She remembered the moment he was asked how he'd convinced so many people to hand over their personal data for his social media platform.

"People just submitted it. I don't know why. They trust me. Dumb f*cks."

Lana stared at the screen, the words echoing in her mind.

Like a warning too long ignored.

Chapter 24

Lana's thoughts drifted back to a conversation she'd had with her friend just after the protests a week earlier. Robyn had been trying to figure out who the organisers could be behind the protests, even wondering aloud if there was Republican involvement—whether officially sanctioned by the party or not. The aggressive tone of the protests, marked by violence and intimidation, reminded Robyn of the control that their Northern Ireland paramilitaries once held over their communities.

But that evening, Robyn had come across a social media post from a local Republican candidate that seemed to refute her suspicions. The candidate had explicitly condemned the protests, proudly proclaiming the party's embrace of multiculturalism in Ireland.

However, as Lana examined the folder in front of her now, everything she saw confirmed her growing suspicions: the post Robyn had seen was likely one of those "dark posts" her source, the former social media employee, had warned her about. These posts were crafted for a very specific audience, like journalists, Irish citizens who supported immigration, and the new immigrant community itself, whose votes the Republican Party sought to capture. For everyone else, these posts remained hidden, disappearing from their feeds like whispers in the dark. It was a clever strategy, Lana thought, a calculated effort to project an image of the party as immigrant-friendly to those inclined to hear it, while keeping the message invisible to others.

The folder she'd just opened laid bare the sinister sophistication of dog-whistling politics. Inside, she found an unsettling form of verbal manipulation—statements laced with carefully chosen words designed to subtly convey a controversial message. These messages were crafted to be understood by the party's supporters yet remain ambiguous enough for plausible deniability. It was a delicate balancing act: saying something, while simultaneously, not saying it at all. It allowed the party to broadcast one message to the general electorate, while sending the exact opposite signal to a more selective, covert audience.

What Lana read in the folder labeled "Immigration" epitomised this tactic. The party's social media strategy involved posting content opposing the establishment of new "Direct Provision" centres, but not for the overtly racist reasons that truly motivated them. Instead, the posts were framed as criticisms of the "inhumane" conditions within the system. It was true that few could argue in favor of the regime, which housed immigrants in substandard accommodations and left them struggling to survive on a mere €38 social welfare payment, unable to work as their asylum cases languished in bureaucratic limbo. But the far-right's sudden concern for these immigrants was nothing more than a perverse ruse.

They didn't care about the well-being of the people suffering in "Direct Provision," but only insofar as it could be taken advantage of for their own racist ends.

Instead, Lana realised, they seized on many Irish people's disquiet over the system's flaws as a way to mask their true intentions. They weaponised the "inhumanity" of "Direct Provision" as a dog whistle to rally other racists, while also co-opting well-meaning citizens who genuinely sought to reform the system. It was a nauseating sleight of hand that allowed them to manipulate communities across Ireland. As she read through the morally bankrupt strategies detailed in the folder, Lana felt physically ill. The far-right was exploiting the good intentions of those who believed they were standing up for vulnerable immigrants, twisting their empathy into unwitting support for the very people who sought to oppress them. The sickening realisation of just how effective this strategy was, how it could inflame communities and draw unwitting allies into the fold of far-right extremism, left Lana feeling as though she could throw up. She pulled the bin in the corner of the room closer to her, in case she just did.

File after file exposed a disturbing trend: various segments of Irish society had been deliberately targeted for online manipulation. Completely unknowingly, anyone who expressed an interest online in traditional Irish music, Irish dancing, Irish history, the Irish language or Republicanism or even had their children in "gaelscoileanna" (Irish language schools), was being singled out as ripe for manipulation. These individuals were then targeted with content designed to stoke "cultural nationalism," feeding the false narrative that their cherished culture could be diluted or threatened by the presence of foreigners. But any Irish person who had ever lived abroad, or even just gone on holiday abroad, would know the opposite was true. Being around foreigners only deepened one's sense of Irishness. It heightened our appreciation for Irish traditions, whether it was music, language, or even just Irish pubs. This was true for every culture. Yet, the Russian agents of chaos behind this manipulation had made it a priority to spread fear, using it as a tool to divide Irish society.

The segmentation of the Irish electorate according to psychological profiles allowed them to manipulate the Irish psyche even further, seeking out those vulnerable to their messages and the neurotic, for special attention. What Lana saw in those files—rows upon rows of Irish names and addresses—made the situation so surreal. These people had been targeted with groundless fears, preyed upon by a sophisticated online apparatus. After planting seeds of doubt and anxiety, the manipulators would follow up with deniable posts, subtly nudging these individuals with carefully crafted and deniable dog whistles, urging them to vote for the Russia's chosen government for Ireland—the Republican Party.

One such dog-whistled meme Lana examined featured a group of black Irish teenagers standing innocently at a bus stop. Above the image, bold text asked: "Are you thinking what we're thinking?" The insinuation was vague, but the intent was clear—designed to appeal to the basest instincts of fear and prejudice, hoping to ignite the worst in human nature based on nothing more than a simple, innocent scene.

But the deception didn't stop there. The files contained countless memes filled with vile, anti-immigrant rhetoric, queued up to be unleashed the moment a target engaged with one of the more subtle dog-whistles. One video, however,

CHAPTER 24

stood out to Lana—not because it was the most vile, but because of its sheer cunning. The video showed a peaceful march in County Wicklow, where people had gathered to support immigrants struggling under the "Direct Provision" system. Yet the manipulators behind Russia's disinformation campaign had taken this video and repurposed it. They posted it to a Facebook group in County Longford, which was opposed to a new "Direct Provision" centre in their locality. But they had edited the description, falsely claiming that the Wicklow march was *against* "Direct Provision" and that these were fellow Irish citizens who opposed housing immigrants in their area too. It was disinformation at its most malicious, twisting the truth into a weapon to mislead and manipulate. The sheer audacity of it all made Lana's stomach heave but at least it was dry-heaving—she hadn't eaten in hours. What she was witnessing wasn't just propaganda, it was a methodical effort to destabilise Irish society, preying on fears, manipulating perceptions, and pushing people toward decisions they wouldn't have made, if not for the lies fed to them online.

She couldn't shake the thought that the relentless bombardment of anti-immigrant messages directed at the Irish public could have serious consequences for the country. If left unchecked, it could pave the way for the rise of far-right extremism and neo-Nazism in Ireland. As Election 2020 loomed, Lana made a mental note to discuss with Robyn using her journalism to start a public campaign to counter this tide of hate. Highlighting the tangible benefits of immigration would be key. At a time when Ireland was experiencing near full employment, the influx of foreign workers was not only beneficial, but essential. Labour shortages were already taking a toll in sectors like healthcare, nursing, dentistry, caregiving, taxi and truck driving, mechanics, and hospitality roles such as chefs, bar staff, and waiters.

The healthcare system, in particular, relied heavily on foreign workers, and Lana knew it would collapse if those workers staged even a one-day protest against racism, let alone if they left the country due to feeling unsafe here. This reliance underscored a harsh reality: without immigrants, critical services could falter. Beyond filling vital roles, the economic advantage of allowing immigrants to work in Ireland was staggering. Over a lifetime, a foreign worker on the average industrial wage would contribute a net amount of over half a million euros in tax to the Irish exchequer. At a time when the national pension fund had a significant deficit and the pension age had to be continuously raised as a result, the need for more workers to support an aging population, was undeniable.

It made no economic sense to keep asylum seekers trapped in "Direct Provision" centres, unable to work, sometimes for years, while their applications were processed. This policy was not only a human tragedy, but also a missed economic opportunity. Yet, the persistent disinformation clouding public discourse left little space for education about the benefits of immigration to Ireland. Countries like Germany had long recognised the value of foreign labour. For decades, it welcomed immigrants to fill gaps in its workforce, helping to build its position as the economic powerhouse of Europe. Ireland, with its current labour shortages, was at a similar crossroads. Unless it welcomed and integrated more workers, its economy risked stagnation, or worse, decline.

Beyond the economic rationale, the refusal to allow people

fleeing drought in Africa—drought exacerbated by global warming caused by the emissions from cars, heating fuel, and industries in developed countries—was morally indefensible. Many of those seeking refuge in Europe were escaping the very consequences of climate change for which Western nations were largely responsible. Civil wars in Africa, often driven by the political and economic interference of Western countries aiming to control Africa's vast natural resources, represented another tragic factor fueling migration to Europe.

In Asia, the return of the Taliban to power in Afghanistan was triggering waves of desperate immigrants to try to reach Europe. The haunting images of people clinging to US military aircraft as they took flight out of the country, highlighted the sheer human desperation of those left behind after two decades of a failed US-NATO deployment in the region. Afghans who had worked with, or helped the US military, were now marked targets for torture and execution by the Taliban. Yet, the US and its European allies, having abandoned these people to the horrors of their new reality, were refusing to offer them asylum.

Denying immigrants a chance to escape such unimaginable horrors wasn't just shortsighted economically, it was morally reprehensible. It stood in stark defiance of any sense of natural justice. The idea of turning our backs on those who had suffered due to Western actions, whether through military intervention or environmental negligence, was ethically appalling.

The Irish public, like all those across the Western world, needed to be re-educated about the realities of immigration. The pervasive lie that immigrants are a drain on society had to be proved wrong by the actual economic numbers. Aside from that, these men, women, and children were fleeing conditions created, in part, by the West, and it was well past time that we acknowledged our collective responsibility to help them. Immigration was not only an economic opportunity, welcoming refugees and migrants was a moral imperative, one that could restore our sense of justice and humanity in an increasingly interconnected world.

As the first light of dawn crept through the slit in the curtains, Lana felt a rising sense of urgency to wrap up her investigation of the Serbian server. The pressure to uncover more, before time ran out, gnawed at her already frazzled nerves. She shut the folder on immigration, and hesitated for a moment, before clicking open the next one—labeled "Climate Change." Among the files within, one called "Strategy" caught her eye, and with a sinking feeling, she chose to open it next, fearing the worst.

What she found was deeply unsettling. Those seeking housing were being specifically targeted by the puppet masters in Russia, working either knowingly or unknowingly on behalf of the Republican party. Anyone visiting housing or apartment rental websites, browsing auctioneers' listings, or searching for mortgages, was bombarded with content either urging them to "kick out the government" or "put Republicans in charge," with the language tailored to their personality to exploit their frustrations and fears. It was manipulative, but not unexpected. But Lana couldn't understand how strategy related to the Irish housing crisis was filed under "Climate Change", until she stumbled upon another file that left her reeling.

While she hadn't expected the Russians to have any genuine interest in Ireland's housing crisis, what she read made her stomach lurch once more. The file revealed a list of Irish environmental protection organisations—groups that Russia had been secretly funding through anonymous cryptocurrency donations. The goal? To support the organisations' expensive legal battles against housing developments across the country. It became clear that Russia was deliberately worsening the housing crisis, fueling public frustration and despair, all to tip the scales in favor of the Republican party. They were not just sowing chaos for chaos' sake, Lana realised in despair, they were playing a calculated game, weaponising Ireland's housing crisis to manipulate the electorate.

Lana stood up to take a break from her computer hoping to shake off the overwhelming nausea she was feeling, but her legs wobbled beneath her, forcing her to sit right back down. She reached for a bottle of water on the desk, taking a cautious sip, but it only seemed to make her stomach churn harder. The cruelty of deliberately worsening the housing crisis and people's desperation for a roof over their heads, purely for political gain, had left her shaken. The housing crisis wasn't just due to failed policies or economic mismanagement—it was being actively provoked by foreign actors with cold, calculated intent. She felt as if she was drowning under the weight of it all. She held her head in her hands for a few moments, reeling from the scale of the manipulation. She wanted to throw in the towel for the night, but as much as her body wanted her to, she just couldn't give up on these people. Sickness and exhaustion aside, she had to keep going. She tried standing again and this time her legs held firm. She paced the room for a few moments, lost in thought. The computer screen glowed with blue light in the darkness, but even still, she noticed the night was beginning to recede outside, with the curtains slowly illuminated with the beginnings of morning light.

Lana opened the window a little for fresh air and walked down to the kitchen, instinctively going to make coffee. But she thought better of it as another wave of nausea washed over her. A bottle of Lucozade, her anti-sickness drink of choice since she was a kid in Ireland, was what she opted for from the fridge instead.

As Lana sank back into her chair, her mind reeled at the sheer cruelty of what she had uncovered. The housing crisis, which had left so many Irish families struggling, was being used as a tool for political manipulation. Worse still, the very people caught in this nightmare—desperate for a place to live—were being exploited for their votes, only to have their suffering deepened deliberately by the same forces claiming to help them. Lana recalled a conversation she'd had with Robyn after one of her latest county council meetings. Robyn had mentioned how the Republican party had consistently objected to every housing development proposal in the county for over a decade. And yet, they were now using the very housing crisis that they had helped create, as a platform to drum up support, cynically playing on people's frustrations. On top of that, their covert allies—the Russian government— were also jumping on the bandwagon to exacerbate the crisis in order to install their preferred Irish government, the Republican Party.

But the more Lana uncovered, the darker it became. The climate change "Strategy" file revealed more sickening tactics from the Russian intelligence operatives. The strategy laid out a calculated plan to portray the fight against climate change as an attack on rural Ireland, its traditions, and its way of life. In this twisted narrative, environmental activists weren't just fighting for the protection of the planet—they were painted as enemies of rural communities. The message was clear: one couldn't support environmental protection and still live peacefully in the Irish countryside. The operatives were determined to frame the two as mutually exclusive. You had to pick a side—save the earth or preserve rural Ireland—you couldn't have both.

Farmers and rural dwellers were to be targeted with a barrage of misinformation, pitting them against climate advocates in a false dichotomy. The lies were bold and dangerous: the EU and Ireland's mainstream political parties were supposedly plotting to take all cars over ten years old off the road, while excise duties on fuel would be raised to levels that would make it impossible for anyone on an average income to afford to drive. Rural Ireland, where public transport links were poor, was told that this would be the death knell for their way of life.

But the misinformation didn't stop there. An even more insidious narrative was being pushed that within twenty years, laws would be enacted to force people out of the countryside and into cities, robbing rural Ireland of its population and identity. Farmers would be bought out by the government, with their land sold to large multinational corporations that would take over food production in Ireland.

It was a dystopian vision designed to strike fear into the hearts of rural communities. The plan was to weaponise their anxieties about the future, driving a wedge between them and those advocating for environmental reforms. Farmers, rural families, and those connected to Ireland's countryside were being manipulated into believing that environmental protection came at the cost of their livelihood and traditions.

But the file contained an even more sickening twist. Buried within the "Strategy" folder was a list of far-right organisations operating in Ireland, along with the names of their leaders and detailed records of undercover financial donations made by Russia to each. It was clear now that the far-right in Ireland wasn't just fighting against immigrants, they had now co-opted the climate debate, claiming to be the true defenders of rural Ireland and its farmers. Russia's financial support was funneled directly to these groups, giving them the resources to spread panic-inducing misinformation. They were slyly positioning themselves as champions of rural dwellers, accusing environmental activists and mainstream political parties of betraying the rural Ireland. With Russia's backing, they had the means to build a dangerous grassroots movement that, not only fought against climate reforms, but also stoked dangerous racist sentiments. But the manipulation wasn't just happening online—it was now being carried out on the ground, with real money backing it.

And yet another folder revealed even more stomach-curdling hypocrisy. It also confirmed something Lana had been beginning to suspect, that the Russians may have had input from someone in the Republican Party with in-country knowledge. She had thought that maybe Russians on the ground here in Ireland, working at the Russian embassy, could have been the source for the intel on cultural and political movements in this country. But the next folder had to have come from a Republican source: it was contained in a file labelled "Corporate Class v. Working Class". Now the Russians were intent on stirring class warfare in Ireland too.

Lana scrolled through the files, which contained more

CHAPTER 24

malicious social media content, this time aimed at creating a divide between the business elite and the working class. The messages targeted businesspeople in Ireland, subtly assuring them that although the Republicans were campaigning hard for the working-class vote, the real loyalty of the party lay with the corporate class. It was cynical and deeply manipulative. The strategy involved courting the working class to win the election, but at the same time, making it clear to wealthy supporters, through covert "dark posts", that once in government, the Republicans would reward "the real wealth creators" as they referred to business people, with government contracts and lucrative opportunities. Laws against corruption didn't seem to apply apparently.

The messaging to corporate Ireland was tantalising: Support the Republican Party in the election, and they would inherit the mantle of Ireland's great Republican heroes—Padraig Pearse, Arthur Griffith, W.B. Yeats, Daniel O'Connell, and Countess Markievicz. It was a pitch designed to inflame national pride while subtly promising that the spoils of power would go to those who helped the party into government. But the party's plans to swiftly dismiss the Irish working class once elected, in favour of the business class, was shocking to Lana given how hard the party was campaigning for their support.

By now, the pitch-blackness of the night had given way to a soft morning glow. Exhausted, Lana pushed herself away from her computer and stood, stretching her aching arms. She walked to the window and drew back the curtains, with the brightness of the morning light burning her tired eyes. Opening the window fully, she hoped letting in a burst of fresh air would help to clear her mind. Then it was back to pacing the room again, as she struggled to process all she had uncovered that night. With each step, her mind churned and struggled and churned, grasping for a solution in the quiet before the world awoke.

The sheer magnitude of the corruption and deceit she had discovered felt overwhelming. But despite the mountain of incriminating evidence from the Serbian server confirming the Republican Party as the beneficiary of those underhanded schemes, one key piece of evidence was still missing—a concrete link to Russia. Lana only hoped that her friend Robyn might have desperately thought of something overnight, though she knew it was the longest of long shots. But it was the only hope she had as the hour approached 9:00am.

Outside, it was a frosty, tranquil morning—that gave no hint of what lay ahead.

Chapter 25

Lana wasn't the only one doing a spot of hacking that day.

Someone else was as well.

A young man named Peter, aged 23 years was glued to a computer set-up in front of him, drinking mug after mug of coffee and chain-smoking cigarette after cigarette. The dim glow of the triple monitor set-up was the only light in his dingy apartment, where the curtains were drawn tightly shut, blocking out any hint of daylight. The air inside was thick, a stifling blend of stale cigarette smoke and the lingering smell of coffee. Empty mugs were scattered across the desk, alongside half-eaten bags of snacks and an ashtray overflowing with cigarette butts.

But Peter's concentration never wavered, despite the chaotic surroundings. The apartment was a mess of spare electronic parts—circuit boards, cables, and old laptops strewn haphazardly across the floor and stacked on shelves. It was as though he had built himself a fortress of technology, with only his screens to keep him company. Each screen displayed a different feed: one flickered with lines of code scrolling rapidly, another showed network maps and IP addresses pinging in real-time, while a third streamed traffic cams, public servers, and unprotected Wi-Fi connections he could easily tap into.

He took another drag from his cigarette, his eyes narrowing as he traced a connection he'd been chasing for hours, maybe days. It was hard to tell in this windowless haze. Time seemed to blur in that single-room apartment, marked only by the number of mugs piling up beside him and the constant cycle of cigarettes he chain-smoked to keep himself sharp.

Peter wasn't your average hacker. He was meticulous, patient, and, above all, untraceable. His fingers danced over the keys, navigating from one encrypted system to another with ease, as if he were born for this. Somewhere across the network, firewalls gave way, and Peter smirked, leaning back slightly in his chair. He didn't care about the politics or the chaos he helped stir from behind his screens. For him, it was all about the game, the thrill of bypassing security, the rush of slipping undetected through systems thought to be impenetrable.

As he munched on a packet of crisps, his mind flitted between tasks. His spare computers, scattered around the room like forgotten toys, were processing large data sets—bots working quietly in the background to scrape information and map weak points. Every once in a while, Peter glanced at one of the secondary screens, making minor adjustments or checking the status of a system he was trying to crack. He cracked his knuckles, took another swig of coffee, and focused again.

Today's target was different though—something big was in the air. His encrypted messages hinted at major moves

CHAPTER 25

being made, and Peter had been pulled into the action from a distance, part of a much larger operation. But for now, it was just him, his computers, and the glow of his monitors in this dim, smoke-filled room.

As his screen pinged with a confirmation—a door he'd been trying to open for hours now unlocked—Peter couldn't help but grin. Somewhere out there, things were about to get interesting. He didn't know where this would lead, but that didn't matter. For now, he was in.

*****

All over Ballina on Ireland's north west coast, people were struggling with the ongoing water crisis. Recent tests conducted by Irish Water had revealed elevated levels of manganese—a naturally occurring mineral in the soil—in the town's water supply. Unlike the more common outbreaks of *E. coli* that sporadically plagued County Mayo due to cattle slurry contamination, the manganese issue was far more serious. While boiling water might solve bacterial contamination, it did nothing to eliminate manganese. Ingesting too much of this mineral posed a significant risk to the nervous system, and residents were forced to collect water daily from a county council tanker, re-organising their day or their work around the timing of the tanker's arrival in their locality.

For Jennifer Davenport, a 32-year-old single mother of two small children, the disruption only added to her already overwhelming daily routine. She lived in an apartment complex on the outskirts of town with her two-and-a-half-year-old toddler and one-year-old infant. Every evening felt like a test of endurance. After collecting her children from crèche, she would navigate the stairs to her second-floor apartment, juggling the baby in her arms while dragging the collapsed double buggy behind her. All the while, she would try to coax her exhausted toddler to walk alongside her after a long day.

But today, even the promise of a treat after dinner wasn't enough to calm her toddler's tantrum. As her daughter wailed in defiance, Jennifer's patience was stretched to the breaking point. She felt the sting of tears welling up in her eyes, the weight of exhaustion and frustration overwhelming her. It was then that a familiar voice saved her from the edge of despair —Thomas Fitzgerald, her neighbour from the first floor, called out to offer help. Thomas was a 55-year-old man living with multiple sclerosis and had always been a kind neighbour, despite his own serious health struggles.

"Jennifer, can I give you a hand there?" he asked coming down the stairs to meet her.

"Tom, that would be great. I'm sorry for all the commotion from little missy here," she said, looking at her over-tired little daughter, as Tom took the buggy from her. "I hope I didn't wake you?" she asked. Jennifer knew her neighbour's exhaustion due to his illness meant he had to nap a couple of times during the day in order to cope.

"I was just up. Couldn't sleep today but what do you do. This water crisis is bothering everybody at the moment."

"My mother dropped in earlier on her lunch break with drums of water for me. You're more than welcome to some, Tom. I know you don't drive. Do you have anyone helping you to pick up water and carry it back?"

"I got a taxi as far as the tanker today and he dropped me back again. I've enough water now that should do me for three days and I can go out again then."

"Mum's picking up water for me, herself and her neighbour, Mattie Hughes. He's 80 and in a bad way with his joints from arthritis. She has to pick it up each day at lunch time, so I'll ask her to stick an extra drum in the car for you too, Tom. I know she'll be glad to help you, Tom. It's a nightmare for people who have their health, never mind those who don't."

"Your mother's an angel, Jennifer," he replied, leaving the buggy inside the door of the apartment.

"I know. Everyone thinks their own mother is the greatest, but mine really is. Come in for a cuppa with us, Tom."

"I won't this evening, Jennifer. I've chicken in the oven and I better keep an eye on it."

"Well then, here's an extra drum of water for you," she said, heaving one off the kitchen counter."

"I feel bad taking this," he said.

"Don't, Tom. Plenty more where they came from. We all have to pull together in a crisis like this."

"I'll remember that, Jennifer. If there's anything I can do for you and the little ones, or you need me to mind them for you some evening, just let me know."

"Oh Lord, you've no idea what you'd be letting yourself in for with these two little crazies, but thanks for offering Tom, I appreciate it."

As Jennifer and Thomas parted ways, across town at the local Spar shop outside Glencullen estate, shop owner Des Killallen was facing another layer of frustration, on top of collecting water to run the deli in his shop. The usual after-work rush had hit, with customers streaming in to pick up a few groceries. But earlier that day, around midday, the card payment system had gone down, throwing Des's routine into chaos. He'd spent the entire afternoon scrambling to find enough change to keep the shop running.

His first stop was the bank, but they were out of cash due to the sheer volume of businesses in the same predicament. Next, he tried the local bookie's office, only to find he'd been beaten to it by other desperate business owners. His last attempt brought him to the parish priest, who luckily, hadn't yet deposited cash from recent masses. With that, Des managed to scrape by for most of the day. But now, as the clock neared half past five, he knew his change would run out by six. After that, he'd only be able to serve customers who had the exact cash on hand.

For a small business owner like Des, having to turn away customers was frustrating. But it was just as exasperating for shoppers who didn't have change to pay for their groceries. Des resolved to allow his regulars to take their groceries "on the slate"—a system of trust where purchases would be noted in a book and paid for later. Despite the chaos, his spirits were lifted whenever he saw customers in the queue helping out complete strangers by exchanging change with them. It was a small but heartwarming reminder that, even amidst all the frustration, the world wasn't gone to hell after all. There was hope for humanity.

Meanwhile, it wasn't just in Ballina or North Mayo where people's patience was being tested. Other towns across Ireland were dealing with their own local crises too. In some areas, repeated E. coli outbreaks necessitated constant water boiling, frustrating families and businesses alike. Rush hour traffic chaos was a feature of poor road planning and traffic management in Ireland for years. But repeated problems with traffic signaling had, in recent weeks, been driving people

CHAPTER 25

in those towns insane with stress with miles of tailbacks for commuters.

One particularly maddening incident in Galway even made the national news. In order to allow massive transport trucks carrying wind turbine parts to pass through during the night, engineers had turned off the city's traffic lights. However, when they tried to switch them back on the next morning, the system failed, plunging the entire city into gridlock for nearly twenty-four hours. The resulting traffic jams lasted for hours, and with tens of minor collisions, the city's A&E department—already stretched to its limits—was flooded with patients. It was a day that tested the patience and endurance of everyone affected.

In Dublin city, the M50 ring road was an everyday stress trap for city workers who had to run the gauntlet of it twice a day. Any disruption to the traffic flow—a car breaking down in one lane or, even worse, a collision that blocked two or more lanes—was enough to push even the calmest commuters to the edge. For 33-year-old Carol Kenny, these nightmare days seemed to be happening more frequently than usual. Local traffic reports had been blaming signaling issues with traffic lights feeding into the M50 from surrounding roads, but whatever the cause, the result was the same: gridlock.

Every evening as she left work at 5:30 p.m., Carol anxiously checked traffic updates on her phone, hoping for a clear route home. But even if it looked like she had a clear run at 5.30pm leaving work, that didn't mean it would remain that way for the rest of her commute. The unpredictability of it all left her on edge. And like most commuters, the worst part of getting stuck in traffic wasn't just the delay itself, but the mounting stress of having children to pick up.

Especially for parents of children at crèche. Most crèches fined parents in increasing increments for every ten minutes late. Crèche fees were already astronomical—considered a second mortgage by most young parents—so adding fines for being late on top of that pushed parents' stress levels into orbit.

But it wasn't just parents who felt the strain. Crèche owners and staff were under pressure too, juggling the responsibility of caring for children all day while having to hold staff late to cover for parents stuck in traffic. It was no party either for older kids waiting at the school gates to be picked up from sports or other activities, for their parents they thought were never coming.

To make matters worse, some evenings brought another layer of chaos: phone coverage issues. Carol, like many parents, would frantically try to call someone—her own parents, a friend, anyone who could help with the pick-up—but if the phone network was down, there was no way to get through. The sense of helplessness was overwhelming, a rising panic as the minutes ticked by and traffic crawled along, her children waiting, and no way to reach them. Every day felt like a high-wire act, with no guarantee that the next commute wouldn't bring yet another disaster. And all the while the commuters were looked down from on high by Jennifer Fitzgerald, the Republican Party leader spouting "change" from a billboard in the most prominent position above the traffic trap. The M50 was more than just a road—it was a battleground, where traffic, time, and stress collided.

Vigilante attacks on mobile phone towers were quietly escalating, fueled by disinformation circulating online about the so-called "dangers" of 5G networks. Fearing more

CHAPTER 25

copycat incidents, authorities had been keeping the news of these attacks under wraps, but the telecom companies were becoming increasingly anxious. They were pushing the government to address the issue, urging a discreet crackdown. In response, the government tasked the Department of Communications to launch a social media campaign aimed at countering the rampant misinformation about 5G.

And it wasn't just phone networks that were being hit. The government was concerned about the increasing number of internet outages and the cost to the economy it was causing, not just in terms of business lost during the outage, but also the risk to Ireland's reputation as place to do business amongst the multinationals based here. There was a growing fear that if the infrastructure remained unreliable, these companies could relocate, leading to massive job losses.

The ripple effects of these outages were widespread. Employees couldn't receive their wages on time, ATMs were going offline, card payment systems were disrupted, and businesses were scrambling to not let down customers. But the most profound stress caused by infrastructure failures wasn't financial—it was human. And no one felt that stress more intensely than Conor O'Brien.

Conor had received a text message from the HSE (Health Service Executive), informing him that his scheduled hip replacement surgery at Castlebar General Hospital had been postponed due to overcrowding in A&E. The news hit him like a hammer. For two long years, Conor had been waiting in unbearable pain, his life a misery. Whether he was sitting, standing, walking, or even lying down, the constant gut-wrenching pain from his deteriorating hip had brought him to the brink of suicide. This operation had been his only hope, and now even that had been taken away.

To make matters worse, Conor's pleas for stronger pain relief were caught in a bureaucratic nightmare. Irish doctors, under immense pressure not to over-prescribe opioid painkillers in light of the opioid epidemic in the US, seemed reluctant to prescribe him anything more effective than mild painkillers. The authorities, however, failed to acknowledge that the US crisis had been caused by excessive, high-dose prescriptions. In Ireland, there appeared to be an almost blanket ban on prescribing opioids, except in the most extreme cases. Even when opioids were prescribed, patients like Conor were forced to endure a grueling, incremental process of starting with the lightest dose and waiting months in agony for even small increases. For patients in their 80s and 90s with incurable conditions like Conor, these restrictions felt like the worst kind of cruelty. While concerns about addiction and tolerance were valid in younger patients, applying these same rigid standards to elderly individuals, especially those with severe, lifelong pain, was senseless. Doctors' intentions may have been well-meaning, but in Conor's case, they were leaving him to suffer in silence, his quality of life deteriorating day by day, with no relief in sight.

As Conor sat in pain in the quiet of his home day-in day-out, the text from the HSE felt like a final blow. He wasn't just another statistic lost in Ireland's crumbling healthcare infrastructure. He was a man nearing his breaking point, struggling just to survive each day.

A government committee looking into the pros and cons of introducing assisted suicide in this country heard from a palliative care consultant who dismissed the necessity for an assisted suicide regime. He claimed that patients could be made comfortable with pain relief medication and depression could be taken care of his colleagues in psychiatry. Conor nearly threw the radio across the kitchen in despair when he heard it on the news, his lived experience being the total opposite. But instead, he buried his head in his hands and sobbed. He hadn't cried that hard since he was an 8-year-old little boy, who lost his mother to cancer on the day before Christmas Eve.

It was the sick and elderly who also bore the brunt of the raft of electricity outages happening across the country. Ireland's booming data center industry had been making headlines for some time, drawing attention to the enormous strain it was placing on the national power grid. Reports highlighted how often the system entered amber and red alerts, signaling the possibility of outages, and so the public had come to accept the likelihood of power cuts as an inevitable consequence of a system under pressure, assuming they were just minor hiccups until the government and industry figured out a long-term solution.

So when smaller, localised outages occurred, people barely questioned them, chalking them up to the larger energy crisis. It was only when an outage in Mayo caused a fire at an electricity substation that it received more publicity when local journalist, Robyn Mayhew investigated it further and uncovered the cause as an external hack.

While the story itself was chilling, it was even more terrifying for people like Kathleen Hanahoe. At 65, Kathleen had been battling COPD (chronic obstructive pulmonary disease) for years, relying on an oxygen machine at home that needed a constant, stable power supply. Even a brief interruption in electricity could put her health, and potentially her life, at serious risk. The thought of a power outage was no minor inconvenience for her— it was a source of daily anxiety.

The same was true for 14-year-old Russell Jackson, who had been living with cystic fibrosis since birth. His condition caused thick, sticky mucus to build up in his lungs, making it incredibly difficult to breathe. Russell relied on medical equipment to help clear his lungs and keep his airways open. For people like Kathleen and Russell, even the suggestion of an electricity outage increased their daily stress to panic levels. For them and their families, it wasn't just about keeping the lights on, but keeping them alive.

*****

Elsewhere, Peter's eyes blurred as he stared at the lines of code on his screen, his brain growing sluggish from hours of intense focus. The urge to abandon his work and dive into one of his computer games gnawed away at him, but he fought it off. He had a new program to finish—a key piece in his latest venture—and distractions were costly. Yet, despite his best efforts, his concentration was slipping. He needed a break.

With a sigh, Peter decided to get some fresh air. The thought of walking down ten flights of stairs to the ground floor was a curse in itself, but it was nothing compared to the climb back up. The lifts in his building hadn't worked in years. Despite living in what was considered a better-than-average tower block in this city, things were always breaking down and never got fixed. Broken lights, cracked walls, malfunctioning systems — everything was dilapidated here.

Not that he had to live like this. By comparison to most people here, Peter was wealthy. His illicit online activities had

CHAPTER 25

made him rich beyond what his neighbours could imagine. But he chose to stay here, in the tower block where he had grown up. The crumbling environment didn't bother him, it felt familiar. Comfortable, even. The only indulgence of his wealth was a collection of supercars he stored in a rented garage across the city. They were the lone symbols of his success, tucked away from prying eyes.

He would have loved to indulge in something bigger, traveling the world maybe, seeing the places he had only read about. But that was impossible. His shady business dealings meant there were international arrest warrants with his name on them. So for now, he was confined to his own world, one where his wealth stayed hidden and his life was bound by the limits of his chosen seclusion.

Peter descended the flights of stairs, his footsteps echoing in the cold, dimly lit stairwell. When he finally reached the street, he breathed in deeply, the cold February air biting his lungs. Ironically, as he took in the fresh air, he reached for a cigarette, lighting it and taking a long drag. He stood there for a moment, looking out over the cold grey streets, his thoughts distant. He was a man trapped by his own choices, bound to a life of secrecy and isolation. For a moment, he let his mind wander to places he could never go, the corners of the world he would only ever see through the glow of his computer screens. Then, with a resigned sigh, he took another drag of the cigarette and turned back toward the stairs. It was time to get back to work.

Shivering in the cold, he zipped his coat all the way up, pulling the fur-lined hood over his head and ears, bracing himself against the cold. It was a freezing cold February day.

Even for St. Petersburg, Russia.

Chapter 26

Although their frustrations were tempered somewhat by the kindness of strangers and neighbours in the midst of crisis, Jennifer, Tom, Des *et al*, all went home more stressed than usual that evening. And it wasn't just them—across Ireland, from town to town, the same stories were playing out.

Ballina had borne the brunt that day, but other places had suffered similarly disruptive breakdowns in recent weeks. In Ennis, it was an electricity outage; in Wexford, it had been the water supply and in Wicklow town, an unexpected road closure caused gridlock for hours.

While the outages made headlines in the local media in the counties where they occurred, none made the national headlines. So nobody was connecting the dots. No one, that is, except Robyn Mayhew. You see, her job path as a journalist was a bit different to that of others. Most journalists enter the profession by one of two paths—either working in an unpaid internship in the national media in Dublin hoping they'll eventually get a paid role, or working for a local paper for a couple of years until they built up experience and then,

CHAPTER 26

if they wished, they'd move to the national media. But when Robyn finished journalism school, she was eager to start work and so applied for jobs in several different counties, not just her home town. When a job came up in *The Mayo Herald*, she jumped at it. Working in local news in a county other than the one in which she grew up, gave her a unique advantage—it meant she knew what was going on in two counties at all times. People living in Mayo thought it was only their county that was struggling with infrastructural issues. But Robyn knew it was happening in Galway as well. So there was a good chance it was country-wide and nobody had yet realised that. Well, the water and electricity companies probably did, but they were keeping quiet for their own reasons.

To see if her hunch was correct, Robyn decided to ring around to friends, cousins and acquaintances from various counties around the country. Thanks to these connections, Robyn was fully in the picture—outages and breakdowns were happening in those counties as well, ones that seemed to mirror what was happening in Mayo. With friends scattered across Ireland and a network of colleagues keeping her informed, she couldn't help but notice a pattern emerging. It almost felt as if Ireland was starting to break down. Could cutbacks during the austerity years after the recession of 2008 have resulted in neglect of national infrastructure that was only coming home to roost now? Robyn wondered to herself.

But maybe it wasn't the fault of successive governments since either. Maybe the fault lay with the tech that we'd come to rely on so heavily in the past two decades. If the development of the internet and social media had taught the world anything, it was that tech titans often failed to foresee the problems their innovations would create. They built, released, and rushed out new products, only coming back to fix problems later, an approach that hadn't worked out well in hindsight. Major societal concerns like content moderation, disinformation, and child protection on social media had been treated as "bugs" to iron out later, rather than the existential threats to society right now that they truly were.

Robyn made a mental note to look into the whole conundrum after the election was over. Then she thought better of it and put a note in her phone instead. With all that was swirling around in her head these days, there was a good chance it could slip her mind to follow up on it. But what Robyn didn't know that day was that she was both right and wrong in her thinking. The fault did lie with technology, but also with government—just not the Irish government.

The Russian government, on the other hand, had a vested interest in sowing civil disruption throughout the West. Russia had long used infrastructural breakdowns as a tool of chaos, starting with the former Soviet republics of Georgia and Ukraine in 2008 and 2014. Back then, Russia had tried to destabilise elections and install friendly governments in those countries. When those attempts failed, they resorted to military invasions. This tactic was now being replicated across Europe and the US in a more subtle form: using breakdowns in infrastructure to fuel frustration and instability.

For Vladimir Putin, the goal was clear: disrupt the social and political fabric of Western nations to discredit the idea of liberal democracy. By sowing frustration with constant failures in everyday systems, from power outages to water supply disruptions, he hoped to convince the Russian people that they were better off under the autocratic system of government in Russia, with him at the helm.

But how could Putin engineer infrastructural breakdowns in a country like Ireland? It sounded like something out of science fiction. Unfortunately, it wasn't. There was a single thread running through all the outages and breakdowns.

They were all connected by the same antivirus software.

It had been developed by a company in the UK in the early '90s and, in order to make inroads in a market dominated by McAfee, the software was sold at a massive discount to retailers, who then had a significant profit motive to push the sale of that anti-virus software over others. This resulted in large-scale purchasing of this software by big corporations, public utilities and many private households throughout Europe and the US. What no one realised at the time was that this widespread adoption would one day become a critical vulnerability, one that foreign actors like Russia could exploit.

Through carefully orchestrated cyberattacks, Russia was able to infiltrate the systems of key infrastructure providers, targeting them through the very software meant to protect them. And now, Robyn was beginning to unravel the threads of a much larger and more dangerous plot than she had ever imagined.

The key thing about antivirus software is that, in order for it to function effectively, it requires deep access into the user's system. This level of access, combined with the intentional backdoor left in the software by its developers, meant that any system running the software could be remotely controlled by the people who created it. It turned out that the parent company of the software developer was based in Moscow. While that might sound alarming now, the landscape in the early 1990s was different. With the Cold War over, the West was optimistic about Russia's shift toward capitalism, eager to foster relations and trade. No one could foresee that, by 1999 with the rise of Vladimir Putin to power, that optimistic chapter would soon close and indeed, take a very dark turn.

The developers of this particular antivirus software were now known to have close ties to Russian military and intelligence officials. And, despite Putin's aggressive policies, Russian software was still running on critical infrastructure across the West, giving Moscow a backdoor and deep access into vital municipal and industrial systems. It was these Russian intelligence officials who brought Peter Gogachev into the fold, a world-renowned Russian hacker tasked with doing the dirty work of Russia's intelligence services. Gogachev's expertise had been cultivated under the watchful eye of Russia's FSB (the successor to the KGB), the SVR (Russia's external intelligence service) and the GRU (Russia's military intelligence arm). These agencies often turned a blind eye to the activities of hackers like Gogachev, as long as they confined their illegal exploits to targets outside of Russia. Much like their arrangement with the Russian mafia, the "Vory," the government tolerated certain criminal activities in exchange for the criminals' cooperation when the state required it. This allowed the Russian government to maintain plausible deniability while engaging in cyber warfare.

And so, Robyn's friend, Lana wasn't the only hacker at work that day. Peter Gogachev was busy hacking Ireland and had been for some time. Gogachev, a programming prodigy in his mid-thirties, had turned to hacking at a young age after growing up amidst the economic turmoil of post-Soviet Russia. He became a key asset for Russian intelligence, running a vast botnet of millions of computers that spanned the globe. This botnet gave him the power to launch devastating cyberattacks, all from the safety of his apartment.

This was why cybersecurity experts always advise it's so important to power down your devices at night. Gogachev's malware, installed secretly on millions of computers across the world, allowed him to control them without the owners' knowledge. When left on overnight, these computers became unwitting slaves in his botnet, often used in distributed denial-of-service (DDoS) attacks. These attacks worked by flooding a website's server with an overwhelming amount of internet traffic, effectively crippling it and denying users access. By the time people returned to their devices the next morning, they would have no idea their computers had been hijacked in the middle of the night to carry out criminal activities. For hackers like Gogachev, the digital world was a playground. And Ireland, much like the rest of the West, was simply another target in his ever-expanding web of cyber subterfuge.

When Russian intelligence services first enlisted Peter Gogachev, it was initially to deploy his massive botnet for cyber operations around the world. His task had been simple at first: direct the botnet toward global targets and disrupt networks as needed. But as time went on, they realised his potential went beyond mere sabotage. They began to ask more of him, pushing Gogachev to take a more hands-on role in their covert operations, hacking directly into specific industrial systems. This time, they had set their sights on Ireland.

Gogachev's mission began with Ireland's public water utility. Using his botnet and a few stealthy commands, he slipped into their servers unnoticed. He knew from his experience hacking into Ukraine's infrastructure that water contamination was a surefire way to cause mass panic. His eyes scanned the lab readings from recent water tests in Mayo. He immediately recognised manganese as his weapon of choice. At elevated levels, manganese was highly toxic to the human nervous system, and simply boiling water wouldn't eliminate the threat. The only solution would be to bring in water tankers, forcing local residents to queue for their daily supply.

With a few clicks, Gogachev manipulated the readings, doubling the manganese levels to well beyond the safe limit. He sent the altered results into the system and moved on, repeating the process across several counties, randomly increasing E. coli levels in some and cryptosporidium in others, just to sow more chaos. Once finished, he erased all traces of his digital fingerprints, vanishing from the system as quickly as he had entered.

Next, he turned his attention to electricity. The outage that had crippled North Mayo wasn't a stroke of bad luck—it was Gogachev's handiwork. Breaking into the smart meters of almost two hundred homes, he used his botnet to remotely switch them off, creating a sudden and significant drop in electricity demand. The abrupt change in load caused the local substation's equipment to overheat, igniting a fire. This plunged the entire region into darkness, cutting off power from towns right along North Mayo.

Gogachev didn't stop there. He replicated the attack across several regions in Ireland, timing the blackouts to coincide with the peak frustration of parents arriving home from work. Exhausted, with hungry children in tow, these families found themselves in cold, dark homes, unable to cook, bathe their children, or carry out any of their evening routines. The disruption was more than just an inconvenience, it was deeply distressing, particularly for families with vulnerable children. Parents of children on the autism spectrum were hit the hardest. Their kids, already struggling with sensory processing, went into meltdown when they were overwhelmed by the sudden darkness and, being unable to use tools that usually calmed them like laptops or tablets that offered a source of comfort.

For elderly people, the situation was equally grim. Many managed with candles, not knowing how to use the flashlight on their smartphones or hesitant to drain their phone batteries, worried they would need to make an emergency call in case of a fall or other accident. For the sickest among them, especially those dependent on nebulisers or oxygen machines, there was no choice but to call for an ambulance, as the sudden loss of power threatened their health. Ambulances rushed to homes, transporting these patients to overwhelmed A&E departments, where at least backup generators kept the lights on. The emergency rooms, already overburdened, were pushed to their limits by the influx of elderly and chronically ill patients.

But not that hospitals were out of Peter Gogachev's reach. Far from it. He simply hadn't unleashed a major cyberattack on them—yet. Thanks to the Russian antivirus software running on their systems, Gogachev could access hospital networks with ease. The strange case at Mayo General Hospital that Robyn had noticed—elective surgeries being mysteriously cancelled unknownst to the hospital's doctors or management—was a simply another instance of Gogachev's handiwork.

Once inside the hospital's network, Gogachev found a web

text application that sent automated messages to patients. Within the system was a template used to notify patients of elective surgery cancellations. After some digging, he located the list of patients scheduled for procedures the following day, along with their phone numbers. With a few keystrokes, he populated the template, sending out a wave of cancellation texts.

The next morning, surgeons and nurses showed up at the operating theaters, scrubbed in and ready to operate, only to find not a single patient had arrived. Confusion reigned in the hospital corridors, and while the HSE (Health Service Executive) suspected a cyberattack, they kept it quiet, pending a full investigation. Meanwhile, patients waiting for vital surgeries such hip replacements, gallbladder removals, hernia repairs and more were left in pain and in limbo, with their procedures postponed for weeks. Gogachev's attack wasn't just a digital annoyance, it was a calculated strike that delayed critical care and brought unnecessary pain and hardship on innocent people.

Traffic light outages, though not as life-threatening as hospital delays, still had the potential for massive chaos too and even danger. A malfunction at a major intersection could snarl traffic for miles and Gogachev knew how to exploit that as well. The incident in Galway, where traffic lights were turned off overnight to allow massive transport trucks carrying wind turbine parts to pass through the city, had all the hallmarks of a Gogachev attack. The following morning, city officials found themselves unable to turn the lights back on, leading to gridlock that lasted for hours. While local authorities battled to unravel the technical glitch, Gogachev was behind the scenes, laughing at the chaos he had sown on

CHAPTER 26

Ireland's west coast.

The same pattern appeared on Dublin's M50 motorway, a critical commuter route that circled the city and funneled hundreds of thousands of people to and from work each day. By subtly manipulating the traffic light sequences, Gogachev created long tailbacks, causing immense frustration. Mile after mile of tailbacks, honking horns and growing delays became the norm, while traffic control officials were left baffled. And to Gogachev and the Russian puppet masters, every fender-bender or collision that resulted from these disruptions was a welcome bonus, further entrenching the confusion and disorder.

And so, the seeds of discontent were quietly sown, well in advance of the upcoming election, turning daily frustrations into simmering anger directed at the government. To the cynical masterminds behind the operation in Russia, the strategy was simple: make people's lives harder, then urge them to "vote for change."

However, the disruption couldn't be too obvious. Gogachev and his associates knew better than to knock out water, electricity, and traffic lights all on the same day, a triple event that would make national headlines. No, the success of this civil disruption campaign depended on subtlety, on keeping the chaos just under the radar. It had to be covert at all costs. Some days it was just a simple knocking offline of card payment systems that would do the trick. Phase I of "Operation Ireland" was designed to stir frustration without sparking outright suspicion, and it was working.

As Ireland's citizens grappled with outages and breakdowns, the infamous troll factory at 55 Savushkina Street in St. Petersburg began its digital offensive. The puppet masters at

Russian intelligence believed that if you made people's daily lives harder, the next step was easy: push the narrative that they deserved better and offer them an alternative.

In Wexford town, phones buzzed with social media content in the wake of the water crisis. Each night for a week, carefully crafted posts flooded Instagram, Facebook, and Twitter feeds, telling citizens that clean drinking water was a basic right, one the current government had failed to deliver, and that a Republican government would take charge of the situation and fix it. Some posts took a more aggressive tone, calling out the government for its perceived weakness: "This government needs to be taken out and put those with balls in charge." Each message was tailored to the personality of the viewer, using data-driven techniques on how best to manipulate their frustrations.

Meanwhile, on phones geolocated to drivers all along the M50 where drivers, trapped in miles of tailbacks thanks to Gogachev's tampering with the traffic lights, had social media videos served up with from local Republican candidates. "The M50 has become a nightmare. It's stealing away the time you get to spend with your family and robbing your quality of life. We've endured this for too long. It's time to vote for change." The message was drilled into commuters, night after night, as they sat in traffic with little else to do but absorb the carefully constructed narrative. The operation was effective precisely because it was so insidious. Every frustration, every inconvenience, every moment spent waiting in the dark or stuck in traffic was weaponised against the government, with Russia's hand quietly guiding the anger towards a Republican Party government.

Two thousand miles away in the troll factory in St. Petersburg, those feeding us those messages knew everything about us, but they were unseen and anonymous, like ghosts in the wires. They knew our names, where we lived, and even what thoughts occupied our minds. They were experts at pressing the exact buttons that would elicit the strongest reactions from us, timing them perfectly for when we were most stressed or vulnerable. Each piece of social media content they delivered was tailored and personalised to manipulate specific personality types, designed to push us towards their objectives with frightening precision.

And it wasn't just in the aftermath of civil disruption campaigns that the ghosts of 55 Savushkina Street appeared. They had other active campaigns too, including the anti-5G movement. Russia's intelligence services had marked 5G technology as a threat to their interests, knowing that it gave Western economies a competitive edge. As a result, pushing concocted 5G conspiracy theories in the West became a priority for them, and their operatives worked tirelessly to fan the flames of misinformation falsely linking 5G tech to heart defects, autism, cancer, infertility and a host of other false claims. The Newport, County Mayo, phone mast incident was a direct result of their efforts. Ironically, the mast damaged in that case was a 4G tower, but the puppet masters never let their followers know that public maps showed the difference between 4G and 5G towers. To them, it was all about spreading as much chaos as possible.

Another favorite campaign pushed by the Russian powers was anti-vaccine propaganda. They weren't anti-vax because they believed vaccinations were dangerous, far from it. In fact, according to academic studies, Russian citizens themselves enjoyed a high vaccine uptake rate. The intelligence services' goal was to sow disruption and hardship in the West, and promoting anti-vax movements was an effective way to weaken the social fabric. As people in Europe and the US became more skeptical of vaccines, public health suffered, and that instability served Russian interests.

The anti-vax and anti-5G campaigns were worldwide, but for the months of January and February 2020, the infrastructural chaos campaigns just had Ireland in its sights. And while the outages and outbreaks appeared to be sporadic at first, they were anything but. They were all cleverly located, timed for maximum effect and followed a clear pattern.

The disruption campaigns targeted fourteen towns and electoral areas across the country—electoral areas where the government held seats that they were in danger of losing to the opposition.

Each time these disruptions occurred, local residents were flooded with anti-government, pro-Republican messaging the moment they logged onto social media, urging them to "vote for change."

And there was one other campaign being waged by the Russian puppet masters that tied it all together seamlessly. It targeted a key tenet of Irish democracy, one which a frustrated Robyn Mayhew in County Mayo had long suspected was being manipulated. But as to the exact nature of that manipulation, she hadn't quite able been to put her finger on. Those damned polls—they were just too bloody fantastical to be real.

But that was because they weren't real.

For months, Putin's hackers had been quietly sitting inside the servers of every major polling company in Ireland. They'd infiltrated the secure online platforms used for gathering public opinion and had carefully calibrated the "results" to present a consistent, manipulated picture of public sentiment. Each poll painted the same story: a groundswell of support for the opposition, dissatisfaction with the government, and the inevitability of "change" on the horizon. The goal was to create the illusion of momentum to make it seem as though the tide had turned irreversibly against the sitting government.

But the hackers hadn't accounted for one variable.

Tom Doherty.

His new polling company had only opened its doors a few months before the election, and so his systems were untouched by the foreign interference.

His polls, grounded in real data, told the real truth. The Republicans were nowhere near the twenty plus per cent support levels other polling companies had stated. Instead, they were exactly where they had been only a few months earlier during the local elections.

Firmly under ten per cent.

Chapter 27

Robyn woke with an unusual heaviness in her chest, an invisible burden she hadn't felt the morning before. The silence in the house was telling. If Lana had made a breakthrough during the night, she would have come to her, no matter the hour. But no knock had come, no whisper in the dark. The stillness was its own quiet confirmation of failure. Their usual morning chat would no longer be about progress or hope—it would be about panic, and what came next.

Throwing his head in the direction of Lana at the kitchen table, Ger opened the back door to Robyn and correctly surmised: "I don't think that one slept a wink all night. You two are up to something, I reckon."

"Yeah, up to no good," Robyn responded in an unusually deflated tone.

Lana glanced up from her laptop, her tired eyes meeting Robyn's. No words were needed. The look they exchanged was one of mutual disappointment, a silent acknowledgment of their shared frustration. Without a word, Robyn crossed the kitchen and flipped the switch on the kettle. The soft hum of

CHAPTER 27

the water heating up filled the quiet space as Lana closed her laptop with a sharp snap, signaling the end of her exhaustive search. They walked together to Lana's room, the air heavy with a sense of defeat.

"I've every last detail on a massive election manipulation campaign," Lana began, sinking into her chair, "but nothing that ties it to Russia. It's infuriating. I found piles of data, gigabytes of information on the Irish electorate, stored in foreign computer systems in Serbia. But it's all useless unless we can confirm who's really behind it." She rubbed her temples, exhaustion evident in every word. "I'm sorry, Robyn. I know how badly you needed concrete evidence of a Russian link before the election moratorium kicks in this morning. I've tried everything, but my brain is fried. I'm done. There's nothing left I can think of." Her voice trailed off, the weight of her failure hanging between them.

"It was always going to be a moonshot, Lana. Here, relax. Drink this and take a break for a while."

"I'm so exhausted, Robyn, but I just wouldn't be able to sleep if I tried."

"What if we look at this another way?" her friend suggested.

"How do you mean?" Lana asked, with no energy left to summon even a modicum of enthusiasm.

"We've been in their computer systems, looking around inside. Now that we're in, why don't we try looking out the way?"

"You've lost me, Robyn."

"What I'm trying to say, Lana, is there any way, you can activate any webcams where that server is based in Serbia?"

"I probably could. But what would that achieve? We'd get a shot of some randomer Serbian guy at a computer screen."

"If we could get that far, I might be able to come up with the goods after that."

"It looks like long shots are our specialties these days, Robyn," she said dejectedly, as she turned to her computer again to begin, what she was sure would end up being another wild goose chase.

But fifteen minutes later, Lana called out to Robyn who had gone into the kitchen to do some work of her own. "I've got it."

"You got the shot?" her friend shouted, coming back down the hall excitedly. It was an image of a male in his early 30s, clean shaven and buzz-cut hairstyle. Definitely military or intelligence services, Robyn thought.

"Yeah, but I don't know what you're so excited about. This will be like trying to find a needle in a haystack.

"Ok, leave it with me. While I'm trying to put a name to this face, can I ask you another favour?

"Sure."

"Is it possible for you to find the IP address of that server we're investigating?" Robyn asked.

"Yeah, I can. But what will that prove? Other than the server is based in Serbia, which we know already," Lana asked, not entirely sure where her friend was going with it.

"Well, can you find a physical address then based on the IP address?"

"There are ways you can, yeah."

"If you can find the building address, that would be a big help and it might take us a lot closer to find our Russian link."

As Robyn's heart began to lift, sensing that the trail might not be gone completely cold on them, other dangers lurked that morning that she had no way of knowing about. She'd

CHAPTER 27

been at Lana's house for over half an hour, focused on the task at hand, unaware that someone had chosen this exact moment to slip around the back of her own home. The intruder moved swiftly, knowing the neighboring houses had a clear view into Robyn's backyard.

Equipped with lock-picking tools, the figure made quick work of the back door, gaining silent entry. He moved cautiously, staying on the ground floor, slipping from the utility room into the kitchen, and then through to the living room. It was the fireplace that drew his attention, because he had been here before on a recce. His movements methodical, the intruder pulled on a pair of gloves and gently slid the fire guard to the side. From the inside pocket of his jacket, he produced a neatly folded piece of plastic, red and blue in colour. It was only when he opened it out fully that its exact nature was revealed: bizarrely it was a six-pack bag of cheese and onion Tayto-branded crisps.

Meanwhile, at Lana's house, Robyn was hard at work completely unaware of the silent visitor to her house. She had started to run PimEyes, plus another reverse image searching tool, RevEye, to search across Russian social media, to try to find the identity of the man behind the screen. It was an eerie feeling, searching for such a stranger, having just photographed him the way they did, almost as if they were hunting for a ghost. All she had to go on was this fleeting shot and a lingering hope that he was indeed Russian, and not another Serbian cut-out meant to mislead them.

Her eyes looked across to Lana, who was deep in concentration in her own hunt for the Serbian IP address. The tension was palpable, each second stretching into an eternity as they desperately clung to the possibility of a breakthrough.

"How are you getting on there, Lan?" she asked, almost whispering with trepidation.

"I'm running this tool that I've used before, SudVPN LookUp, and hopefully it will do the trick. You enter the IP address and it should return a geographic location for that IP address. Got it!" she exclaimed. "That was easier than I thought. I was sure there would be an extra layer of security that I might not have been able to penetrate."

"Yes, Lana!" Robyn exclaimed, trying to keep her voice down, while high-fiving her friend excitedly at the same time.

"It's 14, Jovan Dobric Street, Belgrade."

Just as Lana announced her results, Robyn's computer pinged as her results came up. "We've got him!" she whisper-screamed to her friend. "He's on VKontakte. His name is Dimitri Sidorov!" Robyn beamed at her friend. VKontakte was Russia's most popular social media platform. Lana rushed over to see.

"I'll need you to help me with the Russian, Lan," Robyn asked.

"Sure. Let me take a look."

The friends scrolled through an avalanche of personal posts until they got to one that looked like a graduation picture. Robyn took note of the address and then left Lana to continue the trawl through the VKontakte platform to see if she could find out any other details about the nature of his work or whom he worked for.

This was where Robyn decided to crowdsource the investigation to some friends—an online international community of journalists, hobbyists and online investigators working in the area of, what was known as, "open-source intelligence." She put out a call for further information on the college that

CHAPTER 27

Dimitri Sidorov attended to see if it threw up anything of interest.

"Lana, I've reached out to the OSINT crowd online to see if they can help me with that photo. So park your search on VKontakte for the moment until we see if we get anywhere with that photo first. But, in the meantime, just getting back to the building address where the IP address is based, is there any way you can access security cameras on that building?"

"I can have a look and see. CCTV cameras are often hooked into a network wireless router with a built-in modem, and organisations do not always update the default network name and password. So it could be a simple hack, if that was the case. But assuming they take more care over the security of their cameras, I could just access the network and weave my way into the cameras that are connected to it."

"Ok, let's go for it and see if you can, Lana."

"On it," her friend replied, her exhaustion after a long night's hacking, evaporating in seconds with her new-found enthusiasm.

"Right, I'm in Robyn. What do you want me to do?" Lana told her excitedly.

"Ok, what is the quality like on those cameras? Is it decent?"

"Yeah, it's pretty good," Lana assured her.

"Ok, if we can capture stills of everyone entering and leaving the building for the next while and I'll reverse image search them as you send them to me."

"Brilliant, Robyn. I'd never have thought of something so simple."

"That's me—simple!" Robyn joked with her friend, who laughed back at her. "But I just hope we don't end up getting a bunch of images of Serbian people. We don't know if that building is multi-occupant or sole occupant, so it could be a big fat waste of time too. Oh, and just one other thing, Lana," she paused. "Could you see if there are any cameras facing onto the parking area. If there are, see if you can get any shots of registration plates. I just thought of something I read about a while back that might produce results."

While Robyn was deep in concentration, brainstorming ways to definitively link the Russians to the sabotage of the Irish general election, someone else was busy sabotaging the security of her home. Kneeling on the hearth of the fireplace, he carefully unfolded the large plastic wrapper. With the plastic laying on top of a fisted hand, he reached up into the chimney with it, wedging it into place well above the fire grate. Once satisfied, he got up and put the fire guard back in place, making everything look untouched.

His eyes scanned the room, searching for something specific. After a moment, he spotted it—on the top shelf of a cluttered bookshelf. He reached up, carefully removed the batteries from the carbon monoxide alarm, and then returned it to its original spot, almost exactly as he found it. But now, the once-bright red indicator light that ensured Robyn's protection from the silent, deadly gas, had gone dark.

Back at Lana's house only a few hundred yards further down the Rathbawn Road, Robyn leaned back against the headboard on Lana's bed as tears started to escape from her eyes and stream down her face.

They had done it.

After countless hours of work and frustration, they had found the Russian connection and could now go to the Irish government with proof. She had sent the photo they uncovered—an image of a younger Dimitri Sidorov, their

CHAPTER 27

webcam guy—out to the open-source intelligence community online. It didn't take long for confirmation to flood back: the academy Sidorov had graduated from in Volgograd, Russia was a known GRU training center. The GRU, Russia's military intelligence branch, was now undeniably linked to the Irish election sabotage campaign.

Lana looked across at her friend and she knew instinctively when she saw the tears. She got up from her desk and came over to hug her friend. Robyn filled her in on her find.

"I'm so proud of you Robyn."

"Of me?" she exclaimed. "Who has fought this battle every step of the way with me, Lana?"

Her friend smiled back at her. "We did it," she said quietly, her eyes welling up now too, proud of the fight she too had put up for her adoptive country.

"But I've a bunch more stills of car registrations for you if you still want them," Lana told her.

"Yeah, the more evidence the better," Robyn quipped, excitedly.

Robyn knew they were running out of time, but she knew every piece of evidence would be crucial to make their case to the authorities, so for another precious half hour, she continued to work. She started by accessing the Tor onion network to navigate the dark web. She had read recently that a searchable database of Russian vehicle registrations had surfaced after a hack of the central vehicle registration authority, and it would cement the Russian connection if she could find more evidence by that means.

With her heart pounding, Robyn began entering the registration plates they had photographed at the Serbian facility. One after another, she typed them in, but the results were strange. Every single vehicle returned the same registered address, but with different owners. Frustration mounted—was the database compromised? Desperate for answers, Robyn copied the mysterious address and entered it into Yandex, Russia's equivalent of Google. She wasn't sure what she expected to find, maybe a dead end, but what appeared on the screen made her blood run cold. The address—3 Grizodubovoy Street, Moscow—was the headquarters of Russian military intelligence, the GRU.

But even in her triumph, a nagging feeling tugged persistently at the back of her mind, an unease she couldn't shake. Something wasn't right, but she couldn't put it into words. It was probably just her nerves reacting to the intensity of everything she had just been through.

But her instincts, as always, were bang on the money. Though she had no idea just how close the danger really was.

Chapter 28

Robyn struggled to catch her breath, as she processed the enormity of what she'd just uncovered. But before she even got to share the breakthrough with Lana, her phone rang. She fumbled for it on the bed, her makeshift office for the morning, her hands still trembling from the shock of their discoveries.

It was Dara. His familiar voice echoed in her ear, but his words blurred as her mind raced ahead with what to do next. Robyn tried to focus on the conversation, catching a snippet—something about an update, something urgent—but her thoughts kept drifting back to 3 Grizodubovoy Street, to the GRU, to the proof she now held in her hands.

"Robyn, what the hell is wrong with you? You sound all over the place," Dara asked, concerned.

"Brain fog from the election," she blurted out, without thinking.

"Look, I need to talk to you about something. Where are you? Castlebar? Westport?"

"Castlebar, Dara. But I'm a bit tied up. Can we leave it until the weekend?"

"No, it's urgent, Robyn."

Now, it was her turn to be alarmed.

"Urgent?" she repeated. "Why is it urgent, Dara?"

"I need to show you. I have a picture you need to see."

"Are you at the house?" he asked her. Can I meet you there?"

"Yeah, OK," Robyn replied, reluctantly. "Just give me five minutes and I'll be there." Robyn exhaled dramatically after she rang off the call. Lana looked at her, now her turn to be concerned.

"Is everything OK?" she asked.

But Robyn beamed over at her friend, finally able to tell her they'd gotten the solid proof they'd be searching for, for days and nights. Lana was elated. The two friends hugged each other close, relief and triumph washing over them in waves. Tears rolled down their faces, a release of the tension and exhaustion they had been carrying for over a week.

They had done it.

Robyn would have to run meet Dara, but they agreed Lana would continue to reverse image search the pictures of those entering and leaving the Serbian facility on Russian social media so they could gather as much evidence as possible. When she was done, they would meet at Robyn's house and then start the process of informing the authorities. Time was of the essence, but for the first time in a long while, they both felt hopeful. The endgame was in sight.

Ger and Mike, Lana's trusty security detail who had been by her side 24/7 for the past number of weeks, were going to be their lucky shortcut to the top of the national security chain and intelligence division of the Gardai. The Close Protection

CHAPTER 28

Division was part of the Special Detective Unit which had responsibility for national security and counterintelligence. It had been a source of comfort to Robyn whilst investigating the Russian threat for the past couple of weeks that she would have rapid access to the authorities as soon as she had enough proof to present to them. That hour was nearing.

As she pulled up out outside her house, a freezing cold looking Dara was already outside, waiting at the front door, hopping from foot to foot to try to warm up.

"That was a long five minutes, Rob," he said, looking miserable with the cold.

"I'm sorry, Dara. Things have been insane. I'm not joking."

"You're telling me. I went out on a dive this morning and I don't think my bones are ever going to defrost in this lifetime."

"You went out on a dive? Are you mad, Dara? What they hell took you out in this kind of weather?"

"Wait till you see," he responded, his furrowed brow indicating his seriousness.

"Will you stick on the kettle?" she asked him, as she unlocked the front door, "and I'll throw a match on the fire. I think I have it already set so it shouldn't take too long to warm up." Luckily, it was, and it didn't take long for Dara to appear with two mugs of steaming hot coffee from the kitchen.

"Thanks, Dara. That was quick. I think I'll turn on the heating as well," she said as she left her warm drink on the coffee table in the living room and went into the utility to flick on the heating switch. Whilst there, she had another good idea and reached inside one of the drawers and produced a pink fluffy hot water bottle. She re-filled the kettle and shouted to Dara that she'd be in in a minute. As it came to the boil, she carefully filled it and replaced the cap, making sure it was good and tight.

"This will warm you up fast. Just put it inside your jacket," she said to Dara as she reappeared in the living room.

Looking quizzically at the pink fluffiness of it all, Dara, who would normally have some cheeky quip at the tip of his tongue, was too frozen that morning, brain included, to be his usual cheeky self. Plus, there was a seriousness to him that Robyn didn't see in him that often.

"Thanks, Rob. I appreciate it," he replied, with an uncharacteristic solemnity. As he was about to put the hot water bottle inside his jacket, he stopped and pulled his phone out first. He laid it on the table in silence before settling the hot water bottle against his chest.

"What's up?" Robyn asked, concerned by his demeanour and the urgency of his request to meet. "What's that you have?"

Dara quickly got to the point. He was still concerned about the two "Swedish" guys who had turned up at the pier a couple of weeks ago, claiming to be diving a shipwreck—a shipwreck which, from his years sailing out of the bay, he knew didn't exist in that spot. The location the men had dived wasn't random. It was right above the underwater fibre optic cables which linked the U.S. to Europe and made landfall in Clew Bay. Alarm bells rang for both of Dara and Robyn at the time and then things got even stranger. Robyn had discovered that the same two men had shown up at the Castlebar protest marches—one march supporting the Far Right and the other, against the Far Right. Then, when Robyn rang him yesterday evening and told him that she had discovered the two same guys again at the Brexit disturbances in the North, he knew

CHAPTER 28

he had to do something.

Dara contacted a dive buddy with underwater camera equipment and asked him to meet him early that morning for a dive in the bay. His friend had thought he was out of his mind. Diving in those freezing temperatures was one thing, but when he asked Dara what the point of the mission was, Dara had no choice but to ask for a second favor: not to ask. He explained that in a few days, he'd be able to come clean about everything, but for now, he needed him to trust that they weren't doing anything illegal or dangerous. His friend doubted his sanity, but in the end, he agreed to help. Dara paused for a minute as he pulled the hot water bottle out of his jacket again.

"Have you warmed up?" Robyn asked.

"No, I'm feeling a bit sick. A bit queasy. Is that milk off that's in the coffee?" he asked, lifting the mug to his nose and sniffing it.

"No, it seems fine to me," Robyn replied, tasting her coffee herself. "What did you eat last night?" she asked him, knowing that he usually skipped breakfast. "A take-away?"

"No, I just threw some pasta in a saucepan and had that with sauce and pine nuts. Stuff with lots of preservatives, so there's no chance of any of that being off for about another century or so," he assured her.

"I hope you didn't pick up *E.coli* or some other dirty bug in the water this morning."

"Oh, crap. I hope it's not that," he exhaled, dejectedly. But, just in case, Robyn brought the bin that was in the corner of the living room, over to him. She went to the kitchen and got him a glass of water before he resumed where he left off in his story.

Then he produced a picture on his phone of what they had found at the dive spot.

It looked like a long black cable snaking along the sandy seabed, with fluorescent stripes every few feet of its length, as a marker. But at the centre of the image was a rusted round metal disc, no thicker than a few inches at a guess, sitting on top of the cable. Then, just beyond that was a black rectangular box that looked as if it was clipped around the cable.

"I know someone who will be able to tell me if this is what I think it is," Robyn said in a worried tone. "Can you send me the image file?"

"Yeah," Dara replied. "There. I've sent it."

Robyn tapped away on her laptop for a few minutes. Then looked up at Dara, who was shifting uncomfortably in his seat.

"You're a brave man Dara for doing this. And Paddy too." Paddy Concannon was an award-winning underwater photographer from Westport who had taken spectacular images of coral reefs around the world, as well as hauntingly beautiful images of shipwrecks and epic images of marine flora and fauna.

"Because I couldn't tell him what the purpose of the dive was, please don't mention his name to anyone in connection to this until I get his OK. It was a big ask and he did it no problem, so I don't want to take the proverbial by linking his name to it without running it by him first."

"Yeah, of course, Dara. I understand."

"Look, I'm going to head off, Robyn. I feel like crap. Just give me a ring when you hear back from your contact. I have to go and have a lie down for a while. I've a bad pain in my head now as well. It must be some sort of flu I'm coming down with."

CHAPTER 28

"You poor devil, Dara. It's funny, I've a bit of headache now too. Go home for a while, take two Panadol and get a rest. I'll give you a call later to see how you are."

"I'll be fine, Rob. I've been through a lot worse after an average night out," he said, standing and going to the door.

"Hang on a second, he's back," Robyn said as her phone beeped, with a message from her contact to whom she sent the underwater image. He was a fellow journalist from the UK whom, when he became a stay-at-home father, developed an interest, and later a specialty, in identifying military equipment and war materiel during the Syrian civil war after the Arab Spring.

"You're exactly on the money, Dara," Robyn exclaimed.

"You and Paddy just found a cable tap and a mine planted on the main US to Europe fibre optic cable." She was stunned. Dara stood at the front door, dazed from what he had just heard, combined with the effects of the headache and sickness he was feeling.

"Can you deal with that for me today, Robyn?" he asked his friend, in a weaker voice now than when he first arrived. "Tell whomever needs to be told. I don't know—is it the Gardaí or Army Bomb Disposal Unit you go to with stuff like this? I just don't know my ass from my elbow, at the minute. I'll be able to give a statement later this evening or tomorrow, or whatever."

"Yeah, no problem, Dara. I'll look after it. You've already done the hard part. Lana and myself were planning to go to the authorities by lunchtime today anyway with what we've gathered so far. Just go home and get some sleep, Dara, OK? And I'll give you a call later. Put your phone on silent if you're sleeping."

"Will do," Dara assured her, clearly not able to take in the import of what he and his dive buddy had discovered.

Robyn, still reeling from the shock herself, gave him a hug as she said goodbye, closing the door after him to keep in the heat. As he got into his car, he pulled out past a black Transit van that had just parked up outside the neighbours' house next door, and he drove out of Robyn's estate.

Robyn, for her part, returned to the living room for a quick lie down to see if it would relieve the headache she was starting to feel as well. It was probably caused by her adrenal glands giving out after all the stress she had been through with the election, she thought to herself. She turned on the news to hear the last of the election coverage before the broadcast moratorium on election coverage kicked in the following morning. She couldn't afford a rest right now. Lana and herself were cutting it so close to the wire, but she knew her friend would be here soon. She turned up the sound on the TV so she wouldn't accidentally fall asleep in the meantime.

But Lana would never make it to her front door.

And, with the television turned up, Robyn wouldn't have been able to hear the commotion outside when Lana and her security detail pulled up outside her house.

The moment their vehicle came to a stop, chaos erupted. Her security detail—Ger and Mike—barely had time to react before they were ambushed. The driver and front-seat passenger of the black transit van that had been parked in the estate jumped out, moving with precision and speed. Within seconds, both Ger and Mike were hit with pepper spray, their well-trained martial arts moves doing little to help them avoid the stinging cloud that sent them crashing to the ground, choking and blinded.

CHAPTER 28

Before they could recover, a third man slid open the side door of the van. He moved swiftly, grabbing Lana from behind and forcing a cloth soaked in what was likely chloroform over her face. She struggled, but the chemical took hold quickly, and within moments she was unconscious. The man hauled her limp body into the van, the front-seat passenger tossing her legs inside before jumping in after her. The driver slammed the van into gear and took off at speed, out of the quiet Brookhaven estate.

In the small cul-de-sac of just six houses, not a single soul had seen or heard a thing. The abduction was flawless, executed in seconds, leaving no trace except the two incapacitated Close Protection officers on the ground. And Robyn, still inside, remained completely unaware of what had just befallen her best friend right outside her living room window.

A phone call roused her from the half-slumber she was in on the couch. She grappled with the phone, all thumbs, as she tried to answer it. "Dara, I didn't think I'd be hearing from you so soon," she said sleepily.

"Robyn, I'm after pulling in and throwing up on the side of the road. I'd throw out that milk in your fridge if I were you or you'll be next, puking your guts up," he advised her.

"No...alright...fine," came her slurred reply.

"You sound half asleep?" Dara said, wondering what was going on. "I thought you and Lana were going to the cops in the next while or so?" he asked, confused. "Rob? Robyn? Are you there? Robyn, can you hear me? ROBYN," he shouted into the phone.

But a worrying silence was all he got in reply.

The 999 emergency number was the next one he dialed before turning around on the road and speeding back through town in the direction of the Brookhaven estate on Rathbawn Road.

Chapter 29

As the final preparations were being put in place for the General Election the next day—stacks of ballot papers had been transported to local Garda Stations for secure storage overnight, voting booths were being brought to polling centres, signage to guide the public was being put up, election staff were being given final briefings, everything down to extra pens and extra light bulbs were being organised—two of the election's closest observers, Robyn Mayhew and Lana Volkov, were by now far from the scene. Having fought so hard to maintain the integrity of the election, they were now fighting for their lives.

Somewhere on a winding country road far outside of Castlebar, Lana Volkov was lying in a distressed state in the back of a van, bleeding from an open head wound and passing in and out of consciousness. The force of her abduction had been brutal. She had been thrown into the back of the black Transit van with such violence that her injury now jeopardised her captors' plans. They had already switched vehicles once to avoid detection.

Lana couldn't abate the panic that was rising in her chest. The voices surrounding her were loud, frantic and speaking in a language she couldn't fully grasp.

If she had had the presence of mind at the time, she would likely have realised that the row between the assailants was due to her unnecessary injury, which now required them to find a quiet country pharmacy somewhere to buy bandages. The sheer terror of her kidnapping, knowing her fate was certain death, was too much for her in order to be able to think clearly. Little could she know that her blood was congealed all over the back of the van which would now require switching to a third vehicle. Aside from the logistics hassle and delay that would result, this wasn't the main problem. Their associates would be well able to source such a vehicle on demand and meet them along the way to switch. It was burning out the second van to dispose of DNA evidence which was the cause of the explosive row—an action which would surely set off alarm bells with the Gardai when two burning vehicles would be found within close proximity of each other.

Meanwhile, in the quiet Brookhaven cul-de-sac off Castlebar's Rathbawn Road, an ambulance had pulled up outside No. 3, its blue lights still flashing. The back door was left open, awaiting the patient to be brought out. Three paramedics emerged from the house, carefully guiding a stretcher along the sloping driveway. Robyn Mayhew, unconscious and strapped in, was barely recognisable, her face pale and still. Neighbours had gathered in shock, whispering to each other in disbelief. None of them had any idea what had happened and now they watched, frozen, as Robyn was loaded into the ambulance. The siren wailed to life once again as the vehicle sped off, leaving behind two Garda cars and a growing scene of inquiry.

As Lana drifted closer to unconsciousness, she fought to stay awake, summoning every last shred of mental strength. The voices around her were sharp and unfamiliar, but she strained to identify the language her captors were speaking. It was hard to concentrate through the pain and panic, but she knew her captors could only be working for the Belarusian government. But what was the language they were speaking? It had a lot of throaty, guttural sounds. But it certainly wasn't any variation of Belarusian or Russian. But could it be Chechen?

It wasn't out of the realm of possibility. Belarus' dictator could have easily requested help from his powerful ally, Vladimir Putin, who had long been known for outsourcing such dirty work to unsavoury networks. The Chechen strongman, Ramzan Kadyrov came to mind. Once a separatist leader in Chechnya, he switched sides in the Second Chechen War and became President of the country in 2007. He was now seen Putin's loyal enforcer and Kadyrov's men were often called upon for covert operations that required brutality. Their involvement would fit perfectly with Putin's strategy of maintaining plausible deniability by using criminal gangs or mafia groups for "wet work", the euphemism for assassinations and torture. But just as the thought crystallised in her mind, unconsciousness came for her, wrapping her in darkness.

As Lana was slipping away, elsewhere in the county at Mayo General Hospital, her friend Robyn's eyes finally fluttered open as oxygen surged through her veins. She had been caught just in time, saved from what could have been a fatal dose of poisoning in her own home.

Slowly, as the fog in her mind began to ever so slightly clear, the gravity of what had happened started to sink in. That Lana's minders would be informed so she could be moved to a new safe house was all she could think about. But sadly, she had no idea that it was too late to try to bring her best friend to safety—she had been violently abducted and her whereabouts were unknown.

"Lana...Lana," she tried to say to the nurse standing over her. With that, a Garda came to her bedside.

"Just whisper," he said, knowing the effort it was for her to try to get words out.

"Lana. Volkov. Belarus," she got out before falling back into semi-consciousness, from the sheer effort of speaking. Blackness rolled over her once again.

Hour by hour, as the oxygen made its way through her bloodstream, Robyn began to recover, feeling her strength slowly returning.

By the time evening rolled around, she was sitting up in bed, speaking with the nurses. They explained that she had suffered from carbon monoxide poisoning. Robyn was puzzled. How could that have happened when she had just replaced the batteries in her carbon monoxide alarm less than two weeks ago? She distinctly remembered testing the device afterwards and everything was in working order. She frowned, wondering if the batteries she bought had been faulty and drained quickly. She also remembered having had the chimney cleaned last winter too, as she loved to light an open fire in the evenings. Still, the mystery would have to wait. There were far more urgent matters at hand, starting with moving Lana to safety.

Robyn's attempts to get any information from the Garda stationed outside her hospital room were frustratingly futile. In typical fashion, he would neither confirm nor deny anything, merely stating he would pass her concerns about her friend on to the Garda Superintendent. He did, however, agree to have a colleague retrieve her phone from her handbag back at her house. The twenty minutes it took for the phone to arrive felt like an eternity, as Robyn's anxiety grew. She needed to act quickly, not only to check in on Lana, but also to warn the authorities that the integrity of the general election had been compromised.

Finally, her phone was handed to her. She dialled Lana's number immediately, her fingers trembling after her ordeal. The call rang out without an answer. She tried again, and again, but by the third attempt, the phone on the other side simply went dead, probably out of battery, Robyn concluded.

Panic crept back into her chest. Time was dissipating rapidly to warn the authorities about the election interference operation from abroad. She had always thought Lana's minders, Mike and Ger, who were in senior positions within the Gardaí, would be her connection to the government, when the time came. But with Lana uncontactable, they were likely gone to ground with her, Robyn thought to herself.

There was only one other person she could turn to now to help her to warn the government. Given the craziness of what she had to tell him, she knew she would have to meet him face to face.

Before she could do that, she first put through a call to a man called Dick Hansberry, the owner of a car showroom just outside Castlebar.

"Hi Dick, it's Robyn Mayhew from *The Mayo Herald*," she spoke into the phone as quietly as she could from the en suite bathroom in her room. She couldn't have any of the nursing staff overhear the plans she was about to make.

"Hello Robyn. How are you?" he replied.

"Good now," she lied. "Dick, I finally have time this week to write up a motoring feature for the paper. I know I've been promising to take a car for a test drive from you for a while now and I was wondering would you be able to drop one around to me this evening?"

"That would be great, Robyn. I just have the new Ford Kia in that I'd love to get a bit of a plug for. You're down the Rathbawn Road, isn't it?" he asked enthusiastically.

"Well, I'm actually visiting someone in the hospital at the moment and will be here for a couple hours. Would you be able drop it here for me?" she asked, before quickly following up with a fib that her own car was in the garage.

"The hospital?" he repeated back to her.

"Yeah. If you wouldn't mind," she acknowledged, holding her breath and hoping he wouldn't balk at the strangeness of her request.

"Yeah, no problem. I can do that. Will I meet you outside the front door to give you the keys?"

"Actually, there's a porters' desk at the back entrance. That's nearer where I am at the moment. If you could leave the keys with them and I'll pick them up there when I'm able to leave." She closed her eyes this time, hoping against hope that he wouldn't find what she was asking, just too strange beyond words.

"Eh, yeah. I can do that," he replied, his ever so slightly incredulous tone, belying the certainty of his words.

"That's great, Dick. I appreciate that. I'll put a good mention in for the garage and I'll make sure it makes next week's paper. Thanks Dick. I'll talk to you again soon,"

CHAPTER 29

her rush to get off the call not helping her in the credibility department.

"It's a dark grey model and the reg is 201-M0-1301."

"I might need that all right, Dick. Good job you've your thinking hat on," she joked hesitantly, before thanking him and saying goodbye once again.

Now all she had to do was think of a way to get past the Garda posted outside the hospital room.

"Mark, I'm just going down the wards to check on my friend Dara, who was in the house with me at the time, just to see how he is."

"Oh, Jesus. I can't let you do that. You'll have to stay in that bed until the doctors let you go home, I'm afraid," he said, in a panic that she was even up out of bed.

"Ah, look Mark. I'm bored stupid lying there. No one will know the difference," she pleaded, giving him the best puppy dog eyes she could muster.

Shaking his head at her he said: "Don't get me fired, ok. I'm not on the best terms with the Super at the moment. That's why I'm stuck here. So be back in five minutes, ok? No longer."

She felt awful having to take advantage of his kind gesture, but there was nothing she could do for now. She might try and explain to the Superintendent at Castlebar Garda Station next week when this whole mess was behind her. It was all she could offer her conscience for now.

Robyn had learned from one of the nurses that Dara, too, was on the mend, which gave her some comfort. She hoped to catch up with him later that night or the following day, but for now, her focus was on getting out of the hospital undetected. As she made her way slowly down the corridor, dragging the oxygen tank she was hooked up to behind her, she could feel an unfamiliar strain in her lungs—a reminder of just how close she had come to not making it. Each step was a struggle, and by the time she reached the lift, her head was spinning with dizziness and nausea from the physical effort.

Once on the ground floor, she took a seat near the back door, trying to catch her breath. She had planned her escape meticulously in her head, but executing it was proving harder than she had imagined. The hospital porter, seated behind the desk, held the keys she needed, and she knew she'd have to wait until he was called away to make her move. Her patience paid off when the phone rang, and the porter left his post.

Robyn quietly claimed the keys and made her way back outside, where her car was parked just beside the bays reserved for doctors. Moving quickly, she opened the door and, with all her remaining strength, wrestled the oxygen tank into the driver's seat, then pushed it over to the passenger side. She didn't look around—she couldn't afford to. In her hospital gown, barefoot and shivering from the cold, she was a sight to behold. The paramedics had used scissors to cut her clothes from her collar all the way to her toes, so a hospital gown was all she had to preserve her modesty. It wasn't her finest sartorial moment, but she had no time to worry about how insane she looked. Security would soon be alerted to the desperate escape attempt unfolding in the carpark, so she needed to be long gone by the time they got there.

As she pulled onto the main road, Robyn kept a close eye on her rearview mirror. Hospital security wasn't her only concern. Whomever had tried to poison her might still be lurking nearby, waiting for another opportunity to strike. Her eyes flicked to the side mirrors as she navigated the roads,

CHAPTER 29

ensuring no one was tailing her. After getting through town, she turned left onto the Turlough Road and pulled over, letting traffic pass while scanning for anyone who might be following her. Once she felt certain she wasn't being tracked, Robyn continued on her route, eventually arriving at her destination.

She pulled up to the electric gates outside an elegant two-storey Georgian style home. With her heart pounding, she rolled down her window and leaned into the intercom.

"It's Robyn Mayhew from *The Mayo Herald*. Can you tell Éanna that I need his help urgently?" she said, her voice steady despite her nerves.

Éanna Kilbride, a Castlebar native and former Taoiseach, had never forgotten the early support Robyn had given him when his political career was hanging in the balance. At the time, Fine Gael was on the verge of electoral collapse, but Robyn had admired both his integrity as a politician and his fairness as party leader and gave him her backing in the paper. He held onto his seat in his home constituency of Mayo long enough to rebuild the party and later ascend to the country's highest office. Now, she was banking on him to help her in her time of greatest need.

She waited, her breath shallow, hoping her old ally was home and would answer the call before it was too late. She closed her eyes as she waited for the reply and holding her breath, she thought to herself: I made the mistake of letting Russia take my little brother. I'm not going to let them take my damn country as well.

Chapter 30

The Garda motorcycle outriders were back on the road once again, this time escorting the government Mercedes of the former Fine Gael Taoiseach, Éanna Kilbride from his home outside Castlebar, County Mayo to Dublin. Accompanying him was a very sick and exhausted Robyn Mayhew, by now clothed in a warm cosy tracksuit and cream putter jacket, all borrowed from Eanna's wife, Fidelma. A local doctor was called and asked to join them for the journey to ensure Robyn's safety, given the vital importance of her testimony for the looming election crisis.

It had taken almost an hour of fervent phone calls back and forwards to the government for the decision to be taken by the National Security Committee, or Cabinet Subcommittee F as it was known, led by the current Taoiseach, Liam Varley, that in such a constitutional crisis, the advice of the Council of State would be required to determine the correct course of action to be taken.

So former Taoiseach Kilbride's Garda escort wasn't the only one on the road that evening. Members of the three

CHAPTER 30

branches of government—the executive, legislative and judicial branches—had to be summoned to the Council of State at Áras an Uachtaráin. The Taoiseach, Tánaiste, Ceann Comhairle of the Dail, Cathaoirleach of the Seanad, Chief Justice of the Supreme Court, President of the Court of Appeal, President of the High Court and the Attorney General, as well as the former Presidents, Taoisigh, Chief Justices still living, plus seven further advisors nominated by the President, were all summoned to convene that evening, resulting in an unprecedented number of ministerial Mercs with Garda escorts criss-crossing the country and the capital, rushing to get officials to the Dublin "conclave." It would take a Herculean effort to keep what was taking place out of the media.

Having an hour to lie down in the guestroom of former Taoiseach Éanna Kilbride's home had given Robyn a brief moment to collect herself, but she was still struggling to cope with the enormity of it all. At the forefront of her mind was gratitude that she had been believed, and that the organs of the state had moved into action so quickly. What she hadn't realised was, that it was the kidnapping of her friend earlier in the day, a protectee of the State at the request of the European External Action Agency, that had alerted the powers that be that Russia and its agents were in the country. It had set off alarm bells at the highest levels of government. So by the time Robyn contacted former Taoiseach Éanna Kilbride, the state was already on alert. But Robyn now had the proof of an election interference operation they needed as well.

Sadly, however, Robyn still had no idea that Lana, her close friend and collaborator, had been kidnapped earlier that day. She had alerted the Garda on duty at the hospital to make a call to the Special Detective Unit who provided the close protection officers for Lana, to warn them of a potential danger to her following Robyn's own near fatal poisoning. But unknownst to her, that threat had already materialised. Lana had been taken just moments before Robyn herself had succumbed to effects of carbon monoxide flooding her living room. The severity of Lana's security situation meant no one could inform Robyn even of what had happened to her—at least not yet.

But even before Lana's abduction, another incident had sent ripples of shock through Government Buildings a week earlier. A highly respected pollster, a man by the name of Tom Doherty, sent word through his connections in government that there was something amiss in his polling data in recent weeks. All the major polling companies had been reporting a meteoric rise in popularity for the Republicans, but his data was in direct contrast to this. It was deeply concerning to all, particularly given Tom Doherty's credibility and good standing in official circles meant his findings couldn't be dismissed easily. While word of his concerns had quickly circulated within Leinster House, it sparked concern, but not immediate action. At the time, there was little anyone could do.

But just days later, another source—a confidential intelligence informant—had come forward with even more sensitive political information through different channels. That intel had pushed the government to quietly raise the election alert level even further.

As they drove through the gates of the Phoenix Park, Áras an Uachtaráin loomed majestically, its neoclassical facade illuminated spectacularly against the evening sky, making

CHAPTER 30

the building appear almost ethereal amidst the surrounding darkness. A tear escaped out of the corner of Robyn's eye. Why hadn't she fought Russia this hard for her little brother? she battled with herself inside her head. Whatever she did now, it would be too late for Alexei, no matter how hard she crushed the Russian leader's efforts to damage Irish democracy.

"Will you be alright, Robyn?" Éanna Kilbride asked his young friend.

"I think so," Lana replied, with as much confidence as she could muster strapped to an oxygen tank. The weight of her mission weighed heavily upon her, a burden that seemed to only grow with each passing moment. The doctor did one last check on her oxygen levels, with the oximeter on her fingertip indicating she was just barely above critical levels. But even Éanna himself wasn't looking too good that evening. With strawberry blonde hair and boyish good looks belying his age of 68, it was obvious that the shock of the crisis which was unfolding had knocked it out of him, and consequently, he was looking a lot paler than he usually did.

With the furthest to travel that evening, Éanna Kilbride's motorcade was the last to arrive at Áras an Uachtaráin. The journey from the West of Ireland had been just two hours long, rather than the usual two and a half, thanks to the police escort. As Kilbride's car came to a stop, no time was wasted. Robyn Mayhew, pale and still visibly weak, was immediately escorted through the grand entrance. Her borrowed tracksuit hung loosely on her frame, and though her physical strength had yet to fully return, the determination in her eyes was unmistakable.

She was guided through the grand hall of the presidential residence, past gilded portraits of statesmen and stateswomen from Irish history, towards the state reception room, where the country's most powerful figures had gathered, awaiting the testimony that could determine the future of the nation.

Éanna Kilbride, walking beside her with a steadying hand on her back, gave her a reassuring nod as they entered. The atmosphere in the room was thick with gravitas. The walls, lined with rich tapestries and polished wood, seemed to echo the gravity of the moment—a palpable weight of history that only a very few were ever privileged to witness.

The air carried the faint scent of polished mahogany and leather-bound books, imbuing the space with an aura of solemnity that underscored the seriousness of the proceedings. Each detail, from the intricate woodwork to the muted, reverent lighting, spoke of tradition, authority, and the significance of what was about to unfold.

The President, the Taoiseach, the Chief Justice, and all the members of the Council of State were seated and speaking in hushed tones amongst each other. But they rose to stand as their guest entered the room, before taking their seats again in silence, their faces a mixture of anticipation and solemnity.

The President, a figure of immense calm and authority, remained standing and with no delay or preamble, introduced Robyn to the gathered officials. Every eye turned to her, not with curiosity, but with the expectation that she carried the key to unraveling the crisis gripping the nation.

Robyn, despite her fatigue, felt a surge of clarity as she stood before them. Years working in journalism had honed her ability to be concise, to present the facts with razor-sharp precision, and now, more than ever, those skills were vital. In as steady and as composed a voice as she could muster,

CHAPTER 30

she laid out the facts of what she and her friends, Svetlana Volkov and Dara Wall had uncovered—a deliberate and covert campaign of Russian interference in the Irish general election.

She spoke of their discovery of Irish voter data on Serbian servers, the psychological profiles developed of millions of Irish social media users, the strategies for manipulating various groupings in Irish society, not just to get them to vote for the Republican Party but also to tear apart Irish society, the suspected agents' presence on the ground at the protests in the West and the North, the discovery of a tap and a mine on a key fibre optic cable coming ashore in the West where the agents had recently dived, and the photographic evidence of those working at the Serbian facility that tied them to Russian military intelligence, the GRU.

But what surprised her was the silence that followed her account. She had expected questions, objections, or even skepticism from the Council. But the assembled grandees listened intently, offering no interruptions. The lack of immediate questions left Robyn slightly unsettled, though she pushed the feeling aside. What she didn't know was that three other critical pieces of evidence had already been presented to the Council earlier that evening. The weight of her testimony was not isolated, but rather the final thread in a web of damning information that had already convinced the nation's highest authorities of the seriousness of the Russian threat.

With her testimony complete, the decision was swiftly made. Robyn had done her part, but her physical condition was fragile. The President insisted she be taken to the Mater Hospital in the city centre for further medical care. A car was readied immediately, and within moments, the star witness was being gently escorted from the grand State rooms.

As she left Áras an Uachtaráin, the historical weight of the evening's events seemed surreal, yet she could barely process it because, now that it was out of the way, her brain filled with thoughts about Lana and where she could be. The nation's leaders would act on what she, Lana and Dara had uncovered, but for now, she had to focus on regaining her strength and finding her friend.

After what felt like an endless and tedious check-in process at the hospital, she was finally led to a two-bed room for recovery.

But it was her fellow patient in that room that left her utterly stunned.

There, lying in the adjacent bed, was Lana.

For a brief moment, Robyn couldn't reconcile what she was seeing. Her mind spun in confusion and relief as she rushed toward Lana, embracing her tightly, tears streaming down her face. Both girls, having survived unimaginable ordeals, clung to each other in grief and gratitude. They wept for the danger they had faced and the pain they had endured.

Through tearful words, Robyn insisted that it was her relentless pursuit of the Russian agents that had been reckless and had drawn danger straight to her friend, who had fled to Ireland specifically to escape Putin's reach. The Chechen operatives had followed, and Robyn felt 100% responsible for leading them right to Lana. But Lana wouldn't have any of it, arguing that it was her refusal to move away for a short while and give Robyn space to investigate the election that had put them both in harm's way.

They both laughed through their tears, knowing their friendship was stronger than any danger that had pursued

CHAPTER 30

them. Hours passed as they recounted their harrowing experiences, shared in their guilt, and found solace in each other's company. Exhausted from the emotional release, they eventually fell asleep, side by side, in the early hours of the morning.

As dawn broke over Ireland, the country stirred to life for General Election 2020. But few knew that, in a quiet hospital ward, the fate of Ireland's democracy had been defended by two brave young women who had stood against forces far darker than any ballot box could reveal.

Robyn slept deeply, the sleep of someone who had finally found peace after weeks of stress, anxiety and stomach-churning fear. But, still badly shaken from the trauma of her kidnapping, Lana had only managed a fitful night of sleep. She awoke at 7:00 a.m. and spent the morning pacing the hospital corridors, keeping an eye on Robyn, relieved that her friend at least was getting the rest she desperately needed. When Robyn finally woke, she found a nurse in the room, gently changing the dressing on Lana's head wound before she would be discharged.

"Morning, Sleepy Head!" Lana greeted her, laughing. "That was one serious night's sleep."

"Oh God, how long have I slept?" Robyn moaned, through the cobwebs of sleep.

"A good twelve hours but you needed every minute of it," her friend replied.

"Twelve hours?" Robyn exclaimed and sat bolt upright in bed. "What time is it?"

"About lunchtime."

"Crap, where's my phone?" she said in the panicked tone of someone not used to such a marathon night's sleep. She rummaged frantically under pillows and around the bed.

"What's wrong, Robyn?"

"The election. What happened? Was it deferred?" she blurted out.

"Deferred?" the nurse said, half laughing. "Why would it be deferred?"

"Eh, I dunno. What day is it? I think I'm a bit confused." Robyn lied, trying to cover up her outburst.

"Oh, here. I got it," she said having found the phone at last and lying back on the pillow to check the daily papers and RTE news.

"Take it easy for a while, Robyn," the nurse said to her. "You might need to sleep off what happened yesterday a bit more. It's normal for people to be a bit confused when they come into hospital, but a bit more shut-eye should help," she offered, pulling the sheets up over Robyn as she kept scanning her phone.

But her heart dropped right into her stomach when she saw the headlines.

"Exit Polls Reveal Republicans Are Leading the Charge."

What in hell, she thought to herself, as tears began to well up. What had happened? Why hadn't the Council of State decided, at the very least, to warn the public about what had gone on and bear that in mind when voting? Why hadn't the Taoiseach addressed the nation about it?

"Is everything ok?" Lana asked, not having a phone to check herself. She hadn't even asked anyone that morning what had happened. Her mind was so shattered by her ordeal, she couldn't even summon the mental strength to enquire about the election.

"The Republicans are leading the polls," Robyn replied

looking her friend directly in the eye, who got the message not to show a reaction in front of the nurse.

But now it was Lana's turn to feel shocked. What had all this been for? she thought frantically to herself.

As more medical staff appeared to get the girls ready for discharge, the two friends sat in silence unable to speak, both out of shock and for a lack of privacy. But as soon as the doctors and nurses left, there was a knock on the door and four plain clothes members of An Garda Síochána stepped into their room.

"Ladies, you're on the mend, we hear. Well, physically at least. It might take a while longer to get over the shock of what you've been through," a guy who identified himself as Derek, said. They introduced themselves as members of the Special Detective Unit, assigned to close protection. Robyn was now also deemed to need Garda security for a while, but they couldn't say for how long.

"Lana, the bad news I'm afraid is we'll need to move you. We can't keep you here in Ireland after what has happened."

"Not keep me here?" she exclaimed, stunned.

"It's for your own safety," Derek explained. "The EU External Action Agency want you moved to a third country. The details are being finalised, so I don't know where exactly you'll be going yet, but we're here to take you to Weston aerodrome. Your belongings in the house in Castlebar have all been packed up and we have them waiting for you."

"Hang on," Robyn interjected. "She can't leave yet," she said, shooting a pleading look at her devastated friend. "Look, can you give us five minutes?" she asked the four guys.

"Yeah, of course" came the reply, and they left the room.

"Look Lana, I haven't a damn clue what's going on today,

but we at least need to get to the bottom of that before you go anywhere. It's not fair. You were as much a part of this investigation as I was."

"I know, Robyn, but it's not that. I just don't want to leave. I've already been forced out of Belarus where all my family and friends are. I don't want to be forced out Ireland now as well, where my only other friend in the world is. I need your support to get over what has happened to me."

"Of course, Lana. I know," Robyn replied, hugging her friend closely. "What will we do?"

Before Lana got a chance to answer, another knock came on the door. It was Derek again.

"Robyn, I've just gotten word that a friend of yours, former Taoiseach Éanna Kilbride wants to speak with you."

"Oh, thank God," she exclaimed, exhaling deeply. She knew at last she might be able to get some answers as to what the hell happened in Áras an Uachtaráin after she left the Council of State meeting last night.

"But can you wait until I get back before you take Lana anywhere?" she pleaded with him. He popped his head out of the door again and conferred with his colleagues.

"We have half an hour to spare," he said. "But that's all."

Robyn embraced her friend. "Don't let them take you anywhere Lana until I get back. We'll figure this out. I promise" she said, hoping like hell nobody would pull a fast one and disappear her friend again, while she was gone.

Two of the Gardaí took her in an unmarked Garda car back to the Phoenix Park where Éanna Kilbride was waiting for her at the band stand.

"Well, Robyn, how are you recovering?" he asked, giving her a warm hug before they took a seat on the steps of the beautiful Victorian-era park feature. Looking worn and tired, he clearly hadn't slept much overnight.

"It was going well until I saw the news. The election went ahead?" she replied, her disappointment clear from both her tone and facial expression. "What the hell happened?" she asked, immediately regretting the disrespectfulness of her words to a former Taoiseach. "Sorry, Éanna. I'm still in shock."

"No, I understand. Well, after hours of heated debate until 5.00am, it was decided that that would be the best course of action. You have to understand, Robyn that if we did otherwise, Putin would have won the day."

Robyn sat quietly, letting the words sink in.

"His goal," he continued, "isn't just to interfere in elections—it's to undermine democracy itself, particularly within the EU. By creating chaos and eroding trust in our institutions, he's trying to make us look like a dysfunctional mess to his own citizens. The idea is simple: if we fall apart and if we can't hold a secure and legitimate election, then his people will see his regime as the only stable alternative. Stability under Putin or chaos under democracy. That's the narrative he's pushing to his own citizens."

Robyn exhaled slowly, her mind racing. She knew the stakes, but hearing it spelled out this way made the gravity of the situation painfully clear.

"If we had deferred the election," he continued, "and informed the entire country about the interference operation, the fallout would have been catastrophic. For a start, we wouldn't have been in a position to guarantee the public that it would never happen again. Faith in the electoral process would have been shattered overnight. People would lose complete trust in voting, and if democracy falters in a country as strong as Ireland, the ripple effects would be devastating."

Robyn nodded, but as a journalist through and through, she couldn't stop herself from arguing: "But the country deserves to know what happened."

"Yes, but at what cost?" Éanna replied. "We would have been finished. The instability would have been immediate. Multinationals that rely on Ireland's political and economic stability would have started pulling out straight away. Capital flight would have followed. Investors wouldn't wait to see how we resolved things, they would just take their money and go. Our economy could've been set back by decades. And that's not even counting the social unrest. Once people lose faith in the system, it's virtually impossible to restore it."

The silence between them was heavy. Robyn could see the logic in their decision, yet the thought of keeping it from the public, weighed on her conscience.

"Putin doesn't need to win militarily, Robyn," Éanna explained. "He wins by just sowing doubt, by making democracies crumble under their own weight. And if we had let this crisis derail us, that's exactly what he would have done."

Robyn rubbed her temples feeling the onset of a migraine, still processing the enormity of it all. "I understand," she conceded, with the heaviest of hearts. "I didn't look at it quite this far, Éanna. I guess that's why I'm not on the Council of State," she smiled, quietly.

"Maybe you should be. Only for you, Lana and Dara Wall, we would have been trotting miles behind in our investigations," he replied.

"Investigations?" Robyn looked startled. "You mean the government had wind of this already?"

CHAPTER 30

"We hadn't a lot to go on, but the Russians were definitely on our radar."

"In what way?" Robyn instinctively asked, her journalist's antennae going up immediately.

"Anything I tell you today is bound by the Official Secrets Act, Robyn. Do you understand? Not a word about any of this to a soul. I hope you will respect that."

"Of course. On pain of imprisonment if I breach the Act. I know the drill. I give you my word, Éanna."

"I've always been able to trust you in the past, Robyn. So don't let me down."

"Of course not."

"We were alerted about a week ago to something unusual in the polling data from one of the newer polling firms," he elaborated. "This particular firm had been showing the Republicans polling at 9%—the exact same figure they received in the local elections over the summer—consistently, with no deviation. But all the other major polling companies were reporting numbers that seemed fantastical. Out of nowhere, they were showing the Republicans surging into the low twenties, a leap that just didn't make sense. The managing director of this polling company was baffled. He couldn't explain why his data was so far off from the rest, but he stood firmly behind it. He believed in his numbers and his methods and was confident that there was no error on his end. Still, something about it didn't sit right with him. He knew the stakes, and despite the risk to his own professional reputation, and the future of his business, he decided to take a risk and do the patriotic thing. He reported the discrepancy directly to the government."

"I knew it. I knew those figures were off the wall. But

nobody was questioning it. I couldn't understand it."

"I saw your piece in the paper about it, and I have to say, it made me think. But the country had another guardian angel watching over us as well and I'm afraid to say, Robyn, this is where I've bad news to tell you."

"Bad news?" Robyn repeated, bracing herself. "What, Éanna?"

"Your good friend, German Joe. I'm afraid he has been a casualty in all this."

"German Joe?" her voice creaked. "What happened?"

"They got to him."

"The Russians?" she said, already knowing the answer.

"I'm afraid so," he said.

"What happened?" she asked, her eyes welling up.

"It could have been just after they were at your house, but he was found dead in the kitchen of his own home. And it was bad, Robyn. I'm not going to tell you anymore."

"Tell me, Éanna. I need to know."

"Oh, the savages did what they always do when one of their own turns on them. I'm afraid his body was found mutilated, Robyn. His tongue had been cut out."

"Oh God," she said, the pain painted across her face. "Joe..." she gasped, holding her head in her hands, as Éanna put his arm around her to comfort her. As she cried softly with the former Taoiseach, she lifted her head to ask: "What did you mean 'one of their own?'"

"German Joe was actually, Russian Joe, Robyn," he said. She looked at him confused, amongst the pain.

"German Joe, as they called him, had been a member of the KGB stationed in East Germany at the time the Berlin Wall came down. An awful lot of KGB operatives took flight

CHAPTER 30

to the West when that happened and then lived under false identities abroad. German Joe was one of them. In fact, he had been stationed in Dresden alongside one agent in particular, a ruthless operator by the name of Vladimir Putin. So he had seen first-hand all those years ago the cunning and cold-bloodedness of that man and he never forgot it."

Robyn was aghast, but he continued. "He chose Ireland to move to because it was a small country with a very small intelligence complement and therefore was less likely to have a KGB mole already in place. But being a true gentleman, he informed us of his presence in the country and gave us his full back story. We left him alone in Newport aside from a few friendly meetings when Vladimir Putin came to power in 1999 to find out a bit more. In fact, it was he who approached us, to let us know that he had worked alongside him."

"Gosh, I'm shocked," Robyn reacted, trying to wipe her way her tears, but to no avail, they just kept streaming down her face. "It must have been the people of Newport themselves that gave him the name, German Joe, since Germany was where he last lived."

"Must have been. But he came to us last week with information he had gleaned from your good self, Robyn."

"From me?" she asked, momentarily confused.

"Yes. He warned us first of all that your life would be at risk if the information he gave us got out and to make absolute certain it wouldn't be leaked. Then, he told us you had infiltrated the Republican Party headquarters and that you had discovered a Serbian guy was running their social media."

"Yeah, I did," Robyn acknowledged. "But I thought I would just be written off as a paranoid journalist if I went to anybody with that information without proof first of an election interference operation."

"Well, German Joe went to one of the meetings undercover himself to see if the guy really was Serbian. Just as he suspected, he wasn't Serbian. He was a Russian masquerading as a Serb. Joe confirmed the Ruskie accent. And that's when he came to us. So you got the ball rolling sooner than you thought, Robyn, with the assistance of your good friend, German Joe. God rest him."

"I can't believe he did that," she replied. "He gave me no indication he was going to go there at all."

"He was a man of few words, is what I've been told," Éanna added.

"Yeah, he kept things brief, alright," Robyn agreed. "But knowing his background now, I can see why."

Éanna continued: "Then we got word that Lana was grabbed on the street, so we knew we had a serious problem on our hands—a Russian problem to be precise. And that the Russians were in deeper than we thought here."

"How do you mean?" she asked

"Well, we knew the Russians had been sniffing around for a good few years. I'd say since after the invasion of Eastern Ukraine in 2014 when sanctions were imposed by the EU. They were probably doing a recce in case war broke out with Europe."

"Are you serious?" Robyn spluttered, clearly shocked.

"Yep. A couple of Russian fellas, who'd had their passports spot-checked just by chance coming off the ferry at the Dun Laoghaire, were followed by Gardai all the way to Kerry, where they were checking out the fibre optic cables coming ashore there."

CHAPTER 30

"So that's been going on for a while now," Robyn surmised. "And Dara just happened to stumble across them doing the same thing in County Mayo."

"It's not just the fibre optic cables that are of interest to them. There have been intrusions on the electricity network as well. They've been scoping that out for some time too, likely because Ireland is a world tech centre with all the major social media and internet companies having their EMEA headquarters (Europe, Middle East & Africa) in Dublin. So in a time of war, they'd know where to go in the system to just pull the plug, literally."

"Who would have thought little old Ireland would be of such interest to a country as far away as Russia?" Robyn surmised. "And there I was thinking I'd have been written off as a mad woman if I even suggested it in the paper without having solid proof first," Robyn said, shaking her head at how naive she had been.

"It wasn't just our tech that was being checked out either. Our airspace was as well."

"How do you mean?" Robyn asked.

"We don't have primary radar in this country to monitor our own airspace, just what's called secondary radar for air traffic control for the airports. For primary radar, we rely on the UK. They monitor Irish airspace for threats from the sky and there is an agreement between the UK and Ireland, permitting the Royal Air Force to enter Irish airspace, if deemed necessary. But there were a number of recent incursions into Irish airspace by Russian long-range bombers, triggering the RAF to scramble fighter jets in order to confront the Russian aircraft," Éanna Kilbride informed her.

"Bombers?" Robyn repeated, incredulously.

"Yeah. They were likely testing the limits of UK and NATO radar to find the gap in radar coverage that controls the entrance to the North Atlantic and oversees transatlantic shipping routes. And they were likely gauging NATO and UK response times as well, while also trying to antagonise the UK and its allies, and sow discord within the NATO alliance. There is currently a disagreement among NATO members about what constitutes an appropriate response to such provocation by Russia and their goal would be to exacerbate this disunity as well."

"I'm literally stunned," Robyn responded, visibly shook by all she had heard.

"It gets worse," Éanna warned her.

"Worse?" she stated, her voice gone up an octave.

"As a result of the dolphin kill off the West Coast that you reported on as well, our investigators from the Marine Casualty Investigation Board brought forward the dive to investigate the cause of the sinking of *The West's Awake*. Their report came in just a couple of days ago and it makes for unpleasant reading."

"How so? Aside from the obvious, the loss of life of the fishermen on board, of course."

"Well, it seems, again as you reported for the paper, that the loss of their lives was completely needless."

"Oh, no. You're not going to tell me there was a Russian sub lurking off the coast at the time, are you, Éanna?"

"I'm afraid I am. The nets were cut, which indicates they probably got caught in something. But residues found on the cut ends are of a chemical used in, what's called 'stealth paint', a type of radar absorbing paint used by the military. There would be no reason for French or UK subs to be in those waters, so the only logical explanation was, what you and German Joe put forward—a Russian sub."

"I'm sick. I'm literally going to throw up, Éanna."

"Here, I have a bottle of water. Take a sip."

"No, I'm fine. I'm just so shocked. The Molloy family has been decimated by that tragedy," she responded, with tears welling up in her eyes again.

"If it's any consolation, the government has ordered the army divers to stay in the area to search for the bodies for another few days, to see if they can be recovered. It would be the only tiny bit of comfort we could offer the Molloys."

"It would mean a lot to them to recover the remains for a proper burial. But I don't know what the chances are of recovering any remains this late in the day."

"Well, they're sticking at it for the next few days. Then they have to move on to the Corrib gas pipeline, off the Belmullet coast. With Russian military vessels in the waters off Mayo and Russian agents active in the country, the security of the pipeline needs to reviewed and checks made for any mines that might have been laid."

"You don't think the Russians are forward planning to that extent, do you?"

"They may have taken it beyond reconnoitering and gone a step further, we don't know. But we'll have to find out. Gas exports are one of Russia's main sources of income, so they have an economic interest alone, aside from a military interest, in being able to disrupt our gas supply. All of our civil infrastructure in the country is going to have to be reviewed in light of this new paradigm."

"I guess that would be the wise thing to do. I just can't believe how different the world is that I've woken up to this morning," Robyn added, shaking her head in disbelief.

"But we should have been more on the ball with the security of our election," the former Taoiseach conceded. "It's not like we weren't on notice of Russia's capabilities in this sphere. We saw how they interfered with Brexit, the Scottish referendum and the French and German elections—undermining Angela Merkel in Germany, helping Marine Le Pen's Far Right Front Nationale in France, and promoting Scottish independence to break up the UK. I suppose we put too much weight on the fact that we're not members of NATO and therefore, thought we'd be no threat, and of no interest, to the Russians."

"Yeah, I'm still astounded to know they were here and in as deep as County Mayo. I really thought I'd be seen as a mad woman to even raise the subject to anyone. I thought Lana was the only one who'd get it," Robyn added.

"But we did begin to see in the last few weeks that Northern Ireland's unique position within the UK, could provide Russia with a back-door access to interfere in British affairs. We just received intelligence only a few weeks ago that so-called 'diplomats' from the Russian embassy in Dublin had meetings with both Republican and Unionist paramilitaries in the North. The Russians supposedly made contact with Republican dissidents under cover of discussing history at public meetings and lectures. But again, we understood that the aim was to cause trouble for the UK. We were so busy looking outward, instead of looking inward, at our own election."

"The government knew there had been contact between the Russians and the IRA?" Robyn said, stunned. "So the evidence I presented to the Council of State—that I had found images of the Russian agents I had uncovered in Mayo, also at Brexit protests in Belfast—was no surprise?" she asked. "I was wondering why there weren't any questions."

"It was no surprise, but it was still shocking, nonetheless. All the parties worked so hard to bring peace to Northern Ireland and peace has brought untold advantages to the North. So to think that that could all be undone by Russian saboteurs is soul-destroying," Éanna said, as he shook his head at the possibility.

"But it brings up the question of collusion between the Republicans and the Russians in relation to the election. Did the Republicans know they were getting an assist from Moscow? They may have just been "useful idiots", to use the old KGB Cold War parlance for unwitting assistants, in terms of stoking the Brexit divisions. But Lana's kidnapping in the Republic provides us with evidence that there's now a direct line of communication between the Russians and the IRA."

"How so?" Robyn queried, growing ever more worried.

"Lana heard her captors speak a foreign language which she described as having lots of guttural sounds and guessed it to be Chechen, given that the Chechen leader, Ramzan Kadyrov, is a close ally of Putin. But it now looks like it was the IRA that kidnapped her on behalf of the Russians and that it was Irish that was being spoken in the van so she wouldn't know what their conversation was. Because that's how the Gardaí were able to find them. They had planted a listening device in the jeep of a Dublin gangland figure they were investigating for allegations of torture and assault, including the waterboarding, of a guy who sold him a defective motorbike. Shockingly, this guy was also a Republican politician sitting on Dublin City Council, Jake Donoghue. He was bringing the leader of the Hennessy gang to the North for a meeting with the IRA to seek their assistance in sorting out a feud with another Dublin gang. In the course of their conversation in the jeep, Councillor Donoghue, said: 'I heard the lads grabbed the Russian babe earlier. Fair play to them.' So the Gardaí set up a checkpoint, just outside Sligo, to intercept the van before it crossed the Border."

"Jesus, poor Lana was petrified it was the Chechens. Ramzan Kadyrov's men have a savage reputation. She wouldn't have been so traumatised if she thought it was the IRA, although you and I know their reputation for savagery would be up there with Kadyrov. Do the Gardaí have any information on whether it was the IRA or Russians who tried to off me?"

"Yeah, they're working on the assumption it was a Russian assassin who tried to poison you. Poisoning has been the favored method of dealing with their enemies for decades. They found a large crisp package—you know, from a 6-pack of crisps—stuffed up the chimney breast. This would have prevented the release of carbon monoxide from the fire up the chimney, which would have filled the living room air and killed you before you'd have even realised it. Forensics have revealed that there were no fingerprints on the packaging indicating tradecraft—that it was a professional at work. The batteries had also been removed from your carbon monoxide alarm too."

"Jesus. I distinctly remember replacing them only a fortnight ago."

"You had such a lucky escape, Robyn. Within minutes you could have been dead only for your friend, Dara had the good foresight to ring you."

"I know. I'll be forever indebted to him for his quick thinking to ring an ambulance."

CHAPTER 30

"He's a smart cookie, that's for sure," Éanna agreed. "You all are—you, Lana, Dara and German Joe. What you accomplished all on your own was nothing short of miraculous for four private citizens," Éanna told her.

"But what was it all for in the end, Éanna? The election went ahead without any warning or caveat to the public and the Russians just get away with it because we can't run the risk of destabilising our democracy."

"They won't get away with it. There were already measures under discussion last night," he intimated.

At this, Robyn looked up hopefully. "Measures? Like what?"

"I'm sorry Robyn, but because they're still under discussion I can't make you privy to those discussions yet. I'll have to do the Council of State that courtesy, but we'll catch up again soon at home," he told her.

"I understand," she acknowledged, as they got up to make their departure, embracing each other once again.

As the phone began to ring in Robyn's pocket, they waved each other off. It was Dara's name on the call screen. Robyn burst into tears as she answered.

"Dara," she blubbed, barely able to get the words out through the tears. "You've no idea how thankful I am for you."

"My God. You're definitely not right yet, Robyn Mayhew, if you're telling me that. What's wrong with you, Rob. Will you pull yourself together for God's sake!" he exclaimed, laughing wholeheartedly at his friend, but also in an effort to hide his own emotions. "You know I will be holding that over you for the rest of your life?" he continued to Robyn's sobbing. "Ok, that's enough of that. The Guards told me you're in Dublin.

What brought you there? Was your condition that serious?"

Robyn had already discussed a plan with Éanna Kilbride as to what reason to give family and friends for being in Dublin. "There's a specialist doctor that deals with poisoning they wanted me to see here," she bluffed, feeling horrible lying to the friend that had just saved her life. "But I'm on my way home."

"Good, because I have an envelope for you. It's marked 'private and confidential'," he told her.

"If it is, why the hell do you have it?" she asked, laughing.

"Because—that's the weird thing—it was shoved under the door of the wheelhouse on my boat. I've no idea who left it there for you or why."

Robyn had no idea either, wiping away the last of her tears. Nor had she any idea that there were still lots more tears yet to come.

Chapter 31

As election results continued to pour in from constituencies across the country, the political picture grew more and more stark. The country was experiencing a profound political upheaval, with each new tally of votes further highlighting the seismic shift happening in Irish politics. With every passing hour, the future of the government, and perhaps the nation itself, seemed to hang in the balance, as the full impact of the vote came into focus.

The Republicans had won the popular vote and won the day. It was a heretofore impossible feat for a party backed by paramilitaries, whose murderous sectarian campaign, the party continuously tried to legitimise. Yet despite their impressive tally, the Republicans only managed to secure the second-highest number of seats at 36, behind Fianna Fáil's 38 and Fine Gael's 35. The country's longest established left-wing party, the Labour Party—a party older than the state itself—won a mere six seats by comparison.

But the Republicans' shortfall in seats wasn't due to a lack of voter support, but rather a lack of foresight from the party. The Republicans, having been decimated in the European and

Local Elections just months prior—losing half their seats—simply hadn't anticipated the overwhelming success they won in the General Election. And who would have in those circumstances? It would have made no logical sense to field extra candidates and risk spreading the party vote too thinly. As a result, they had fielded far too few candidates to fully capitalise on their surge in popularity. The magnitude of their resurgence, a complete reversal of their earlier misfortunes, took even the party's most experienced strategists by surprise. But the sudden wave of support they garnered came too late to alter their strategy, and while they dominated in terms of overall votes, their seat count fell too short to form a government.

The most glaring and shocking examples of just how stratospheric the rise in the party's fortunes were in seven short months, involved six Republican candidates who, after failing to win seats on their local councils in June, suddenly found themselves elected to Dáil Éireann by the following February. They went from only a few hundred votes in the local elections to over 10,000 votes each in the General Election. It was the stuff of political miracles.

But the most egregious Republican victory of all belonged to the Republican candidate who, seven months earlier barely scraped her way onto her local authority with a paltry 630 first preference votes. Then, within a few short months she managed to pull in over 10,000 in the General Election—a stunning result by any account but especially considering she had spent the bulk of the three-week general election campaign away on a pre-booked holiday! You quite literally couldn't make it up.

All over the country Republican party candidates' votes

surged, topping the polls in constituency after constituency, as the political establishment looked on in shock and despair. The Republican Party had just become the biggest political party in the North in recent elections there, and now they were on their way to becoming the biggest party in the South.

As the last votes were still being counted, the Republican Party leader, Jennifer Fitzgerald, wasted no time in calling for a border poll on Irish reunification, declaring that the political momentum demanded it. This call—while electrifying for the party's supporters—sent shockwaves through the political establishment. Fine Gael's leader, Liam Varley, swiftly moved to counter the Republican leader's challenge, accusing her of destabilising the country's fragile political balance. He quickly reminded her that there had been zero mention of a border poll in the Republican Party's manifesto, and to bring up such a contentious issue at this moment was, in his words, "a reckless move, typical of a party being manipulated by unseen forces." His insinuation that the Republican Party was controlled by shadowy forces in the North pulling the strings from behind the scenes, only heightened tensions further. Departing Republican Party members in months to come would later allege widespread campaigns of intimidation and bullying within Republican ranks, painting a disturbing picture of a party that was clearly anti-democratic and authoritarian, with strict central control and intolerance of dissent that evoked unsettling echoes of fascism.

Behind the scenes in Irish national security circles, speculation was rampant about the implications of Republican power and whether the price of their success would be political payback to Russia. Rumours now abounded of a grand deal: if the Republicans succeeded in holding a border poll and reunifying Ireland, it would be with Moscow's assistance. The installation of the Republican Party in power wasn't just a matter of a party with a recent violent past ascending to government—it was, in the eyes of some, a case of Russia installing its preferred regime in Ireland. This looming spectre of Russian influence conjured fears of far-reaching consequences. Would Russian gas flow through the liquefied natural gas (LNG) terminal planned for the port of Foynes, just outside Limerick? Even more ominous was the question of whether Russia's growing foothold in Irish politics might eventually lead to a military presence? Could a Russian military or naval base in Northern Ireland become a reality, right on NATO's westernmost flank? The sight of Russian navy ships setting sail out of Kaliningrad, Russia's naval base on the Baltic Sea, bound for Ireland would, just months earlier, have seemed implausible. But to Russia, their new ally would have to be kept an eye on. And so Russian ships conducting military exercises off the Irish coast could potentially become a familiar sight. With the Republicans poised to reshape Ireland's political future, these fears seemed all too real.

The shock to the political system was so profound it was described everywhere as a political earthquake, sending tremors not just across Ireland but around the globe. The Irish general election became a topic of international interest, covered extensively by national media in the United States, Australia, Asia, Africa, South America, and yes, even in Russia. But as the political aftershocks from Ireland reverberated, an even greater earthquake was building momentum across the world, a seismic event with its epicenter in China. This global quake wasn't political, it was biological—a pandemic that soon gripped the entire world in fear and uncertainty.

CHAPTER 31

The COVID-19 virus, spreading rapidly from China to the U.S., Europe, and beyond, began to shake the world to its core in Spring 2020. It was the first time in over a century that humanity faced such a deadly and far-reaching health crisis. And it was edging closer and closer to home. The nightly scenes on the news of the arrival of the virus in Italy, with its epicentre in the Lombardy region where the fashion capital Milan had close commercial ties with clothing manufacturers in China, shook Irish people to the core. Italian hospitals were overrun and there were distressing scenes of tarpaulin-covered military trucks carrying the dead away from the hospitals, the cities having long run out of hearses to transport human remains with dignity. The outbreak was on the verge of becoming a global pandemic, an event so all-consuming that even the monumental political shifts in Ireland, would soon be overshadowed.

What had seemed like an unstoppable wave of political transformation in Ireland quickly became background noise in the face of this worldwide catastrophe. As the virus edged closer to Ireland, arriving on its shores on February 28, 2020, the country braced for impact.

Just four days later, the caretaker Irish government—still holding power until a new one could be formed—made a decision that under normal circumstances would have made news headlines. In an unprecedented move, they revoked a planning permission that had been granted five years earlier in 2015, for an extension to a property on Orwell Road, located in the genteel suburb of Rathgar, Dublin 14. In any other circumstances, the decision would have sparked intense debate and scrutiny, given the unusual timing—five years after the permission was originally granted.

However, with the nation's media and public attention now focused squarely on preparing for the imminent spread of COVID-19, the story barely registered on the public consciousness. It appeared in a small column at the bottom of page four in *The Irish Observer*, the country's national newspaper of record, drowned out by the rising panic over the pandemic. What might have been a headline-grabbing controversy in usual circumstances was instead reduced to a footnote in the face of the unfolding global crisis.

But 184 Orwell Road was no ordinary address. It was, in fact, the home of the Russian Embassy in Ireland. But bizarrely, it was also now one of the largest Kremlin operations outside of Russia. Yet it hadn't always been this way. In 2015, the embassy was granted planning permission to vastly expand its existing five-acre site. The proposed development would increase the embassy's footprint by adding 86,000 square feet of new buildings to the existing 21,000 square feet, effectively quadrupling the compound's size. Included in the plans was a large underground structure, supposedly designated for storage. However, the Irish government had serious concerns about this underground building, noting that its design appeared to include military-grade security features.

Another troubling feature of the proposal was the construction of an underground car park at the rear of the embassy complex, capable of accommodating 23 vehicles. Irish officials were baffled by this addition. The embassy compound already had ample above-ground parking, so why go to the extraordinary expense and effort of building a second underground facility? These details, coupled with mounting concerns about Russia's global espionage activities, set alarm bells ringing in Irish intelligence circles.

CHAPTER 31

On March 4th, 2020, less than a month after the general election and just four days after the first COVID-19 case was reported in Ireland, the Irish government made the time, in the midst of the global health crisis, to hold a meeting to re-examine the embassy's expansion plans and scrutinise them further. After "reinterpreting" the original documents, officials revoked the planning permission that had been granted five years earlier. It was a move that was unprecedented, but it was deemed necessary in the face of the potential security risks the embassy posed.

One of the chief concerns fueling the government's action was the unusually large number of staff at the embassy. Officially, the Russian Embassy housed 30 declared diplomats. By comparison, Ireland with a population of just 5 million, only had four staff members in its embassy in Russia, a country of 144 million people. What exactly then were 30 Russian diplomats doing in such a small country like Ireland? And these were only the declared personnel. The presence of undeclared staff—intelligence agents operating in the country covertly—was also highly likely and evidenced by the discoveries of Robyn Mayhew. The imbalance was glaring. Ireland had minimal trade or cultural ties with Russia, and the Russian population in Ireland was estimated at fewer than 9,000 people. Even in larger, more influential countries like France and Germany, Russia maintained embassies with only 10 or 12 diplomats. So why did Ireland require three times that number?

The answer, many suspected, was that Ireland had unknowingly become a major espionage hub for Russia. Intelligence agencies elsewhere speculated that the Russian Embassy in Dublin was being used as a center for gathering, intercepting and analysing intelligence from throughout Europe—an extensive AI-driven operation that could explain the embassy's unusually high energy consumption which the government officials had also uncovered.

German Joe had been keeping a close eye himself on Russian activities here after the Skripal poisoning in the UK, when a former Russian spy who had defected to Britain was poisoned with a nuclear nerve agent brought onto British soil. It wasn't the first time either. A similar attack had also taken place in 2006 against another Russian defector, Alexander Litvinenko. German Joe called the government's attention to the suspicious size and scope of the Dublin embassy. But he also warned that if Russia was denied its embassy expansion, they might simply establish a secret "black site" elsewhere in Ireland, a hidden facility that would be much harder to monitor than the embassy compound itself.

Once word came through to the Irish government that "diplomats" from the Russian embassy were holding secret talks with dissidents on both sides of the political divide in the North, the Garda's Security and Intelligence Unit with assistance from the Army Ranger Wing, began quietly surveilling suspected Russian agents operating out of the embassy. The situation grew more tense as the Irish government began refusing accreditation for new Russian diplomats and expelling others. In the two years after the election, the number of Russian personnel was reduced by half, as those whose activities were "not in accordance with international diplomatic standards", were designated *persona non grata* and sent back to Russia.

But it wasn't just the Russians who were holding secret meetings. Behind the scenes, the main Irish political parties were making Herculean efforts to counter the Republican Party's shocking gains in the general election. What began as covert discussions, soon spilled into the public eye: the two main opposition parties, Fianna Fáil and Fine Gael—bitter rivals since the Irish Civil War over a century ago—were now joining forces in a historic alliance. Their goal? To block the Republicans from forming a government. In an unprecedented political move, Fianna Fáil and Fine Gael, adversaries for generations, now united against the threat of the Republicans, who were only recent converts to politics over violence, taking the reins of power in this country, including control of An Garda Síochána, the Army and their respective arsenals of weapons. Chief amongst the fears of Republicans entering government was that, once given the reins of power, would the Republicans—known for subverting institutional norms and their authoritarian approach to internal politics—cede those reins if ousted from government in a future election? It was a very real fear for Irish democrats at that turning point in history.

But even this extraordinary political realignment was quickly eclipsed as the COVID-19 pandemic escalated. Overnight, the country's focus shifted from political intrigue to survival in the face of a global health crisis. Any suspicions or concerns the public might have harboured about backroom political deals faded into the background as the gravity of the pandemic became clear. Yet, beneath the surface, a quieter but equally significant change was in motion, one that received almost no attention at the time. The government quietly initiated plans to move future election days from Saturday back to Friday. Officially, this decision was framed as necessary to bolster a better "work-life balance" for politicians, a seemingly benign and enlightened justification for the move. However, there was a much deeper, more strategic motive behind the shift. The generation that had overwhelmingly supported the Republicans—young people, particularly college students—traditionally weren't motivated to transfer their voting cards to their term-time addresses. By holding elections on Fridays, when most students were away at college, only the most determined and politically engaged would make the effort to transfer their voting card to the city in which they attended college. But thousands of students would fail to do so, effectively denying themselves a vote. In essence, this quiet move to shift the voting day back to Friday was designed to curb the youth vote that had been heavily influenced by Russian-backed social media campaigns in favor of the Republicans. It was just one small change, but one that would have an outsized effect in shifting the political landscape.

Soon, the general election itself became little more than background noise. What might have been the most consequential political moment in decades was swept away by the larger wave of the pandemic. COVID-19 had overtaken every aspect of life, and the once-dominant political headlines faded as greater, more immediate concerns took hold. The nation—and the world—was now grappling with an unprecedented public health crisis, leaving the political drama of Ireland's election almost forgotten in its wake.

*****

The bay shimmered under the early morning light as Robyn navigated the winding coast road towards Rosmoney Pier. The water, usually calm and inviting, now held a haunting weight. A Navy vessel sat anchored in the distance, close to the spot where the trawler, *The West's Awake* had tragically gone down. The search for the bodies of the lost fishermen continued, a grim task that weighed heavily on everyone in the close-knit coastal community of West Mayo.

Robyn felt a knot of grief tighten in her chest. Russia's suspected involvement in the sinking was still impossible for her to fully accept, a cruel twist that added to the unbearable loss. She hoped, more than anything, that the government would be able to share the full truth with the Molloy family. They deserved answers, no matter how painful. The thought that vital details might have to be withheld on the basis of national security pained her deeply. As horrific as it would be to hear the truth, knowing what caused the sinking would at least give the family a sliver of closure, something they so desperately needed.

As Robyn rounded the final bend in the road, the pier came into view. She spotted her friend Dara in the distance, standing by the boat that had become his refuge. During the summer months, Dara usually lived on the boat moored in the bay, drawn to the sea as if it were an inseparable part of his being. But despite the bitter February cold, he had returned here as soon as he was released from the hospital, seeking the solace and safety that only the water could offer him after the events that had shaken their lives.

He had begged Robyn to join him, worried about her safety after everything that had happened. She had considered the comfort it would offer by having one of her closest friends by her side. But the biting cold of the Irish weather had made the decision for her. Instead, she chose to stay in a temporary safe house assigned to her by the Gardaí, under constant security for the next few weeks. While she had convinced them to let her drive out to the Bay today herself for the sake of her sanity, they had followed her all the way. The powers that be would carry out a "safety assessment" again in two months to review the situation, but it all felt so surreal to Robyn—like living someone else's life. She longed for normality again, just to walk freely, to return to her routines, and to put this nightmare behind her. But for now, she had to wait, holding on to the hope that soon, she could reclaim her life.

But despite the calm of the bay and the temporary sense of safety, Robyn couldn't shake the lingering depression the hung over her after the recent election. The memory of how perilously close the country had come to having a Republican government still haunted her. Age-old questions around the Republican Party had re-surfaced again: Who was really pulling the strings in the party? For years, whispers had circulated that "those in the shadows," the IRA, still dictated the party's actions. The idea wasn't mere conspiracy; it had been confirmed once again just a week after the election by the Garda Commissioner, the highest-ranking Garda officer in the country. During a press conference, he revealed that intelligence suggested the IRA Army Council oversaw both the IRA and the Republican Party, reinforcing the long-held belief that the Republicans were little more than a front for the remnants of the IRA.

For Robyn, this was chilling confirmation of what she had always suspected: that the Republican Party, despite its left-wing platform, was a façade. In reality, they were right-wing wolves in left-wing sheep's clothing, fascists masquerading as progressives. The thought of such a group seizing control of the government, potentially with covert backing from Russia, was deeply worrying.

These worries circled her mind relentlessly, a constant undercurrent of fear and uncertainty. The weight of what she knew, and the knowledge that she was forbidden from discussing it with her family and friends, left her feeling like the loneliest girl in Ireland. Each conversation she had with her loved ones felt incomplete, burdened by the unspoken truth she carried. The isolation was suffocating at times, knowing she couldn't share the full extent of what was happening, not the secrets and not the danger. All of it had to remain locked inside her, making her world feel smaller, more distant, and achingly silent.

Still, she found some comfort in the unprecedented efforts of Fianna Fáil and Fine Gael to counter the Republican threat. These two parties, sworn enemies since the Irish Civil War, had put aside their decades of opposition to form a historic coalition, united by the singular purpose of keeping the Republicans out of government. The very idea of a Republican-led government posed a grave threat to Ireland's democracy, not just because of their own controversial history, but because their rise to power was orchestrated by foreign hands. The spectre of Russia loomed large, and Robyn knew that any support from Moscow would come with significant strings attached. Sooner or later, Putin would demand payback—whether in the form of political influence, military cooperation, or something far darker.

"Ahoy there, landlubber!" Dara shouted across to her, pulling her out of her sombre thoughts. He stood on the deck of his boat, waving enthusiastically as she stepped out of her car, a temporary one she had been using while waiting for a new vehicle to replace her old jeep. It was part of the effort to keep a lower profile and avoid being easily tracked by those who might wish her harm. Ever since her life had been upended in the past few weeks, Robyn had been forced to take precautions she would never have dreamed that she would ever need. Even the idea of leaving Ireland altogether had crossed her mind. She could work remotely for a while— conduct interviews via Zoom, file her reports from abroad— but the idea left her unsettled. Reporting from afar wasn't the same as being on the ground and meeting people face-to-face.

But it wasn't just Robyn's world that had turned upside down, the whole entire world's had. As the virus invaded country after country, people everywhere were forced into isolation, travel came to a standstill, and in-person reporting had become almost impossible. For now, Robyn was caught in a strange limbo, her personal safety and the global crisis intertwining in a way that made her long for some kind of normality, even though she wasn't sure what that would look like for her anymore.

As she stepped out of her car, the two friends embraced, laughing and crying at the same time. How had they survived?

"We're hard to kill," were Robyn's first words to her friend.

"Yep, it's like they always said: 'It's hard to kill a bad yoke,'" Dara laughed, mock-insulting her for the laughs.

"That goes for you too then," Robyn told him, flinging the insult back at her friend.

"Will you have a beer for old time's sake? While we can? While we're still alive?" Dara asked her.

"Go on. You've twisted my arm," Robyn replied.

"I didn't even touch your arm!" he joked back.

"Ok, where's this letter then?" she asked. "I'm half afraid

CHAPTER 31

to open it after all that's gone on the past few weeks. It might have anthrax in it. I actually brought a mask and disposable gloves with me."

"I thought of that too. Maybe open it off the boat."

She deliberately hadn't told her security team about the letter, wanting to cherish the one last shred of privacy she had in her life. But now she was questioning the wisdom of that very decision.

Dara produced the envelope with Robyn's name handwritten on the front. Just her first name—no surname—which at least looked friendly.

They left their beers on the boat and jumped ashore to take the letter up to a piece of rough ground to open it. Robyn donned the gloves and mask with her back turned to where her security team was parked. She ripped the envelope open and pulled out the pages it contained, but no powder seemed to be amongst the contents, which was a relief.

There was a photograph and a letter. She sat on the grass and laid the photograph down, as she tried to pull off the gloves, craning her neck to look at the picture as she was doing so. Her eyes scanned the image and her brain scrambled to recognise who it could be.

But then it hit her.

So hard, it was as if she had been hit by a train.

Unable to take her eyes off the face in the picture, but with the air punched from her lungs with shock, her only word to her friend was: "Alexei," in a barely audible whisper.

Then she said it again: "Alexei." And again, and again. It was like her brain went on repeat, it was so stunned.

"That's your brother?" Dara quizzed his friend gently, sensing that she was going through something right there. "I thought he was a lot younger when he disappeared, Robyn?" he said, eager not to upset her in any way.

But it was too late. The tears appeared at the corner of her eyes and then huge droplets landed on the picture before her. Dara had no tissues to hand but gently tried to rub the tears from her eyes.

"He was. Much younger. But this is him now," Robyn spoke, like a robot.

"How do you mean: 'this is him now'?" Dara asked, confused. "Where did the picture come from? Who got a picture of him? Where did they get it?"

His questions shook her out of the reverie she was in, looking at her little brother who had grown into a teenager. She reached behind the picture for the letter that was also in the envelope. Dara had hoped she'd read it aloud. But she barely had any oxygen in her lungs. The tears came in torrents now, as she struggled to wipe them out of her eyes to read.

She turned back to the picture again: "Alexei," she exclaimed, in an almost primal cry as she hugged the picture to her chest.

Elated, she turned to her friend, smiling through a waterfall of tears: "He found Alexei! He found Alexei!"

Dara looked at her bewildered. "Who found him?"

"German Joe," Robyn whispered now, barely able to breathe through all the tears.

She hugged her friend tightly, not even letting him go while he tried to ask: "How did he find him? Where did he find him?" Dara was incredulous now as well.

Robyn pulled away to smile the biggest smile of her life at her friend. "He went all the way to Belarus, Dara, after I told him what happened to Alexei. He went all the way there and

CHAPTER 31

used his old contacts to track him down and find him. He found him in the end in a state institution there for special needs teenagers," she told him, her voice changing as she told him the last part. "But he's on his way now."

"On his way where?" Dara asked, still struggling to put it all together.

"On his way home. The letter says that he'll be on a flight to Dublin by tomorrow evening and he'll be landing at 9.30pm. He'll be accompanied by an old friend of Joe's."

"Jesus Christ. This is just amazing, Robyn. After all you and your family and Alexei have been through. This is just unreal," Dara beamed, pulling Robyn in for another hug.

"God bless you, German Joe, God bless you," Robyn cried.

"That's for sure. God bless you indeed, Joe," Dara agreed, looking up to the sky as he spoke the words towards heaven.

"I can't believe I ever doubted him, Dara. He's done so much, not only for my family, but for this country, Dara. Stuff I can't even tell you," she said.

He looked at her quizzically.

"I'm bound under the Official Secrets Act, but someday I will tell you. I'll probably have to abide by that 30-year rule. You know the one where they release government archives after 30 years? But I will tell you the whole story someday when you're older."

"I don't think anyone has ever said to me 'they'll tell me when I'm older' since I was about five years of age," Dara laughed. He hadn't a clue what she was talking about but could forgive her for being a bit delirious after the news she just received.

Robyn lay down on the sandy grass, trying to calm her racing thoughts as she stared up at the wintery, grey sky. She had never forgiven herself for not asking enough questions about why her brother had to return to Belarus. Every day of her life since, she kept asking questions about everything and anything, never letting anything go, until one day—today—all those questions paid off and she finally got her little brother back. She struggled to believe it was even happening, but she had the letter and picture still in her hand to prove it.

She thought back to that first meeting with German Joe at Daly's Hotel on the Mall in Castlebar. It was a fortuitous, but fitting setting for their encounter—Daly's Hotel, the birthplace of the Land League, where the seeds of the Irish State were sown so many years ago. At the time, Robyn had no idea that the man she met that night would play such a pivotal role in saving Ireland from the grip of a foreign power, or that he would deliver a long-lost member of her family back to her. German Joe, or Russian Joe as he really was, was an Irish patriot and would go down in history as having saved the Irish state. Those who founded the Land League at Daly's Hotel may have begun the movement for Irish independence from Britain, but Russian Joe ensured Ireland stayed independent and didn't just go on to swap one coloniser for another. His quiet heroism saved Ireland's sovereignty in an era where new powers sought control in subtler, more insidious ways. He became the guardian of the very freedom those early revolutionaries had fought to secure.

Robyn's thoughts then shifted to Eileen Heaney, the weather forecaster with the quiet, enigmatic way about her. Eileen had a way of seeing things others overlooked. When Robyn first met her, it wasn't the usual talk of rain or wind that Eileen brought up. Instead, she spoke of "the lights beneath

CHAPTER 31

the sea," words that had stayed with Robyn ever since. Those lights beneath the sea, the vital undersea communication cables that linked Ireland to the world, carried information, secrets, and power. Eileen had foreseen that threat when few others had even considered it, sensing that these unseen networks, pulsing silently under the waves, would become a battleground in ways no one could have predicted. If only Eileen could know just how close her warning had come to reality, how fragile those lights beneath the sea truly were, and how the messages they conveyed had nearly brought Ireland to the brink of catastrophe.

Even her prediction of increasing east winds had proven more prophetic than anyone had realised. It wasn't just a shift in the weather, but a metaphorical warning about the winds of change blowing in from the East—from Russia. People often dismiss the elderly when they speak but Robyn understood the weight of Eileen's words. She saw in her, a kindred soul, someone not afraid to speak up and challenge accepted thinking. Eileen had been right all along, in more ways than she could have imagined.

Robyn closed her eyes and took a deep breath, trying to find some measure of calm. The world felt so much more complex now, as if unseen forces were constantly swirling beneath the surface, affecting everything. But despite the uncertainty, one thing was clear: people like Joe and Eileen, those who saw what others missed, were the ones who would protect the future. And as Robyn lay there, she knew she, too, had a role to play in this unfolding story.

Suddenly, there was a noticeable uptick in activity from the Navy boat out in the bay. Robyn squinted and could just make out divers clambering aboard a small inflatable boat before it sped off across the bay, pulling up alongside the larger Navy ship. She and Dara exchanged glances, a silent question hanging in the air between them.

Moments later, the low hum of an engine grew louder behind them. Robyn turned to see a hearse rolling to a stop near the pier, its presence haunting and unexpected. Instinctively, she took a deep breath as the pieces fell into place. The Navy must have recovered remains of one of the fishermen from *The West's Awake,* the trawler that had sunk a few weeks ago after being sunk by a Russian submarine in Irish territorial waters.

It was a poignant moment for Robyn after having followed the story for weeks, never letting up in the quest for answers for the family. As the Navy rib returned to shore with the remains, two Navy sailors solemnly passed a blue body bag to the waiting undertaker. Robyn and Dara stood in silence. Dara made a sign of the cross and Robyn bowed her head and putting her hand to her heart. The wind seemed to die down, as if nature itself was bowing in respect for the souls lost at sea. The grief in the air felt palpable and she acknowledged how fortunate she was in comparison to the Molloy family, to have her brother that she thought was lost to Russia, return home to their family tomorrow.

But the bodies of these men lost to the sea weren't just one more tragedy that befell this part of Mayo. Just like the tragedies which fulfilled the Achill Prophecies, which had foretold centuries earlier the coming of rail travel long before trains ever appeared, this tragedy too foreshadowed great change ahead for the entire country. The sinking of *The West's Awake* by a Russian sub off the Mayo coast wasn't merely a random act of misfortune—it was a harbinger of something

CHAPTER 31

much larger, a chilling sign of bigger changes to come. In ways no one could yet fully grasp, the tragedy of the sunken trawler, *The West's Awake*, had prophesized the Russian threat to Ireland's very democracy. And so, from this small and seemingly forgotten corner in the West of Ireland, it had proved true—that the West was indeed, truly awake.

Note to Readers

If you enjoyed this book and have a few moments to spare, I would be ever so grateful if you could leave a review on Amazon.ie or Amazon.co.uk. Positive reviews on this platform can be of immense support to a new author and your efforts would be gratefully appreciated.

Plus, if you would like to be notified of future new releases, just email the words "mailing list" to:

LMcSimonBooks@gmail.com

Many thanks for your kind support and I hope we will meet again!

Acknowledgments

First and foremost, thank you dear reader for your support. It's an incredibly humbling experience to know that you shared so many hours of your precious time with the words I wrote in a world I created. I hope this book has at the very least entertained you and hopefully, even intrigued you too.

To all those who work in the journalism profession (and especially those whose work inspired this story), thank you for your tireless dedication and your vital contributions. In these darkening times, a robust and vigorous media stands as one of the last great pillars of democracy. While the spirit of that mission endures, the resources do not. And as long as that imbalance persists, we cannot afford to take the media's strength—or survival—for granted.

To little Fiadh and Carla for all the hugs, kisses, cuddles and giggles.

But most of all, to my mum, Ann. You gave me that greatest of all gifts as a child—a love of books and reading—which has given me endless hours of entertainment and comfort throughout some of the most trying times of my life. And that was just beginning. Your great heart, your compassion and enormous personal strength is a gift that keeps on giving to all of us lucky enough to have you in our lives. Without your unwavering love and support, this book would never have come into being—not least because you saved it from the "delete" button. Twice. Thank you for nurturing both me and this story, and for showing me that a mother's love, particularly this mother's love, knows no bounds, no matter how old I get. Thanks Mum!

Glossary

- Áras an Uachtaráin — the Irish presidential palace
- Brexit — the British referendum held in 2016 by which the majority of the people of the UK (51.9%) voted for the UK to leave the EU. Following years of negotiations, the formal exit took place on January 31st, 2020.
- Dáil — the principal and lower chamber/house of the Irish parliament
- Fine Gael — centre-right political party that grew out of one of the old Civil War factions. One of the three main political parties in Ireland (with Fianna Fáil and since 2020, Sinn Féin also.)
- Fianna Fáil — centre to centre-right political party and also one of the old Civil War factions. One of the three main political parties in Ireland (with Fianna Fáil and since 2020, Sinn Féin also.)
- Garda — a member of An Garda Siochána, the Irish police force
- Gardaí — the plural of "Garda"
- IRA — Irish Republican Army, a paramilitary force, designated a terrorist organisation, that sought to end British rule in Northern Ireland and reunite North and South in an independent Republic.

- Luas — the name of the Dublin city tram system. It's an Irish or Gaelic word that translates as "speed"
- PSNI — Police Service of Northern Ireland
- 'Ra — slang abbreviation of IRA (the Irish Republican Army)
- Republicans — in this story the term "Republicans" is used as shorthand for the fictional Irish Republican Party.
- Taoiseach — the prime minister of Ireland
- TD — Teachta Dála (or TDs plural) Irish member of parliament
- Unionists — those of the Protestant tradition in Northern Ireland who support the province remaining in union with the United Kingdom. (The nationalists or republicans being of the opposing side.)

Printed in Dunstable, United Kingdom